Forgotten Dreams

KATIE FLYNN

WILLIAM HEINEMANN: LONDON

Published by William Heinemann 2007

2 4 6 8 10 9 7 5 3 1

Copyright © Katie Flynn 2007

First published in Great Britain in 2007 by
William Heinemann
The Random House Group Limited
20 Vauxhall Bridge Road, London SW1V 2SA

www.randomhouse.co.uk

Addresses for companies within The Random House Group Limited
can be found at: www.randomhouse.co.uk/offices.htm

The Random House Group Limited Reg. No. 954009

A CIP catalogue record for this book
is available from the British Library

ISBN 9780434017720

Mixed Sources
Product group from well-managed
forests and other controlled sources
www.fsc.org Cert no. TT-COC-2139
© 1996 Forest Stewardship Council

The Random House Group Limited makes every effort to ensure that the
papers used in its books are made from trees that have been legally sourced
from well-managed and credibly certified forests. Our paper procurement
policy can be found at: www.randomhouse.co.uk/paper.htm

Typeset in Palatino by Palimpsest Book Production Limited,
Grangemouth, Stirlingshire
Printed and bound in Great Britain by
Mackays of Chatham plc, Chatham, Kent

Forgotten Dreams

Also by Katie Flynn

A Liverpool Lass
The Girl From Penny Lane
Liverpool Taffy
The Mersey Girls
Strawberry Fields
Rainbow's End
Rose of Tralee
No Silver Spoon
Polly's Angel
The Girl from Seaforth Sands
The Liverpool Rose
Poor Little Rich Girl
The Bad Penny
Down Daisy Street
A Kiss and a Promise
Two Penn'orth of Sky
A Long and Lonely Road
The Cuckoo Child
Darkest Before Dawn
Orphans of the Storm
Little Girl Lost
Beyond the Blue Hills

For John Emms, and any other members of the Rhyl Tennis Club who played with us in the sixties; happy days!

Acknowledgements

My very sincere thanks to John Emms, who starred at the Wellington Pier Theatre in the eighties, and put me right on things which I was no longer able to check for myself since the old theatre has been demolished. However, he floored me by assuring me that the theatre did not have a green room; the cast congregated in the bar. But this did not suit my story because of under-age performers, so I'm afraid I invented a green room. Thanks again, John.

Chapter One

1921

It was a hot afternoon in August and Lottie Lacey was sitting on the top step of No. 2 Victoria Court staring unseeingly ahead of her whilst her tongue checked her small pearly teeth, as it had done so often this past week. Of course the result was always the same: she had a wobbler. Several of her friends had already lost some baby teeth, which was not unusual at seven years old, but they could regard such a loss with equanimity. Some even put the tooth under their pillow and next day found it gone and a round brown penny in its place. But even if their parents could not afford to hand out pennies whenever a tooth came out, there would be no dire consequences for the tooth losers.

Lottie, however, knew her own case to be very different, for her mother had impressed upon her the importance of looking 'sweet'. It was one of the first prerequisites for a child star – a subject on which Mammy had been very bitter recently, for while Lottie had been in hospital she had been forced to employ another little girl to appear nightly in the current production at the Gaiety theatre just off the Scotland Road. But Merle sang flat and could not be persuaded to mime her songs,

1

so she had been told to go. Consequently, Mammy had had to do a solo act until Lottie had been well enough to perform once more.

Sweetness, however, was not merely a matter of small pearly teeth; it encompassed hair as well. Lottie's hair was brown and straight but her mammy had decided that it simply would not do. 'You see, queen, when you're part of a double act – a mother and daughter act like you and me – then it's best to look alike,' she had said, giving her appealing smile and twisting a strand of Lottie's hair into a ringlet. 'So this very evening I'll lighten your hair up a bit. It won't take more than an hour and I'll buy a comic paper so that you've got something to read while the peroxide works.' She had smiled lovingly at her daughter. 'Then you'll be as fair as me and the audience won't ever know that we aren't both true blondes.'

That had been when Lottie was only six, but even at six she had been well aware that Mammy was no more a true blonde than herself. She had not been tempted to comment, however, for Mammy could be reduced to tears – or temper – when unpalatable facts were pointed out. So Lottie had submitted to a long evening of boredom and discomfort whilst her mother covered her hair in a thick white paste, then rinsed and shampooed, and finally rubbed her head briskly before settling her on the hearthrug before the fire to dry out. Later, Lottie had looked in the mirror and had been shocked to find her hair not merely lighter but as yellow as her mother's. She had hated it at first, but soon grew accustomed though it was a nuisance having to have her roots done every few weeks. 'Stage lighting is strong and it wouldn't do for you to come on half brown and half blonde,' her mother had explained. 'But like most theatricals I am a perfectionist, so even though it's a bother I shall make sure you always look your best, as I do myself.'

Cautiously, now, Lottie's tongue probed the wobbly tooth. She wondered whether it would be possible to glue it into place, perhaps with chewing gum, then remembered Baz O'Mara telling her that first teeth did not so much fall out as get pushed. 'It's your grown-up teeth wantin' a place in the front row and pushin' your baby teeth out o' the way, you little idiot,' he had said crossly. 'You can't stop it. All you can do is hope your new teeth will come through small. But I expect they'll be huge, like horses', and then, when you don't look sweet any more, your mam'll kick you out, same as she did with Merle, and it'll serve you bleedin' well right.'

Lottie took most of Baz's remarks with a liberal pinch of salt because she knew Baz and Merle had been great pals and he had bitterly resented her dismissal, but this time Baz's remark had scared her a bit. After all, he was ten, three whole years older than herself, and had been connected with the theatre all his life; and though he made no secret of the contempt he felt for Lottie at least he often answered her questions, which was more than her mother did. She knew her mother would never really turn her out, but she guessed that she might be relegated to being merely a daughter, which was nothing compared to being a performer.

Lottie herself had also been connected with the theatre all her life, of course, but ever since the accident her memories of the years before it happened had been vague and muddled. When Lottie had come round to find herself in a hospital ward, she had not recognised her own mammy – imagine that! She could still remember the trembling terror of finding herself lying in a narrow white bed whilst a beautiful blonde lady clutched her hands and wept and begged her not to die, not to leave her mammy, whose fault it was . . .

Apparently, Mammy had blamed herself for the accident because she had decided to leave Rhyl, where she had worked at the Pavilion theatre, and return to Liverpool, the city where Lottie had been born six years earlier. Mammy had explained that Lottie had been so excited at the thought of seeing the birthplace they had left while she was still a baby that she had dashed ahead, straight into the roadway, where she had been knocked down by a passing lorry. She had suffered from something called concussion and had been unconscious for three whole weeks and in hospital for more than three months, for she had broken both her legs and such fractures take a considerable time to heal. When she had come to herself, she could remember nothing, not her own name, not her mammy, nor anything that had happened over the past six years. It had been a bit as though she had been born in that hospital bed, and although a whole year had passed since then, her memories of the time before the accident were fuzzy and unreal. If she tried to make sense of them the headaches came back and this was bad for her: the doctors at the hospital had said so. Her favourite doctor had also said not to worry about the memory loss. 'You may wake up one day remembering every tiny detail of your past life, or it may come to you in dribs and drabs,' he had said. 'But don't try to force it; let it happen naturally, if you can.'

As her mother had pointed out, however, this had not been possible. The dance routines and songs which Lottie had been performing over the past year had gone along with everything else, and had to be relearned as quickly as possible, and in the process Mammy had let slip a great many details about their past life together. Lottie had fastened on to these eagerly.

If they had returned to Rhyl, of course, she might have remembered a great many things for herself, but in Rhyl her mother had been assistant to a conjurer with whom she had fallen out, which was why she had left the Pavilion theatre and come to Liverpool to work with Baz's father. Mr O'Mara was also a conjurer, though he preferred to be known a magician, and Mammy, whose stage name was Louella, handed 'Mr Magic' his equipment, climbed into the disappearing cabinet and disappeared, and, as a finale, was sawn in half to reappear, two minutes later, miraculously unhurt. In their mother and daughter routine, Louella and Lottie tap-danced to popular tunes and sang a few songs, and then Mammy did cartwheels and flick-flacks all round the stage whilst Lottie, in a frilly pink tutu and pink satin ballet shoes, stood on her points, pirouetted with her arms over her head, and smiled sweetly at the audience to encourage their applause.

It had been suggested by one doctor that mother and daughter might return to Rhyl, just for a few days, in order to aid Lottie's memory, but Louella had been horrified by the idea. It seemed that her former partner had been violent and had bitterly resented Louella's abandoning him, even though she had stayed until the end of the holiday season. 'He'd likely kill the pair of us if we went back,' she had told anyone who suggested a return to Rhyl and Lottie was glad, for she dreaded the thought of facing more strangers, particularly one who disliked both herself and her mother.

'Hey, what on earth are you doin' starin' into space like a great mooncalf? Your ma's in a reg'lar takin' 'cos you ain't been down to the theatre so's you can get her messages. I offered to get 'em but she said she wouldn't trust me to pick out the freshest fruit, nor to know what sort of tea an' that to buy, so you'd best get yourself over there afore she decides you've got yourself kilt stone dead runnin' under another perishin' bus.'

Lottie's eyes, which had been half closed, shot open. 'Great mooncalf yourself, and it weren't a bus, it were a lorry,' she said quickly. 'Will you come with me, Kenny? Mammy usually gives me a penny for doin' the messages so we'll go halves. What d'you say?'

'Oh, awright,' the boy said amiably. He was a ragged urchin, a year older than Lottie, and her best friend in Victoria Court. Indeed, Mrs Brocklehurst 'gave an eye' to Lottie when her mother was busy, as well as cleaning No. 2, and taking the Lacey washing on Monday mornings and bringing it back clean and freshly ironed on the Wednesday evening. She was a fat, motherly woman with five children of her own but thought nothing of taking on an extra one, and only charged Louella a nominal sum for childminding, though she enjoyed the privilege of being able to have a free seat at the theatre whenever she had time to see a show.

Everyone living in the court assumed that Louella and Baz's father were married since they lived in the same house, but Lottie knew it was not true. 'Only don't say anything to anyone because folk don't approve of theatre people,' Louella had said, thoroughly confusing her daughter. 'Let them believe what they want to believe, that's what I say.'

Of course Baz must have known that Louella

and Max O'Mara were not married, but he never remarked on it, so it was easy for Lottie to keep her own counsel. The neighbours referred to Max and Louella as Mr and Mrs Magic, and were friendly enough in an offhand way, though they seldom mixed much, of course. When the other residents of the court were coming wearily home after a day's work on the docks, or in the factories and shops, Mr and Mrs Magic were setting out for the evening performance at the Gaiety. Thursdays and Saturdays they did matinée performances, and on Sunday they stayed in bed until noon and then went to the theatre, if they wished to do so, to rehearse whatever act they were going to perform the following week, for the management liked to vary its programme since this encouraged the audience to return. But quite often neither Max nor Louella felt the need to rehearse so Sunday was usually a holiday.

At Christmas, the entire cast abandoned their own acts and put on a pantomime. Baz, who despised the theatre, or said he did, always moaned and grumbled that he would not be dragged on to the stage, but usually ended up as the rear end of the cow in *Jack and the Beanstalk*, or a servant to the Marquis of Carabas when they did *Puss in Boots*. They all loved the pantomime season when every seat in the theatre was filled and the money rolled in steadily for six glorious weeks, and when it was over the theatre was closed for a whole fortnight so that everyone could go off for a well-earned rest.

8

'Well? Are we goin' or ain't we? Honest to God, Lottie, I don't believe you listen to a word I say. You sit there with your gob open, dreamin' away, when I *telled* you your mam were in a takin'.' Kenny seized Lottie's hands and heaved her to her feet. 'What's gorrin to you today? You're always dreamy but you ain't usually this bad.'

'Sorry. I'm a bit worried like, Kenny,' Lottie said apologetically. 'The fact is . . . If I tell you, will you promise you won't tell no one else?'

'Cross me heart and hope to die, slit me throat if I tell a lie,' Kenny said rapidly, drawing a finger across his throat and making a peculiarly horrible choking noise as he did so. 'What's up then? Don't say you've remembered you killed someone afore your accident?'

'I'll kill you if you don't shurrup,' Lottie said automatically. 'No, but do you remember me tellin' you how my mam had to get rid of Merle 'cos she weren't sweet no more? Well, one of my teeth is wobbling, and that means the rest will start to wobble too quite soon. Baz says Mammy will kick me out, like she did Merle . . .'

'Course she won't. Merle weren't no relation so that were different,' Kenny said bracingly. 'You're daft, you are! Oh, I grant you teeth's important if you're on the stage, but you'll grow some more, same as everyone else does.' He grinned like a crocodile and tapped his own front teeth with a grimy forefinger. 'See them? Them's me second teeth, even better than the first lot if you asks me.

Most kids lose 'em when they's five or six – I did – so you're lucky to have hung on to 'em for so long. I guess it's because you're small for your age,' he concluded wisely.

Lottie stared doubtfully up at him. She supposed he was right because Mammy and she loved one another but she still wished she could do something which would stop the wobbler from wobbling. Hesitantly, she suggested gluing it with a wodge of chewing gum but this only made Kenny laugh. 'You're always tellin' me how wonderful your mam is and I know she's a kind woman,' he said. 'She'll tell you not to open your mouth when you smile until the new teeth have growed in, but then you'll go on as before.' He heaved an exaggerated sigh. 'I never met a girl what worried more over less.'

By now, the two of them were making their way along the crowded pavement and Lottie stopped short, grabbing Kenny's arm so that he stopped too. 'You'd worry if you couldn't remember a great big dollop of your life,' she said accusingly. 'Anyone would.'

'No, no, only a stupid girl,' Kenny said tauntingly. 'Just wait till I tell me mam that you think Mrs Magic would kick you out 'cos you'd lost your front teeth!'

'If you tell anyone, you're a horrible liar,' Lottie said. 'You swore you wouldn't.'

Kenny began to say that such an oath only applied to other kids, but Lottie was having none

10

of it. She hurled herself at him and in a moment the two of them were rolling on the ground, Lottie making a spirited attempt to punch her companion on the nose whilst Kenny, giggling helplessly, fended her off.

It was a friendly fight, for Kenny never used his full strength, but when they drew apart and lurched into a shop doorway – for passers-by had not been pleased when the fighters had barged into them – Lottie realised there was a salty taste in her mouth. When she checked the wobbler, she discovered why. Her tooth had come right out. She gave a wail of despair and spat it into the palm of her hand. It looked very tiny, but when she probed at the hole it had left, still wondering if she could stick it back, she felt the sharp edge of the new tooth and realised it was hopeless. She had lost her first tooth and could not possibly hide the fact from anyone, and of course Louella would have to be told.

'What's up?' Kenny said, staring. 'I didn't hurt you, did I? There's blood on your chin.'

'Me tooth's come right out,' Lottie quavered, holding out her hand to show the evidence. 'I must have jammed me teeth together or something. Oh well, once it started to wobble there weren't much I could do. I'll just have to tell me mam an' see what she says.'

'I'm tellin' you she won't mind. All mams know their kids lose teeth,' Kenny said reassuringly. 'And if you put that tooth under your piller, chances are your mam'll take it out and put a penny there instead.'

Lottie grinned at him. For some reason, now that it had actually happened, she realised she had been worrying for nothing. Mammy would never turn her out, no matter what horrible Baz might say, and besides, there had been times when she had wished that she was an ordinary child and not a theatrical one. If losing a tooth meant she did not have to perform for several weeks, what was wrong with that? When she had first started work again, after coming out of hospital, she had been so tired the day following a performance that she had repeatedly fallen asleep in class and this had not pleased her teachers. Because of her memory loss she had had a lot of ground to make up and the head teacher of the school in Bond Street had told Louella that her daughter should miss matinées rather than school. It was the summer holidays now, but of course theatres did not close down, like schools, so she was only able to play out when she was neither rehearsing nor performing and often she was too tired to join in the more energetic games played by the children in Victoria Court. Yes, a break from working in the theatre would not be so bad after all.

She said as much to Kenny but he looked at her with incredulity. 'Wharrabout the money, queen?' he asked. 'Your mam's got Number Two real nice but she's bound to miss your money.'

They had almost reached the theatre by this time

and were about to go down the jigger which led to the stage door, but once again Lottie pulled her companion to a halt. 'Money? But no one pays me money,' she said. 'They pay Mammy . . . I must remember to call her Louella because she doesn't like me sayin' Mammy in the theatre, I don't know why. What makes you think anyone would pay me, Kenny?'

'Course they does,' Kenny said impatiently. 'Why, half the folk in the stalls goes there pertickler to see you; they think you're sweet.' He sounded disgusted. 'Anyroad, let's see what your mam – I mean Louella – says when you tell 'er about your tooth.'

Both children had forgotten that Kenny had already seen Louella in the box office or they might have gone in through the front. As it was, they found the stage door uncompromisingly locked so they had to retrace their steps. There was a short queue for tickets, for the theatre put on extra matinées during the school holidays, giving a shortened performance and charging half the usual price. They joined the queue but several people looked round and Lottie was immediately recognised. Faces beamed and there were murmurs of 'It's little Miss Lottie come to visit her mammy' as the folk in the queue pushed her gently to the front. Lottie had grown used to being hailed when she was with her mother or near the theatre, but she did not like it. However, she smiled brightly, keeping her lips

13

clamped together and reflecting that at least being recognised meant she could speak to Louella at once, rather than having to wait her turn.

It was apparent, however, as soon as she reached the front of the queue that her mother was not in a very good temper. 'Lottie, you bad child, where on earth have you been?' she snapped. 'I was beginning to think you must have had an accident. You know full well that you're supposed to come down to the theatre for my messages as soon as Mrs Brocklehurst has given you your dinner. What were you doing? I must say you're usually . . . oh, my God!'

Wordlessly, Lottie had opened her mouth, indicated the gap, and then held out her hand with her small tooth in its palm. 'Me bleedin' tooth come out, Louella. I'm awful sorry but I couldn't help it,' she said humbly. 'I wanted to stick it back in with chewing gum only Kenny said that wouldn't work. Will it – will it mean—'

Her mother interrupted her. 'Losing a tooth doesn't take over an hour, nor should it make you as dirty as though you'd been rolling around on the pavement,' she said accusingly. 'And how many times have I told you not to use bad language? It's vulgar and unnecessary.'

Lottie stared at her mother with considerable respect. How on earth had she known about the fight on the pavement? She opened her mouth to enquire but Louella was producing her purse, a list and their marketing bag, so she said nothing.

After all her worry it seemed that a missing tooth wasn't even an acceptable excuse for being late. But Louella was standing up and coming round to the little side door. She emerged into the foyer, holding out the marketing bag with one hand and fluffing up her blonde curls with the other. She smiled sweetly at the queue of people, then bent to give Lottie a quick kiss and to smooth a hand over her daughter's rumpled curls. 'Off you go then, pet, and you may buy a couple of iced buns for you and your little friend,' she said gaily. Then she turned her sweetest smile on her audience. 'Aren't children little wretches?' she enquired laughingly. 'When I left home to come to work earlier little Miss Lottie was clean and neat as a freshly picked flower, and look at her now!'

'Well, missus, the kid ain't born what can spend a couple of hours out in the street wi'out gettin' muck up to the eyebrows,' someone remarked, and there were murmurs of agreement from those around.

'Very true,' Louella said. She turned back to Lottie. 'Don't be long, darling. I'm dying for a cup of tea but there's no milk – or tea for that matter – so I'm relying on you to buy me some.'

She turned away but Lottie followed her, saying in a low undertone: 'Can I go on this evening, Mammy, without me tooth? I'll try to smile with me lips closed but I might forget . . .'

Louella whipped into the box office, then turned and faced her daughter. 'Of course you'll go on tonight,' she hissed, her voice losing its sweetness and becoming merely impatient. 'And you'd better practise smiling with your lips closed.' And with that, she slammed the box office door, causing Lottie to jump backwards, for had she not done so she might easily have lost another tooth.

Rather chastened, the two children left the building and headed towards St John's market, for Louella was a great believer in fresh fruit and vegetables and always bought quantities of both.

'Your mam were in a rare old temper,' Kenny said presently. 'An' it weren't your tooth, though I aren't denyin' it shook her up a bit. Don't she like doin' a turn in the box office?'

Lottie shrugged. 'Dunno,' she said vaguely. 'I think it was me bein' late and her worrying about the messages which made her a bit short like. Actresses is all the same. And it ain't temper – it's temperament what they've got.'

'Looked like temper to me,' Kenny said shortly. 'Tell you what, queen, we'll go to the nearest shop for a tin of conny-onny and two ounces of Typhoo and take it straight back to the theatre. I knows women, I does: she'll be sweet as apple pie once she's got her gob round a cuppa tea.'

Lottie agreed that this would be sensible and the two children hurried to the corner shop to buy the tea and a tin of condensed milk. Then they returned to the theatre and went straight to the foyer. Kenny tapped loudly on the box office pass door, then thrust it open. 'We brung you some conny-onny and some tea, Mrs Magic,' he said in a loud and cheerful choice. 'We guessed you'd be gaspin' for a cuppa, but we'll get on now and do the rest of the messages.'

'Ah, you're a good lad,' Louella said gratefully. 'I'd ask you to put the kettle on but Mrs Mulvaney arrived ten minutes ago so I dare say she'll make a brew, and I'm about to close the box office anyway. You'd best go straight home with the rest of the shopping.'

'All right, Mammy,' Lottie said, as her mother shut and locked the box office window and came out of the pass door to close off the foyer. 'Will – will you be coming home before the performance?' She glanced at the clock which hung just over the door leading to the stalls. It was only half past three and the first house started at seven: plenty of time for Louella to get back to Victoria Court and fix them both a snack before they returned to the theatre together.

Louella cocked her head on one side, considering. 'I suppose I'll have to since you've got yourself in such a mess,' she said, her voice softening. 'Now off with you. If you're home before me, queen, you can start the tea.'

'Yes, all right, Mammy . . . I mean Louella,' Lottie said as she and Kenny were pushed out of the foyer and on to the pavement. 'What do you want for tea, though? There's some cold mutton . . .'

'That'll do. Butter some bread and buy a piece of slab cake from Sample's,' Louella said, and the children heard the bolts being drawn across as they turned away, heading once more for St John's market.

Lottie always went to the same stall since it was a well-known fact that if you shopped regularly with the same stallholder he or she was unlikely to risk losing custom by selling you inferior fruit or vegetables. Nellie Crabbe was a tiny wizened old lady with dyed ginger hair, a pair of enormous spectacles and a face wrinkled as a prune. Once she had been wardrobe mistress at the theatre but failing eyesight had led to her retirement and now she ran the greengrocery stall for her son, William, who farmed on the Wirral and provided her with excellent fruit and vegetables in season. Everyone in the theatre patronised her because they knew she would never cheat them and also from a sense of loyalty to one who had, in her time, worked well for them. When Louella did her own shopping, which was not often, she would not have dreamed of going to any other stall first, though if Mrs Crabbe had run out of a particular fruit or vegetable she would buy from another source, though she would make sure to do so where Mrs Crabbe could not see her.

For her part, Lottie did very well out of Mrs Crabbe for she personified the two loves of the old lady's life, the theatre and little girls. Mrs Crabbe always made up Lottie's order with meticulous honesty and then added little extras. At this time of year there might be a peach with a bruise on it,

18

a handful of late blackcurrants or the fat, red dessert gooseberries, sweet and juice-filled, which Lottie and Kenny particularly loved. Later, there would be apples and pears, and when winter came an orange with a split in it, or a banana whose yellow skin was turning black, for William Crabbe bought from the wholesalers such fruit and vegetables as he could not grow on his own farm.

The children arrived at the stall and Lottie handed over her list. Mrs Crabbe pursed her lips and frowned down at the writing, then handed it back to her small customer. 'Just you read it to me, my love; it'll save time and reading small writing makes me eyes ache,' she said. 'And don't forget, read out the heavy things first – spuds, drumhead cabbage and such – so's they go into the bottom of your marketing bag and don't crush the fruit.' She chuckled softly. 'I knows your mam of old; she don't think logical, but there, that's actresses for you.'

Lottie scanned the list, then began to read it in reverse order, thinking indulgently that Louella wrote her list in order of her own preference so that peaches entered her head long before mundane things like potatoes. When the list was completed, Mrs Crabbe selected a brown paper bag from the hooks behind her and regarded her stall. 'Them grapes will be mush by tomorrer,' she murmured, popping a bunch into the bag. 'An' them plums won't go till Sat'day.' She picked up two large Victoria plums, put them carefully

19

beside the grapes, then named the sum which Lottie owed for the rest of her goods.

Lottie fished out her purse and paid up, beaming at her old friend. 'You are kind to us, Mrs Crabbe,' she said gratefully. 'I wish I'd been in the theatre when you was, though Mrs Jones is very nice and hardly grumbled at all when I told her I'd growed out o' me tutu an' needed a new one. She made me a beauty, too,' she added reminiscently.

Mrs Crabbe chuckled indulgently. 'I trained that young woman so she's bound to be capable,' she remarked. Mrs Jones was Mrs Crabbe's daughter and was in fact very good at her work, though Lottie would not have dreamed of saying so to the old lady. In fact, Mrs Crabbe had retired before Lottie was born, but Lottie knew what a formidable reputation the old lady had had for making costumes out of nothing, and at a moment's notice.

Now, she consulted her list as soon as Mrs Crabbe moved to serve the next customer. 'Not much more, Kenny,' she informed her friend. 'Most of it we can get on our way home.' She dug a hand into the basket and produced the plums, and soon both children were eating the fruit, juice dribbling down their chins. 'Don't let me forget Mammy wanted some slab cake because it ain't on the list, and she likes to cut little bits off the slab to dip into her tea.' She glanced ahead of her. 'Race you to Pringle's.'

*

Louella usually enjoyed her stint in the box office, but today, she thought as she went to join Mrs Mulvaney in the green room, she could have done without it. And now, on top of her disagreement with Max, she would have to face up to the fact that her daughter was beginning to lose her teeth and might easily lose her appeal as well.

When she reached the green room, Mrs Mulvaney, who was responsible for the hiring and firing of usherettes and made tea for the cast, was not there, but the kettle was steaming gently on the paraffin stove, so Louella tipped tea into the big brown pot and let it brew for a few moments. Finally she poured herself a large mugful, flopped into an armchair and began to sip. She was still cross, however. She and Max had fallen out when he had suggested that she might begin to pay a fairer share of the rent of the house in Victoria Court – half, in fact – and she had reminded him, pretty sharply, that he earned more than she and the arrangement had always been that she should pay one-third and he two. After all, she pointed out, she kept the place clean, did the marketing and cooked the food, as well as keeping his stage clothes spotless and the paraphernalia of his magic act in tip-top condition. This included feeding two white rabbits and four white doves, though to be fair young Baz always looked after the animals and birds. He bought their food and the sawdust with which the cage floors were lined, but she had not mentioned this fact to Max, of course.

The argument had started soon after they had got up, when they were sitting in the kitchen, toasting rounds of bread and spreading the slices with strawberry jam. Usually they had porridge, but Louella had forgotten to buy milk or conny-onny the previous day, and Max liked his porridge creamy. Perhaps it had been that which had led to his grumbling that money seemed to go nowhere these days. 'It's not so bad for you because the management pays you pretty well for little Miss Lottie,' he had observed. 'What's more, you don't need no rabbits nor pigeons nor disappearin' boxes to perform your act. I reckons it's time we split the rent down the middle, 'cos there's two of us an' two of you and it 'ud be fairer all round.'

Louella had glanced at him expectantly, hoping to see a teasing smile cross that handsome face, but Max was staring at her challengingly, so she waded straight in on the offensive, listing all that she did in the house.

'But it's not you who cleans the place,' Max pointed out. 'Mrs Brocklehurst does that, as well as the washing and ironing, to say nothing of some cooking and any shopping that you and Lottie don't have time for. And it's me who usually pays her, remember.'

'Ye-es, you usually do,' Louella admitted unwillingly. 'But that's because it was your house for a couple of years before I moved in, and Mrs B has always worked for you. If you ask me . . .'

'And it's Baz who feeds and cleans the animals

and birds, not you at all,' Max continued remorselessly. 'I'm telling you, Lou, it's not fair and it's time we sorted things out.'

Louella had jumped to her feet, realising that she had been unwise to claim to do so many jobs which were in fact done by other people. 'You're in a bad mood because you lost your bleedin' shirt on the horse what one of your pals said was a dead cert,' she announced firmly. They had been sitting on either side of the kitchen table, but then she had crossed the room and as Max had struggled out of his chair had flung herself at him, throwing her arms up round his neck, for he was a good deal taller than she. 'I'm sorry, I'm sorry. I know you back the horses and go to the races for relaxation,' she said, pushing her head into the hollow of his shoulder. 'But oh, Maxy, darling, I do pay more than my share of the housekeeping, you know I do. Don't let's quarrel. Suppose I pay all the housekeeping; would that do?'

Max had heaved a great sigh. 'You know very well I'm not the sort of feller to check up on you when you tell me what the food has cost,' he said, but to Louella's relief he no longer sounded angry. 'What's wrong with paying half the rent, anyway? No, tell you what. You pay Mrs B for the work she does – the whole lot, mind – and we won't argue over the rent.'

Louella had had to agree but she had not been at all pleased. She and Max had been together now for a year and this was the first time he had questioned her contribution to household expenses. Louella knew that many men would have expected her to hand over most of her earnings, so before she had moved in she had made it plain how things were to be. She was an independent woman with a child to bring up. One day, she would need money for her daughter's schooling and so on, which meant she must have savings. Max had agreed to all her conditions, for apart from his work on the stage he was both lazy and easy-going, and he had been quite content, in the past, for Louella to manage their finances.

Now, sitting in the green room sipping her tea, Louella cursed the wretched horse, which had proved to be not a dead cert at all but had run as though it only had three legs. But for Flying Finish's abysmal performance Max would never have dreamed of querying how she spent their money. Indeed, he would have shared his winnings with her, taken her somewhere exotic for a meal, and bought her a pretty necklace or some of the thin silver bangles which she wore in her stage act. However, Louella thought she had been lucky that Max had not asked to see the household bills. The arrangement was that she should purchase everything for the house and then split the price of such items down the middle. In fact, he usually paid somewhat more, and Louella salved her conscience by telling herself that Baz ate at least twice as much as Lottie, and that Max himself ate a great deal more than she. This was true but did not take into account the fact that Max thought fruit and salads were miserable fare, whereas she and Lottie ate masses of vegetables and fruit all the year round, even when the latter was expensive, as it was in winter.

Louella's train of thought was interrupted as the green room door opened and several members of the cast entered. They surged into the room led by the comedian, Jack Russell, a small, sharp-faced man with bristly grey hair and shrewd twinkling brown eyes. Louella did not know if Jack Russell was his real name since it was a part of his act to bound on to the stage, yapping like an excited terrier, and his first line was always: 'Well folks, was I named after the dog or was the dog named after me? C'mon, c'mon, c'mon, answers on a post-card and if youse wrong I'll come down and nip your ankles!'

Just now, however, Jack's mind was on other things. 'Fee, fie, fo, fum,' he boomed, pointing to the pot, 'I smell tea in the auditorium. Who's goin' to pour Giant Jack a cup, eh?'

One of the chorus girls smiled at Jack and patted his bristly head. 'I'll do it,' she said, beginning to get mugs down from the shelf. 'Anyone else gasping for a cuppa?'

Lottie and Kenny completed their shopping in good time and tea was on the table when Louella arrived home. Her temper had clearly improved for she was singing as she entered the kitchen and smiled approvingly at her daughter as her eyes took in the tidy kitchen, the kettle steaming on the hob and the table neatly laid with cold mutton, bread and butter, and slab cake set out ready. 'You are a good girl, my pet. I knew I could rely on you,' she said, taking off her light jacket and fluffing out her hair with the gesture Lottie knew so well. 'I'm sorry I was cross earlier, but Max and I had had a bit of a barney and I was still upset. You know how I am.'

Lottie smiled forgivingly at her parent; she did indeed know how Louella was. Up one minute and down the next, blowing first hot and then cold, tears turning to laughter in a moment, that was Louella, but of course it would not do to say so; instead she went over to the fire intending to make the tea but Louella forestalled her. 'I'll do that, pet, if you'll run up to my room and fetch down my sewing box. There's a hole in the knee of my fishnet tights which I'll have to mend before I can go on stage again. Ah, I see you didn't wait for me to get home but had a good wash and brushed out your hair.' She finished pouring the hot water into the teapot, then swooped on Lottie and gave her a hug. 'I won't even ask if you got all my messages because I know you will have done so. Oh, you didn't forget Max's Woodbines, did you?'

Lottie giggled, feeling waves of warmth and reassurance wash over her. How could she ever have worried that this gentle loving woman could turn her out? But you had to laugh; Louella had said she knew Lottie would have done all the shopping and in the same breath had asked if her daughter had remembered to buy Max's cigarettes. Since they were on the list and Lottie had worked her way conscientiously through it, it was scarcely likely that she would have forgotten. So she returned her mother's hug, pointed out the cigarettes on the Welsh dresser, and then ran upstairs for the sewing box.

When she returned to the kitchen, Louella was sitting in one of the fireside chairs with a cup of tea in one hand and a piece of slab cake in the other. She was dipping the cake absently into her tea but stopped when she saw her daughter and got to her feet, carrying tea and cake over to the table. 'Max would have my guts for garters if he saw me doing this,' she said cheerfully, standing the tea down on the table. 'He says only old ladies need to dunk.' She turned to Lottie. 'Now let's have a look at the gap in your teeth.' Lottie obediently opened her mouth, and after a moment's scrutiny her mother said that provided Lottie remembered to keep her lips together when she smiled she was sure no one would even notice. 'I had a bit of a talk with Jack Russell,' she said, gesturing to Lottie to take her place at the table. 'He said as how kids without front teeth went down pretty big on the silver screen because audiences think it's cute – American audiences that is – and he thought Liverpool folk would feel the same. In fact, he suggested that when we take our final

27

bow you should give a great big smile at the audience to show the gap in your teeth. I wasn't too sure, but, thinking it over, he may well be right. We'll try it tonight, at any rate, and see how it goes.'

'But what about when the new teeth come through?' Lottie asked rather apprehensively. 'Baz said some people's teeth come through huge, which isn't pretty. And you let Merle go because she stopped being sweet.'

'They won't be huge, because you're very like me and I've always had small, even teeth,' Louella said. 'But I didn't let Merle go because of her teeth, queen. It was because she didn't sing too well. Truth to tell, sweetheart, I only employed her because she was related to Max. And it's always a mistake to employ someone you don't know yourself.'

'Related to Max?' Lottie squeaked. 'I never knew that, Mammy. What sort of relation?'

'She's his niece,' Louella said briefly, helping herself to another slice of cake.

'Well, I'm blowed,' Lottie said. 'Baz never told me that! So that makes Merle his cousin, don't it, Mammy? No wonder they were such big friends, her and Baz. It did seem odd because she were only with you for a couple of months, weren't she? While I were in hospital, I mean. But I reckon her and Baz had probably known each other for ages. An' if she's his cousin, where is she now?'

'With her parents, of course,' Louella said. 'Her

pa is Max's brother and he's a conjurer like Max, only he's with the circus. Well, Max started off with the circus too, but he soon realised he could do a deal better for himself on the stage. So you see I took Merle on as a favour to Max, really.'

'But she was only a kid, so why did they let her come to you?' Lottie asked. 'Mammies don't usually leave their kids, norreven with an uncle, do they?'

'Sometimes they do,' Louella said. For some reason a faint pink blush stole up her neck and invaded her cheeks. 'But Max's brother knew poor Merle couldn't read or write because they never stayed in the same place long enough for her to get any schooling. They thought if she lived with us for, say, a year, she might catch up. Only it's no good denying she couldn't sing, and when I knew you were coming out of hospital we sent her back to the circus. And since she sagged off school whenever she could and was dreadfully cocky to the teachers, they weren't sorry to see her go, I can tell you.'

'I see,' Lottie said slowly. She felt greatly relieved. All her worries over losing her teeth had been completely groundless. I should have guessed that Baz was only trying to frighten me, she thought, helping herself to cold mutton. But I wonder why he never told me Merle was his cousin? I'll ask him sometime, if I can catch him when he's in a good mood, that is. And how odd that I never knew Max had a brother, either. I wish *we* were in a circus! If we were, I shouldn't have to go to school and I could learn to be a tightrope walker and swing on a trapeze in spangled tights and a frilly top. Just wait till I tell Kenny that I'm as good as related to a circus conjurer!

Chapter Two

1922

It was July and this was the last day of term. Lottie, cleaning her teeth vigorously and spitting into the slop bucket, remembered how frightened she had been a year ago that her second teeth would turn out to be large and yellowy, and prevent her from performing on stage with her mother. How things had changed in that year! Her teeth had come through as Louella had predicted, small and even. And she had grown a little as well, only a couple of inches, but enough to make her mother eye her thoughtfully. 'I'm beginning to wonder if Max is right and you should go to proper ballet lessons,' she had said, only a few days earlier. 'In a couple of years we shan't be able to call you little Miss Lottie any more and the management may want you to do an act of your own. What would you think of that, eh?'

Lottie had stared at her mother, round-eyed. 'I'd hate it,' she said truthfully. 'I always tell myself that the audience is looking at you, not me, else I'd die of fright. Honestly, Louella, I couldn't do a solo act, not to save me life.'

Louella had laughed and looked pleased – though she had said, soothingly, that Lottie would soon grow accustomed – and the subject had been dropped. But Lottie was sure her mother was wrong. She would never get used to being stared at and the thought of being alone on the stage terrified her. She was grateful for her school uniform and the fact that, offstage, she was allowed to plait her hair into a thick rope so that most folk did not realise she was little Miss Lottie, and was even more grateful to Kenny, for he had discovered how she felt and had bought her, off a jumble stall in Paddy's market, a pair of steel-framed spectacles. He had knocked the glass out of them and she wore them whenever she thought there was the least danger of being recognised. She had never let her mother see the spectacles, but valued them as a sure disguise and was thankful to Kenny for the gift of anonymity which the spectacles bestowed.

Now, Lottie finished cleaning her teeth, rinsed her toothbrush and poured her washing water into the slop bucket. Today was a very special day and she was full of excitement at the thought of it. It was also the first time she had ever deceived her mother, but she did not feel guilty over so doing. Why should she? Today was the day of the school trip. Her mother knew that, and approved, but what she did not know was where the coaches were bound. 'This year we shall set off at eight o'clock sharp and stop halfway to the coast at a café which caters for coach parties,' Miss Bradshaw had said. 'We shall arrive in Rhyl at noon. Bring a packed lunch to eat on the beach. You will have the whole afternoon to play in the sand, to paddle, and to visit the amusement arcades. Then we will all gather under the clock on the promenade and go to the Seagull restaurant for a high tea, which will be paid for by the school governors. When the meal is finished, we shall return to the coaches and get home again between eight and nine in the evening.'

The only part of this information which Lottie had failed to pass on to her mother was their destination, and even then she had not exactly lied. She had, however, talked of the Great Orme and the excitement of taking a tram to the very top, without actually saying that the trip would be to Llandudno. Had she admitted that they were going to Rhyl she was honestly afraid that her mother would have refused to let her go. However, she did not intend to let her conscience trouble her over such a small matter. Though the memory of her early years had still not returned, she was pretty sure that her mother had not bleached her hair then, so it seemed highly unlikely that anyone would recognise her as Louella's daughter. Why should they? She meant to take her glassless spectacles, just in case, but was pretty sure that there would be no need to put them on. And if someone did know her, what would it matter? Two whole years had passed since Louella had fled from the violent conjurer – Lottie could not remember his name – so surely his rage would have cooled, probably had disappeared altogether, by now.

Having washed herself thoroughly and brushed her hair until it bushed out round her face, giving her a marked resemblance to a dandelion clock, Lottie made her way downstairs. The school trip was a combined one which meant that Lottie had been forced to beg Baz not to tell Max, or Louella, where they were bound. Baz was tall and broad for his age and was beginning to look very like his father, who had thick black hair, very dark eyes and a commanding high-bridged nose, for though Max had lived in England for most of his adult life he had been born in Spain of an English father and a Spanish mother and looked very foreign, Lottie thought.

Baz had recently stopped teasing Lottie, apparently thinking it beneath his dignity to make fun of a child so much younger than himself, so she had put her request to him with more hope than she would have done a year earlier. Baz had stared at her hard, his black eyes curious. 'Why?' he had demanded brusquely. 'Rhyl's a grand place. The sand is all covered with little shells, and there's pools for the young kids to paddle in, and the lovely shallow sea for us big 'uns. And the amusements is great. There's a shootin' gallery, penny falls, grab a gift and peep shows: what the butler saw and that. I've been saving up me paper round money for weeks.' He stared even harder at his small companion. 'Your mammy won't stop you going, you little idiot: is that what you're feared of?'

Lottie had hesitated. You could never tell with Baz. Sometimes he was really nice but he could be such a beast. However, there was no sense in lying; truth will always out, and generally when it could cause you the most embarrassment, she reminded herself.

'Well? Is you goin' to tell me or ain't you?'

'I am,' Lottie had said resignedly. 'Before we came to Liverpool, we were in Rhyl. Mam was working for another magician but she'd heard your dad wanted an assistant and the Rhyl magician was mean to her. So we ran away from Rhyl and came to Liverpool, and Mam – Louella, I mean – won't ever go back there in case the magician kills 'er.'

Baz had guffawed noisily. 'Stupid little halfwit. Of course he won't kill her. And anyway, he was with the circus, wasn't he? Circuses move on. They don't stick around in one spot.'

'I thought we were at the Pavilion, Louella and me,' Lottie had said. 'Well if you're right and he's moved on then I dare say Louella would let me go to Rhyl. But I'd still feel happier if you'd not tell her, Baz. Remember last year?'

The school trip the previous year had been to New Brighton, but at the last minute Louella had decided that her daughter should not go. She had said that the fair at New Brighton was a rough place, and the teachers would have their hands full and might not be able to supervise the children properly. Lottie had been bitterly disappointed but there had been nothing she could do about it. This time, she had told her mother bluntly that she did not mean to miss out because the other kids had had such a good time the previous year. Louella had stared at her, round-eyed. 'I wouldn't stop you going, pet; Llandudno is a most respectable resort,' she had said. 'I'll give you half a crown to spend on the pier and when you get home you can tell me all about it.'

That had sounded perfectly reasonable but Lottie was taking no chances. 'Please, Baz, don't forget last year,' she had said again. 'She wouldn't let me go to New Brighton, remember . . .'

'Oh, awright, no need to run on,' Baz had said impatiently. 'I won't tell on you and that's a promise.'

And so far, Lottie knew, he had kept his word. So now she started down the stairs, no longer worrying that the treat might be snatched from her. It was early still and the kitchen was deserted, but there was nothing strange in that. Lottie always cooked the breakfast porridge for herself and Baz because Louella and Max seldom got up before mid-morning, and the youngsters had to be in school by nine. Baz usually made the toast, squatting on his haunches and holding out the slices of bread, impaled on a toasting fork, towards the fire. He complained in summer that it was a horrible job and that he'd far rather make the porridge, but on the only occasion upon which he had insisted upon changing he had somehow managed to produce a panful half burnt, half raw and full of lumps. So now each did their own task without more than a token grumble.

The porridge was actually in the bowls and the tea steaming in the mugs when Baz bounced into the kitchen. He grinned at Lottie and sat down at the table, beginning to eat at once. 'I don't reckon I'll make toast today,' he said, taking a noisy drink of his tea. 'We don't want to be late and our teacher said the coach would stop halfway to the coast, so I dare say that'll be for elevenses. Have you made our sarnies yet? We're supposed to take a packed lunch, remember?'

'Louella said she'd make them and leave them in the meat safe,' Lottie said. She got to her feet and went over to the small pantry, returning with two bulky packages wrapped in greaseproof paper.

She pushed her own packet – the smaller one – into her satchel, but Baz immediately unwrapped his and examined the contents. 'Well I never! Your mam's done us proud for once,' he said. 'Mine's corned beef and brown sauce – lovely grub.'

He began to take one of the sandwiches out of its wrapping, but Lottie darted across the kitchen and laid her hand over his. 'Don't start on them yet,' she said urgently. 'They're for us dinners. If you're still hungry, have some bread and jam.'

Baz sighed, but replaced the sandwich and

reached for the loaf. 'I'll cut a slice for each of us,' he said gruffly. 'Then we'd best be mekkin' a move, else we'll be late.'

'Right,' Lottie said breathlessly, beginning to wash up the crocks, but she had scarcely sunk her teeth into the round of bread and jam which Baz handed her when someone banged on the door and it shot open to reveal Kenny and his small sister, Daisy.

The two children tumbled down the passage and into the kitchen, both beaming. 'C'mon, youse,' Kenny gabbled. 'We don't want to be late. Got your nib-nabs? Mam has give us pilchard and tomato paste and an apple. Wharr've you got?'

'Corned beef,' Lottie and Baz said in unison. Baz had jammed his sandwiches into his jacket pocket but Lottie picked up her satchel, which already contained her packed lunch, then glanced guiltily around the kitchen. She always tidied and washed up before leaving for school but today there had not been time. Should she just whisk round quickly or . . .

She was about to turn back into the kitchen when Kenny seized her arm and pulled, and Baz pushed her so hard in the small of her back that she popped into the court like a cork out of a bottle.

'Gerra move on, our Lottie,' Baz said. 'Here, take your perishin' jacket an' don't worry 'cos you haven't washed up. Today's special, after all. Your mam knows that.'

'Right you are then,' Lottie said, falling into step

between the two boys. She was relieved to have had the decision not to linger taken for her and suddenly she felt light and carefree, looking forward to the day ahead. The sun was shining, there was a light breeze and she was off to the seaside! Dancing along and chattering to Kenny and Daisy, Lottie was sure she had never been happier.

'Tuck your dress into your knickers. I'm gonna roll me trouser legs up. I'd take all me clothes off and have a swim, only you can be sure if I do, some teacher will spring up and send me back to the coach in disgrace,' Kenny said, as the two of them, up to their knees in seawater, surveyed the happy scene. Daisy had gone off with a crowd of little friends and Baz, having eaten his sandwiches aboard the coach, had disappeared in search of fish and chips, leaving Lottie and Kenny to the joys of the beach and each other's company.

'The teachers did say we should just paddle, and not go in above our knees,' Lottie reminded her friend. She had no wish to see Kenny get into trouble, and besides, since he had neither towel nor swimsuit, she thought going further into the water ought to be out of the question. 'What about collecting shells? My mam has a box all covered with the most beautiful shells. It's on her dressing table and she keeps her jewels in it. I say, Kenny, are you going to take your mam a present? I expect shell boxes are very expensive, though.'

'Mam said not to bother – she said she'd give us some money so's we could enjoy ourselves, not so's we could buy a present for her. But there's four of us on this here trip – only Jimmy ain't here, bein' at work now – so we all got together and Patsy took tuppence off each of us. She's goin' to spend it on the biggest stick of rock she can find, 'cos our mam loves peppermint rock.'

'Rock! That's a good idea,' Lottie said enthusiastically. 'That's what I'll get for my mam, and I'll buy another stick for Max. Oh, look – there's a big curly shell. It's a bit deep for me to pick it up here unless I can grab it with my toes . . .' This was easier said than done and presently she began to kick it nearer the shore until it reached a spot shallow enough for her to plunge her hand in and bring it up from the watery depths. She moved her hand gradually nearer and nearer to the magnificent shell and as she did so the sight of her small white hand, wavering like some exotic fish through the clear water, reminded her of something . . . somewhere. She had done this before, fished around for a shell, seen her hand beneath the waves . . . but she could not remember anything else about the incident. I suppose Mam brought me on the beach when we were in Rhyl before, Lottie told herself. But she did wish she could remember! What a nuisance that nice things were no longer in her head to be enjoyed, though perhaps there were nasty things best forgotten as well. She was musing on this when she felt the

shell beneath her fingers and grabbed triumphantly, which meant a good deal of splashing,
though what did that matter? She had the shell,
the biggest one she had ever found, despite the
fact that by the time they regained the beach her
dress was decidedly wet. She pointed this out to
her companion but he merely grinned and told her
that such a wonderful shell was worth a bit of a
ducking. 'We'll go and sit on the soft sand higher
up the beach and eat our sarnies while you dry
off,' he said cheerfully. 'Then we'll build the biggest
sandcastle in the world, bigger'n anything else on
the beach.'

Lottie agreed to this and presently the children
settled themselves comfortably just by the tideline,
for the sea was coming in and this would make
filling the moat which they intended to dig round
their castle less of an effort.

Lottie lay on her tummy on the sand, enjoying
the sandwiches and every now and then taking a
bite out of the tomato which Louella had included
in the greaseproof wrapping. It had got rather
squashed but was still very welcome, for the bottle
of lemonade which she and Kenny had shared for
elevenses seemed a long time ago. When they
finished their food Lottie pointed out that they had
nothing to dig with, unlike the children around
them who were enthusiastically wielding small tin
shovels or large wooden spades, but Kenny waved
such a defeatist remark aside. 'Me mam always
says fingers was made before forks, so it stands to

reason hands was made before spades,' he told her. 'D'you see that little dog, with its nostrils all clogged up from diggin' in the sand? Well, that's how we'll do it.'

Lottie giggled. 'He digs a hole then shoves his head down it, an' I don't mean to do that, even if you do,' she said. But presently they began on the great work of construction, and when one of the teachers came along and announced that everyone had been set to making sandcastles and that he, personally, would give a prize of a sixpenny piece and a stick of rock to the makers of the best and most elaborate edifice, Lottie and Kenny were already well on their way to winning. They piled and patted until the castle was as tall as Lottie herself, and then collected shells, feathery red and rubbery green seaweed, and round white pebbles with which to decorate their enormous monument. They duly won the prize, though Kenny donated the sixpence to the children whose castle had come second, and then he and Lottie, tired but happy, made their way back to the promenade where they shook off large quantities of sand, donned their footwear and headed for the pier, for Lottie's half-crown was still intact.

They paid their pennies to join the bustling crowds. Lottie was fascinated as they drew near the end of the pier by the fact that she could see the sea through the gaps in the wooden planking. It gave her a delicious thrill to think that she was over deep water, though when she said as much to Kenny he said, reassuringly, that it would probably only reach up to her shoulders. Then the two of them found an empty bench and knelt upon it, to look over the side. Lottie saw what looked like round transparent balls with pinkish markings bobbing under the calm surface, and Kenny told her that these were jellyfish. 'Good thing none of 'em come up to us when we was paddlin' 'cos they've got poisonous stings on the end of them trailing things what'll kill you in a second,' he said impressively.

Lottie was about to say that she would never paddle again when one of the teachers, overhearing, cuffed Kenny playfully and called him a wicked little liar. 'There are jellyfish which can sting you but they're usually only found in tropical waters,' the teacher assured her. He turned to her companion. 'The ones you see round this coast are absolutely harmless, so don't you go scaring your pal, young fellow-me-lad. And don't forget to come to the clock at five because I popped into the restaurant just now and there's a grand spread laid out ready for us.'

'Is it fish and chips, sir? I does love fish 'n' chips,' Kenny said eagerly.

The teacher grinned but shook his head. 'No, but I saw sandwiches, sausage rolls, meat pasties and all sorts of jellies and cakes, besides bottles of ginger beer and lemonade,' he told them. 'If you ask me, it's better than fish and chips because you don't have to sit down and wait to be served. They

give everyone plates and tell you to help yourselves, and last time the kids just ate until there
wasn't a crumb left on the tables. So I do advise
you, my little friends, not to be late at the
rendezvous.'

'Gosh,' Kenny breathed, clearly almost unable
to believe his ears. 'Don't you worry, sir, we won't
be late ... we'll be *early*, won't we, Lottie? We
wouldn't want to miss grub like that!'

After the teacher had wandered off, Kenny
checked the time on the clock. 'We've got a whole
half-hour before we need come back here. What'll
we do?' he enquired. 'If we go into town we could
go to the rock shop. Ever been there? You can go
inside and watch them making the rock, pulling
it until it's thin enough to chop up into sticks.'

'No, I've never been there,' Lottie said uncertainly, then was suddenly sure that she was
speaking the truth. She knew she had lived in Rhyl
once, Mammy had said so, but she was positive
she had never watched rock being made. She
accompanied Kenny, sure that she was in for a
treat. And so, presently, it proved. The rock factory
smelt deliciously of sugar and mint, and it was a
real thrill to see the girls taking a large ball of the
warm, soft sweetmeat in their hands, two girls to
each piece. Then both girls began to pull,
smoothing their hands along the rock and keeping
it the same thickness throughout. Then they laid
it on the long chopping board at the back of the
shop where a young man using a cleaver cut it

44

into lengths. Kenny told Lottie importantly that though the girls' job was interesting to watch, the cutting of the rock into even-sized pieces was a real art, since it had to be soft enough to cut but hard enough to keep its shape otherwise the ends would seal and it was important that the lettering inside each stick should be clear and readable.

Having admired the work for ten or fifteen minutes, Lottie bought two sticks of rock for her mother and Max, and they emerged on to the pavement once more. 'We'd best be making our way back to the clock,' Kenny said. 'We dursen't be late; I'm mortal fond of sausage rolls.' He took Lottie's hand and began to hurry her along the crowded pavement.

A group of lads was coming towards them, talking, laughing and arguing, each one holding a newspaper packet containing chips, well salted and vinegared judging by the delicious smell which came wafting towards the two children. Kenny pulled Lottie into the road to avoid them, and as he did so someone shouted. 'Hey, Sassy, hang on a minute! What the devil are you doing here?'

Lottie ignored the call and would have walked on, but someone caught her arm, dragging her to a halt. It was a boy, very thin and brown, whom Lottie to her knowledge had never set eyes on before, but he was gripping her arm so hard that it hurt and he dragged her on to the pavement, giving her a little shake. 'Sassy! The old 'un's been desperate worried ever since you left! When you weren't at the Tower I asked around, but no one knew a thing ... oh, Sassy, we've been that worried!'

'I don't know what you mean,' Lottie said helplessly. 'Do I know you? And who's Sassy?'

The look of blazing indignation on the boy's face faded into uncertainty. 'Sassy?' he said again. 'It *is* you, ain't it? I was dead certain, but now I look closer ... oh, my God ... but you're real like her, honest to God you are, only your hair's quite different ... what's your name?'

Kenny had been staring, open-mouthed, but now he stepped forward and pulled Lottie away from the other boy. 'She's Lottie Lacey, if that means anything to you,' he said angrily. 'What d'you mean, grabbing the kid like that? And who's this Sassy, anyroad?'

The boy dropped back a pace. He was older than Kenny, probably thirteen or fourteen, with straight, golden-brown hair and eyes so light that they were almost golden too. He had a strange face, with a broad brow tapering to a narrow jutting chin, which gave him a look of great determination. He was wearing ragged denim trousers and a grey shirt, open to the waist, and now, Lottie saw with some pleasure, a blush was stealing across his high cheekbones. 'Sorry,' he muttered. 'I – I mistook you for a pal. I'm real sorry, I didn't mean to scare you.'

Lottie opened her mouth to say indignantly – and untruthfully – that he had not scared her, but it was too late. He had turned and melted into the crowd, and though she stood on tiptoe and tried to follow him with her eyes, he had disappeared as completely as a raindrop in a puddle.

For a moment, she and Kenny stood just where they were, staring at one another. Then Kenny took her hand and began to tow her along the pavement towards the clock on the promenade. The boy had gone in the same direction but Lottie was certain they would not see him again. Indeed, she wondered if she would recognise him, for the encounter had been brief, but then she remembered the blazing golden-brown eyes and thought, with a little shiver, that they would remain in her memory for some time to come. They were strange eyes, the sort of eyes which normally belonged to cats or tigers, not to thin brown boys in ragged kecks. She had a feeling that he might have been barefoot, but when they reached the clock and she had time to cross-question Kenny, he was quite positive that the boy had been wearing ancient black plimsolls with a hole in the toe. 'So he weren't here on a school trip, 'cos if he had been, he'd have wore shoes. Come to think of it, his mam wouldn't have sent him out in kecks all covered with holes.' Kenny thought this over and then added, ruminatively: 'If he's got a mam, that is.'

'What makes you say that?' Lottie asked.

Kenny looked surprised. 'I dunno,' he said slowly. 'I just . . . I dunno. I say, Lottie, you know what he said about your hair?'

Lottie nodded vigorously. 'I were thinkin' the same: me hair's only blonde because Louella bleaches it so's we look more alike. But it *couldn't* be me he were talking about, could it? I mean Sassy sounds nothing like Lottie.'

Kenny considered, then shook his head. 'Nah, I reckon he made a mistake, like he said. Only it's kind o' weird, him thinkin' he knew you an' you havin' forgot such a big chunk of your life. Why, the only thing you know is that you were in Rhyl before you came to Liverpool, and this is Rhyl.' He struck his forehead dramatically with the back of his hand. 'We should have asked him his name, told him that you *had* lived in Rhyl! If he really did know you when you were here, he could fill in a lot o' gaps. Who's the old 'un, for example? Did he mean your father?'

'No, of course not. My father wasn't old. And anyway, I thought he said "she" when he talked about the old 'un,' Lottie said. 'I'm almost sure he said "she".'

Kenny, however, was adamant that the boy had said 'he' and they were still wrangling over the point when the other children began to join them under the clock. And presently they were ordered to form into a crocodile so that the teachers might count them before marching them to the Seagull restaurant.

Naturally, Kenny and Lottie were almost at the head of the crocodile since they had been the first to arrive, and as they marched briskly towards the restaurant Kenny was struck by an idea. He turned to Lottie. 'Tell you what. Ask your mammy what your billing was when you lived in Rhyl,' he suggested. 'And if she says it was Miss Lottie, like now, you could ask her who Sassy is.'

Lottie frowned thoughtfully down at the pavement. 'Maybe Louella was right when she said it might be dangerous to come back to Rhyl; that boy was certainly cross enough to box my ears when he thought he knew me,' she said rather confusedly. 'To tell you the truth, Kenny, I were so frightened when he grabbed hold of me that I didn't listen awfully well. What *had* Sassy done that made him so cross?'

'Gone off without telling anyone where she were bound,' Kenny said briefly. 'I don't gerrit. If this Sassy was a kid, like you are, she couldn't just go off, 'cos kids can't. You were only five or six when you left Rhyl, weren't you? Well, there you are then. He were definitely talkin' about someone else. But I still think you ought to ask Louella what your billing was and whether she's heard of a girl called Sassy.'

'But that'll mean telling her I've been to Rhyl,' Lottie said uneasily. 'I don't like to deceive Mammy – I mean Louella – but it seems more sensible than letting her get in a state. And you know, in a way she were right: I come to Rhyl, and what happens? Some boy I don't know comes slap bang up to me, grabs me arm and thinks I'm someone he knows. No, I don't reckon I'll tell Mammy anything at all.'

Kenny was beginning to argue when he suddenly gave a crow of laughter and poked Lottie so hard in the ribs that she gasped. 'Oh aye?' he said. 'You're going to stick to your story that we spent the day in Llandudno, and you're going to hand her some rock with "A present from Rhyl" writ all the way through it! You stupid little sausage, that rock's a dead giveaway, so it is!'

Lottie groaned, then giggled. 'Oh well, then I'll have to tell her, I suppose. But I shan't say anything about that horrid boy; it would only upset her. I'll just say we had a grand day out, which is true, and sort of drop Rhyl into the conversation . . . I'll say she must have misunderstood me . . . after all, I never *said* we were going to Llandudno.'

'I'll back you up,' Kenny said heroically. He craned forward, for by now they had reached the double glass doors of the restaurant and could see what awaited them inside. 'I say, that teacher weren't foolin'! Look at them sausage rolls . . . and the Cornish pasties!'

'I'm looking,' Lottie said reverently. 'There's a huge iced cake, all pink and white, on that side table, and heaps of jellies. Me favourite's the green one . . . or do I like orange best?'

'It don't matter. We're first in line so we'll have time to help ourselves to both,' Kenny hissed. 'Mam said we'd get a meal afore we left Rhyl so she wouldn't save us no supper, and I thought I'd be missin' out, but what do I care now? She and Dad was only havin' scrag-end stew and spuds, but we can eat ourselves square on this little lot!'

They did eat themselves, if not square, at least round-stomached, and when they tottered back to the coaches the teachers freely prophesied that their charges would sleep all the way home. However, if they were looking forward to a peaceful journey, they were to be disappointed. Comfortably full of the best food they had eaten for a long time, the children still bounced up and down, occasionally fought, jeered at one another and eventually began to sing. The coach driver bawled for some quiet, but he had little chance of being heard. This was the school treat and the pupils intended to enjoy themselves, come what may. They sang 'Pack up your troubles', 'It's a long way to Tipperary', and 'I'm forever blowing bubbles', before rounding off a perfect day with a drunken-sounding rendering of 'Show me the way to go home'. Lottie leaned against Kenny's shoulder and almost fell asleep, but when they arrived back outside the school she and Kenny were amongst the first to climb down. They thanked their teachers sincerely for a lovely day and then Lottie hung around until the coach carrying Baz drew up. Kenny, with apologies, had gone off as soon as the coach arrived back, for little Daisy was jiggling up and down and longing, she said, for a piddle, and her older sisters were nowhere to be seen, so he meant to hurry her off home before she disgraced him, he confided to Lottie, by squatting in the gutter. Normally, Lottie would have accompanied the Brocklehursts, but she had decided that this was a good opportunity to talk to Baz and ask him a few questions. He would be mellow and happy after his day out and thus easier to approach than he sometimes was, she thought.

And so it proved. Baz looped a long arm round her shoulders and asked if she'd had as good a day as he himself had enjoyed, and Lottie was able to assure him, truthfully, that she had. 'But an odd thing happened,' she said as they walked along the Scottie in the direction of Victoria Court. 'A feller came up to me and called me Sassy. He – he said he remembered me from way back. You know I can't remember anything, really, from before the accident. We didn't think to ask his name and when he realised I weren't this Sassy he backed off and disappeared. What d'you think, Baz? Might it have been someone who really knowed me, from the time before?'

'It could have been, I suppose, but then it's easy to think you recognise someone from a distance and then discover, when you get closer, that it's someone completely different – I know, for I've done it meself. Did you enjoy yourself today, queen? That tea were grand, weren't it?'

They chatted happily until they reached the court, where they hurried up the steps of No. 2 and through the door, which had been left unlocked for them. The pair of them staggered into the kitchen, Lottie almost asleep on her feet, to find Max and Louella about to go up to bed. Louella came sleepily over and kissed her daughter fondly, then said, on a yawn, that they would hear all about the coach trip on the morrow, and would Lottie like a cup of cocoa before she went up?

Lottie, full to bursting, said that she couldn't eat or drink another thing, and the four of them went their separate ways, for though folk might think Louella and Max were married, they went to their own rooms each night. Lottie meant to rehearse her story of how they had come to end up in Rhyl before she slept, but though she did her best to stay awake, it was useless. She fell asleep as soon as her head touched the pillow.

And dreamed.

The dream started ordinarily enough. She was on the Rhyl promenade, walking towards the clock, knowing that something exciting was about to happen. There were people about though no one took any notice of her. She saw a teacher she knew and smiled but the woman seemed to look straight through her. And this was odd because Lottie could feel the warmth of the sun on her shoulders and a gentle salt-scented breeze in her face. When the boy came slap bang up to her, she recognised him at once, even though his golden-brown eyes were gentle now. She half expected him to walk past her as the teacher had done, but he stopped right in front of her and spoke urgently. 'You'll have to go back,' he said. 'You'll have to go back even further than Sassy, right back to the very beginning. It's the only way, you see.'

'Back where?' Lottie said blankly. 'Back to Victoria Court? But I've not had me tea yet and Kenny's teacher said there were a grand spread. Besides, the coach doesn't leave for ages and I don't believe I could walk all the way home. It would take days and days.'

She tried to dodge, to sidestep the boy, but though he never appeared to move he was always in front of her, barring her way. Suddenly frightened, she turned round, meaning to run in the opposite direction, but it did not work. He was in front of her again and this time he was smiling. It was not an unpleasant smile, though there was an edge of mockery to it. 'You can't escape, you know,' he said gently. 'Not if you *really* want to know what happened. You've simply got to go back . . . back . . . back . . .'

As he said the last words, his voice became fainter and fainter and rang hollowly in her ears, reminding her of the dreadful day when Mammy had taken her to the dentist to have a tooth removed because it was growing sideways and impeding the one next to it. The dentist had held a mask to her face and the room had whirled round and round, getting smaller and smaller until it was no bigger than a full stop, and the dentist's voice had boomed strangely, echoing round her skull until it faded to a whisper.

54

Now, she tried to resist, to escape from the boy's gaze and from the whirling dance of promenade, sky and people. Thoroughly frightened, she gave a choked little gasp, and began to fight her way up from sleep to the reality of wakefulness. She half opened her eyes and saw her own little room, with the clutter of her possessions all about her. Thankfully, she sat up on her elbow. What a horrible dream! And yet it had only turned frightening when she had decided to run away from the boy. Perhaps if she had been sensible, allowed him to explain what he meant . . .

Once more, Lottie glanced thankfully around her room. It was a nice room, furnished especially for her. There was a little dressing table with a mirror and three drawers, and a marble-topped washstand upon which stood a jug and ewer, brightly patterned with poppies and cornflowers. The curtains at the window were cream cotton with more flowers printed upon the material, and the little wardrobe, which Mam had bought on Paddy's market, had a garland of flowers stencilled round the door. There was a shelf for books, for Louella always encouraged her daughter to read, and another shelf for toys. Golly, Baby Susan and Teddy were prime favourites at present, but there was a pink rabbit with only one ear, a rag doll whose features had been rubbed away by constant use, and a wooden zebra which had once had a red handle and four wheels, although such appurtenances had fallen off years ago.

Lottie had no idea what the time was but she knew it was still night, so she hopped out of bed, grabbed the rag doll and the teddy bear, and snuggled down once more. She would go back to sleep, and if she dreamed the dream again, she would be more sensible. Why had she tried to run away from the boy with the golden-brown eyes? He had seemed to be telling her that if she wanted to know about the past, then she must go back, whatever that might mean. Drowsily, she looked around her once more and remembered Mrs Brocklehurst saying that Louella had put a lot of care into the making of this room. It just goes to show how much my mammy loves me, not that I ever doubted it for one moment, Lottie thought sleepily. I'll tell her the truth about Rhyl because I'm sure she'll understand, and now I'm going back to sleep and I'll try as hard as ever I can to dream myself back to that boy and find out what he meant.

But dreams are tricksy, fickle things which do not simply come because you want them to. Lottie dreamed about Rhyl and the golden sands, and her own small feet, seen through the glittering water, but she could not feel the sun on her shoulders or the water washing around them, and when she picked up the little pink shells, she could not feel them in the palm of her hand. Nevertheless, it was a good dream, and when she woke she had only the haziest recollection of what the boy with the golden-brown eyes had said. She knew it was something about going back, but it no longer seemed important.

When she went downstairs, her mother and Max were sitting at the kitchen table eating porridge and planning a trip to Prince's Park because the weather was hot and sunny, and the theatre did not have a matinée on Fridays. 'Ooh, can I ask Kenny to come with us?' Lottie begged. 'We had such a good time in Rhyl.' She handed over the sticks of rock she had purchased. 'We gave two of our pennies each to the Punch and Judy man. He was ever so funny, Louella. We ought to have a Punch and Judy man at the theatre. He said: "Squashages? Who's going to cook these lovely squashages for my breakfast?" And then Dog Toby grabbed the sausages and Mr Punch pulled one end and Dog Toby pulled the other, and the string of sausages broke and they both tumbled off the stage and into the audience. I picked Dog Toby up. He looked soft and cuddly but he's really made of wood. Then we went to the rock factory . . .'

Lottie thought her mother had stiffened when she had mentioned Rhyl, but as she chattered on she saw Louella relax and when she had described in detail how the young ladies in the rock factory created sticks of the sweetmeat simply by pulling, she was pretty sure that her mother would never again try to stop her visiting Rhyl.

'Well I never! I don't know where I got the impression that you were going to Llandudno, but I reckon Rhyl's more fun for youngsters,' Louella said when her daughter had finished her recital. 'Did you see anyone you knew besides kids and teachers from your school?'

'Norra soul,' Lottie said cheerfully and with complete truthfulness, for the boy might have thought he knew her but she most definitely had not known him. 'Mind you, we didn't really go into the town. We were on the beach, the prom and the pier, and we had our high tea in the Seagull restaurant, so I don't suppose there were many local people around, just holidaymakers. Where did we live when we were in Rhyl, Louella? Were we there for ages? Baz said something about a circus . . .'

Louella looked startled, then nodded slowly. 'Yes, we were with a circus for a little while but we were mostly at the Pavilion theatre. And don't say "norra", darling; it's common. We were in Rhyl for a couple of years, I suppose, and before that we were in several different places. I doubt you'd remember them, even if you hadn't had the accident, because small kids don't remember much, do they?'

'I don't know; I can't remember,' Lottie said, giggling. 'But the doctor thought I'd remember one day, didn't he? And you've helped me an awful lot, teaching me the dances and the songs and that, what I'd forgotten, and reminding me how I had a little travelling bed and slept in it beside you, whenever we were on tour. And how you gave me Golly when I was one, and Baby

Susan when I was two, and Teddy when I was three.'

'And don't forget that your daddy gave you Raggedy Jenny, just before he died,' Louella said, dropping her voice impressively. 'Poor Daddy. He'd so looked forward to having a little daughter of his own, and was so excited when he heard you'd been born, that he bought the doll and ran into the road to hail a tram so he could come and see us in the maternity ward. Only he didn't notice the brewer's dray thundering down upon him until it was too late. His last act had been to buy you that rag doll.'

Lottie opened her mouth to remind her mother that the last time she had mentioned the fatal accident, it had been a Guinness lorry which had ended her father's life, then bit back the words. Her mother was a true actress, she reminded herself, and a born storyteller, fond of embroidering every tale she told or incident she described. She simply could not help it, and already Lottie had heard several versions of her father's sad demise, including the best one, when he had slipped off the roundabout at the fair just as the traction engine which powered the amusements had come trundling past, ending his life in a manner most dramatic and terrible.

Max had been sitting at the kitchen table, eating his porridge, but now he looked up and cleared his throat. 'Lou, my dear,' he said, and there was definitely a note of amusement in his voice. 'I was under the impression that Denham was killed by a Guinness lorry. You really must keep your imagination in check, you know.'

'Oh, didn't I say it was a Guinness lorry?' Louella said, looking surprised. 'But of course I wasn't there myself, I was still in the maternity ward, with my darling little daughter. When they came and told me that poor Denham was dead I saw the whole scene so clearly in my mind's eye that it was as though I had actually been present, but I dare say I got things a bit muddled.'

'To be sure,' Max said mildly. He grinned at Lottie, a companionable sort of grin which said *we know how she is, but we love her anyway*. 'And now what about getting a few sandwiches and some fruit into a basket and heading for Prince's Park?'

'Of course; and if you think Kenny would like to come, Lottie darling, then you'd best go round and tell him to get himself ready,' Louella said lazily. 'I've got plenty of pilchard and tomato paste and some cheese so I can make sandwiches in a trice.'

'I'll help when I get back from next door,' Lottie said eagerly as Max lounged out of the room. However, thinking it over she decided that right now would be a good time to ask a few questions herself. 'When we were living in Rhyl, Louella, did we know someone called Sassy?'

Louella had been collecting her sandwich ingredients on the big wooden table, but for a moment it was as though she had been frozen in one position. Then she reached for the bread knife and the loaf and gave an exclamation of annoyance. 'Oh, dammit, we've not got nearly enough bread! Nip round to the corner shop, darling, and ask Mr Andrews if he can spare me a loaf.'

'I'll go on my way back from seeing Kenny,' Lottie said, knowing that the remark had been made simply to divert her thoughts whilst Louella decided how to answer. 'But Mrs Brocklehurst makes her own bread and usually has some over. Shall I ask her if she can spare a loaf?' Out of the corner of her eye she could see the bread bin standing on the pantry shelf, see the big white loaf inside it as well, and decided to persist. 'Mam, I asked you if we knew anyone called Sassy . . .'

'So you did,' Louella said with apparent placidity. 'And now I come to think, I bought a loaf as we left the theatre last evening – Sample's were selling them off cheap – so there's no need to trouble Mrs B. But if you truly want Kenny to come with us you'd better go round there right away.'

'Mam . . . Louella . . . Mrs Magic . . . I asked you a question,' Lottie almost shouted. 'Did we know someone called Sassy when we lived in Rhyl? All you have to do is say yes or no.'

Her mother turned and gave her a long, speculative look. Then, smiling primly, she said, 'No. Why do you ask?'

It was a masterly table-turning, and for a moment Lottie could only stare. Then she spoke, her voice a nice blend of sulkiness and defiance. 'Someone shouted "Sassy" in the street, and came over to us, then – then mumbled a bit, said I looked like someone called Sassy, and went away.'

'Often happens,' Louella said. She sounded pleased, Lottie thought. 'Anyway, Sassy isn't a name. It's what Americans call a cheeky, uppity girl or boy. I believe it's a corruption of "saucy". So you see it's not a name at all.'

'Oh!' Lottie said, considerably taken aback. Trust Louella to get out of answering any question which might embarrass her! She was tempted to continue, to describe the boy and repeat what he had said, then changed her mind. Louella was quite capable of telling a whopper if she thought that the truth would not be good for her daughter. But I will find out, Lottie told herself. One of these days I'll go back to Rhyl and find that boy and learn what he knows. I will, I will!

Chapter Three

It was a fine summer afternoon towards the end of August. Lottie was standing in the wings, ready to go on when she heard her cue. She was wearing her frilly pink ballerina frock, long white tights and her pink satin shoes with the blocked toes. But instead of the familiar fluttering in her stomach at the thought of the performance ahead, she was feeling a trifle rebellious. After good weather at the start of the month they had had a great deal of rain, and now, on the first really fine day for ages, she would not be joining Kenny in a trip to Seaforth Sands, or her friend Betty, who meant to take some bread and jam and go down to the canal to watch the boats unloading at the wharf. Instead, she would be stuck in the stuffy theatre, performing before a hot and restless audience, smiling an artificial smile, and being sweet when she felt as sour as any lemon.

When her mother had called her in from the court where she had been playing skipping, she had suggested that she might be allowed to miss the matinée performance as it was a lovely sunny day for a change. 'There won't be much of an audience, norron such a nice day. Kids won't come,

63

'cos in another ten days they'll be back in school,' she had pleaded. 'Honest, Mam – Louella, I mean – no one will miss me. You know you can do the whole act by yourself. Kenny's goin' to skip a lecky out to Seaforth Sands, and, oh, I do love the seaside! Mrs B will make us a carry-out – she's awful good like that – so you wouldn't have to worry about feeding me.'

They had been in the kitchen by then, sitting opposite one another at the big wooden table and eating cold ham and salad. Max had already left for the theatre because the stagehands who took his magical apparatus into the wings at the end of his act had dropped the disappearing cabinet and the sliding panel had been knocked out of true. It had happened before but Max did not trust anyone but himself to put it right, so he had made himself a thick cheese and pickle butty and had left a good hour earlier. This was unfortunate since Max might have taken Lottie's side – his own son did not work in the theatre, after all – but as soon as she had finished speaking, Lottie had realised that she might as well have saved her breath. Louella had been tapping her fingers on the table, a sure sign that she was not going to give in. 'How can you suggest such a thing, Lottie?' she had said plaintively. 'I'm far too professional to miss a performance and you should be the same. And if I've told you once, I've told you a hundred times that you may call me "Mam" at home and "Louella" in the theatre. Are we in the theatre now, may I ask?'

64

Lottie had stuck a forkful of lettuce into her mouth and counted ten whilst she chewed it. 'Sorry, Mam, but how about if I call you Louella all the time? Then I shan't keep stumbling over what I say and you won't get cross with me. You've no idea how difficult it is to remember where you are whenever you talk to someone!'

She must have sounded more plaintive than she had intended for Louella had jumped to her feet, run round the table and given her a loving squeeze. 'I'm sorry, darling, I didn't mean to snap at you. The truth is, I'd love to take an afternoon off and go with you to Seaforth Sands, but it wouldn't be fair on the audience, would it? Some of them, particularly the old ladies and the stage-struck kids, come to the theatre 'specially to see Louella and little Miss Lottie. They pay their money and choose their seats and really look forward to our act, so we would be cheating them if we didn't appear. Can you understand that?'

There had been a longish pause before Lottie had replied. 'Ye-es, but I'm sure they come to see you more than they come to see me,' she had said at last. 'I mean, I try my hardest but I'm nowhere near as good as you.'

Louella returned to her own side of the table and sat down once more. 'You're good in a different kind of way,' she had explained. 'You've got a sweet little voice and you sing all the songs that children enjoy. You've come on no end at tap-dancing since – since we came to Liverpool, but most of all, you remind the old people what it was like to be young. They watch you doing the hopscotch dance, and the song you do with the skipping rope, and they remember the games they played, as long as forty or fifty years ago perhaps.' She had smiled encouragingly across at her daughter. 'Do you see, darling, why we must turn up for every performance and never disappoint our audience? And besides, management pay us extra for matinées, you know, and I won't deny that the money is useful. Why, Max and I have been saving up and after the pantomime we mean to take you and Baz somewhere really nice for the whole two weeks. Max wants to go skiing in Scotland but I think it would be better to go to London because there's so much to see there. Wonderful stage shows with famous people in the lead roles, to say nothing of museums and art galleries and exhibitions. But that's for later, of course. So am I forgiven for insisting that the show must go on?'

She had glanced across at Lottie, her big blue eyes so appealing that in her turn Lottie had abandoned her salad and run round the table to give her mother a hug. 'Of course you are,' she had said, kissing her mother's delicately rouged cheek. 'I hadn't thought about the money, though I know it's important really. Why, Kenny often says how his mother likes working for us and how much easier their lives have been because of the extra cash coming in, and of course it's the same for us.

66

I'm really sorry I grumbled and I won't do so any more. After all, tomorrow may be another sunny day and there's no show, so Kenny and I could go to Seaforth Sands then.' She had added, with serpentine cunning: 'And since we're better off than the Brocklehursts, you might give Kenny an' me our fares for the overhead railway.'

Louella had laughed and, getting to her feet, had begun to clear the table. 'OK, sweetheart, it's a deal,' she had said joyously. 'I'll give you some money for your train fares when the show finishes tonight, and make you some butties to take with you tomorrow. And now we must get a move on or we'll be late.'

Now, standing in the wings and waiting for her cue, Lottie remembered that Kenny had not been too pleased when she had asked him to delay his seaside trip until the following day, though he had submitted with a good grace when she had explained that her mother would give them both a carry-out and their fares on the overhead railway. 'And you can go today anyway, just in case it rains tomorrow,' she had said persuasively. 'You don't mind going two days running, do you?'

Kenny agreed that he didn't mind and Lottie had dashed back to No. 2 just as her mother had emerged from the house. 'Kenny says thanks very much and we'll go tomorrow,' she had said breath- lessly, falling into step beside her parent. 'Can I have an ice cream in the interval, Louella? Because the theatre's going to be like a perishin' oven.'

And now here she was, standing in the wings whilst Jack went through his comic routine. She had been right as well, for it was extremely hot on stage and not a lot cooler in the wings. From where she stood, Lottie could see beads of sweat running down the back of Jack's red neck, but that did not prevent him from giving his usual excellent performance, and the waves of laughter which greeted all his jokes made Lottie feel quite guilty for her earlier rebellion. Louella had been right: if Jack was prepared to do his act and the audience were prepared to spend a sunny afternoon in the stuffy auditorium, then she should be happy to go through her songs and dances and grateful that the management were prepared to pay her to do so.

Jack finished his act and bowed deeply, so deeply that the panama hat he had perched on his head fell off. He caught it adroitly, however, waved it at the audience, and headed for the wings. He grinned at Lottie as he passed her. 'It's perishin' hot out there; wish I could prance around in a frilly pink skirt and satin slippers,' he whispered, making Lottie giggle as she pictured Jack in such a costume. And perhaps that was what he intended, for as she ran on to the stage to join Louella, coming on from the opposite direction, she was smiling as brightly as anyone could wish.

The audience began to clap as the orchestra struck up their first number, a dreamy ballad during which she and Louella faced each other holding hands and singing alternate lines of the verses, though they sang the chorus together. When it was over Lottie performed her skipping dance whilst her mother sang, and then Lottie disappeared into the wings for a moment to change into her tap shoes. She ran back on to the stage to the opening bars of 'Tiger Rag' and they began to dance. It was a brisk number and the orchestra always increased the pace as it neared its end. Lottie felt sweat trickling down her back and was grateful when Herman, the conductor, kept the tempo slower than usual. Then it was time for her to sing her last song, during which a large paper moon was lowered from on high, a cue that the act was about to end. Louella and Lottie held hands and ran towards the footlights, smiling and blowing kisses, and then – oh bliss – the tabs were lowered and mother and daughter were able to return to their small dressing room and pour themselves two tall glasses of lemonade, which they gulped down thankfully.

'No curtain calls for a matinée,' Louella said, unbuttoning her tap shoes and kicking them off in order to wiggle her toes. She smiled across at Lottie who had collapsed on the small pouffe in one corner of the room. 'Only one more performance, sweetheart, and you'll be off to the seaside. Oh, I do envy you.'

'You could come as well,' Lottie said, but she knew that Louella would not dream of accompanying them. Her mother's idea of a restful break was to stay in bed late before going to the nearby public baths where she would lie for ages in steaming hot scented water, and then spend even longer curling her hair, painting her nails, and generally titivating.

So it was no surprise to her when Louella said immediately: 'Darling, I wouldn't dream of it. I don't want to cramp your style. You and Kenny will want to paddle and dig sandcastles and do all sorts of energetic things, whereas I want a nice restful day. Which reminds me, I've not yet given you the train fares. You said Kenny liked the idea, didn't you?'

Lottie laughed. 'He certainly did. He skipped a lecky and went today anyway, just in case tomorrow's wet,' she said cheerfully. 'But two days at the seaside is twice as good as one, and a ride on the overhead railway is a favourite treat. And I do love going to the beach, though Seaforth is nowhere near as good as Rhyl.'

'Never mind. At least it's sand and seawater,' Louella said vaguely. 'Maybe next summer we'll take our act on tour – that usually means seaside towns. You'd like that, wouldn't you? We might go to Scarborough and Whitby, places like that.'

'Are they near Rhyl? I'd love to go to Rhyl again,' Lottie said eagerly. 'There's no end of things to do in Rhyl, quite apart from the beach, and I'll bet the theatre is full every night.'

Louella, however, shook her head. 'No, darling. Whitby and Scarborough are on the east coast, and so is Great Yarmouth. There are two piers there which means two shows and they get enormous audiences. Yes, we might try for a booking in Great Yarmouth. Max would like that because he's awfully fond of bloaters and they say the best ones come from Yarmouth.'

'Right,' Lottie said. It was clearly useless to expect her mother to talk about Rhyl, and anyway, now that she came to think about it, Rhyl was not that far away from Liverpool. Louella was generous over such things as pocket money so it was quite possible that Lottie could save enough money for a return train fare for herself and Kenny.

But here, unfortunately, her imagination gave out. Just what she meant to do when she reached Rhyl she truly did not know, for finding one boy amongst the thousands who thronged the prom might well be beyond her even if she had a week at her disposal.

She and Kenny discussed the situation as they sat on Seaforth Sands the next day, chucking pebbles into the grey sea, for though it was warm enough, the sky was cloudy. 'I don't see why you want to find that feller again anyway,' Kenny said, when she explained why she wanted to revisit Rhyl. 'He called you Sassy, which ain't your name, and he ran off before you could ask him what he meant. What good would it do, meetin' up with him again?'

Lottie screwed up her eyes and rubbed her nose. The truth was, she had no more idea than Kenny whether a meeting with the strange boy would be any use. She remembered she had dreamed about him but could not recall any details. She wondered whether to mention the dream to Kenny but was sure he would only scoff. Instead, she told the truth. 'I don't know if I just looked like this Sassy and the boy simply made a mistake,' she said honestly. 'But I do want to know about the years before my accident. I think it's important that I know.'

'But you *do* know. Your mam told you,' Kenny said impatiently. 'Ain't that enough for you?'

Once more, Lottie hesitated. But if she was to go to Rhyl to find the strange boy, then she knew she needed Kenny with her. It was far too big an undertaking for an eight-year-old to venture on alone, which meant she had better come clean. 'Louella is my mam but she's not like other people's mams,' she said slowly, picking her words. 'Sometimes she says things which aren't true. It's part of her being an actress . . .'

Kenny had been gazing towards the sea and preparing to hurl another pebble, but at her words he stopped short. 'D'you mean she tells lies?' he asked. 'If you means she says she's put the rent money aside when she ain't, or she likes someone's new hat when she really hates it, all mams do that and I don't think it counts as lyin'. Everyone's gorra pay the rent money in the end, an' sayin' you like somethin' when you don't is what my mam calls a white lie, 'cos it does no harm and makes folk feel good. And think o' the marvellous stories Louella tells you sometimes. Why, when she told us the story of Moses in the bulrushes, it was clear as clear . . . she made a picture, like, an' it went into our minds. I could see the big ole river, an' the crocodiles what were tryin' to get the baby out o' the reed basket so's they could eat it for their dinners, an' the beautiful girl walkin' along the river bank an' singin' a song an' not even thinkin' about babies . . . I'd heared it in church, an' school, an' I'd even read a bit of it in the Bible, yet when your mam told it . . . d'you know wharr I mean, queen?'

'Yes, I do. She's a perishin' wonder at tellin' tales. Max says she's a real actress – that's why she can make you see what she sees, inside her head. But I didn't say she told lies, I said sometimes the things she says aren't true,' Lottie pointed out, remembering her mother's marvellous stories with real pleasure. 'Max says she embroiders and Jack Russell says she exaggerates, but what I'm trying to say is that sometimes she gets a bit muddled between what's real and what's not, if you understand me.'

Kenny's brow lightened. 'Oh, you mean like telling you your dad were killed by the traction engine one day and a Guinness lorry the next,' he said. 'But those things don't matter, queen. What matters is that your dad were killed in a traffic accident, and your mam told you that. D'you see what I mean?'

'Yes. But when Louella talks about what happened to me before my accident she's always sort of vague, and I don't want a story, I want the plain, unvarnished truth,' Lottie said a little plaintively. 'She told me we lived in Rhyl for two years but when I wanted to know where we lived before Rhyl, she said we were on tour, going all over the place, and that I wouldn't remember anyway because little kids don't. Sometimes – oh, Kenny, sometimes I think she's hiding something from me, hiding it on purpose I mean, and that's kind o' worrying.'

'Yes, it would be,' Kenny acknowledged. 'But what makes you think that, queen? I mean, what reason would your mam have for keeping you in the dark? It don't seem to make sense.'

'No, it doesn't, though there must be a reason,' Lottie said. 'But you know how I've always loved circuses? Yet Louella never told me that we were with a circus for a while in Rhyl and she must have known how it would have thrilled me. Of course I'd have asked lots of questions, but surely that wasn't enough for her to keep it from me? It was Baz who told me about the circus, but when I wanted to know all about it, Louella just said we weren't with them long, and went out of the room. Oh, I know she thinks circuses are low, which could be the reason she fobbed me off, but I still want to know what happened before the accident. Kenny, it was six whole years, just gone, disappeared. Sometimes I feel as though I'm only half

74

a person, as if I only began to exist after the accident . . . it's horrid, I'm tellin' you.'

'It sounds as though you've been cut in half, like your mam is in Max's magic act,' Kenny said. He guffawed at his own wit and Lottie smiled too, though somewhat reluctantly.

'Yes, all right. I know it sounds silly but it might help if I could go back to Rhyl some time and see what I can find out.'

'Awright, awright, don't get upset. You know I'm your pal and I'll do everything I can to help you,' Kenny said quickly. 'I'll even go wi' you to Rhyl, though I don't see it's goin' to help much.'

'Thank you, Kenny. You are kind to me,' Lottie said humbly. 'Though I reckon it'll be next summer before I can save up enough for us to have a day in Rhyl again.'

'Mebbe so,' Kenny said, heaving her to her feet. 'And now let's see who can make a pebble hop the most times when we skim it across the waves!'

He picked up a couple of flat pebbles as he spoke and handed one to Lottie; then the two of them headed for the sea. Lottie had never quite got the hang of skimming pebbles, but on this occasion Kenny showed her exactly how to do it and very soon her pebbles were skipping almost as lightly across the surface as Kenny's. Then the sun came out for the first time that day and when Kenny suggested going into the water for a swim it seemed like a good idea, though Lottie thought that a paddle would be more in keeping with the cool breeze which was getting up. Accordingly, she tucked her skirt into her knickers and Kenny rolled up his trouser legs as far as they would go, and the two of them gambolled in the sea until the sun hid itself behind the clouds once more and Kenny decided it was time to eat the remains of their carry-out, most of which had been devoured within ten minutes of boarding the train.

Wet and sandy but happy, they gobbled paste sandwiches and swigged milk from the bottle Louella had provided. Then they began scraping around in the sand, for this time they would make not a castle but a racing car. Lottie, digging industriously, was suddenly sure that, with Kenny's help, anything was possible. She would either remember of her own accord what had happened in her life before the accident, or she would be a sort of detective, like the ones in the books Louella was so fond of, and track down anyone – not just the boy with the golden-brown eyes – who knew anything about her past.

Together, the two youngsters worked hard on the creation of their racing car, though by the time it was finished the tide had crept rather too close for comfort and was within six inches of the car's long bonnet. 'If we dig a little channel all round it and then down to the sea, it will be a car moat, like a castle moat only more interesting,' Lottie said, but Kenny shook his head.

'We can't do that if we're to get home in time for that high tea your mam promised us,' he pointed out. 'And just look at yourself! Honest to God, Lottie, you're a right mess. If we go up to the recreation ground, there's a drinking fountain where we can rinse off the salt and the sand, and then run around a bit until we're dry. I say, your mam gave you money for ices, didn't she? There's nearly always a "stop me and buy one" cycling round any sort of park. I wouldn't mind an ice.'

Lottie agreed that this was an excellent idea and soon both children were a good deal cleaner, though still damp. They bought ice creams, for as Kenny had said there was a vendor hanging about the gate to the recreation ground, and then they made their way back to the dockers' umbrella. Tired but happy, they finished their ice creams and climbed aboard a train. Lottie leaned back in her seat with a satisfied sigh. 'I've had a grand day, Kenny; don't I wish we could do this every day,' she said as the train began to pull out of the station. 'I wonder what Louella is doing now? Making our tea, I hope.'

Louella had had a quiet sort of day and now she was lying on her bed wondering just where she had gone wrong. She knew herself to be both pretty and desirable for she was always fending off the attentions of young men, yet for some reason Max, though a dear friend, seemed impervious to her charms. Well, perhaps impervious was not quite the right word, she corrected herself, remembering several incidents, but despite the

closeness of their relationship – and her expecta-
tions – he had not yet asked her to marry him.

Looking back, she remembered her first
marriage, the union which had resulted in Lottie's
birth. She had been seventeen and working in the
theatre when she had met Denham Duncan, and
she was certain that it had been a case of love at
first sight on both sides. At any rate, he had asked
her to marry him within a month of their meeting
and she, of course, had been delighted to accept.
Denham had been ten years her senior and already
a very successful magician, performing feats of
illusion which left other magicians gasping. He
and Louella had been idyllically happy, and just
before Lottie's birth Denham had landed an important engagement in a London theatre. 'My name
will be up in lights, sweet Lou,' he had said excitedly when the letter had arrived, seizing her hands
and whirling her round and round. 'As soon as
the baby's born you can start working again as my
assistant, and we should be able to afford a full-
time nursemaid. We've got our feet on the ladder
of success at last!'

'Oh, Den,' Louella had breathed. 'Your name in
lights! How proud we shall be, me and my baby!'

But there had been little opportunity for pride,
for within a week Lottie had been born and
Denham had died, and for a while life had been
incredibly hard for Louella. Then the opportunity
had come for her to join a touring company which
consisted of a number of different acts, going from

one small theatre to another. The conjuror needed an assistant, as did the knife thrower, and the manager told her that they always staged a melo-drama or a comedy at the end of every performance. 'We need someone young and pretty to play the heroine, so you see we shall keep you busy,' he had said in a fatherly fashion, though the glint in his eyes as they roamed across her slender figure had been anything but fatherly. 'You will get a great deal of much-needed experience, and a decent wage, I can promise you that.'

Louella remembered those days with nostalgia, for she had begun to enjoy her independence, and it was during that time that she had learned to repel unwanted attentions without giving offence. She had continued to do so, in fact, until she met Max. He was very like Denham to look at, being tall, well made and dark of hair and eye, and when she had applied for the position as his assistant he had taken her on at once. He was living at No. 2 Victoria Court with his son, but had not at first offered her a room in his house. Afterwards, he had told her that he wanted to be very sure they would get along before so doing, but it had not taken him long to decide that a house share would suit them both.

And so it has, Louella wailed inside her head. I've been happier sharing this house with Max than I've been since poor darling Denham died, and I know Max is happy too. He often gives me a kiss and a cuddle, he spends money on me and treats Lottie with genuine affection and warmth, yet he has never so much as entered my bedroom, let alone tried to share my bed. Of course I don't want to fling myself at his head because I would just die if he repulsed me, but I've had quite a bit of experience with men and I know he likes me. If he's still married to Baz's mother, I realise we could not have a proper legal marriage, but what would be the harm in simply pretending? Everyone in the court thinks we're married already – that's why they call us Mr and Mrs Magic – and I'm sure everyone in the company thinks the same. So even if Max can't actually ask me to marry him, he could suggest that we live together and pretend. I'm sure I've given him every sort of hint that I'd be willing and I do like him so much. Well, if I'm honest, I'm the sort of woman who needs a man, but Max makes all the others seem dull. Goodness, why can't I be honest, even to myself? I love Max O'Mara and I want him for my very own.

Louella had been lying on her bed, staring up at the ceiling while she thought, but now she leaned up on one elbow, took a cigarette from the packet on the bedside table, lit it with the little silver lighter Max had given her last Christmas, and inhaled luxuriously. Her thoughts continued. If Max really was still married, what was wrong with divorce? She was pretty sure that his wife had run off with somebody else, but from what Max had occasionally let drop, it had happened soon after Baz's birth, and Max's son was eleven now. She knew all about the seven-year rule, and even if the first Mrs O'Mara had remained with her husband until Baz was two, that meant nine years had elapsed since the defection. Louella had never mentioned divorce for the same reason that she had never mentioned marriage, but now she thought she might just drop it into the conversation if an opportunity ever occurred.

Lying on her back, gazing up at the ceiling, she smoked the cigarette until it threatened to burn her fingers, then stubbed it out. She got off the bed reluctantly and went over to the mirror propped on the washstand, hearing as she did so the front door open and close, and footsteps approach the kitchen. Hastily she checked her appearance. She licked her finger and ran it over her eyebrows, then fluffed out her hair, straightened her blouse and slipped her feet into the soft flat sandals she wore in the house. She had promised Lottie and Kenny high tea when they returned from their trip to Seaforth Sands, and Max had said he and Baz would be sure to come home in good time with a parcel of chips to go with the very large meat and potato pie she had made earlier in the day. Max was very fond of her meat and potato pie, and of course all children love chips, so high tea tonight would be a treat for them all. Louella had made a bowl of jelly and another of blancmange which would do very well for a pudding, and would not involve more cooking. All I've got to do is put the kettle on and mash the tea, she thought happily.

She let herself out of the bedroom and began to descend the stairs. She could hear Max's deep voice coming from the kitchen, and even as she reached the last stair the door opened again and Lottie and Kenny burst into the hall.

'We've had a wonderful day, Louella. We built a sand car – a car, not a castle – and Kenny taught me to skim stones properly. I skimmed eleven hops once and then we went to the rec and bought ice creams with the money you give us . . . are we in good time for tea?'

Before Louella could answer, Kenny was in full voice. 'That were a grand carry-out you give us, missus. We ate the lot,' he announced. 'But I dunno how it is only we's starvin' again, ain't we, Lottie? I 'spec it's because we ran all the way from the station 'cos you said to be in for high tea by five, and the station clock said quarter to the hour when we got off of the train.'

'You couldn't have arrived at a better time, Kenny,' Louella said, pushing open the kitchen door. 'I'll just put the kettle on . . . ah, I see Max has already done it. Thank you, Max. You're very thoughtful.' She beamed at him. Max was laying out plates whilst Baz fetched salt, vinegar and Flag sauce from the pantry. 'I was going to heat up the pie but I see the fire's almost out, so what say we have it cold? After all, the chips are still very hot indeed.'

Lottie, who had wandered over to the dresser, gave a squeak of excitement at this point as she peered into the two china bowls on the surface before her. 'Red jelly and blancmange! Oh, Louella, you're the best mam anyone ever had.' She turned to beam at Max. 'And Baz has the best dad in the world, I reckon. Don't you think so, Baz?'

Baz grinned. 'Don't you go givin' my dad a swollen head or I'll use *my* magic trick and gobble up all the chips before you kids have so much as smelt 'em,' he said. 'C'mon, everyone, dig in.'

They all had a hearty meal, even though at first Lottie was worried in case she filled herself up with pie and chips and could not eat her share of the jelly and blancmange. However, her worry proved groundless, and by the time she and Kenny had washed up whilst Baz put away, she found herself quite anxious to climb the stairs and get into her own little bed.

'It's been a grand day but I've ate too much,' she sighed as she let Kenny into the court. 'See you tomorrow?'

'Aye, of course you will. Monday's washday,' Kenny reminded her. 'Your mam will get all the stuff she wants washed made up into a big bundle and I'll come round to collect it. My mam likes to get to the washhouse early so she can bag the best lines for hangin' out. Of course, if it don't rain she can use the line in the court, but if it does – rain, I mean – there's always a rush to get the one nearest the door 'cos the women reckon linen dries quicker in a bit of a draught.'

'I'll come along and give you a hand,' Lottie

said eagerly. She loved the washhouse in Lime Kiln Lane, with its rows of stone sinks crowned by huge brass taps, the big mangles at one end and the lines criss-crossing the long, high-ceilinged room, but most of all she loved the atmosphere of good-will and jollity which always prevailed. The washhouse was open all week, of course, but it was busiest on a Monday, and though the women were quite willing to help one another, it would save Mrs Brocklehurst a good deal of time if Lottie and Kenny went along to wring, rinse, fold and mangle.

'Oh, all right,' Kenny said rather reluctantly. 'I meant to go down to Lime Street station with me pal Hugh to collect engine numbers. I ain't got a notebook yet but I've picked up some odd scraps of paper and a stub of pencil so's I can write the numbers down. Still, I can do that another day, I suppose. When'll your mam have her stuff ready, d'you suppose?'

'Early,' Lottie said positively. 'I'll explain that you and me are going to take it round to the washhouse and we need to get away immediately after breakfast. So if you come round about eight o'clock . . .'

'Right,' Kenny said. 'See you then, queen.'

Lottie stood on the doorstep until Kenny had disappeared through his own door, then she turned back into the house and headed for the stairs. She really was very tired indeed and wondered whether she had been foolish to suggest that Kenny should call for the laundry at eight o'clock. Suppose she overslept? She decided she would not pull her curtains across so that the light might wake her and then, having climbed between the sheets, she would bang her head seven times upon the pillow. This time-honoured action had been successful in the past in waking her at seven o'clock so she hoped the magic would work next morning.

For a while she lay in bed, her mind too active for immediate sleep, tired though she was. It had been such a lovely day, starting off with the train journey, then the fun they had had on the beach and ending with a high tea so glorious that Kenny had scarcely spoken a word throughout the meal. But gradually Lottie's lids grew heavy and presently she slept.

The dream started at once. Lottie was lying on her back in something which looked like a basket. It was some sort of woven material at any rate, wicker or reed, and though it surrounded her she could see out. She was aware at once of being gloriously safe and wonderfully comfortable, yet she knew she was not lying in her own bed, for there was no ceiling above her but only the blue arch of the sky, and as she watched she realised she was gently moving, for now and then the branches of a tree appeared and disappeared, and a small white cloud scudded across the blue.

Am I in a boat, Lottie wondered. She thought

she caught the sound of lapping water, but then her attention was distracted, because a face appeared. It was not a face she recognised, yet in the dream she knew and loved it well. She smiled up into eyes dark as damsons and a face brown as a walnut, and the woman smiled back and spoke, her voice full of love and gentleness, though Lottie could not understand one word.

This might have been frightening – should have been frightening – but somehow it was not. The feeling of warmth and security which had surrounded Lottie was with her still, and remained even when the woman's hand came out, smoothed the hair from her forehead, and then went round her and picked her up.

Goodness, I'm a baby, Lottie thought, astonished. Well I never did! She tried to look around her but could not focus on anything beyond the woman's face, and now she could no longer see that face because the woman was cradling her close to her breast and then she was pushing something against Lottie's lips, and Lottie found her mouth opening eagerly to accept a rubber teat. She began to suck and warm, sweet milk filled her mouth and was gulped down with such enthusiasm that presently the teat was pulled gently away and she was laid across the woman's shoulder. A hand rubbed her back until a huge burp emerged, and then the baby that was Lottie was replaced in what she now realised was a cradle, a soft knitted blanket was tucked round her, and, though she tried to fight it, very soon she slept.

Lottie woke to find the room flooded with light and realised that she had slept the whole night through, though she was sure the dream had only lasted a matter of minutes. She had no idea of the time but guessed that it must be around seven o'clock when she heard sounds coming from the next room. Baz had a newspaper delivery round and set off to fetch his papers from the corner shop at around seven, so she had best get a move on. She washed quickly, pulled on a faded cotton dress and slid her feet into ancient plimsolls; no point in dressing up to go to the washhouse. Then she brushed her hair vigorously and set off down the stairs. Whoever was up first would start making breakfast, Lottie dealing with the porridge whilst Baz riddled the fire in the stove and made it up with fresh fuel.

Today, Baz had clearly got up earlier than usual and was in a good mood. The fire burned up brightly, the loaf had been sliced and Baz was squatting in front of the fire with a piece of bread on a toasting fork held out to the flame. A couple of slices, already toasted, were propped up near the stove, whilst the lid of the kettle was beginning to hop as it reached boiling point. Baz's newspaper bag, full to bursting with the papers he would presently deliver, sat on the floor by the kitchen door.

Baz looked round as she entered. 'You're early. Make the tea, will you?' he said gruffly. 'Too hot for porridge; besides, I hate cleaning out the pan afterwards and there's plenty of toast. How many pieces can you eat?'

'Two please,' Lottie said promptly. 'I think I'll take Louella a cup of tea in bed. It's Mrs B's day for doing our laundry, and Louella promised she'd put it out so Kenny and I could carry it to the washhouse for his mam.' She glanced around the kitchen. 'But it doesn't seem to be here, does it? So if I take her a cuppa she can tell me where she's put it. The washing, I mean, not the tea.'

As she spoke, Lottie was pouring boiling water on to the tea leaves in the big brown pot. She gave it a few vigorous stirs, then carried it over to the table and plonked it down. 'Is there any fresh milk left?' she said hopefully. 'Louella loves fresh milk in her first drink of the day, though if there isn't any she'll have to put up with conny-onny.'

In the rush of getting up and getting ready for the day ahead, she had completely forgotten her strange dream, but as the words 'fresh milk' left her lips she remembered it, right down to the tiniest detail. She went to the pantry and fetched the jug of milk, poured some into her mother's best china teacup, then put the strainer in position and began to dispense the tea with great care, for the pot was heavy. After a moment she said: 'Baz? Can you remember being a baby?'

Baz was carrying the toast across to the table.

He reached for the margarine and began to spread it on each slice before answering. 'Remember being a baby? Course I can't. No one can, you stupid thing. Why d'you ask?'

'Because I dreamed I were a baby last night, a baby in a cradle,' Lottie said, and could have kicked herself when Baz guffawed loudly. I should have known he'd only make fun of me, she thought bitterly, snatching one of the pieces of toast and reaching for the jar of jam. 'You're the stupid one because dreams aren't supposed to be sensible,' she said tartly. 'Why, I dreamed once that I were about to sit down on the lavvy when a crocodile came out of it and tried to bite my bum. I suppose you'd say that that was a stupid dream because everyone knows a crocodile wouldn't fit into the lav.'

She expected Baz to say something cutting, but instead he grinned at her rather sheepishly. 'Sorry, but keep your hair on – you didn't tell me it were a dream straight off, did you? Fancy dreamin' you was a baby, though! If it were me, I'd rather dream a crocodile were snappin' at me bum. I don't like babies. Horrible squawking brats, always guzzlin' or pooin' and ugly as a pan o' worms, most of 'em. I aren't havin' no babies when I'm growed up.'

'No, you won't, because no sensible woman would marry you,' Lottie said, hoping to take Baz down a peg or two. 'And the baby in my dream was sweet, really she was.'

89

Baz stared thoughtfully at her across the table as she cut the crusts off the slice of toast – Louella did not like crusts – and arranged the quarters on a pretty china plate. 'Look, I said I were sorry, didn't I? But you've got me puzzled. You said you dreamed *you* were the baby so how could you possibly know it was sweet?'

Not surprisingly, this question completely floored Lottie. She had been about to sweep out of the room, carrying her mother's tea and toast, but she stopped short, staring at Baz. For once, he looked neither mocking nor cross, but just interested. 'I really don't know why I said the baby was sweet, except that the woman who picked me out of the cradle was very gentle and loving, so *she* must have thought I was sweet, don't you think?' she said at last, rather uncertainly.

'Yeah, I reckon you're right,' Baz said. 'But you're a rum kid and no mistake! What else did you dream? I mean about being a baby, not about crocodiles and that.'

'Well, not a lot, only that I were in a cradle made of wicker or reeds or something, and it were moving and I were outside, norrin a room, because I could see the blue sky and the little white clouds.'

Baz reached for a slice of toast and took a large bite, then spoke thickly. 'I reckon you dreamed like that because you ate such a huge helping of meat and potato pie. Don't say you didn't – it were as big as the piece I ate. I noticed it pertickler. Then you had all that jelly and blancmange, and a cup of cocoa. That's enough to make anyone dream odd dreams.'

Lottie was beginning to reply indignantly that her slice of pie had been half the size of the piece Louella had placed in front of Baz when a far likelier cause of her dream occurred to her. 'I've got it!' she exclaimed. 'It were nothing to do with our high tea, it were that story Louella told us the other evening when Kenny came round with Daisy. You know, Baz, the one about Moses and the bulrushes! Gosh, no wonder I thought I was sweet – the baby I mean – because in the story the princess loves the little baby so much that she takes him to the palace and brings him up as her own little boy. Oh, I'm so glad there weren't a crocodile in the dream, trying to grab me out of the basket, like there were in Louella's story.'

'Well, there you are then,' Baz said. He poured himself a mug of tea and added a large spoonful of sugar, then stirred it briskly. 'And if you don't take that tea and toast up to your mam before it goes cold, she'll give you what for.'

'You're right; she hates cold tea and leathery toast,' Lottie said. She went over to the sink and poured the cooling tea away, then seized another slice of bread and crouched down to hold it to the flame. 'Please, Baz, do me a favour and pour my mam another cup of tea, would you?' she said over her shoulder. 'Only I promised Kenny I'd have the washing ready by eight . . .' she glanced up at the clock above the mantel, 'and it's twenty to already.'

She half expected Baz to tell her to do her own work but he lounged to his feet, picked up the pot and poured the tea, then actually took the toasted bread from her and spread it generously with margarine and jam. She thanked him, took the plate and cup and headed for the stairs. She was on the bottom one when Baz spoke from behind her. 'I wouldn't mention that dream to anyone else,' he said casually. 'They might think you'd gone off your bleedin' head. But if you have any more dreams like that you could tell me. I'd not laugh, I promise you. If you ask me, there's a bit more to a dream like that than Moses and the bulrushes.'

Lottie stared at him for a moment, then began to climb the stairs once more. 'All right, I won't tell anyone else, not even Kenny,' she said. 'But I don't suppose I'll have any more dreams like that. Besides, I mostly forget my dreams as soon as I wake up.'

Baz made no answer but disappeared into the kitchen, and as she continued up the flight Lottie reflected that boys were odd creatures. Baz had never seemed to have any time for her, had always mocked or teased, or been downright obstructive, yet just now he had seemed truly interested in her dream and anxious that she should confide in him rather than in anyone else.

She reached her mother's door, tapped gently and crept quietly into the room. Louella's curtains were still drawn across and Lottie almost stumbled when she walked into something large and soft at the foot of her mother's bed. She stepped over it, however, without spilling a drop of tea, and placed cup and plate on the bedside table before whispering: 'It's getting on for eight o'clock, Louella, and you promised you'd get the laundry ready so Kenny and meself could take it to the washhouse. It ain't . . . isn't, I mean . . . in the kitchen, so where have you put it?'

'It's in a pile at the foot of my bed,' Louella said sleepily. 'I've tied the whole lot up in a sheet, but if there's anything you or Baz want to add, you can do so. You might pull the curtains back a tiny bit so I can see to drink the tea, but I don't mean to get up yet. It's far too early.'

'Right you are,' Lottie said cheerfully. She lifted the bundle of washing, which was pretty heavy, and made her way out of the room, closing the door softly behind her. Then she propelled the laundry ahead of her, watching as it bounced from stair to stair. What did it matter if it got dirtier, after all? Mrs Brocklehurst would make sure that everything was clean and ironed before it was returned to No. 2. She even starched Max's evening shirts until they could have stood up alone, and put blue bag in the rinsing water so that they fairly sparkled when he walked on to the stage.

The washing landed in the hallway and Lottie's hand was reaching out towards the knob of the kitchen door when it opened and Baz emerged. He was still chewing toast but had his newspaper bag across one shoulder and his cap on his head.

Clearly, he was about to start work. Lottie pushed the laundry to one side and was about to re-enter the kitchen as Baz opened the front door, but before she could do so she heard Kenny's voice.

'Mornin', Baz! Is Lottie about yet? I know it's a bit early but I thought as I were ready we might as well get ourselves a head start. It's washday and . . .'

'I know, I know,' Baz said impatiently. 'You might tell your mam the kid kicked the washing down the stairs so it'll be twice as dirty as usual. But that's girls for you: always take the easy way out.'

Well, his friendliness didn't last long, Lottie thought ruefully, heaving the washing up into her arms. Aloud she said indignantly: 'Just you shut your gob, Basil O'Mara, and mind your own bleedin' business. Kenny's mam cleans them stairs twice a week and you could eat your dinner off 'em. Besides, the laundry's too heavy for one person to carry, especially downstairs.'

Baz laughed. 'Good thing Louella can't hear you, swearin' like a perishin' docker,' he said mockingly, but his tone was a good deal friendlier than it had been. 'What have the pair of you got planned for today, eh? After you've lugged the sheets round to the washhouse, I mean?'

'Dunno,' Kenny said briefly. 'But we're both goin' to help my mam and that'll take up all the morning and most of the afternoon, I reckon. And of course Lottie's on stage this evening.'

Baz nodded and ran down the steps into the court, and Kenny closed the door and came up the hall towards Lottie. 'Are you ready?' he said briskly. 'If so, we'll get goin' at once. Mam's gone to fetch the washin' from old Mrs Ruddock and from Mrs Tennet at her canny house, so she'll start their stuff first. But the sooner we get your mam's stuff to the sinks the sooner we'll be free to have a bit of fun.'

'What sort of fun?' Lottie asked suspiciously. Hanging round the stalls in St John's market to see if they could nick something was not her idea of fun, but she knew Kenny often obtained fruit by this method. 'Don't forget I'm on stage this evening.'

'Oh, you,' Kenny said, grinning. 'You keep saying you want to learn to swim, so I thought we might go down to the Scaldy. I know you won't go in because it's mostly lads there, but if I swam slow, like, you could watch. Likely you'd learn how it's done without even getting your feet wet!'

Lottie giggled. 'We'll see what time your mam finishes with the washing,' she said diplomatically. 'And now let's get moving, or we won't reach the laundry till lunchtime!'

Chapter Four

1929

'Do you know, Lottie, you're nearly as tall as me now? It never occurred to me before that you might grow tall, but I suppose I should have guessed it was possible. Your father, after all, was almost six foot, but being petite myself I thought you would be the same. Yet here you are at almost fifteen years of age, almost as tall as me.'

Louella's voice was reproachful, as though Lottie had deliberately set out to grow tall, and her daughter looked at her with some puzzlement. She had not, after all, grown overnight – she had been this tall for a good few months, she was sure – so why was Louella suddenly remarking on it? Lottie knew she was no longer a fluffy little child star, but she still did the tap-dance routine with her mother, sang all the songs and tried, to the best of her ability, to smile winningly at the audience. She had realised, however, that a fifteen-year-old does not cause the audience to coo as appreciatively as an eight-year-old, and in fact it had been her suggestion that they should drop the ballet portion of their act. 'My legs and arms are too long and thin to look sweet,' she had told her mother, at least a year earlier. 'The tap-dancing's fine and the singing of course, but the ballet just looks silly.'

They had been in the green room at the time and when her mother had demurred, both Max and Jack Russell had said that Lottie had a point. 'In a few years' time, when she's filled out a bit, she'll be able to do all sorts,' Max had said tactfully. 'But right now, all her strength is being put into growing.'

'And you won't need to shorten your act,' Jack Russell had pointed out. He had clearly realised that a shortening of the act would mean a dwindling of the money, and no one wanted to see their pay packet grow lighter. 'You could put in an extra song . . . no, I've had a better idea! I seen an act which went down real well when I were in Great Yarmouth doin' a summer show a coupla years back. You know Mackintosh's Carnival Assortment? Toffees and chocolates and that? Well, remember the picture of Harlequin and Columbine on the lid? This young gal dressed up as Columbine and did a dreamy, stately sort of dance with a big tin of Mackintosh's under one arm and she threw toffees to the audience and they loved it. Of course, folk in the audience knew who she were meant to be because of the picture on the tin lid which she kept flashin' at 'em, and I reckon the toffees in the box were the cheap sort you can buy for a penny a quarter, so it wouldn't cost you much.'

Louella had been excited by the idea. 'Why can't

I dress as Columbine and Lottie as Harlequin?' she had asked excitedly. 'They are easy costumes to make – I'm sure Mrs Jones could do it standing on her head.'

Max, however, had vetoed this. 'If you want to make your daughter look a laughing stock – and yourself of course – then go ahead,' he said with unwonted frankness. 'Darling Louella, a Harlequin even a couple of inches shorter than his Columbine would make both look ridiculous.'

'But I can't be Harlequin; I've far too much hair and my bosom would show,' Louella had said. 'Suppose we both dress as Columbine and throw toffees.'

Lottie had beamed at them all, seeing a way out. 'If we move the Columbine piece to the end of the act and Louella does it by herself, then I could leave the theatre a bit earlier. I'd go straight home and start getting supper,' she had added with serpentine cunning, and had then turned to Jack. 'You *are* clever, Jack; it's a wonderful idea. I'm sure management will love it as well as the audience.'

'Especially since you won't be askin' them to pay for the perishin' toffees,' the little man had said. He turned to Louella. 'Well, since it were my idea I reckon I deserve a cut. I'll take it in toffees: two for each performance. Howzat?'

To Lottie's enormous relief, everyone had liked the new finale to their act, though Mr Quentain, the theatre manager, had insisted that Lottie should be Columbine and not Louella. In the end, they had compromised: Lottie was to be Columbine and would throw the toffees, and Louella would dress as a Victorian lady – the company already had such an outfit – and throw a few toffees on her own account.

Now, the two of them were in the kitchen getting Sunday lunch, or rather Louella was getting Sunday lunch whilst Lottie made a cake for their tea. Lottie was pouring the mixture into the tin which she had prepared and greased earlier, and remarking: 'I'm not *that* tall, Louella; I mean I still look my age, don't I? And now that I don't do the ballet no one laughs where they shouldn't. Has someone in the theatre said something? You know I'd be happy not to go on stage at all if you'd rather I didn't.'

Louella had been whipping up batter but now she dropped the whisk and came over to give Lottie a hug. 'Why, darling, I can't imagine the act without you,' she said, dropping a kiss on the top of her daughter's head. 'You're still my little girl, even if you aren't quite as little as I'd thought. And it will be summer quite soon and Max and I have had an excellent offer from the Wellington Pier theatre in Great Yarmouth, which of course includes you.'

'I know; I auditioned too,' Lottie said, rather surprised. 'But the manager said mine was only a tiny part of the act so I only did some tap-dancing and sang about three lines of "Bye, Bye, Blackbird". D'you mean to say they've changed their minds and don't want me after all?' She tried not to sound too hopeful and must have succeeded, for Louella gave her another squeeze.

'Darling, of *course* they want you. But the thing is, one of Max's nieces is looking for work. She's a dancer and – and we wondered, Max and myself, if we could include her in the act. Her speciality is modern dance – she does the Charleston, the Black Bottom and the Tango, and the Shimmy. She needs a partner, however, and we thought . . . we wondered . . .'

Lottie could see what was coming. 'If you mean me, I don't know any modern dances, and I don't mean to learn them, either,' she said firmly. 'Just what have you got in mind, Mam? If you want to drop the tap-dancing and the songs . . . you know I wouldn't mind, don't you? The show must come first, as they say.'

Louella gave a trill of laughter and did not remind her daughter that she wanted to be called Louella all the time now. 'Darling, how absurd you are!' she said gaily. 'No, I've something quite different in mind. I thought we would bill ourselves as "The Three Lacey Sisters" for the songs and the tap-dancing, and then you and Merle could do the modern dances. Merle would have to dress up as a boy because she's seventeen and probably taller than you, but I dare say she won't mind that.'

'I dare say she will,' Lottie said positively. 'If she's used to taking the girl's part and wearing those wonderful waistless dresses with the skirts several inches above her knees, and having long necklaces and feathers in her hair, she won't take kindly to a feller's evening suit.' Something struck her even as she said the words and she peered suspiciously across at her mother. 'Merle? Did you say she was seventeen and her name was Merle? Oh, Mam – Louella, I mean – is she the girl who took my place when I was in hospital? The one you said couldn't hold a tune?'

Cornered by her own eloquence, Louella could only nod unhappily. 'Yes, Merle did stand in for you whilst you were in hospital,' she acknowledged. 'But of course she was a lot younger then and Max says her voice has improved no end. She's left the circus and has been working in Birmingham, I think he said, doing a three sisters song and dance routine with two other girls, but they've moved on, so as I said she's out of work. Darling, do be sensible! If the three of us can work up a good act, we can bring it back to Liverpool when the holiday season's finished. I'll still be Max's assistant, of course, but I've been thinking for some time that our mother-daughter act isn't as appealing now you're older. Merle can be made up to look sufficiently like us Laceys to make the audience believe we really are sisters. But of course if you hate the idea I suppose I'll have to think of something else.' She took the cake bowl from Lottie and plunged it into the sink, then went over and grasped both her daughter's hands, gazing earnestly into her face. 'Darling, I'm going to let you into a secret and I want you to promise me that you'll never say a word to a soul about what I'm going to tell you.'

'Oh, Mammy,' Lottie breathed, far too excited at the thought of a secret to consider forms of address. Perhaps, at last, her mother was going to divulge a bit more information about her past! Over the last two years she had told Lottie that Denham Duncan had been a stage name and that her father had really been Alf Denham, a name which Louella described with scorn as being far too commonplace for a magician. She had also admitted that the name Lacey was not her own maiden name but her mother's, since it seemed that Lottie's grandmother had been Jane Lacey before her marriage to Walter.

'What was Walter's surname?' Lottie had asked, intrigued. She knew both her grandparents were dead, but now it seemed her mother was about to flesh their image out a little. 'If Grandmamma had been Jane Lacey, then when she married she would have become Mrs Walter Something, wouldn't she?'

'Yes, that's right. My father's name was Henning,' Louella had said, with a darkling look. 'What a perfectly dreadful name! If I'd used it on stage, people would have made clucking noises and flapped their wings – elbows, I mean. They might even have thrown eggs. So I called myself Louella Lacey. And of course when you were born,

Denham and I decided that Lottie Lacey sounded just perfect.'

Now, Louella squeezed Lottie's fingers and then released them. 'Max said that if I decided not to include Merle in our act, he would feel obliged to take her on as his assistant,' she said, eyes widening with horror at the very suggestion. 'I couldn't believe he meant it because we work so well together, but Max's family feeling has always been very strong. And of course Baz and Merle were brought up together when they were little and are still close friends. So as soon as Max said that he'd take Merle on as his assistant I just burst into tears and said I didn't know what I'd done to deserve such cruelty. He gave me a cuddle and promised me I wouldn't lose out and could continue to share the house and so on. But of course that isn't all that matters. So I agreed to include Merle in the act, which will mean changing it to fit her in. He made me swear on the Bible to do as I'd said, as if I was the sort of person to go back on a promise. I was deeply hurt – and when it was all decided he gave me another cuddle and admitted he hadn't meant a word of it, and would never replace me, but had invented the threat to make me realise how important it was to him to see his niece in a respectable job.'

'Well I'm blessed!' Lottie said, genuinely astonished. She was very fond of Max and often wished that he and Louella would regularise the situation and get married, though this would make Baz her stepbrother, she supposed. Not that she would particularly mind that, since the two of them had got on very much better of late. But Louella was still speaking, so she dragged her mind from her own thoughts and listened to her mother's words.

'Yes, I was surprised myself that Max would stoop to threatening me,' Louella admitted. 'But I'm sure it's for the best, darling, because as I said, the mother-daughter act was only really a winner whilst you were small. Now, three sisters will be very much better. Merle can tap-dance, so that's all right, though of course she'll have to learn our routines, and both you and I have strong voices so if she does wander from the tune a little the audience won't notice.' She smiled winningly at her daughter, her big light blue eyes sparkling. 'It's all agreed then? We'll be the Lacey Sisters and you'll learn modern dance so you can partner Merle? If she wants you to do so, of course.'

'But where will she sleep? We've only got the two big bedrooms on the first floor and the two attic rooms that Baz and I have . . .' Lottie began, only to be swiftly interrupted.

'Why, she'll share with you, of course, darling. You have a really big room with plenty of space for another bed, so that will be no problem. In fact, it will be nice for you to have another young girl in the house. I envy you, honest to God I do! You'll be able to discuss the theatre and your friends . . . you'll be like sisters, only even better because sisters don't always get on. Oh, yes, you're a lucky girl . . . I always wanted an older sister when I was your age.'

Lottie began to object, to say that it would never work, but Louella cut her short. 'Nonsense, darling. Don't forget I'm far more experienced than you and I'm sure it will work beautifully,' she said gaily. 'Never meet trouble halfway, that's my motto. It will all go like a dream, I promise you. And now I must get on with the Yorkshire pudding or the men will be back before it's even in the oven.'

That night, in bed, Lottie lay awake for a long time, wondering about the changes which were to come. She knew she was very lucky to have a room of her own; almost everyone in her class had to share with at least one sister, and, as Louella had said, her attic room was very large, with plenty of space for another bed, another occupant, in fact. It was spring, though there were few enough signs of it in Victoria Court, but from what Max had said as they ate their Sunday lunch, Merle would be joining them in another couple of weeks so that the Lacey Sisters could put their new act together and rehearse every move until all three of them were both word and action perfect.

Lottie told herself severely that Merle must be a nice girl, for she was Max's niece, and also Baz's friend. At eighteen, Baz was easier to get along with than he had been. Lottie supposed he felt himself too grown up to tease and torment someone of her age, but it might not be just that.

Ever since she had dreamed what she always thought of as the 'Moses dream' he had been friendlier, sometimes walking her to school or meeting her out of it even after he himself had left, so that they could discuss her most recent sleep-adventure, as she thought of them. For the dreams had not stopped with the Moses one, though they were rare and sometimes so vague that she could not remember them clearly next morning.

True to her promise, she had never told anyone else about the dreams, though she had nearly given herself away to Kenny. It had been not long after the Moses dream and they had been walking alongside the canal, peering interestedly at the boats drawn up at the wharf, and perhaps it was the sound of lapping water or the rocking motion of the nearest boat when another chugged past, but a thought had popped into Lottie's head and she had spoken without thinking. 'I know the baby in the basket was Moses, but he was found by a beautiful princess. The woman who picked me up wasn't beautiful at all, and she wasn't young either. She was old and brown and wrinkled, not a bit like a princess.'

'Wharrever are you talkin' about, dumplin' head?' Kenny had said, staring at her. 'Are you still on about that story your mam told us? Because if so, you've forgot an awful lot. Your mam telled us the princess had long golden hair which reached to the back of her knees, and big blue eyes, and she wore wonderful clothes all covered wi'

106

jewels. So what's this about a wrinkled old woman a-grabbin' hold of the baby?' He had given a loud, rude laugh and poked Lottie in the ribs with a sharp elbow. 'Next thing you'll be sayin' it were a crocodile what whipped the baby out o' the rushes. Crocodiles is all wrinkled and brown.'

By this time Lottie had recollected her promise, and she walked on in silence. 'Well?' Kenny had demanded presently, when Lottie did not speak. 'You're gettin' in a rare old muddle if you ask me. Babies in the bulrushes indeed! Whatever *are* you on about?'

So she had said humbly: 'Sorry, Kenny. I suppose the canal made me think of that there Egyptian river – the Nile, weren't it? – and I got kind of muddled. Don't you wish you lived on a canal boat? I wish I did. Then no one would expect me to be sweet and put on a silly little frilly little pink skirt and throw kisses to old folk what I don't know from Adam.'

'The money's all right though,' Kenny had said rather wistfully. He did what he could to earn a few extra pence for his family each week, chopping up orange boxes for kindling, which he sold for a ha'penny a bundle, carrying heavy bags of shopping home for elderly ladies, queuing at the tap in the yard and delivering the full buckets to the kitchens, and even minding children if the parents had to go out for an hour or two. But none of these things brought in regular money and Kenny was looking forward to the time when he could leave school and skip aboard a freighter, as his older brother had done.

'Regular money is nice,' Lottie had acknowledged, glad to see that her unwise remark had been forgotten. 'Want to come back to my house for tea? Mam's going to make pancakes.'

She had not again been tempted to confide in Kenny, and unfortunately, as time passed, they had grown apart. Relations between them had suffered considerably during the National Strike in May 1926. Then, Lottie had followed the lead of most theatre folk who deplored the meanness of the bosses and backed the strikers to the hilt, but Kenny had seen an opportunity to get himself a job and earn some money. He had had to sag off from school and lie about his age, of course, but he had been well grown and anyway, people were desperate. So Kenny had become, for a short period, a deck hand on a small coaster and had gloated over his sudden change in fortune. Audiences at the theatre had been too small to make it worth opening up the auditorium, so for the first time in Lottie's memory money had been truly scarce, with everyone living on their savings. Lottie had grown used to scanty meals and to being confined to the house, since Louella had said the streets were dangerous. Then, having met Kenny one day when returning from the St John's market with a string bag full of damaged and therefore cut-price vegetables, she had taunted him. 'You're a bleedin' Blackfoot,' she had yelled at him across the street and had been mortified when he had given a shout of laughter, and not been in the least offended.

'Blackfoots is Indians, you ignorant kid; you means blackleg,' he had said between guffaws. 'Oh, wait till I tell me pals you called me a Red Indian!'

So it had not been her intended insult which had caused the rift but his mockery. But that had been almost three years ago, and though the two were back on speaking terms the old warmth had gone. Now that Kenny was in permanent employment they saw little of each other and, truth to tell, Lottie missed him and was often lonely.

The other side of the coin, however, was the good relationship which now existed between herself and Baz. He did not exactly include her in any of his pursuits, but she was welcome to watch when he played football with his mates or joined a game of pitch and toss, though this happened rarely since Max did not approve of gambling and had told Baz that he would thrash him within an inch of his life if he caught him taking part in a toss school.

This threat always made Lottie laugh because Max was the least aggressive of men and never raised his hand to anyone, let alone his son. Indeed, when one of his white rabbits, Snowy, had died, Max had taken it out into the country so that it might be buried in a wood with wild rabbits nearby, and had wept as he shovelled soil on to the corpse. On the way out of the city, the bus conductor had looked at the large white bundle in Max's string bag and had said, conversationally: 'Someone's going to have a grand dinner!' which had caused Max to give him an extremely cold look, though Lottie had seen Baz stifling a giggle. Lottie had felt her own lips twitch, but knowing how fond Max was of the creatures who helped in his act, she could understand why he would not dream of eating the rabbit; one did not devour one's pals, after all.

Now, however, lying in her bed, her thoughts went to her dreams. Sometimes they were just tiny snatches of life, and though she tried hard to make sense of them she had never really done so, and had come to the conclusion that they were delightful but meaningless. She had tried to will herself into dreaming, but had long ago given up. She was pretty sure that something she did in the real world triggered the dreams, but she simply did not know what the trigger was, so now she let her mind wander delightfully, thinking how nice it would be to catch a bus into the country, perhaps to the very wood where the late lamented Snowy was buried. There would be wild flowers; primroses and violets at this time of year. She imagined herself picking a bunch and bringing them back to her mother. She imagined rabbits coming out of the wood at dusk to crop the sweet green grass of the verges, and slid into sleep, and straight into a dream.

She was sitting on a comfortable seat, a cushioned bench, and before her on a brightly painted table was a round blue pottery bowl full of something white and soft. Sitting beside her on the bench, with an arm about her small shoulders, was a very large woman. The woman held a spoon in one hand, which she was dipping into the blue bowl. She said something in a strange language which Lottie could not understand, yet she knew enough to open her mouth to accept the spoonful of warmed bread and milk. It was delicious; even though she was dimly aware that this was a dream, she could taste the bread and milk, taste the sugar which had been stirred in to make it more palatable. When she had swallowed the first delicious mouthful, she clutched the woman's arm, saw her own hand, small and white and soft as thistledown, and as the spoon travelled towards her mouth once more she spoke, and heard her own words for the first time in the dream. 'Nice,' she said contentedly. 'Nice, nice, nice, Mumma.' The woman chuckled, a rich contented sound, and then the scene slid away and Lottie slept dreamlessly for the rest of the night.

She awoke with the dream as clear in her mind as though it had really happened and lay there, not trying to interpret what she had dreamed but simply enjoying it. Once more, peace and contentment had been her chief emotions. She did not know who the old woman was, or where she was, but she knew the woman meant her nothing but

111

good, and she was beginning to believe that the dreams had some significance and would eventually tell her what she wanted to know. She had realised some time before that the boy who had told her to 'go back' must have meant it literally. She was going back to her baby days, and eventually, surely, the dreams would take her to a time when speech was not confined to single words. If this was so, then surely she would be able to find out just where the things she dreamed fitted into her past. It was odd that Louella never appeared in the dreams, but Lottie supposed that the woman must be some sort of childminder and that Louella hovered just beyond the scene, waiting to enter it when the time was right.

'Are you awake, love? Only there was a telegram waiting for us when we got back from the theatre last night. Well, I say for us but it was really for Max, and it was from Merle. She's coming to join us in a week, so I thought we'd get your room ready, which will take us most of the day ... do get up, sweetheart!'

Lottie rolled over and pulled herself upright in bed; then, with some reluctance, swung her feet out on to the chilly linoleum. 'I don't know what you mean by getting my room ready, Louella,' she said sleepily. 'Surely all we need do is to buy another bed? There's space for her clothes as well as mine on the rail behind the curtain which you put up, and we can use the same washstand.'

As she spoke she was stripping off her thin

nightie and hurrying over to the basin. Louella, standing by the door, was holding the kettle, so she took it from her and poured a generous dollop into her china bowl, then topped it up with cold water from the ewer and began to wash. Behind her, Louella sank down on the bed.

'Yes, but Max thinks Merle should have her own dressing table and even a small wardrobe and a few other things, because she's older than you, I suppose. But we're off to Great Yarmouth at the end of May and you never know, Merle might not want to return to Liverpool when the summer season's over, so I don't mean to spend a lot of money on turning your bedroom into a twin, so to speak.'

'I expect Max will pay for it; he's awfully generous over things like that,' Lottie said, and saw her mother's reflection frown in the small mirror. Louella would not want to be reminded that it would be Max who would pay for the additions to Lottie's room. 'Has he told you what he wants to spend? You won't get new stuff, will you? You can get all sorts in Paddy's market and I love poking round the stalls down there.'

Louella snorted. 'You can certainly get all sorts from the market, and that includes bedbugs and fleas,' she pointed out. 'I told Max that I wouldn't have infestations in my house, even if it did mean a big saving.' She opened her eyes wide, as Lottie swung round, and pouted at her daughter as though she herself were the younger of the two.

'He got quite cross. He said I was to get a square of carpet from Jacob's – as if a girl of seventeen needs carpet in her bedroom, let alone a new one – and to buy a mattress from Ginsburg's on the Scotland Road. I said it would be all right to get a washstand, a dressing table and the bedstead itself from Paddy's, as well as a chair, as long as it wasn't upholstered, so we're going to have a busy day of it. Thank God it's a Wednesday and we don't have to be in the theatre until this evening.'

'Ooh, Ginsburg's; they have lovely furniture. I often look in the windows but I've never been inside,' Lottie said yearningly. 'Only I don't fancy carrying all that stuff back to Victoria Court. Will they deliver?'

'Ginsburg's might, but they'd charge extra,' Louella said, standing up and heading for the bedroom door. 'So I told Baz to borrow a hand-cart which is big enough to hold pretty well everything. He's at work until half past five, of course, but most of the shops will let you collect stuff in the evenings.'

'I could help . . .' Lottie began, then remembered that she had to be in the theatre by six and groaned. 'No, of course I couldn't, I was forgetting. But Kenny would help. I'll go round before breakfast, to be sure of catching him, and explain.'

She was rubbing herself dry and dragging on her clothes as she spoke, but Louella smiled at her and shook her head. 'No need for either you or

Kenny to help, darling. Baz says his pals Sosso and Roof will give a hand. 'Specially if I get fish and chips for them so they can eat here before going on to the Rotunda to see *The Cocoanuts*. I told Baz that if they'd like to come to the theatre his father and I would give them free passes, but he just looked embarrassed and said that it's the Marx Brothers film they want to see.'

She had been standing in the doorway, but now she began to clatter down the stairs and Lottie, following her, saw she was already wearing her best high-heeled navy pumps to match her elegant dark blue silk suit, which had a long jacket and a skirt so narrow that she could only take very small steps. Lottie smiled to herself; trust her mother to dress up for a shopping expedition, even though she pretended that buying furniture for Merle's occupancy was a real bore. Lottie wondered whether she would be expected to put on her best skirt and jumper, but decided to say nothing and hope that her appearance would pass unnoticed. In fact, she had finished her breakfast and was carrying the crocks over to the sink before Louella realised that she was in her old clothes.

'Leave the dishes, we'll do them when we get home . . .' Louella was beginning, taking her light grey coat down from its hanger and pushing her arms into the sleeves. She stopped speaking and gave a squeak of indignation. 'Lottie Lacey, whatever were you thinking of to put on that grubby old dress? And that cardigan has a hole in the elbow! If you think I mean to take a little ragamuffin into Ginsburg's, then you've got another think coming.'

Lottie turned reluctantly away from the sink. 'Well, what *shall* I wear?' she said plaintively. 'I'm not risking my best jacket and skirt; that's for after-show parties, you said so.'

'Wear the brown check dress, the brown strap shoes and that smart little blazer Max bought you,' Louella said decidedly. 'I want to be proud of my daughter, not ashamed. And do hurry, darling, or we'll not finish the shopping before the theatre opens.'

'That brown dress is tight under my arms and makes me look about seven, and the strap shoes are the sort worn by Little Lord Fauntleroy,' Lottie grumbled, making her mother give a spurt of laughter. 'Couldn't I put on the skirt and jumper I wear for school? They fit me pretty well and there are no holes in the jumper. At least, it was all right last term so I s'pose it's all right still.'

'No, you must wear the brown,' Louella said. 'Remember, you'll be with me and this suit is the latest thing. Now no more arguing, dear, or I shall get cross. What a blessing that it's the Easter holidays, otherwise I should have to shop alone, and I hate doing that. You see, we're buying things to go in your room, so I want you to approve of them, and since we're also choosing for a young girl you may have a better idea of what Merle would like than I could possibly have myself.'

Lottie heaved a sigh but knew better than to continue to argue. She clattered up the stairs, tore off her comfortable old clothes and donned the childish brown dress, noting with satisfaction that the buttons of the blazer would no longer fasten. As she returned to the kitchen, she reflected that with a bit of luck the blazer might mysteriously disappear one day. She knew, of course, that her mother sold both her out-grown clothing and Baz's, and probably garments of her own which she considered no longer fashionable, to one of the stallholders on Paddy's market, though neither of them ever mentioned the fact. Darling Louella! Lottie was sure that her mother put the money she was paid towards buying new clothing, and equally sure that neither Max nor Baz knew about Louella's 'nice little earner', as someone had once phrased it.

'Ready? Good girl. Don't you look nice! Off we go then.'

Outside, the sky was grey with scudding clouds and there was a chilly wind blowing, but Lottie reminded herself that weather didn't really matter when you were in and out of shops. She had hoped to hurry across the court unnoticed by anyone, but Louella paused at the bottom of the steps, looking doubtfully up at the sky. 'I wouldn't be surprised if we had some rain,' she said in a dissatisfied tone. 'This suit is silk and water marks it. Just pop back in, queen, and fetch my navy umbrella.'

'But your coat covers almost all of the suit . . .'

Lottie began, then noticed Kenny and two of his pals approaching, and hastily ran up the steps. If Kenny saw her in the brown outfit, he would be bound to make some cutting remark, and she could not blame him. Nor of course could she give him a punch on the nose, not with Louella standing by. When she emerged cautiously from the house again, she was glad to see that Kenny and his pals had disappeared. *He who fights and runs away will live to fight another day*, she quoted rather irrelevantly to herself as she handed her mother the umbrella.

Louella tucked it into her shopping basket and the two set off, Lottie hurrying along with a light heart. 'Will we be home in time to have some lunch, Louella?' she asked presently. 'There's some of the joint of mutton left over; I know you were going to make it into a shepherd's pie but I doubt we'll have time to do it today.'

'We'll have a proper lunch at Fuller's, or Lyon's, or somewhere smart,' her mother said confidently. 'And if we're not back in time to make the shepherd's pie for tea then we'll have the cold mutton with a nice parcel of chips. Max will understand that we've not had time to cook anything.'

'That will be really lovely,' Lottie said appreciatively, as they turned out of the court and into Burlington Street, then headed towards the Scotland Road. 'Paddy's market is the nearest but I think we ought to do the other shops first, don't you?'

*

A week later, the attic room was ready to receive Merle O'Mara – or Merle Lacey as she would now be known. She was coming by train and would be arriving at Lime Street soon after three that afternoon, and Baz had agreed to meet her, though only in order to introduce her to Lottie, who would then accompany her back to Victoria Court. Baz was now working as a porter on Lime Street station so he would not have to leave his workplace to point Merle out to Lottie. In fact he meant to offer to carry her case – legitimate work for a porter – and that meant he could go with them out of the station and even walk them as far as the tram stop, for no doubt Merle's suitcase would be heavy and she would scarcely relish having to carry it all the way to Victoria Court.

Lottie had thought that her mother should meet Merle since she knew her from times past, but Louella and Max had been engaged by a rich businessman living out at Fazakerley to entertain at a children's party he was giving. Max had said that the money was too good to turn down and that Merle would understand. 'We'll be back in Liverpool in time for the evening performance,' he had said. 'But Merle's a real trouper; she'll know all too well that a performer can't turn down work. So what we want you to do, Lottie, is to meet her, take her back to the court and give her a meal. Louella is going to make a plateful of ham sandwiches and there'll be a bowl of salad and some hard-boiled eggs as well. By the time you've eaten you will have to leave for the theatre. Merle may come with you or she might prefer to go to her room and unpack, get settled in.' He had smiled affectionately at Lottie. 'I know you think it's a pity that Louella and I won't be around when Merle arrives, but it will give you girls an opportunity to get to know one another. All right? Any questions?'

Lottie had grinned and said that everything was fine. She was determined to like Merle and had actually gone out that morning and bought, with her own money, a large bunch of yellow daffodils. She had taken her mother's favourite vase – it was a pale green glass, shaped like a woman, and Lottie considered it very beautiful – arranged the daffodils with care and carried it up the two flights of stairs to the newly furnished bedroom.

Now she looked around the room appreciatively and was sure it would delight any girl, for she and Louella had chosen with care, and the new furniture looked as though it had always been in place there. The piece of carpet was cream, scattered with pink rosebuds, and Louella had managed to match up Lottie's pink bedspread so that Merle's bedcover, too, was the same pink as the curtains which graced the large window. The white walls – Baz had spent a whole weekend redecorating the little room – were hung, not only with Lottie's much-loved pictures of rural scenes, but with a couple of theatrical ones which Baz had said his cousin would much admire. The new wooden chair and chest of drawers had been painted white to match the ones already in place and Louella, who considered herself artistic, had stencilled garlands of flowers round the drawer handles, and had made a floral cushion to enhance the plain wooden chair.

Standing the daffodils carefully on the white-painted windowsill, Lottie took one last look round the room, then headed for the stairs. She had better get a move on; it would be dreadful if she arrived after the train because Baz would think her thoroughly unreliable, might even suspect her of not wanting to make Merle welcome, and she was truly determined that Merle and she should be friends. After all, why should they not like one another? It will be all right, Lottie told herself for the hundredth time. We'll be pals because theatre people are always nice. And now I'd better get moving or I'll be late, and that would never do.

She pushed open the kitchen door, checked the time, then reached her jacket down from its hook. She had been out earlier getting messages for her mother and hoped that the weather was still fine, but it was always difficult to tell in the courts for the houses were tall and hid all but a strip of sky from the court dwellers.

Lottie slipped into her jacket, hurried down the hall, and let herself out into the court. She locked the door with the key on its string, then popped it back through the letterbox. She ran down the three steps, waved to a couple of girls who were sitting on an orange box, gossiping, and set off towards the main road. She liked her classmates, would have enjoyed joining them, but was rarely able to do so. She was a year older than the rest of her class, still trying to make up for her time in hospital and the matinée performances, and because she had respectable clothes for school and worked hard whilst she was there, she knew some girls thought her stuck-up. It did not help that Louella had always discouraged her from playing out.

'Street games are for street kids, and street kids are common,' she had remarked in the past. 'I don't mind you playing with Kenny; Mrs B is a good friend and often kept an eye on you when you were small and I was busy. But some of the children – and their parents for that matter – don't know the meaning of the words soap and water. The kids are forever sagging off school, cheeking their elders and playing tricks on folk who don't appreciate their behaviour. And their language! If I ever heard you talking like the Willis kids, for example, I'd die of shame. So play with Kenny, or that nice little girl from Number Ten, but keep a decent distance from the others; do you understand?'

Since the 'nice little girl' was four years younger than Lottie and was seldom allowed to play out, Louella's commands had cut her daughter off from most of her contemporaries. As she turned into Scotland Road, Lottie thought again that it really would be nice if she and Merle got along. Even though Merle was a couple of years older, they would be sharing the same house and the same stage. Surely they might be friends?

Chapter Five

Lottie arrived at the station in good time and soon spotted Baz. She thought he looked nice in his porter's uniform, with his peaked cap, and felt proud when he came over and spoke to her, particularly when he tugged his cap and grinned. Just as though I were a real lady, Lottie told herself, returning his smile.

'Train's on time,' Baz said as he approached her. 'She'll be arriving . . .' he hooked a large gunmetal watch out of the pocket of his waistcoat and frowned down at its face, 'in eight minutes precisely. It'll be the good old *Lancashire Belle* and Mr Tomkins – he's the driver – is a stickler for timing. Some of the fellers on the footplate will nip out at a station and fetch back a mug of tea but you won't find Mr Tomkins having a drink unless he's arrived early and can spare five minutes. When I'm a driver I reckon I'll be the same.'

'I didn't know you were going to be a train driver, Baz,' Lottie said, awed. 'I wish girls could drive trains, but they can't even be porters, can they? Will it be long before you start driving one?'

Baz laughed a trifle self-consciously. 'First you've got to be a fireman and there's stiff competition for driving jobs,' he told her. 'There's all sorts of railway jobs I could do, though, even if I never get to drive an express. There's signalman, station-master, guard . . . oh, all sorts.' He lowered his voice. 'The thing is, if I can't see my way to advancement I'll mebbe do something different altogether, something not connected with rail-ways, I mean. I wouldn't want to work in the ticket office as a booking clerk. I've got me sights set on an outdoor job and you never know, if I applied for a country station . . .'

'Porter! Over here! Oh, it's you, young O'Mara. I didn't recognise you from the back. Gi' us a hand with this bleedin' cabin trunk; I dunno what the feller's gorrin it but I think it must be house bricks, it's that heavy.'

'Right away, Mr Collins, sir,' Baz said to the grizzled individual, also in porter's uniform, who had addressed him. Under his breath he spoke to Lottie. 'That's Mr Collins. He's been a porter here for thirty years and manages the rest of us. He's a nice old feller but . . .' The rest of the sentence was lost as he turned and left her, shouting as he went: 'I'll fetch a trolley, Mr Collins. You don't want to go tryin' to lift a weight like that, norreven atwixt the pair of us.'

Lottie watched as Baz hurried off, returning presently with one of the sturdy two-wheeled trolleys which stood nearby. She saw Mr Collins and Baz manoeuvre the heavy trunk into position and then her attention was distracted by the arrival of a train which entered the station in a cloud of steam, its brakes screeching as it drew to a halt. Hastily, Lottie looked round for Baz but he and his companion, and their burden, had disappeared. The engine was near enough, however, for her to read the name *Lancashire Belle* emblazoned upon it and her heart gave an uneasy thump. Oh dear, she had arrived on time and so had the train, but where oh where was Baz? She guessed, from what Louella had said, that Merle was fair and would be unaccompanied, but apart from that Lottie would not know her from any other female on the train. Desperately, she scanned the carriages, walking slowly along the platform, but she was pushed and jostled by the people getting off and by others trying to board, and was on the verge of tears when she saw before her a tall slender girl with a merry face. She was wearing a pale blue cloche hat which matched her coat, and beneath the hat Lottie glimpsed curls of an angelic fairness. Eagerly, she hurried forward, one hand stretched out. 'Merle O'Mara? I'm Lottie Lacey. Baz is here somewhere, but . . .'

The girl turned a pair of laughing blue eyes upon her. 'I'm sorry, love,' she said in a gentle voice. 'But I'm not Merle what's-her-name, I'm afraid. Ah, I can see my young man . . . he said he was going to meet me, but the crowd is so dense that he must have . . .' Her voice rose to a squeak. 'Alfred, darling, I was beginning to think you'd forgotten . . .'

The young man who had approached them seized the beautiful girl in his arms and kissed her, then picked up the suitcase which she had stood down as she descended from the train and the two of them hurried away, leaving Lottie scarlet with mortification. How could she have been so silly? She knew very well that Merle was seventeen, and the young woman in the blue cloche hat was probably quite twenty, and now she had lost her chance of spotting Merle when she left the train for already it was almost empty. In fact, there was only one other person getting down from the very last carriage. Lottie cast a desperate glance around her, longing to catch sight of Baz's familiar face, but she supposed he had been given another job to do by Mr Collins and could not escape. She made her way towards the last passenger and hesitated, not wanting to make a second mistake. She cleared her throat and looked enquiringly at the other girl. 'Excuse me, but I'm supposed to be meeting someone . . . her name's Merle O'Mara . . . I don't suppose . . . ?'

The girl had been gathering a large quantity of luggage into a heap but at Lottie's words she looked up. 'I'm Merle,' she said. 'But Uncle Max told my pa that Baz would be meeting me. What's happened to him? Only you and meself can't possibly carry all my traps.'

'He's somewhere about,' Lottie admitted, looking hopefully around her. 'He had to carry a great big cabin trunk for an old gent, but I'm sure he'll be back as soon as possible.' She looked curiously at the older girl. Merle was not at all what she had expected from the chance remarks Louella had let fall. She was very pretty, with a heart-shaped face framed by a great deal of curly light brown hair. Her nose was small and retroussé, her mouth a rosebud, and her teeth, when she smiled, were very white. She was sturdily built and of medium height, and she stood as dancers tend to do, with her feet planted solidly upon the platform and her legs braced. The only unattractive thing about her, in fact, were her eyes, which were small, very dark brown and shiny, though Lottie guessed that with stage makeup these orbs would appear large and lustrous so that Merle would pass as a very pretty girl indeed.

'Well? Know me again?'

The remark might have been meant as a joke, but there was a spiteful gleam in Merle's small eyes which made Lottie blush. 'I'm sorry,' she said humbly. 'Only – only from something Louella said I got the idea you were a blonde, and . . . and . . .'

'I'm as much a blonde as you are,' Merle said, staring very hard at Lottie. 'And if your ma thinks I mean to start bleachin' me lovely locks she's got another think comin'. It ruins your hair, you know. Yours will probably fall out after another two or three years. And what's wrong wit' me hair, anyway? Audiences love it when I swirl round and me hair flies out like a silken cloak. I wash it twice a week, and brush it two hundred times, night and mornin'. That's what makes it shine and look so good.'

'Oh,' Lottie said inadequately. 'I wish you'd tell Louella that; I hate having my hair bleached and last time I went to the hairdresser she said, more or less, what you've just told me. She said I could wear a wig but I haven't dared say anything to my mam because she'd get cross. She thinks – she thinks audiences like blondes better than brunettes.'

'I might mention it if the subject comes up,' Merle conceded. 'As for liking blondes, they just like us to look good, that's all.' Her eyes swept over Lottie, who immediately felt small, skinny and extremely plain. 'Of course I've not seen your act, but I'm blessed if I know what the three of us will look like – I mean, meself and your mam are women, but you're only – what? – fifteen, is it?'

'Yes, nearly fifteen, but the audiences seem to like me,' Lottie said stoutly, but with a sinking heart. 'They – they think I'm sweet, and . . .'

Merle laughed scornfully. 'Oh, when you were younger, I can believe that. But you ain't a child star any more, and you'll be dancin' and singin' wit' meself and your mam, two glamorous women. I don't see . . .'

She would have continued, but at that moment someone threw his arms about her and gave her a smacking kiss on the cheek. It was Baz, beaming all over his face and then bending to pick up the heaviest of the suitcases. 'Merle O'Mara, wharra little smasher you are!' he said. 'You were a pretty kid four or five years ago, but now you knock spots off every other gal in the company! Wait till me pals clap eyes on you; they'll be green wi' envy, I'm tellin' you!' He turned to Lottie. 'There's too much here for a tram, queen, so take that big blue bag and the brown holdall and we'll make for the taxi rank.'

'Right,' Lottie said, seizing the articles at which he had pointed and thinking rather crossly that it left only one lightweight bag for the owner of all this luggage to carry. 'Where did you go, Baz? I went up to the wrong person because you weren't . . .' She stopped. Baz and Merle had walked off, chattering animatedly. Baz seemed to find everything Merle said amusing, for he laughed a great deal and kept giving his cousin admiring glances.

Well, she *is* pretty, and they're both older than me, quite grown up, Lottie told herself, trudging along in their wake. She's right about bleached hair, too, and if she does tell Louella that it's bad for my hair I'm sure I'll be really grateful. But why was she so unfriendly when we first met? After all, if I'm just a kid – and I suppose I am – then why should she be nasty to me, she asked herself, crossing the pavement and going to the end of the taxi queue. But I expect she was disappointed that Baz hadn't turned up and was taking it out on me. She'll be fine once we get to know one another.

And sure enough, when the taxi came, Merle

took the heavy bags from her and thanked her sweetly for carrying them. 'It was too bad of Baz and meself, stridin' ahead and leavin' you behind,' she said, smiling. 'Only we're such old friends that I'm afraid I forgot me manners. Now you hop into the taxi, love; you can sit on one of them little tip-up seats, and Baz and I and the luggage will squeeze up together.'

'Oh, but Baz can't come with us,' Lottie said earnestly, climbing into the cab. 'Didn't you notice his uniform? He's a porter; that's why he had to help that old gentleman with his cabin trunk It's his job.'

'Yes, of course . . . but I thought mebbe they'd give him time off to see me and me traps back to wotsit court,' Merle said. 'Oh, come on, Baz! Your little pal and meself can't possibly manage all this stuff.'

Baz promptly went round to the driver's window and Lottie saw money change hands. Then he returned to explain that he had paid the driver extra to help them to carry Merle's luggage as far as the hallway of No. 2. 'No need to carry it right up to your room – leave it downstairs and I'll take it up when I get home,' he said magnanimously. 'Lottie will get you a drink and a meal before she goes off to the theatre. See you later, gals!' He slammed the rear door and stepped back as the taxi began to move off.

Merle leaned back in her seat and gave Lottie a dazzling smile. 'Phew! Sorry if I were a bit sharp wit' you when I got off the train but it were a devilish journey – folk crammed in like sardines and most of 'em in a bad temper. A young feller gave me his seat but I was squashed between a fat woman whose shopping basket kept diggin' me in the ribs and a dirty old man who smelt of fish. And that were only the last leg o' the journey. I had to change twice, you know. Still an' all, I got here in the end.'

'Yes you did, and you'll be able to rest up a bit once we get back to the court,' Lottie said. 'I have to be backstage by six because we're the second act tonight following Jack's warm-up routine, but you can stay at Number Two or come with me, whichever you like.'

'I'll see how I feel, love,' Merle said amicably, as the taxi slowed to avoid a crowd of people crossing the road. 'What time does Baz get home? He said he'd carry my luggage upstairs so mebbe I'll wait for him.' She glanced down at her dark coat. 'I don't want to make a bad impression at the theatre by turnin' up in this old thing an' still dusty from me journey, but I can't change until I can unpack.'

'I reckon he'll be home between six and seven,' Lottie said. She had just noticed that the glass panel which separated the driver from his passengers was pushed back and wondered if that was why Merle was being nice to her, then scolded herself. Merle had apologised very prettily for what she had said on the platform and if they were to be friends and colleagues, Lottie had best stop expecting the worst.

The car swerved into Burlington Street and drew up before the entrance to Victoria Court. 'We're here,' she informed her companion unnecessarily. 'The taxi can't get into the court so you and I will take the lighter stuff and the driver will bring the two big cases.'

It took some time to get all the luggage to the foot of the stairs but then Lottie paid off the driver with the money Max had given her and ushered Merle into the kitchen. Here she produced the plate of sandwiches and pulled the kettle over the flame whilst Merle took off her coat and hat and hung them on the row of pegs by the kitchen door. Then she looked around the room before settling herself in a chair and reaching for a sandwich. 'I'm bleedin' famished and parched as any desert,' she said, through a full mouth. 'I've not had a bite to eat since breakfast and I could do wit' a pee.' She looked around her once again. 'Where's the back door? I take it you have one?'

Lottie felt her cheeks begin to burn. She had taken it for granted that Merle would know the houses in the court were back-to-backs, which meant that the only way in and out was through the front door. This in its turn meant that all the houses shared the privies at the end of the court as they shared the water from the big brass tap nearby. She explained, haltingly, to Merle, who stared at her, small eyes rounding. 'Is that why there were a queue o' kids waitin' near them hut things?' she demanded. 'I see'd 'em when we were carryin' the luggage in. But what happens if you're in a hurry, like what I am? What happens at night time, come to that?'

'There's chamber pots under the bed if you're desperate,' Lottie said. 'If you really want to go now, though, you might be lucky – there might not be a queue because it's teatime. And it's not cold or raining, so you won't have to put your coat and hat back on.'

Merle got reluctantly to her feet, helped herself to another sandwich and took a quick swig of her tea. She disappeared but was back in a very short time. 'I hope I don't have to go there too often,' she said in a grumbling tone. 'Phew, what a pong! I bet it's a flies' paradise in the summer.'

Lottie vouchsafed no reply but sipped her own tea and thought bitter thoughts. She supposed that it had not occurred to Max to tell Merle what the house was like but wished that he had done so since she did not relish the task herself. For the first time it struck her that Merle might not realise the bedroom she would share with Lottie was an attic room up two flights of steep stairs, and she wondered what sort of digs Merle had occupied when she left her parents' caravan. She was soon to find out. Underneath her navy coat, Merle was wearing an old grey skirt and a shabby pink cardigan, and now she tweaked these garments impatiently, finished her tea and stood up. 'I feel

134

better after a bite and a sup, so I reckon you'd best show me up to me room,' she said. 'I've a change of clothing in the holdall along wit' me sponge bag, so I can spruce meself up an' put on a clean jumper and skirt before Baz gets home.'

'Yes, all right,' Lottie said, crossing the kitchen and heading for the stairs. Neither girl said a word until Lottie threw open the door and they entered the bedroom. Then Lottie said, rather shyly: 'Both beds have got clean sheets on so you can take whichever you like. The chest of drawers is for your underwear and that, and the rail nearest the door is for clothes that want hanging. We hadn't realised how much luggage you'd have, though. Is it all clothes?'

'A lot of it's me stage stuff. Didn't Uncle Max tell you? My act's called "Dance Through the Ages". I start off as an Elizabethan lady in an enormous farthingale – that's a dress, you know – doing a stately pavane and end up with the Charleston, the Twinkle, the Black Bottom . . . oh, you know what I mean, all the modern stuff. So you see I have a great many costumes.'

'But you aren't doing your "Dance Through the Ages" when you're with us, are you? Louella said it would just be modern dance and you'd join us for the singing and tap-dancing,' Lottie said, alarmed. It seemed as though Merle had got hold of the wrong idea all round.

'Is that so? Well, I couldn't leave my costumes behind, could I, even if I won't need them all,'

Merle said practically. 'You wouldn't catch Uncle Max leaving his disappearing cabinet behind, even if he weren't going to use it for a few weeks, would you?'

Lottie agreed that this was so but pointed out that stage clothes would be left at the theatre. 'My Columbine costume has layers and layers of net to make the skirt stick out; it would take up almost the whole of my clothes rack if I brought it home,' she said. She pointed to the daffodils. 'I bought them for you to make our room look pretty. Do you like them?'

'Very nice, I'm sure. But did I hear aright? Did you say "our" room? There's another door opposite this one on the landing. Why can't you sleep there?'

'That's Baz's room,' Lottie explained. She was beginning to wonder whether Merle was a trifle wanting in the upper storey. In big families, the girls would have one room and the boys another. She knew Merle was an only child but she must have realised that Max could not just whistle up a fifth bedroom because his niece was coming to stay.

Apparently, however, Merle had not been told how things stood for she said impatiently: 'Look, you little halfwit, there's two bedrooms on the first floor, right, and two up here. That makes four. One for Max and Louella, one for Baz, one for you and one for me. So why do they expect me to share when I'm a young lady and need a place of me own?'

'Uncle Max and Louella have a bedroom each. They share the house and the bills and that, but they each have their own room,' Lottie said, feeling the heat rush up her neck and invade her face once more. 'They aren't married, you know, they just work together. And anyway, what's wrong with you and me sharing? We're both girls, aren't we?'

'I'm years older'n you, and I have – have women's troubles. I bet you don't even know what that means,' Merle said crossly. Her small mouth had tightened until it looked more like a button than a rosebud.

'Of course I know what it means,' Lottie said quickly, though untruthfully. 'But it's a nice big room and the beds are comfy. Besides, there's nowhere else, unless you want to share with Louella, of course.'

Merle shrugged, her expression sulky, and walked over to peer out of the window, then straightened up. 'Where's the bathroom?' she snapped abruptly. 'I might as well have a wash before I change me clothes.'

Lottie could have slapped her. Merle must know full well that there was no bathroom; she was just being difficult. Lottie said as much, pointing to the washstand, with its ewer full of cold water and soap and a towel laid out neatly by the basin.

Merle approached it cautiously, as though she thought it might bite, tipped a tiny amount of water into the basin and washed her hands and face, then rubbed herself dry and turned once more to her companion. 'It ain't what I'm used to but I suppose I'll have to make the best of it,' she said coldly. 'After all, we're off to Great Yarmouth in a few weeks. But you can clear out when I'm havin' a strip-down wash and I want your word that you won't go interferin' with me nice clothes, 'cos the thought of your dirty fingers pawin' through 'em fair turns my stomach.'

Up to that point Lottie had been determined to remain cool and friendly, but this was too much. 'I wouldn't touch your bleedin' clothes with a barge pole,' she said angrily. 'As for your strip-down wash, you can have a bath, same as other people; there's nothin' to stop you.'

Merle rounded on her at once, the small eyes narrowing venomously, her cheeks scarlet. 'If you think I'm goin' to slosh around in a tin bath by the kitchen range, you're bleedin' well wrong,' she hissed. 'Oh aye, I can just imagine it: me crouchin' in the water while the whole world tramps in and out. It may be all right for you, but it ain't all right for me.'

'If you believe Louella and Max – and Baz for that matter – take their baths in the kitchen, then you're a whole lot stupider than I thought,' Lottie said. 'There's a public baths not two minutes away; that's where grown-ups go. It costs a bob, but Louella says it's worth every penny, 'cos you get all the water you want, a nice bar of Lifebuoy soap and a big fluffy towel to dry yourself on. But of course, if you prefer a strip-down wash . . .' She turned away on the words, shot across the room and began to run down the stairs, too angry now to care what Merle thought.

Behind her, she heard Merle begin to descend, calling out as she came. 'Lottie! Hang on a minute . . . wait, will you! I didn't mean . . . shouldn't have said . . .'

'Can't wait; gorra be at the theatre in fifteen minutes,' Lottie shouted back. 'I'll just grab me coat . . .'

She entered the kitchen and took her coat from its peg, but was prevented from leaving the room again by Merle, who rushed into the kitchen, slammed the door shut and then leaned against it, panting heavily. 'Look, it were the shock what made me so rude,' she said breathlessly. 'It's just that it ain't what I'm used to, bein' in proper digs 'n' all. You see me pa told me that Uncle Max had a big house, a real nice modern place, in the centre of Liverpool, quite near the theatre. When me and the girls split up I'd had several other offers, but . . .'

Lottie buttoned her coat and grabbed at the door handle. 'You'll have to explain another time – if you really want to, that is,' she snapped. 'I'm off. I mustn't be late. *You* know that.'

Looking considerably chastened, Merle nodded. 'Yes, I know; but I've changed me mind. I'll come to the theatre with you, then I can talk as we go.'

'Suit yourself,' Lottie said ungraciously as she opened the front door, waited for Merle to emerge, then locked it and slipped the key through the letterbox. 'I'm sorry Number Two isn't good enough for you but I'm sure you can get lodgings somewhere else once you get your first wage packet, and don't tell me Uncle Max pretended he lived in a lovely modern house because he and Louella are always talking about moving somewhere better, only Victoria Court is right handy for the theatre, and it's cheap as well and near the public baths.'

'I expect it was me pa getting in a muddle,' Merle said. 'He's a real family man is me pa. When us three girls split up, I had several offers of work but Pa thought I'd be better off if I stayed with the family, so to speak. You've not met my pa, have you? He's only a year younger than Uncle Max, and they're like as two peas in a pod, an' real fond of one another. Pa knew Uncle Max would do right by me an' not let me be cheated or taken advantage of. Otherwise I'd have gone with the Dynamos, 'cos Reggie – he's the youngest – was real keen to start up a song and dance routine, as well as what he does already.'

'What does he do already?' Lottie enquired politely. She was not in the least interested but recognised an olive branch when she heard one. 'Was he at your theatre in Birmingham?'

'No, the Dynamos are with Pa's circus. They do a motorcycle act,' Merle explained. 'They're very good, honest they are, but of course they're all fellers and anyhow I've missed Baz and wanted to work with him again, so I settled for Uncle Max.'

By now they were turning into the jigger which led to the stage door and Lottie put a detaining hand on her companion's arm. 'Hang on a minute,' she said urgently. 'Baz has never done anything in the theatre, so far as I know. I told you he is a porter on Lime Street station – well, you saw him yourself. Max wanted to teach him conjuring and magic, all that sort of stuff, but Baz said he weren't interested. He says he'll be a train driver one day, or maybe work on a country station, but even if he doesn't do that I'm certain he'll never want to go on the stage. He says he hates folks staring at him and you've got to like it, you know, or it shows.'

Merle had stopped dead in her tracks but now she began to move forward again, though more slowly. 'Yes, I remember when I were standin' in for you, he never would come on stage, or only to change props when there were no one else around to help,' she said. She was frowning, but then her brow cleared. 'Oh, but he'll be free evenings and weekends when the show's over an' I'm telling you, he'll love Great Yarmouth. So will you. There's beautiful white-gold sand and all sorts of shells cast up by the tide, and a wonderful prom, with all sorts of sideshows and attractions. There's two piers with a different show at each of 'em, and an old fishing harbour where boat trips go right out to Scroby Sands, so's you can see the seals and their babies – they call 'em pups – stretched out on the banks as though they were sunbathing.

There's a great huge fairground, and one year Levallier – he's the ringmaster – took the circus there for the whole month of August. The big top were packed every night an' we took more money in that month than for the whole of the previous three. Yes, you'll love Great Yarmouth, and so will Baz.'

'But he won't be there!' Lottie shouted. She was beginning to suspect that Merle did not listen to a word one said. 'He'll be in Liverpool, working as a porter and keeping Number Two Victoria Court warm for us. Mrs Brocklehurst next door is going to give him his meals and keep the place nice, so you see he won't be anywhere near Great Yarmouth.'

A glance at Merle's face told her that she had got through this time, for the older girl looked shattered. 'But me main reason for joining Uncle Max was so's I could see more of Baz,' she said, sounding so miserable that Lottie felt almost sorry for her. 'Mind you, we're only in Yarmouth for the season, ain't we? Then we'll come back here.'

'Ye-es, but the season's nearly four months,' Lottie reminded her. She risked a grin. 'You'll have to make do with me for that time,' she said.

Merle grinned too, and for a moment Lottie saw that the other girl might be quite fun if she could just make the best of the situation in which she found herself. 'Well, we'll see how the act goes,' she said. 'I suppose there'll be quite a few young men in Great Yarmouth keen to give a girl

142

a good time so mebbe I'll not miss Baz too badly after all.'

At this point they reached the stage door and were greeted by the doorman. 'Evenin', Miss Lottie,' he said, and, noticing Merle, he gave her a nod. 'Evenin', miss. Are you goin' round the front to watch the show or comin' in with Lottie here?' His eyes returned to Lottie. 'Friend of yourn, miss?'

'No,' Lottie said rather unwisely and saw, with a feeling of guilt, the colour deepen in Merle's cheeks. 'I mean, yes, she is a friend of mine but she's joining the company as well,' she amended hastily.

'In you go then,' the man said, stepping back so that they could pass him. 'You're in good time, Miss Lottie; your mam and Mr Magic only went to the green room ten minutes ago and Jack hasn't arrived yet.'

'That's good; we'll have time for a cup of tea before the show starts and I can introduce you to everyone,' Lottie said as they hurried along the gloomy passage towards the green room where, Lottie guessed, she would find all the cast beginning to assemble.

In fact, the only people there were Max and her mother. Lottie announced that their guest had arrived and saw her mother's eyes widen with surprise as they fell on Merle, but Louella rushed forward and enveloped the girl in a scented embrace. 'My dear, I would never have recognised

143

you,' she said, stepping back but retaining her hold on Merle's shoulders. 'I was expecting to welcome a child but you're a young woman, and a very pretty one too. Dear me, what a surprise!'

There was a rather uncomfortable silence which Max broke in his usual tactful manner. 'It certainly is a surprise, and a very pleasant one, too,' he said warmly. He turned and flung a casual arm round his niece's shoulders. 'We mustn't forget that the last time you and Louella met you really were a child, but now you're a glamorous young woman. When the three of you are on stage together you'll have audiences eating out of your hands in no time.'

Merle cast her uncle a grateful look, then turned a somewhat measuring glance on Louella. 'I know we're going on stage as the Lacey Sisters,' she said, 'but you and I are almost the same height, Louella. Somehow, I'd imagined you would be taller, I don't know why. But I suppose we can do our routines with Lottie here between us.'

'Oh, I'll be taller than you on stage,' Louella said airily. She looked meaningly at Merle's court shoes. 'You can't tap-dance in high heels, you know, and when you leave them off you'll lose two or three inches. And we'll have to see about that hair, young lady, because a sisters' act means we should look alike and . . .'

'I'm not bleaching my hair, Louella,' Merle said at once. 'It would ruin the texture, and remember I've got my whole career to consider, not just this summer season. And if you ask me, little Lottie here shouldn't be bleaching hers either.'

Louella was so surprised that for a moment she simply stared at the younger girl, saying nothing. But then she spoke, her voice cold. 'I suppose I can't insist that you bleach your hair, Merle, but I shall certainly not allow you to interfere between me and my daughter. If I say she must bleach hers . . .'

'Louella, I think Merle's right,' Lottie said, her voice very small but as determined as she could make it. 'My hair is growing to feel harsh and horrid. I'm very sorry because I know you think it's important, but I do agree with Merle. I did talk to the hairdresser last time I went there and she said if you were dead set on having a blonde daughter, then you should buy me a blonde wig. She said my hair's growing brittle from too much bleach and she wants to shingle it so I'll look like a boy and let the bleach grow out. It would make it easier to wear the wig as well. I'm sure it would be all right, Louella, and no one would guess that it wasn't my own hair.'

Louella began to reply just as the door opened and Jack Russell bounced into the room. He was already dressed in his stage clothes of a ridiculously exaggerated pair of plus fours, a tartan jacket and a huge checked cap, and burst into speech before even shutting the door behind him. 'Have you heard the latest?' he demanded. 'Miss Tideswell – only she's Mrs really of course – is in

145

the fambly way. Her old feller told me just now; he's pleased as Punch, though of course he'll have to find someone to take her place when she begins to show.'

'Bella? Having a baby? Oh, the poor darling,' Louella said, her mind temporarily diverted from her own troubles. 'It'll be the end of her career on the stage, you mark my words.'

Bella and Andrew Tideswell blacked up and did an act called 'Down the Mississippi' in the course of which they sang Negro spirituals and performed old-time dances. They were popular with audiences and actors alike, and Lottie could not see what was wrong with having a baby. The Tideswells did a good deal of their act aboard a Mississippi steamer made from cardboard, and Lottie thought that audiences were unlikely to notice Bella's condition provided she sat down behind the cardboard gunwale, so that only her top half showed. She started to say as much but was rudely interrupted. 'My dear child, you know nothing about it. You think a baby is all sweetness and light, but that isn't the case at all. Babies ruin a girl's figure and need constant attention. Feeding, cleaning, washing nappies, making sure they don't howl and annoy people . . . stage folk simply can't afford to have families, and that's the truth.'

Lottie looked across at Max and saw that he was frowning, though he said nothing. He had been left to look after a small baby, but his career had

146

not suffered, and she knew other theatricals who had families. 'But Louella, you had me and I don't think I've ruined your career,' Lottie said in a small voice. 'Do you – do you think you'd be on the London stage by now if it hadn't been for me?'

Louella promptly ran across the room and gave her daughter a consoling hug. 'Darling, what a thing to say! You were a perfect baby, good as gold and a great asset so far as my career was concerned. No one ever minded looking after you whilst I was on stage, because you never cried or made a fuss, and as soon as you could toddle you were a part of my act. I was tremendously lucky and I knew it, but I would never take the chance of having another baby. Remember, I was a mere child when I had you and I got my figure back within a few weeks of your birth. That's the way of it when you're young, but neither Bella nor myself could claim to be girls any more. So I think she's mad to have allowed herself to get caught, and even if I were married I'd make absolutely certain I didn't get pregnant ever again.'

There was a short silence and then Max spoke. 'I like kids,' he said mildly. 'I'm sure we all understand your point of view, Louella, only you must keep it to yourself. Andrew told me ages ago that he and Bella wanted a family very badly indeed, and you wouldn't want to hurt their feelings, I'm sure.'

Louella turned her sweetest smile upon him. 'Darling, of course I wouldn't dream of saying anything to Bella except congratulations,' she said at once. 'Each to their own, I say, and I'm sure Bella will be just as happy being a housewife and a mother as she has been on the stage with Andrew. And now let's change the subject.' She looked enquiringly at Jack. 'You're in your stage costume! Why on earth . . . ?'

Jack wagged a finger. 'I'm in my stuff because I'm doing my warm-up in ten minutes,' he said, 'and you're second act tonight and you're not ready, and nor, I see, is little Miss Lottie.' He glanced around the room and, noticing Merle, gave her his cheekiest grin. ''Ello, 'ello, 'ello, I spy strangers,' he said. 'Ho no I don't, I reckon I spy the beautiful Miss O'Mara, what's goin' to swan off to Yarmouth with us for the summer season. Is that right, queen? I guess they'll have told you old Jack's goin' along as well. My, Great Yarmouth won't know what's hit 'em.'

Merle smiled prettily, but Louella's mood was not improved by the realisation that Jack was right. She was meticulous about timing and was usually ready long before her call, and now she and Lottie would have to scramble into their stage clothes or risk Jack's having to ad lib in order to give them time to get on stage. She shot a glance at the clock, and would have hustled Lottie out of the room had Jack not detained her. 'Your mam's right about babies in some ways,' he said quietly. 'But I reckon Bella's littl'un will be an asset because she'll be able to black it up and sing some of them Negro

148

lullabies to it. Be nice that would, and audiences would love it, you mark my words.'

Louella looked back and addressed Merle. 'You'd better go out front and watch from there; you might learn something,' she said nastily. Then, as she and Lottie hurried towards their dressing room, she turned on her daughter. 'Didn't you notice the time? We'll have to get a move on – I don't intend to be late on stage just because that cheeky little madam took my mind off my work. As for you, Lottie, I'm disgusted! You should have told me what the hairdresser said so that I could decide what best to do. Of course, the woman's quite right: bleaching is bad for one's hair, though it doesn't seem to have done mine much harm.'

They reached the dressing room and entered it to find the wardrobe mistress laying out their clothes and turning reproachful eyes on them as they appeared. 'Well, Miss Louella, I never knowed you late before,' she remarked. 'Here's me wantin' to go along to Mrs Rivers to put a stitch in the dress she wears as Marie Lloyd, but I dursen't leave here, knowing as you'd want me to give you both a hand.'

Mrs Rivers was, in her own eyes at least, very much the star of the variety show. She was lucky in that she looked very like Marie Lloyd, the queen of the music halls, and could imitate Marie's voice and gestures exactly. When she gave her rendering of 'My Old Man Says Follow the Van', she brought the house down and soon had the audience singing along with her.

'I'm awfully sorry, Mrs Jones,' Louella said penitently, beginning to tear off her day clothes ready to dive into her stage dress. 'I simply didn't notice how time was passing.' Her head emerged through the neck of the dress and Mrs Jones began to do up the dozens of little buttons which fastened the back. 'You run along now. You really mustn't keep Mrs Rivers waiting, and I can help Lottie as soon as I've done my face.'

Mrs Jones swept out and Lottie scrambled into her own dress, dragged a brush through her hair, and slid her feet into her tap shoes, fastening the buckles and then flying across to the mirror to apply powder to her shiny nose and colour to her lips.

'Ready? Off we go then,' Louella said briskly. 'Mrs Jones is a real pro; she'll be standing in the wings with your Columbine dress and my crinoline minutes before we need them.'

The pair of them arrived in the wings in good time, for Jack had only just begun on his comical interpretation of a golfer trying to rescue a ball which had fallen deep into a sandy bunker. 'Sounds like a good audience,' Lottie said rather timidly as a roar of laughter greeted Jack's latest attempt. 'Louella, I know you feel I shouldn't have mentioned the bleach when Merle were being so difficult and I'm sorry, 'cos I reckon you feel I've let you down. Only – only I'll be fifteen in June, and you've been having my hair bleached for years, and . . .'

'I didn't mean any harm . . .' Louella began defensively, then cast a hunted look at her daughter. 'Oh, never mind, it doesn't really matter. I just wish you'd told me what the hairdresser said. I can't say I approve of wigs, but just for a little while I dare say we can manage.'

Lottie turned and gave her mother an impulsive hug. 'It'll only be for while we're here because once we're in Great Yarmouth no one will expect me to be a blonde,' she said excitedly. 'And you know, Louella, short hair is all the rage. Most of the kids in school have bobs or even shingles, so why shouldn't we? You'd look really lovely . . . and it can't be good for your hair to be bleached all the while either.'

'I'll think about it, but the trouble is Max likes his assistant to have long hair. It goes better with the tights and the spangled tops,' she said. 'I'd like to know what that little madam does with that great mass of hair when she's doing the Charleston and the Black Bottom. That's modern dance if you like.' She brooded for a moment, then added darkly: 'Well, we'll see. After all, if she doesn't fit in with our act even Max can't expect me to put up with her, especially if she's ruining our reputation.'

There was a roar of applause from the auditorium and Lottie saw Jack cast an anxious glance into the wings, then brighten as he saw them waiting. He bowed jerkily, swung his ridiculous golf club in acknowledgement of the clapping, then took the ball from his pocket and bit into it, causing yet more laughter as he came off, munching. Lottie knew that the ball which came out of his pocket was not the one with which he had played golf, but was made of marshmallow. Of course the audience did not know and responded accordingly. He gave Louella an approving pat as he came into the wings. 'All serene?' he muttered beneath his breath. 'Right; then I'll announce you.' He strutted back on to the stage, bowed stiffly, and then announced: 'And now, folks, put your hands together for Louella Lacey and little Miss Lotteeeeee!'

He left the stage as the orchestra struck up the first bars of 'Tiger Rag' and mother and daughter, arms linked, tap-danced briskly from the darkened wings into the bright lights of the stage. Lottie always kept her eyes fixed on the back row of the stalls, but today she looked down and saw Merle sitting in the third row and staring up at them. As their eyes met, Lottie flashed a quick, genuine smile and received a small grin in return. Later, when they were alone in their bedroom, she would try to explain away her mother's sharpness, but for now the smile would have to be sufficient. Lottie danced on.

Chapter Six

Lottie was in her shared bedroom, packing. Thoughtfully, she reflected on the past weeks. Merle had proved to be an excellent dancer, very much better than Louella or Lottie herself, and her demonstration dances – the modern ones – were tremendously popular. For these she tied back her hair into a heavy plait which she then coiled round and round the top of her head and covered with a colourful browband, and wore the long bead necklaces and slinky, waistless fringed dresses which were all the rage. She had several of them in bright, primary colours, and either Lottie or Louella stood with Mrs Jones in the wings to help with the quick changes necessary so that Merle charlestoned off in blue and tangoed back in orange which, of course, delighted the audience as much as her spirited rendering of the half-dozen dances she did at each performance.

As Louella had said, Merle's voice was not strong, nor even particularly melodious, but she did have sufficient sense to keep it soft whilst mouthing vigorously and allowing Louella and Lottie to carry the tune between them. Max had actually had the temerity to suggest that Louella might let the two girls do the tap-dance routine without her, saving herself for the singing and for the end-of-act Columbine performance, but as Lottie could have told him the suggestion had been turned down emphatically. Louella might know her tap-dancing left something to be desired, but, though generous in many ways, she would never relinquish one second of her time on stage.

Lottie finished cramming her last garment into the case her mother had provided and glanced at her reflection in the mirror. Her hair had grown into a neat bob just below her ears. It was dark brown with burnished auburn lights and was far less trouble than her bleached hair had been, for it did not take even a second to run a comb through her new style. Even Louella admitted grudgingly that Lottie's natural colouring was a great improvement and she liked the modern style, though at first she had complained that no one would take them for sisters because they looked so different. Lottie and Merle, however, had banded together to scoff at this idea. 'We aren't pretendin' to be perishin' triplets,' Merle had said, and Lottie had chimed in with a reminder about Kenny's sisters.

'One's got red hair, one's almost yellow as a daffodil and Daisy's quite dark,' she had pointed out. 'Yet all three have got the same mum and dad. And the Trevors at school look quite different, and it ain't just their hair, either; Una's fat and Beryl's skinny, but they're still sisters.'

They had been in the kitchen of Victoria Court at the time. Max had been polishing his shoes but he looked up. 'It's two to one, Lou . . . no, three to one, because I agree with the girls,' he had said. 'What matters to the audience is how well you dance and sing, not whether you look alike. C'mon, let's get breakfast on the table or we'll be late for rehearsal.'

Now, Lottie snapped her case shut and picked it up, giving one last valedictory glance around her room as she did so. It was a good deal changed from the room into which she had ushered Merle several weeks earlier, for Merle had made changes and stamped her personality upon it. The older girl had bought a very pretty Chinese screen from one of the vendors on Paddy's market. It was made of wood lacquered red, surrounding pictures of Chinese scenery painted on some stiff type of paper, and when Merle wanted to wash, dress or change she unfolded the screen so though she and Lottie could exchange remarks they could not actually see one another. And she had bought a full-length mirror which Baz had screwed on to the wall for her. Since this made the mirror a permanent feature, Lottie had offered to pay half but Max had said he would stand the nonsense which meant neither girl had to part with any cash.

There were other signs of the shared occupancy. Merle was a film fan and had acquired a number of enlarged photographs of her favourite stars. Rudolph Valentino, turbaned as the sheik, Douglas

Fairbanks as Robin Hood and Ramon Navarro as himself looked down from the walls on Merle's side of the room. Lottie had once wondered aloud why so many sultry male eyes gazing at her companion as she washed and dressed – or indeed undressed – did not make her feel self-conscious, but Merle had laughed this idea to scorn. 'I wouldn't mind if they was here in person 'cos there's nothing wrong with my body,' she had said boldly. 'I bet they'd jump off the walls and chase me round the room given half the chance.'

Lottie had giggled. 'But you're shy of me seeing you so wharrabout Rudolph Valentino?' she had enquired. 'That's a lovely picture of him you've got on the wall; d'you hang your face flannel over him every time you take your knickers off?'

This remark, for some reason, had infuriated Merle. The two girls had been in bed at the time and Merle had rolled to the extreme edge of her own mattress and taken a swipe at Lottie. 'You're stupid, you are,' she had said scornfully. 'If you were a woman, same as what I am, I wouldn't need no screen. But you ain't a woman, you're just a silly, stuck-up little girl. Get it?'

Lottie, nursing a sore ear, for Merle's swipe had hurt, had said sulkily that she did indeed get it and had cuddled down under the covers thinking that she would never understand Merle if she lived to be a hundred. The older girl could be so nice when she chose, but Lottie was quite bright enough to realise that she was usually at her nicest when an adult was present. It was when the two of them were alone that the unpleasant side of Merle's nature sometimes came to the fore. Lottie wondered uneasily whether Merle's spite was partly her way of getting back at Louella, for Mam was always criticising Merle and finding fault generally. Obviously Merle could not take her annoyance out on Louella without its being plain to everyone, so perhaps she was wreaking her revenge on Lottie. It was clearly unfair, and once or twice Lottie had actually considered bringing the whole thing into the open, but she hated rows and unpleasantness and comforted herself with the reminder that once they reached Great Yarmouth Merle would not have Baz's support and might be glad to be friendly with Lottie.

At this point in her musing, Lottie began to descend the stairs. Her mother and Merle were waiting outside in the court, guarding their luggage, for Max had hired a motor van to take all their paraphernalia to their destination. He had also hired a driver, so he and Louella would be passengers, but the two girls would undertake the tedious journey by rail, arriving some time after the motor van. Jack Russell had left the previous day, and had promised to meet the girls at the station and accompany them back to their lodgings, because otherwise they would not know which bus to catch.

Lottie let herself out of the house, locked the door and descended the steps. Louella looked round and smiled. 'I was just beginning to get worried, because I know Max wants to load up and leave immediately when he arrives,' she said. 'And you two had best get down to the tram stop. Have you got your handbag and your ticket, darling? I feel awfully mean sending the pair of you off on such a lengthy and complicated journey by yourselves, but at least you won't have any luggage to worry about.' She handed her daughter a bulging string bag. 'There's sandwiches, apples and a flask of hot tea here because I doubt you'll have any chance of getting yourselves a meal en route – unless you miss a connection, of course. Baz will see you on to the train and remember Jack is meeting you at the other end. Oh, dear, I suppose I should be coming with you, but Max will need me when we reach the theatre to help with the unpacking.'

'Goodness, Louella, I'm seventeen years old and I've been on a hundred journeys by myself and always arrived safely,' Merle cut in impatiently. 'And Lottie's a bright kid. I'm telling you, the pair of us will be fine.' She grabbed Lottie's arm. 'C'mon, there's bound to be a tram along any minute. No point hanging around here.'

She and Lottie set off down the court, but Louella called after them, her voice sharp. 'Merle, I told you to leave your luggage here. Why have you hung on to that bag?'

Merle pretended not to hear but pulled Lottie along until they reached the tram stop. A tram drew up within seconds of their arrival and when they had climbed aboard and taken their seats, Lottie said breathlessly: 'Why didn't you leave the bag behind, Merle? Louella was only trying to save you trouble, you know.'

'She wasn't; she just wanted to know what was in the bag,' Merle said. 'It's my makeup, my diary, a set of silk underwear I bought with my last week's wages, and the box of chocolates which Baz gave me as a leaving present.' She glanced rather slyly at her companion. 'Baz and me is going steady; did you know?'

'No. But how can you go steady? You're going to be separated for weeks and weeks,' Lottie pointed out. 'Why, I remember you telling me when you first came to Victoria Court that you were hoping to have lots of young men admirers when we reach Yarmouth.'

Merle gave a triumphant little smirk. 'Yes, but I didn't know how keen Baz were going to be,' she said. 'He won't have told *you*, of course, 'cos you're only a kid and don't mean nothing to him, but in a week's time me an' Baz will be seein' each other every day, goin' out on Sundays, havin' a great time.'

'Why? Don't say you're goin' back to Liverpool?' Lottie said, devoutly hoping that this was true. 'Only if you are, why come to Great Yarmouth at all? I'm sure Mr Quentain would have been happy to have you do a solo act with your "Dance Through the Ages" routine. But I thought you said you was keen to have another season in Great Yarmouth.'

Merle tossed her head scornfully. Her hair was braided today into two long plaits, and one of them slapped quite painfully across Lottie's cheek. Lottie jerked her head back, opening her mouth to protest, but Merle was speaking again. 'I always knew you were a little silly what don't understand nothin'. As if I'd change my arrangements just to suit a feller, no matter how much I liked him! D'you remember telling me as how Baz wouldn't mind workin' on a country station? Well, he applied for a job as porter at a station quite near Great Yarmouth. What do you think of that, eh? No feller would move his job unless he were serious. He reckons he'll move to Norfolk in a week or two. So you see, we *are* going steady and one of these days I'm goin' to persuade him to leave the railways and give Uncle Max a hand so's he can learn the game, like.'

'He did say he wouldn't mind a country station, but to move so far from the rest of us . . . his dad, I mean . . . and what'll he do when the season's over? As for joining Max on the stage, he'll never do it . . .' Lottie was saying as the tram drew to a halt outside Lime Street station. Both girls got to their feet, seized their belongings and descended from the tram, though as they made their way into the station Lottie repeated breathlessly: 'Baz won't go on stage, Merle, not for you or anyone else. He gets terrible stage fright. The only time he ever stood in for Louella he had to go off the stage twice to be sick. Some folk are like that, didn't you know?'

'It'll be different when he's working wi' me,' Merle said firmly. She stopped short and waved violently. 'There he is!' She raised her voice to a yell. 'Over here, Baz!' She turned on Lottie. 'And don't you dare say a word about seeing him next week or I'll bloody throttle you in your bed,' she hissed. 'I swore I'd not tell a soul in case Uncle Max tried to persuade him to stay in Liverpool.'

'I won't say anything,' Lottie said rather despondently. The good relationship which had existed between herself and Baz had almost disappeared since Merle's arrival. The older girl and Baz had spent every spare moment together and no matter what entertainment they had planned, they had utterly refused to let Lottie accompany them. Once, of course, she would not have minded but would have gone off happily enough with Kenny, only Kenny, too, had changed. He belonged to a gang of lads of his own age and had no time for a mere girl, especially one who, as he put it, 'made a right spectacle of herself in front of an audience of silly old women at the Gaiety theatre every night'.

So the past weeks had not been happy ones for Lottie. She had felt lonely and more than a little neglected, because Louella had assumed she was going around with Baz and Merle, or with Kenny, and so had made no attempt to take her daughter along when she and Max had a day out. Lottie had begun to look forward eagerly to the move to Great Yarmouth, believing that Merle would be glad of her company once Baz was no longer within reach. Now it seemed that this was not to be, for if Baz was prepared to change his job just to be near his cousin, things were serious indeed.

Now, however, Baz came over to them and gave Merle a hug, then, after a quick glance round, kissed her cheek and whispered something Lottie could not catch. He took absolutely no notice of Lottie, but addressed himself to Merle. 'Wharra grand girl you are, Merle O'Mara, arrivin' in good time an' lookin' as fresh as a daisy, though you must have been up for hours. The train ain't in yet, so do you want to go to the buffet and get yourself a nice cuppa and a bun? I'm on duty so I can't go wi' you, but I can carry your bag and take you to the train and wave you off.'

'A cup of tea would be lovely, but I'd rather be with you, Baz,' Merle said soulfully, fluttering her lashes and turning down the corners of her small mouth. Lottie thought nastily that the older girl would have stuck on stage eyelashes if she had known how inadequate her own looked when fluttered. 'Can't we find some quiet spot where we can be alone for ten or fifteen minutes?'

Baz frowned doubtfully, then his brow cleared. 'Show me your ticket,' he muttered urgently. 'Then I'll pretend there's something wrong with it and we'll go over towards the ticket office. There's a little bit of unused platform where some of the chaps go for a quiet smoke; we'll go there.'

Lottie realised, of course, that she was not meant to be included but felt she could not hang around on the platform alone so followed them and wished she had not when they reached the secluded spot. Baz put both arms round Merle, then appeared to notice Lottie for the first time and scowled at her. 'Buzz off, kid,' he said roughly. 'Find Platform Three: there's a framed timetable there which you can pretend to be studying. We'll join you in ten minutes.'

Lottie glared at him. He would never have treated her like this before his cousin had joined the company. She remembered, wistfully, the long discussions they had had about her dreams and how interested Baz had been in every aspect of them. Since the advent of Merle, he had never even enquired as to whether she had had one, though since she had not she supposed it would be unfair to accuse him of losing interest. Now she came to think of it, it was strange that she had never once dreamed herself back into that other place since Merle's arrival. Perhaps she had been too lonely and unhappy, too confused, to get into the dreams, for there was no doubt that she had been confused, both by Baz's sudden lack of interest in her and by Merle's antagonism. Even Louella had not been as loving towards her as Lottie would have liked. Louella disliked Merle and criticised her, but when Lottie had pointed out, rather timidly, that Merle

163

had still not taught her even the simplest of the modern dances, Louella had heaved a great dramatic sigh and said that no doubt the older girl would do so in her own good time. 'And why do you want to learn modern dance anyway?' she had asked peevishly. 'Once the season's over, I'm sure Merle will take her "Dance Through the Ages" elsewhere and you and I will go back to our own act.'

'Yes, but you said Merle was to teach me so that we could incorporate some modern dance into our routines,' Lottie had pointed out. She had both hoped and expected that her mother would insist upon Merle's teaching her, but Louella had merely told her crossly to run away and get Doris Lavery, their pianist, to teach her 'Ain't She Sweet', a popular song which was sweeping the country.

Remembering the incident, Lottie began to hum the tune beneath her breath, and began to feel more cheerful. So Baz was no longer interested in her; so what? Merle was not the only one who hoped to find new friends in Great Yarmouth. There would be holidaymakers as well as all the theatricals in the show they were to join. Louella had promised her generous pocket money so that she might enjoy all the entertainments on offer, and Jack Russell had said he would teach her how to swim because he thought that a girl who meant to spend a whole summer by the sea ought to be able to bathe with safety, and not merely content herself with paddling and sandcastles.

She found the framed timetable and stood before it, then turned her back on it to survey the hurrying crowds just as a train chugged into the station. Whistles blew shrilly, men in uniform waved flags, others darted off to pile luggage on to trolleys, and Lottie was filled with wild, unreasoning happiness. She was off on a great adventure; she would actually be living at the seaside for weeks and weeks and suddenly she was sure that the dreams would begin again and this time, because she was older, she would look around her more intently, discover why she dreamed such things and what they meant. And Baz can ask me a thousand questions and I shan't answer one of them because he's so besotted with horrible Merle that I wouldn't trust him not to spill the beans, she told herself, just as Baz and Merle came hurrying towards her. And something tells me I'll make a real friend in Great Yarmouth, someone of my own age who will understand how I feel about the theatre and horrible Merle.

But even as she climbed into the carriage behind the older girl and settled herself in a corner seat, she knew she would never tell any new friend about the dreams. They were too personal and too mysterious. Now that Baz was no longer interested, she would keep them to herself.

Rather to Lottie's surprise, the journey went smoothly. They were lucky with all their connections and arrived at Great Yarmouth on time to find

Jack waiting for them. He hustled them on to a bus and presently hustled them off again, conducting them down a street lined with pretty terraced houses, most of which had cards in their windows advertising the fact that they took paying guests. 'We are at Number Fifty-five with Mrs Shilling,' Jack told them. 'She only takes theatricals and we were lucky to get fixed up with her 'cos she's reckoned to be the best landlady in all Great Yarmouth.' He eyed the two girls speculatively. 'Know why she took us in?' Both girls admitted that they had no idea and Jack nodded with satisfaction. 'It's because we're showing at the Wellington Pier theatre which starts rehearsals a fortnight earlier than the Britannia. And that means Mrs Shilling will get an extra two weeks' money.'

'But what about our money, Jack?' Merle said rather plaintively. 'I know the Wellington management pays well – Uncle Max told me – but no one ever pays the same for rehearsals as for the real thing.'

'That's true,' Jack said, nodding his bristly head. 'We get paid half, which is fair enough when you think about it. Some places wouldn't even pay that much. Anyway, for the first two weeks Mrs Shilling charges cut rates and gives us a main meal once a day, but no puddings.' He chuckled. 'Good for your figures, young ladies.'

'I think that sounds very fair,' Lottie said, eyeing the terraced houses they passed with deep interest. Each one had a tiny front garden, crammed with blooms, windows that gleamed with cleanliness and the almost obligatory sign in the front window. In fact she recognised Mrs Shilling's dwelling because the card in her window read 'No Vacancies', a sure sign that Mrs Shilling was indeed the best.

Jack ushered them down a short brick path and into a square hallway. Then he raised his voice in a cheerful bellow which had Mrs Shilling erupting from the rear premises, shaking her head disapprovingly. 'Mr Jack, will you never learn? I were just gettin' a tray of bread out of the oven and when you sharmed out like that I jumped, burned the top of my hand and near dropped the whole perishin' lot on the kitchen floor,' she said. She then turned towards the two girls and beamed at them. 'What an introduction to Number Fifty-five! Now you'll be Miss Merle Lacey, and this must be Miss Lottie. Your mam and Mr Max arrived a couple of hours ago but they've gone down to the theatre. I kept your meal back, so if you'll go up to your room and tidy yourselves, it'll be on the table in twenty minutes.' She flung open a nearby door to reveal a large dining table already set out with a gingham tablecloth, cutlery, and a fine array of sauces and pickles. 'It's cold ham, salad and as much bread and butter as you can eat, 'cos I didn't know for sure what time you'd be a-coming.' She turned to Jack. 'Take the young ladies and show them their room, there's a good lad. My legs have already been up and down them stairs a dozen times today.' She turned back to the girls. 'And don't you be late, my women, the cup of tea I'll have ready in twenty minutes will go cold, and if there's one thing I can't abide it's cold tea. And while you're eatin', we'll talk about our house rules and so on. See you presently, when you've got rid o' the train dirt which I don't doubt is all over you, try though you might to keep yourselves clean.'

Stunned by this flood of eloquence, the girls murmured that they would be down in good time and followed Jack. At the top of the first flight of stairs he turned to grin at them. 'She can talk the hind leg off a donkey, that one,' he said in a low voice. 'Never stops, in fact. Her hubby's a quiet little feller, scarce opens his gob at mealtimes except to shove in his grub, but Mrs Shillin' likes to chat. I wouldn't say she were a gossip because I don't recall ever hearing her say a bad word about anyone, but by God, she says plenty of good words. I've lodged here whenever I've been playing in Great Yarmouth and I reckon decent beds, a clean house and plenty of grub are worth paying for, and I don't mean wi' money, either. Your ear 'oles takes a bashin' from Mrs Shillin', but it's well worth it.' He started to climb another flight of stairs, then stopped, clapping a hand to his brow. 'Heavens above, I'll forget me own name next! You're up in the gods, as they say, but I'd best show you the bathroom first 'cos it's on this floor.'

Lottie and Merle exchanged a quick, delighted glance. A bathroom! And when Jack threw the door open, they were thrilled with what they saw. A large white bathtub with brass claws for feet was surmounted by a huge white object which, Jack informed them, was the geyser which heated the water. 'You have to light it with a match, or a taper, and if you don't get the flame in quick enough the gas builds up and you'll get an explosion which will make you jump six inches. Best let meself, Max or Louella show you how to light it the first couple of times. And of course you can always have a wash in the handbasin, 'cos that's runnin' hot water from the boiler at the back o' the kitchen fire,' he added. And Lottie thought he sounded as proud as though the bathroom, and its contents, were his own invention.

'Where's the lavvy?' Merle asked suddenly. 'Outside in the bleedin' yard, I suppose?'

Jack tutted, wagging his finger at her. 'Don't you let Mrs Shillin' catch you swearing; she don't approve of bad language,' he said. 'The lavvy's the next door along. It's only partitioned off from the bathroom, but it's right convenient to have it separate when everyone's tryin' to get ready at once. There's a downstairs lavvy an' all,' he continued, flinging open the door to reveal a massive blue and white porcelain lavatory with a mahogany seat. 'It ain't as grand as this one, but it's just outside the back door an' to my way of thinkin' it's real posh. It even has its own washbasin so's you can wash your hands after you've done your deed, and a roller towel on the back of the door so you can dry 'em as well.'

He closed the lavatory door and set off up the next flight of stairs, and presently conducted them to what was to be their room, having informed them that the door opposite their own led to the room which would be occupied by the Melias. Gill Melia called herself the Snake Lady and was a very clever contortionist, and her partner – and newly married husband – was Ray Melia, an acrobat. Both girls looked forward to meeting the young couple, for Jack Russell had worked with them before and said they were 'real nice' and performed with great slickness. 'But there's no side to 'em and they're always ready to give a hand if anyone's stuck,' he had said. 'You'll like 'em – everyone does.'

The girls surveyed their domain. It was a large airy room, with a sloping ceiling and a long, low window. There were two small beds with bright patchwork counterpanes, a large chest of drawers and an ornate dressing table. There was also a curtain which, when Merle pulled it back, revealed a long clothes rail, and a washstand, complete with jug and ewer.

Jack was about to leave the room when Merle grabbed his arm. 'Hang on a mo', Jack,' she said urgently. 'Why have we got a washstand? Ain't we supposed to use the bathroom?'

Jack heaved a sigh and wagged a finger. 'How

you jump to conclusions, young lady,' he said severely. 'First you think the lavvy's in the yard, now you think you're not going to be allowed to use the bathroom.' He turned to Lottie. 'What's your opinion, queen?'

'I think the washstand is there because there's only one bathroom and Mrs Shilling won't want folk queuing up for it and being late for meals,' Lottie said slowly. 'After all, you did say everyone lodging here was in the theatre. I suppose someone will make a sort of bath rota – that way everyone will get a turn at the bathroom and there won't be no ill feeling.'

'You're a bright 'un,' Jack said approvingly, turning and making for the stairs. 'It's quicker for you to wash your hands and faces and put a comb through your hair up here rather than traipsing all the way down to the bathroom and mebbe finding someone already in the tub. See you presently.'

Left to themselves, the two girls explored the room thoroughly. Lottie cried out with pleasure when she rushed to the window. 'Oh, Merle, I can see the sea plain as plain over the rooftops,' she shouted. 'An' if I put my cheek on the glass and look to the right, I do declare I can see the funfair. And there's something . . . I bet it's the Wellington Pier, only the wretched chimneys are getting in the way.'

'Oh, how fearfully exciting,' Merle drawled, putting on an affected languid voice, though she rather spoiled the impression she was trying to

171

make by joining Lottie at the window and exclaiming: 'There's a kitten in the garden opposite! D'you know, I've always wanted a kitten of my own – or a dog. When I get married, I'd like to have a dog act. I saw one once. The feller had a dozen little brown and white dogs and there weren't nothin' they couldn't do. One rode a bicycle, two played on a seesaw, they all walked on their hind legs, an' they could all count an' find things which were hidden. An' they were really happy; their tails never stopped wagging for a moment.'

'I'd like a dog, too,' Lottie said wistfully. She crossed the room and poured water into the basin, beginning to wash. 'But Louella says it wouldn't be fair on the dog because we're out so much . . . here, you can use my water, save pouring more. I don't seem to have got very dirty after all.'

She half expected Merle to sneer and refuse, but the other girl splashed her face and hands briefly and then the two of them made their way down the stairs and into the dining room where they speedily dispatched an excellent meal, drank two cups of tea and then asked for directions to the Wellington Pier, since they thought they might as well familiarise themselves with the place.

It was a fine evening. The promenade was not thronged exactly, but there were still people about, and the Wellington Pier took their breath away. When one paid one's penny and walked through the turnstile the first thing one saw was a huge building made of glass, and inside what was in fact an enormous conservatory were wonderful tropical plants, palm trees and other wonders. The girls gasped and exclaimed and Lottie said that no doubt they would be able to enter the conservatory – it was called the Winter Gardens – without having to pay anything once they got the passes which the theatre would doubtless issue.

'I love piers, all of them,' Merle said dreamily, gazing at the shape of the theatre ahead of them. 'It's like being on a ship, only better, because it doesn't bounce up and down, yet you are over the sea and can look right into the water.'

Lottie ran to the rail and gazed down upon the gleaming gentle waves. She turned and grinned at Merle. 'I think we're going to have a wonderful time here in Great Yarmouth,' she said exultantly. 'Race you to the stage door, Merle!'

They rehearsed hard for a fortnight, and, to her own secret surprise, Lottie really enjoyed Merle's company. Despite her hopes, they were the two youngest members of the cast, but Merle, with no Baz to back her up, was quite happy to go about with her. Together, they rehearsed their numbers, and to Lottie's pleasure Merle actually unbent to the extent of teaching her the Charleston. When they were free – which was every afternoon and evening until their season started – they went off together to sample the delights of the town. They explored the narrow rows where the householders could shake hands, if they so desired, with the inhabitants of the house opposite. They went on the funfair and won themselves dreadful kewpie dolls and small bottles of exotically coloured scent. They bought sticks of rock from the stalls on the promenade, as well as small tubs of cockles, shrimps and winkles. But best of all they went on the beach, where both girls forgot they were young ladies and built sandcastles, digging out moats and filling them with seawater, and decorating their edifices with shells and stones. Merle actually bought herself a very glamorous bathing suit, though she refused to go deeper than her knees, vowing that she did not mean to let Jack Russell teach her to swim because he was only small and might let her drown.

Lottie, however, was made of sterner stuff. Louella had produced a hand-knitted bathing costume, old and faded and by no means fashionable, which she had worn as a youngster and Lottie, with squeaks of delight, followed Jack into the waves and proved to be a quick learner; in fact she was doing a very respectable breast stroke after her first lesson. Jack was astounded and preened himself as a first-class teacher, though he did tell Lottie, privately, that she was a natural. 'I've never known anyone to take to it the way you have,' he said. 'Why, you're as good doing a backstroke as I am meself and I've been at it for years.' He cocked a quizzical eye at her. 'Are you sure you didn't use to sneak off to the Scaldy with your pals and swim with them?'

Lottie laughed but shook her head positively. 'No, I never went in the water because the Scaldy's for fellers really, but of course I watched when my friend Kenny was being taught by the older boys. I used to think I could do it easy, given the chance, but I never was – given the chance, I mean.'

'Carry on like this and you'll be able to come down here without yours truly to keep an eye on you,' Jack said. 'Only never forget, gal, that this here beach slopes real sharp like, so one minute you're up to your knees and the next the water's over your bleedin' head and you're still goin' down.'

'I won't forget, Jack,' Lottie said obediently. She was wading out of the water as she spoke and looked down through the tiny waves and saw her own white feet on the beautiful sand, and inside her head a tiny voice said: *You've done this before; you've been here before. This isn't new to you.* She looked round at her companion. Jack was wearing an ancient blue bathing suit which came down to his knees and he was grinning encouragingly at her. It emboldened her to say thoughtfully: 'You're an awful good swimmer yourself, Jack . . . much better than Max, though he's a lot bigger than you. But of course you've been to Great Yarmouth lots of times, you said so when we first came. Jack . . . when you were here before, was I here, as well? Only quite often, particularly when I'm in the

175

water, I get the feeling that I've been here before. I did ask Louella, but she just laughed and said that I was remembering Rhyl, where she and I were before my accident. Only . . . oh, I really don't think it's that.'

'Déjà vu,' Jack said wisely. 'That's wharrit's called, ain't it? Something to do with the two sides of the brain . . . I get it sometimes. And in answer to your question, fair lady, I've been here half a dozen times or more, but I never clapped eyes on you or your mam on me previous visits. And I make a point of visiting all the theatres in the area, to see if I can meet up wi' old pals,' he added. 'So I don't reckon I could have missed your mam, or yourself for that matter.'

Lottie accepted this, but that evening, sitting round Mrs Shilling's dining table and finishing off a large helping of toad in the hole, she mentioned her swimming lesson with Jack and asked Louella whether she had been taught to swim whilst they were in Rhyl. She saw Jack's attention sharpen and smiled at him. 'You see, I've forgotten absolutely everything which happened to me before the accident,' she reminded him, 'so it's quite possible . . .'

Her mother, however, shook her head decidedly. 'No indeed. Who would have taught you? I can't swim; few women of my generation can. I don't deny I took you to the beach a couple of times so that you could paddle and play in the sand, but I'm afraid I never taught you to swim. Why do you ask?'

'She asked because I told her I'd never known anyone pick it up quicker,' Jack broke in before Lottie could reply. 'You've got a real little water baby there, missus. She don't know the meanin' of the word fear.'

Lottie expected her mother to look gratified, but instead Louella frowned anxiously. 'Oh, dear. I never thought I'd worry over her swimming, but what would happen if she got into trouble? Even if I were there, which I probably wouldn't be, I couldn't rescue anyone.'

'Don't worry, Louella, I don't mean to go out of my depth,' Lottie lied valiantly. 'And I promise I'll never go in the water unless someone's with me. Will that stop you worrying?'

Louella's brow cleared and she gave her daughter a loving smile. 'I'm sorry, love, I should have told you what a clever girl you are to learn so fast, but you know what a worrier I am. Still, if you promise never to swim alone, I know you'll keep your word. And now, whose turn is it to help Mrs Shilling with the washing up?'

Chapter Seven

Swimming, and the seaside generally, must have been on Lottie's mind for that very night she found herself back in her mysterious dream. She was paddling, her small white feet clearly visible through the water, her pink gingham skirt tucked into her rather baggy knickers. She glanced back towards the shore and saw the white-gold sand with holidaymakers scattered upon it and knew, without really thinking about it, that this was Yarmouth and that, somewhere, someone was keeping an eye on her. She also knew that she must not go in too far because of what was known as 'the shelf', which meant that one minute the water was shallow and the next very deep indeed. So she kept well inshore and presently heard a voice calling. She turned obediently, though the voice had not called 'Lottie', but the name by which, she realised, she was always known in her dream.

'Come on out now, Sassy, and we'll have a nice paper of chips for our tea,' the loved voice said. Lottie knew she loved the owner of the voice, though she was not sure from whom it came for when she looked shorewards once more she saw that most of the people were looking in her direction. Still, the voice must be obeyed so she began to wade ashore, then saw through the water the long, almost black shape of a razor shell and bent to pick it up. But water is tricksy stuff and every time her small hand delved, the shell seemed mysteriously out of reach. She was still trying to take hold of it when another hand seized hers and squeezed her fingers gently, whilst the owner of the hand chuckled softly – she could *feel* the laughter, coming down his arm and into her small palm – and then he plucked the razor shell from the depths and gave it to her. She looked up, smiling her thanks, and saw that the boy who held her hand was familiar, with light brown hair and eyes of a curious golden-brown colour. He smiled back, revealing very white teeth and a long crease down one lean cheek. 'All right now, Sassy? Did you hear old Gran say we'd buy a paper of chips for our tea? Well, I reckon that means fried fish as well, 'cos Jim went out wi' the fishing boat earlier and came home wi' half a dozen codling. Gran will batter 'em and we'll have a fine feast.'

'I love fish and chips,' Lottie said yearningly. She suddenly realised that she was very hungry, very hungry indeed, and wondered when she had last eaten. 'Does it take long to get home from here?'

The boy laughed and wagged their joined hands together mockingly. 'Why, we're just along the Marine Parade, out by the Denes. We'll catch a bus and be back at the camp in two ticks.'

179

As he spoke they had been walking across the beach, and now he stopped beside an elderly woman sitting in a striped deckchair with a towel laid across her knees. She beamed lovingly at Lottie, then heaved her on to her lap and began to dry her wet legs and feet. 'You'm a good li'l girl so you are,' she said crooningly. 'And this lad do be a good young feller an' all. But I can see we're goin' to have to teach you to swim else I'll never have an easy moment. Folk who live near water, be it broads, rivers, canals or the sea itself, need to be able to swim. You've had a fine time a-playin' on the beach and in the sea, but now it's gettin' late and I've work to do when we get back to camp.' She produced from somewhere a pair of old plimsolls and pushed Lottie's still sandy feet into them. 'Best go shod, else they might turn we off the bus an' call us feckless gypsies, wanderin' folk that don't know no better.'

'They'd better not,' the boy said, but he said it laughingly and Lottie laughed too.

'What's gypsies?' she asked, and was surprised to hear her own voice, very young and high and not at all as she normally spoke. 'We are wanderin' folk though, aren't we, Gran?'

'Some say so,' the old woman said. She struggled to her feet, for the deckchair was low and the sand soft and deep, and held out her hand. 'Time to go, Sassy, my heart. Time to think of our bellies, and our beds. Can you walk or do you want the lad to give you a ride on his back?'

'I'll walk so I will,' Lottie said sturdily, and was once again surprised, this time not by her voice but by the words she had chosen to use. And then, as dreams will, this one became misty and cloudy, no longer real as it had been on the beach. As though she were watching what was happening from high above, she saw the oddly assorted trio climb on to a bus, saw the vehicle go off along the wide road, saw it disappear into the distance . . . and woke to her attic room in Mrs Shilling's lodging house, with Merle snoring in the next bed and the sound of feet ascending the stairs, crossing the landing, opening a door and then closing it quietly.

That would be the Melias, making their way to bed after an evening out, Lottie told herself drowsily, turning over so that her hot cheek met the cool pillow. When everyone had enjoyed a bite of supper the grown-ups had taken themselves off for what they had described as 'a bit of a walk along the prom', which Merle had immediately identified as a polite way of saying that they had gone to the nearest pub for a few drinks, and no doubt they had all come back together.

The return of the Melias had taken Lottie's mind off her dream, but presently it came back to her and she decided it was certain to continue if only she could fall asleep quickly enough. Accordingly, she closed her eyes and willed herself to sleep, and very soon she dropped off, for it had been a long and exciting day. But she did not again dream of the old woman she had called Gran, or the boy with the golden eyes.

Next morning she had only the vaguest recollection of her latest sleep-adventure when she was woken by Merle, anxious – for once – not to be late. 'Get up, you dozy kid,' Merle said without animosity. 'Today we have our first show in front of an audience; have you forgotten? Remember what Jack said about Mrs Shilling's breakfasts? It'll be porridge, then bacon and egg, then toast! Oh, do get a move on, or them others will have ate the lot. And before the evening performance, we've got to buy fishing line. Remember what Archie told us?'

Lottie giggled. Whilst they had been rehearsing, a touring repertory company had produced a number of amusing plays for twice weekly matinées and evening performances. Archie, the leading man, was married to Gwen, the leading lady, so they had the largest dressing room. Not that that was saying much, for all the dressing rooms were tiny. The advantage common to all the dressing rooms, however, was a window overlooking the sea, and Archie had told the girls that several members of the cast threw out fishing lines before they went on stage and pulled them in again when the show was over. Sometimes they caught nothing, but often there would be a couple of nice pollock and once or twice, Archie told them, he and his wife had harvested a codling. Thrilled by the thought of obtaining fish without the boredom of holding a fishing rod for hours on end, the girls had determined to try their luck as soon as they were officially given their own dressing room. Archie had also told them that for some reason the fish seemed to bite better at night so there was no point in the girls throwing out lines whilst they were rehearsing. 'And it don't look good for members of the public walkin' along the pier to see actors fishing for their supper,' he had added with a grin.

Right now, however, Merle and Lottie were more concerned with getting their breakfast than with fishing. Whilst they had been in rehearsal, breakfast had just been porridge, but now that they were actually earning Jack Russell had assured them that it would be bacon and egg and toast as well, treats that seldom came their way under normal circumstances.

The girls washed, dressed and hurried down the stairs, and with no one to remind her the dream simply went right out of Lottie's head. When, later, she tried to recapture it, she had only the vaguest memory of what had befallen her. There had been a boy . . . an old woman . . . the seaside . . . But then she was hurrying along the road which led to Marine Parade, so anxious to get to the Wellington Pier theatre that dreams seemed of little importance. She did mention casually to Louella and Max, as they approached the theatre, that the beach had seemed familiar to her when she and Merle had played on it the previous day, but they both laughed indulgently and Louella said that one beach is very like another and she could promise Lottie that neither of them had ever visited Great Yarmouth before.

'But I hope we shall do so again, because it's easily the nicest seaside place I've been to,' she said. 'There's so much to see and do – the gardens are beautiful, and that great greenhouse place . . .'

'The Winter Gardens, you mean,' Lottie said smugly; she had learned a good deal about the town since their arrival. 'You can have tea there, in ever such pretty cups, and buns and probably little iced cakes as well. Me and Merle mean to go there when we have some money to spare.'

It was only later that she realised Louella had, once again, managed to divert her mind from the subject she had raised. But it did not really matter, she consoled herself. There was bound to be another opportunity . . . only what was the point? Louella had said positively that the Laceys had never visited Great Yarmouth before, and she had no reason to lie. The dreams were just dreams and nothing more; she must stop believing that they had some deeper significance.

They reached the pier and were waved through by the man in the ticket office without having to show their passes since he had grown to know them over the past couple of weeks. They arrived at the theatre and met the others on stage, where the stage manager was allocating dressing rooms. There was some confusion at this point since he had assumed Max and Louella would share, but this was soon remedied. Louella would go with Merle and Lottie, and Max and Jack would share, as they had done at the Gaiety.

Once this had been decided, the stage manager talked earnestly about technical matters, then told them that they had the rest of the day to set up their dressing rooms as they liked them. They had not rehearsed in costume, since the back of stage facilities were cramped and had, in any case, been the prerogative of the repertory company.

The two girls hurried off the stage and found their dressing room. It was very small and only thin wooden partitions separated them from the rooms on either side. The window did not fit very well – in fact there was quite a strong draught coming from round it – but Lottie thought it would do. There would be just about sufficient room for themselves and their costumes, and the mirror, with its surrounding lights, was both large and clear.

She was saying as much to Merle when the door opened and Louella came in. She glanced around her then sniffed disparagingly. 'You can see why theatre folk call these dressing rooms the cowsheds,' she remarked. 'Still, the auditorium's grand, the seats are comfortable and the stage is well lit and will do nicely, both for our act and for Max's. We'd best cut along to the green room now, though, and fetch our traps, because the SM wants anyone who has a change of costume to do a dress rehearsal this afternoon. It's a pretty compact theatre and I believe the wardrobe mistress is helpful and efficient, but I rather agree with Ronnie Radcliffe that we should practise our quick changes before the first performance.'

Both girls groaned but Merle agreed reluctantly that Mr Radcliffe, the stage manager, was right. 'I remember black-bottoming off stage left whilst wrigglin' out of me dress, only to find Mrs Lucy, white as a ghost, holdin' me costume out appealingly from the opposite wings. I had to struggle back into me dress – couldn't do it up at the back, of course – and chassis across the stage wit' a bright red face while the orchestra were one jump ahead, so to speak, and the folk in the front row were all gigglin' and whisperin'. I wouldn't want to go through *that* again.'

Lottie went pale with horror at the thought of such a thing happening to her and decided that a dress rehearsal was a good idea. She accompanied her mother and Merle to the green room, where they spent the best part of an hour sorting out their costumes and taking them back to their dressing room. Each of them had a rail upon which to hang their stage clothing and Louella, who was tidy-minded in the theatre if not at home, got a stick of greasepaint and labelled three drawers with their names. 'These are for gloves, headdresses, tights, stage jewellery and so on,' she informed them. 'I know your ostrich plumes won't fit into a drawer, Merle, but you can perch them on the windowsill.'

'No she can't,' Lottie said quickly. 'There's an awful draught where the edges of the sash don't meet and – and we might want the window open; these dressing rooms must get awfully stuffy when the noonday sun's on them.'

Louella frowned, then her brow cleared and she laughed. 'Archie told me about the fishing; I bet you've planned to make yourself a mint of money selling whales to holidaymakers,' she said cheerfully. 'You're right, though, there's enough draught coming around the edges of that window to sail a yacht. I'll see the wardrobe mistress – maybe she can suggest something.'

Merle, however, speedily solved the problem. 'I'll stick 'em in a string bag and hang 'em on the hooks,' she said, gesturing to a row of pegs on the back of the door. 'Good thing I don't change the plumes when I change me dress, since it takes me a good five minutes to pin the bloody things on me head.'

'Language,' Louella murmured, but without much conviction. Everyone in the theatre swore at times, Lottie knew, and though her mother disapproved, Lottie had heard her cuss with the best when she dropped something heavy on her foot, or missed a cue. 'Now, you two girls, this is a serious dress rehearsal, especially for Merle, so get on with it. Max is treating me to supper after the show, but before it I mean to buy myself a cup of tea and a doughnut in the Winter Gardens. If you get your dress rehearsal over in time you may come with me; my treat.'

Louella's own act did not call for a quick change since management always made sure that Mr Magic's act and that of the Lacey Sisters were separated by at least two other performances. So Louella simply stood in the wings, masterminding Merle and Lottie as they flew backwards and forwards, doing their routines. The only change Louella had to make was for the finale, when she and Lottie left the stage to Merle and her modern dances. It was not far back to their own dressing room, so they were able to get there and become Columbine and the Victorian lady in a few seconds, returning to the stage in plenty of time to help Merle slip into her various slinky little dresses.

There were a few hitches to be ironed out but finally both Louella and Mr Radcliffe were satisfied that the acts would go smoothly, and the two girls rushed gleefully back to their dressing room, changed into street clothes, and took themselves off to a small shop in Regent Street which boasted that it sold everything to do with fishing. When they had purchased their lines, they rushed back and met Louella, just approaching the Winter Gardens. She told them that Max would join them presently and they found a table beneath a flourishing palm tree and ordered tea and cakes for four. The waitress looked rather pointedly at the empty chair, for already the café was crowded, but Louella explained that a friend would be joining them shortly. When Max arrived, they discussed every aspect of the Wellington Pier and its theatre.

'I love it; it's much more fun than the Gaiety ever was,' Lottie said, gazing around her. She turned to her mother. 'I never asked, but do I have to go to school here? I'm fifteen, so no one will think it odd that I'm not in class.'

'But darling, we agreed that because you'd missed so much school, what with your accident and matinée performances, you'd stay on, at least until the end of this term,' Louella said. 'It seems foolish, because you write perfectly clearly and you understand figures as well as I do myself . . .'

'If not better,' Max murmured, giving Lottie the benefit of his wickedest smile. 'You're the one who ought to be going to school, Lou my love, if we're talking about mathematics. I remember when we were in Liverpool, you asking me how I knew the number of people in the auditorium one quiet afternoon and I told you that each row had thirty seats and that, because it was so quiet, Mr Quentain had moved everyone into the front eight rows. So all I had to do was multiply eight by thirty and then count the empty seats. I don't believe you ever really understood what I was talking about!'

'I'm sure I don't know what you mean, dear Max,' Louella said sweetly. 'Can I pour you another cup? Lottie? Merle?'

Max laughed and reached across the table to give Louella's hand a loving squeeze. His eyes

189

were full of affection and Lottie could not help reflecting that her mother had done it again. When asked a question she did not want to answer, she simply changed the subject, and did it so cleverly, and so nicely, that either no one noticed or they simply accepted that Louella did not wish to answer.

Lottie sat back in her chair and thought about Mr and Mrs Magic. She had intercepted the glance which Max had just given her mother and realised, not for the first time, that the couple were really fond of one another. She knew Max had been married, but his wife had left him years ago, so why on earth didn't he ask Louella to marry him? Lottie knew her mother well enough to be certain that she would accept with joy, for Louella often complained that life would be a whole lot easier if she were married and had a husband to ward off the importunate young men who haunted the stage door. And then there were others, directors or producers, who expected beautiful but un-attached women to grant them favours. Lottie had no idea what these favours were, but she had heard her mother and Max discussing them, and knew that this was the reason why Louella fostered the idea, in the theatre at any rate, that she and Max were more than merely stage partners, separate dressing rooms notwithstanding. So why, oh why, didn't Max pop the question and make them all happy?

But he was speaking now and Lottie returned

her attention quickly to his words. '. . . I don't think we need worry too much about your schooling, young 'un,' he was saying. 'I've had a word with our landlady on that very subject. There's a little school, privately run, only a couple of streets away and Mrs Shilling assured me they're used to theatricals and wouldn't turn a hair over you wanting one afternoon a week off for matinées. She says it's a really good school, well worth what they charge, so now we've finished rehearsing I reckon Louella should take you round there tomorrow morning and sign you on.' He leaned across the table to chuck Lottie under the chin. 'Don't look so outraged, sweetheart! I seem to remember you saying you wanted to meet kids of your own age, and this way you'll do it all right. Classes finish at three, so apart from Wednesdays, when you'll be doing a matinée, you'll have two or three hours to yourself before the evening performance. And it's only six weeks till the summer holidays start.'

'It isn't fair! Look at Merle, free to do what she wants from eight in the morning until six at night, pretty well. And I'll be shut up in a horrible smelly schoolroom when I could be on the beach, or having a go on the scenic railway or – or doing a hundred lovely things,' Lottie wailed. 'Oh, Louella, say I needn't go! No one will notice, and I'm sure I look nearly as old as Merle.'

Louella laughed but shook her head. 'It's no use, love; Max is quite right. Think of poor Merle, with no one to go around with until the holidays start. At least you'll be with other kids, but she'll be all on her ownio.'

It was on the tip of Lottie's tongue to say that Merle would not be on her own but would have Baz's company whenever he was not actually working, but then she remembered her promise and shut her mouth with a snap. She would have to make the best of it until the end of term and by then, with a bit of luck, she would have made friends at school so when Merle went off with Baz she would have someone with whom to share things. Sighing, she nodded. 'All right, Louella, I'll go,' she said. 'But I'll tell you something: as soon as I'm grown up I'm going to get me a proper job, nothing to do with the theatre. Then I'll have evenings and weekends off, just like other people.'

Louella laughed, having heard this sentiment expressed before when Lottie particularly resented the long hours which working in the theatre entailed, but Merle looked thunderstruck. 'You can't mean it!' she gasped. 'Everyone wants to be on the stage! Why, your mam told me when I auditioned for the job of taking your place all them years ago that you'd been toddling on to the boards and waving to the audience even before you could talk. You're a real trouper, Lottie; you can't want to give it up.'

'Oh, she doesn't mean it,' Louella said easily. 'She says it to upset me, and make me feel guilty because I got her into the act when she was too young to make up her own mind, but she loved it then and she loves it now, of course.'

Lottie scowled across the table at her mother's fair, complacent face. 'It's all very well for you, Louella: it's what you've always wanted to do,' she pointed out. 'It's different for me. I know you say I loved it when I was a kid and was always running on to the stage and trying to join in your routines, but because of the accident I can't remember any of that. So far as I'm concerned I was, what, six and a half before I danced a step, and when I danced and sang before an audience for the first time I felt sick and wobbly and simply longed to get off, away from all those staring eyes. And it's not fair to say I deliberately try to upset you because I never have and never would.'

'But you don't feel like that now, Lottie,' Merle protested, before Louella could answer. 'You love it, like me. Well, you must, or you wouldn't be any good at it.' She turned appealingly to Louella. 'That's true, isn't it?'

Louella nodded rather uncertainly, but Lottie answered before her mother could speak. 'It's a job, Merle, just a job. I suppose I do enjoy it – the dancing and singing anyway – but I still hate people staring at me, even audiences. It's different for you, and for Mam, because you're both awfully pretty with proper figures, busts and that, but I'm just a skinny kid, all arms and legs.' She frowned, trying to put her feelings into words which everyone would understand. 'I sometimes feel I'm doing my growing up in a very public sort of way, whereas most kids can grow up more privately like.'

Merle gave a hoot of derisive laughter. 'That's rubbish. All child stars do their growing up in public; I certainly did,' she declared. 'My mam used to say that she carried me into the ring for the first time when I was six months old and I waved to the audience and blew kisses.' She turned to Louella. 'And I bet young Lottie here was just the same, whatever she may say now.'

'Yes she was,' Louella said at once. She reached out a caressing hand and rumpled her daughter's hair. 'If only you hadn't had that awful accident! Because you'd simply forgotten your entire past, I'm afraid I made you work tremendously hard to relearn all our songs and routines, and I suppose that gave you a distaste for the stage. As for doing your growing up in public, that's what audiences love, my pet. They're really impressed to see a young girl singing and dancing like the professional you are.' She smiled brightly round the table. 'And now let's talk about something else.'

Max laughed. 'Don't try to change the subject just because you're tired of it, Lou.' He turned to Lottie. 'I know exactly what you mean, because that's why Baz has always refused to start learning magic,' he said. 'He told me that being at school all day and in the theatre all night was like serving two life sentences, and I could see his point of view, so I never pressed him. But I do believe that when he's a bit older – say twenty-five – he may change his mind. And now you two will want to try your luck with a bit of fishing. Have you thought about bait? There's a shop on Regent Street which sells mealworms . . .'

'We're going to use bread pellets,' Lottie said primly. 'Neither of us fancy impaling a wriggling creature on a hook and then chucking it into the sea.' She shuddered eloquently. 'But Jack says he's caught fish with bread pellets, and that's good enough for us, isn't it, Merle?'

'Sure is,' Merle said in an American accent. 'Sure is, honey!'

'Oh, you,' Louella said, getting to her feet as the two girls stood up. 'It won't surprise you to know that I shan't be throwing out any fishing lines, but that doesn't mean I'll turn down any fish you catch. Especially if it's kippers,' she added, and hurried over to the till whilst Merle and Lottie, laughing, left the Winter Gardens and headed for the theatre.

Lottie had always enjoyed school in Liverpool but did not expect to do so in Great Yarmouth, for she knew no one and was afraid they would cold-shoulder her as an outsider, and one who was older than themselves. However, she soon found she was mistaken, for the other pupils were friendly and there was another new girl of about her own age. The teacher introduced them and told them to sit at the same desk. 'Lottie Lacey, meet Angela Capper. You'll soon discover you've a lot in common,' she said, smiling at them. 'And you can spend your break finding out just why I've put you side by side.'

Angela beamed at Lottie. 'Hello. You're appearing at the Wellington, aren't you? My mum and dad are at the Britannia, and so am I, though I only help behind the scenes. Is this your first time in Yarmouth?'

'Yes. We come from Liverpool. What about you?' Lottie said. She did not recognise the other girl's accent, but thought it was rather like that of local shopkeepers and Mr and Mrs Shilling.

'We actually come from King's Lynn. It's still Norfolk, but a good way from here,' Angela explained. 'We've been with the theatre always – my dad does the lighting and props and my mum is wardrobe mistress though she was a performer when she was younger; she was a dancer, actually, with a group called the Melodeons. Only she began to get awful aches in her legs and back – the doctor say it's arthuritis, whatever that may mean – so she had to give up performing,' Angela explained. 'I know all about you, of course. You're the youngest of the three Lacey sisters and you dance and sing and throw toffees at the audience. We always spy on the cast at the Welly, and I reckon someone in your company will have spied on us an' all.'

'I don't know, but you're probably right,' Lottie admitted. 'I'm sorry about your mam, though; arthritis is very painful, I believe. And I don't throw toffees *at* the audience, I throw them out into the auditorium. What do you do?'

'Oh, I help Dad with the lights and understudy the dancers, because I like dancing, and of course I know all the songs by heart, though my voice isn't strong enough to sing solo,' Angela said cheerfully. 'I sell ice creams in the interval and tickets if they've no one else to man the box office, and I go up and down the aisles at the beginning of a performance, showing people to their seats. I help with scenery changes and check props for my dad . . . in other words I'm a sort of odd-job person. A dogsbody, my dad calls me.'

Lottie chuckled. 'And do you have to be in the theatre every evening and for matinées?' she asked wistfully. 'I bet you get more time off than I do. My mother – she's Louella Lacey – never lets me leave before the final curtain. Still, it won't be so bad once the summer holidays arrive: then I'll have all mornings and most afternoons to myself.'

'I'm not always in the theatre, though mostly I'd rather be there than by myself in our lodgings,' Angela said, pulling a face. 'We're with Mrs Masters, on Gordon Terrace. She's a horror, really she is. There are rules and regulations hung up in every room and she's mean with the food, too. Mum keeps on saying we'll move somewhere nicer, but Mrs Masters is cheap and we're saving up for a place of our own when Mum and Dad retire, if they ever do, which I dursen't think about,' she added gloomily, 'since I reckon they'd be lost without the theatre. You're at Mrs Shilling's place, I'd put money on it. We stayed there last year ... the food was just the best!' She looked curiously at Lottie. 'But I'm the only young person – really young, I mean – in the whole company, and you've got your sister to go around with. I envy you that.'

'She's not really my sister, and she's got a young man, so once he's on the spot I don't suppose I'll see much of her,' Lottie said. 'I was dreading starting school because I thought I'd be the only new girl ... how about if you and I go around together? Only I'm pretty tied up until the holidays start.'

Angela agreed that this would be fun, and Lottie went home that afternoon well satisfied with her lot.

To her considerable surprise, however, Merle was waiting for her outside their lodgings and linked arms with her, giving Lottie's a squeeze. 'I've missed you,' she said, sounding unflatteringly surprised. 'I suppose I'd got used to you while we were rehearsing. Let's go down to the prom.'

'Thanks,' Lottie said dryly. 'But once Baz arrives you'll be happy enough to give me the go-by, the way you did in Liverpool. When is he arriving, by the way? When you told me he was coming to Norfolk you said "a week or two". That ought to mean any time now.'

She happened to be looking at Merle as she

spoke and thought the older girl looked down-right shifty, but before she could remark upon it Merle replied, stiffly, that she was not Baz's keeper. 'He's probably here already,' she said, 'but of course he won't get time off immediately. I dare say they'll make him work pretty hard for his first week. And I don't know nothin' about public transport around here. He may have a long walk to catch a bus into Yarmouth.'

They had been walking along Marine Parade as they talked, but now Lottie pulled her companion up short and swung her round so that they were staring one another in the eye. 'Merle O'Mara, if what you told me is true, then Baz won't need to catch a bus! Why, you silly girl, he's working at a station, as a porter, and everyone knows about porters' perks; he'll be able to hop on any train, because they all come to Great Yarmouth. Just what sort of a yarn have you been spinning?'

Merle dropped her eyes to her feet, which were scuffling uneasily on the pink paving stones. 'It's what Baz said,' she muttered. 'He said he were going to try for a job in Norfolk, so's he could be near me. He didn't say which station, exactly, but he thought he'd be here in a couple of weeks.' She glared at Lottie. 'I bet he's here already. It's just as I said; he's too busy right now to come a-visiting. And you shouldn't make out I'm a liar when I'm only telling you what Baz said.'

There was a long pause, then Lottie said slowly: 'I don't think you're telling the truth. I think you only said that about Baz coming to Norfolk because I didn't believe you when you said you and Baz were going steady. I know I promised not to say anything to Louella or Max, but I didn't promise not to write to Baz. Come to that, I reckon I'll telephone Lime Street station and ask to speak to him. Then we'll find out if you're telling the truth.'

This time the pause stretched even longer before Merle suddenly shrugged and gave her companion a sheepish grin. 'All right, all right, it wasn't exactly the truth. Baz said he wished he could get a job in Norfolk so we wouldn't be so far apart, and I suggested he might have a try at getting work somewhere near. He – he sort of said he would, but of course I knew there might not be any jobs going. Only when you wouldn't believe we were going steady . . . oh, I'm sorry, Lottie, it was a mean thing to tell you fibs and I wish I hadn't.' She linked her arm in Lottie's once more. 'I will get in touch with Baz, but I hate letter writing, so I've not done so yet. What about you? Have you written?'

Lottie gave an exasperated sigh. 'How could I when I thought he was leaving Liverpool any minute?' she enquired. 'But I'll write to him now, though I promise I won't tell him why I've not written before. I'll just say we've been hectically busy; he'll understand. And I'll tell him I'm pals with ever such a nice girl whose parents are in the show at the Britannia pier.'

Merle's face brightened. 'In the show at the

Britannia? Well, it ain't such a good show as ours, but I'd like to meet her. What's her name? What does she do in the show?'

'She's called Angela Capper and she helps her parents. Her dad's lighting and props, and her mum's the wardrobe mistress.'

'Is that all she does?' Merle said rather contemptuously. 'I thought you said she was in the show. Who's the liar now, then?'

Lottie took a deep breath and counted to ten; it was plain that her earlier remark had offended Merle more than she had intended. 'She is in the show from time to time, because she understudies practically everyone,' she said rather stiffly. 'She does all sorts, in fact. She's in the box office when there's no one else about, shows people to their seats, sells ice creams in the interval, helps with scenery changes and so on. In fact she's what you'd call a real trouper because she's been in the theatre all her life, same as you and me.'

By this time they were approaching the pier and Fred in the ticket office called out to them, for the previous day Lottie had told him that she was dreading her first day at the new school. The girls went over and peered through the glass panel which separated him from the public. 'Well? How did it go?' Fred asked. He was a small, white-haired man with a face permanently tanned by the summer sun, for he spent as little time as possible in the ticket booth, much preferring to sit outside when the weather was fine.

'It was lovely. All the girls were friendly, but there's one girl from the show at the Britannia, so the teacher sat us together. We're going to be best friends and do all sorts when the holidays start.'

Fred beamed and said he thought this was a good thing, but as they walked away Merle looked reproachfully at the younger girl. 'Wharrabout me?' she enquired plaintively. 'Now I've come clean and you know Baz isn't going to turn up, I'll be awful lonely if you just desert me.'

'We can be a threesome, like the Lacey Sisters,' Lottie said gaily. 'Angela's the same age as me, so I'm sure we'll all get on famously. Tell you what, if we go straight to the green room we can write a letter to Baz between us and post it this evening. What d'you think?'

'It's a good idea,' Merle said at once. 'You can write all the interesting bits about what we've been doing and I'll add a lovey-dovey bit saying how I miss him. Oh, and your mam told me to tell you she'd left us some sandwiches in the green room, a screw of tea, a little jug of milk and some sugar lumps so we can make ourselves a drink. C'mon!'

The letter to Baz turned out to be quite fun, but when they had both signed off Lottie realised that she was longing to tell Baz as much as she could remember of her most recent dream. Yet she felt reluctant to confide in him since she no longer

202

trusted him not to repeat anything she said to Merle. She supposed that it would not matter if Merle knew about her dreams, yet still shrank from revealing them to anyone other than Baz. She wondered whether she might tell Angela, but decided against that as well. The trouble was, the more time elapsed between waking and the present, the fuzzier grew images which had been keen and sharp at the time. No, it would not do. Instead, she decided to keep a sort of dream diary, and the next time Louella handed out her weekly pocket money she spent threepence of it on a notebook in which she recorded all her sleep-adventures, starting with the very first one. She did not write this in straightforward language but made use of a book which she had found in the green room called *Speedwriting for Beginners*. It was quite simple, but an effective way of making sure that anyone who picked up the exercise book and tried to read it would be speedily baffled.

She knew it was foolproof within a week of starting the diary, when Merle came into their dressing room, picked it up and began to leaf through it. 'Is this yours?' Merle enquired after a moment, eyebrows rising. 'Because if so, you've finally gone round the bend. Half the letters are missing by the looks, so it's double Dutch.'

'That's right. Me mam taught me to write double Dutch when I were knee high to a grasshopper,' Lottie said gravely, and was amused when Merle nodded and said that she'd always wanted to learn a foreign language and wasn't Lottie lucky to have a mam who could teach her.

'Yes, I suppose I am,' Lottie said. 'But I can't speak it, I can only write it. It's that sort of language, you see.'

'Fancy that,' Merle said. 'When did she learn you? I s'pose you wouldn't like to learn me an' all?'

Lottie laughed, but capitulated. 'It's not a real language, you dope, it's speedwriting,' she said. 'And no one taught me, I taught myself. I don't see much point in you learning, though, because you're not even that keen on writing letters, so I can't see you keeping a diary.'

'No, you're right there,' Merle said, dropping the notebook into Lottie's lap. 'We've got an hour before we have to start getting ready for the show, so what d'you say we stroll along to the Britannia? The feller in the ticket office will let us in free if we say we've come to see Angela, and there's a stall there which sells ring doughnuts and paper cups of tea.'

'You don't want a doughnut, you want to see that Alex fellow, the one who does a ventriloquist act,' Lottie said accusingly. 'I've seen you goggling at him whenever we meet. If you aren't careful, I'll tell Baz you've got a fancy man, and then where will you be?'

'I can't help it if men admire me,' Merle said pertly. 'And he ain't the only one. That feller in the chorus, the one who sings so nice, he asked me to go for a walk along the sands last time we met only I said no, 'cos of Baz,' she added virtuously.

'You said no because Angela told you the chorus boys were pansies and didn't really like girls,' Lottie rejoined. 'Don't try to fool me, Miss O'Mara.'

Merle and Angela had met and liked one another on sight, though Angela was no more interested in boys than Lottie, and found Merle's preoccupation with the male sex mysterious. For there was no doubt, Lottie mused as the two girls, arms linked, walked through the Wellington Gardens towards the Britannia pier, that Merle eyed up every young man they passed and most of the young men returned such glances with considerable interest. It won't be long before Merle takes up with some feller and poor Baz gets dumped, Lottie thought, as they reached the pier and went towards the turnstile and the ticket office. Poor Baz. But he'll still have me – if he wants me, that is.

The thought of Baz made Lottie remember she had been intending to ask Merle a question for ages. Now she jerked on her friend's arm, bringing her to a halt. 'Hang on a minute, Merle, there's something I've been meaning to ask you,' she said. 'When you came to the Gaiety to take my place in the act, why didn't you come and see me in hospital? I mean, I know you were older than me, but you were still only a kid. Weren't you curious to know what I was like?'

Merle stared at her. 'I were desperate to see you,' she said slowly. 'They had to make new stage clothes for me because your mam said all your stuff was too small, but I really would have liked to visit you, get to know you. There weren't nobody else in the show anywhere near my age, and to tell you the truth Baz was pretty offhand with me for the first week or two. He'd never met you himself, because you'd come from Rhyl, hadn't you? He was quite curious as well, but your mam laid the law down. She said as how you were very ill and didn't remember nothing. She said meeting theatre folk could confuse you and might hold up your recovery. I explained over and over as how me singing your songs to you might help you back, but your mam said it were nonsense and that the doctors said no visitors, apart from your mam herself, that was. So you see, I would have come if I'd been allowed.'

Lottie stared at her companion. 'Whyever did my mam say that?' she breathed. 'I was on a children's ward, but none of the other kids worked in the theatre and when I was trying so hard to remember it really might have helped to have you there. Mammy sang me the songs and showed me a lot of the dance steps when there were no doctors around, but none of it did any good.'

'What's it like to lose your memory?' Merle asked curiously. 'I really can't imagine it; it must be horrible.'

'It is. It's a bit like walking along a path you

206

know well and seeing a thick white mist ahead of you, and knowing that if you walk into the mist, it'll be all around you, holding you back,' Lottie said with a shudder. 'I try not to think about it because it's pretty frightening.'

'Yes, it would be. I've often meant to ask you . . .'

The two girls had been standing just outside the ticket office and now the Britannia pier attendant came out of his booth and spoke to them rather impatiently. 'Are you two comin' in or not? There'll be a bleedin' queue formin' behind you in a minute. C'mon, shift yourselves.'

Hastily, the two girls made for the turnstile. 'We've come to see Angela Capper. We're from the Welly,' Merle said.

The man laughed and clicked the turnstile so that it swung free and let them both through. 'Ah, go on with you; you'll find something on the pier to spend your money on, I don't doubt,' he said cheerfully. 'Enjoy yourselves!'

Chapter Eight

By the time the summer holidays arrived, Lottie's fear that Merle would find herself a boyfriend had proved to be well founded. He was not a holidaymaker, neither was he with the theatre. His name was Jerry and he was with a firm of contractors who kept both piers and a great many of the other Marine Parade attractions in good repair. He had been repainting the Wellington pier when his undoubted good looks had caught Merle's attention, but at first he had not seemed particularly interested in any of the girls, though friendly with them all. That had been rather nice, since it meant that when Jerry joined them they became a foursome rather than a threesome, for despite Angela and Lottie's making every effort to include Merle they were uneasily aware that sometimes she became bored with their talk of school and schoolfellows. However, as August progressed, it became clear to Lottie that Jerry liked her pal, and she was glad of it. She thought him a big improvement on Alex, though she was uneasily aware that Merle was still seeing the ventriloquist from time to time.

Jerry, being local, was a fund of information. One of the first things he had told them, painting away busily at the railings, was that the firm no sooner finished doing one job on the pier than it needed another and this went for the Britannia as well as the Wellington. 'Of course, we do most of the maintenance in the winter when the piers are closed to the public,' he had told them. 'But holidaymakers being what they are, there's usually something which needs mending or replacing during the season itself. So my father – he's Bill Green, and owns the business – sets me and my brother Ted to work because, being as how we're family, he knows we'll do a good job and won't try to claim more hours than we've actually done.'

'That's nice,' Lottie had said approvingly, for she had noticed that though he talked and laughed with them his brush never ceased applying paint in long, even strokes. 'What else do you do, Jerry?'

'Oh, all sorts; I'm a jack of all trades, same as Ted,' Jerry had said airily. 'In the old days there weren't much work for a mechanic, but with all the new rides on the pleasure beach I've had to learn a good deal about engines, most on it from Ted, who's got a real grasp of such things. He's ten year older than me, with a wife and family, so o' course Pa pay him more than he pay me, 'cos that's only fair.' He had cocked a dark eyebrow at the girls, for all three of them had been present at the time. 'I come and saw your show last week; the SM give my dad a couple of comps.' He had nodded to Merle and Lottie and had then turned to Angela. 'But I couldn't spot you, though I did me best. If it were the pantomime season, I'd reckon you were the backside of the horse, but since thass midsummer I must ha' bin looking away when you come on stage.'

The girls had laughed and Merle had explained that Angela was actually at the Britannia and was only on stage when she understudied a member of the cast. Jerry had nodded, using up the last few drops of paint and picking up the empty can. 'Got to go now to get more supplies,' he had said. 'But I shall finish here in half an hour. Want to come up to the pleasure beach for a go on the scenic railway or the helter-skelter? Just until your show start, o' course.'

They had gone with him willingly, enjoying his company and the speculative glances from girls they passed. They had loved both their trip to the pleasure beach and several other outings, but it soon became apparent that it was Merle who interested Jerry most and by the time the school term ended they had split into two couples, Merle and Jerry going off in one direction, Lottie and Angela in another.

Lottie thought little of it until one night when she, Louella and Max were walking home after a show. It was a lovely night, with a full moon that turned the streets to black and silver. Max and Louella strolled along, their arms linked, talking earnestly about a new trick which Max was working on. It involved two identical white doves and would, Max thought, be popular with audiences, who always enjoyed seeing animals apparently perform, though it was usually just clever timing. In this instance, Max and Louella got the audience to choose a figure between one and twenty, and would then tell them, after they had chosen, that the brilliant counting dove would work out how to release himself from his cage and would flutter across to perch on Louella's shoulder when the count reached the number the audience had picked.

Lottie, who knew how the trick was done, speedily grew bored and dropped behind, and it was then, as she approached a dark doorway, that she realised a couple tightly clasped in one another's arms were taking advantage of the shelter provided. Lottie was not particularly surprised, since she knew boys and girls often cuddled in doorways, but what did surprise her was that she recognised them both as they drew apart for a moment. They must have kept very still and quiet until Louella and Max had passed, never dreaming that Lottie had fallen so far back. Then Lottie heard Merle give a muffled squawk and saw her dive back into the deep shadow as Jerry did likewise.

Lottie said nothing at the time, but later she lay in her bed, wondering what to do for the best. If Merle really meant to go steady with Baz, then she should not hide in doorways kissing and cuddling with Jerry. On the other hand, Baz had only written to Merle twice in all the time they had been in Great Yarmouth, and his letters had been little better than notes: a few ill-spelt sentences scrawled on cheap notepaper and often posted days and days after they had been written.

So if Merle chose to change her allegiance, Lottie could not honestly blame her, though she did think that Baz should be told. He might want to get himself another girlfriend, for it did not look to Lottie as though Merle would be accompanying them when they returned to the Gaiety theatre at the end of September. Or he might want to be my friend again, Lottie thought wistfully. She was very fond of Kenny and had missed him when they first left Liverpool, but talking things over with Angela had been a revelation. 'Girls grow up a whole lot quicker than boys do,' Angela had said wisely. 'It's a well-known fact. My mum told me so years ago when my pal Frankie went on playing kids' games after I thought it would be more fun to go window-shopping or help Mum and Dad in the theatre. Frankie's mum and dad are in the theatre too, but he would talk loud when he was in the wings, or start braying like a donkey at something he thought most awfully funny, and I got real impatient with him and slapped him round the chops more than once. Frankie was the same age as me, but Mum said I'd out-grown him, and she was right. We began to go our separate ways and I reckon it's the same with you and your Kenny.'

Lottie had been much struck by this information and realised that it was as true for her and

Kenny as it had been for Angela and Frankie. Kenny was not interested in girls; he wanted to skip a lecky to Seaforth Sands, or nick fades from St John's market or swim in the Scaldy, generally in company with a number of lads his own age, whereas she enjoyed other pursuits. But Baz, three years older than she, had begun to be a good friend and someone in whom she could confide – until, that was, Merle had entered their lives.

Once, she would have told Baz what was going on without a moment's hesitation, but now she found she had divided loyalties. She had grown quite fond of Merle and she could not completely forget how Baz had dropped her, Lottie, in favour of the older girl back in Liverpool. So now, to tell on Merle seemed a worse sin than letting Baz continue in a fool's paradise. She wondered if she could hint without actually telling him what was going on and was still mulling over the matter when she heard Merle's foot on the stairs. As soon as Merle had come quietly into the room, she closed the door behind her and then spoke in the softest of whispers. 'Lottie? Are you still awake?'

Lottie sat up like a jack-in-the-box, causing Merle to give a small shriek and collapse on to her own bed, clutching her throat dramatically. 'You idiot! I nearly died of fright. I thought you were bound to be asleep 'cos I'm awful late . . . I take it you saw me earlier?'

'Yes I did and I've been lying here wondering what the devil you're playing at,' Lottie said with unaccustomed frankness. 'One minute you tell me you and Baz are going steady, the next you're carrying on in a dark doorway with Jerry Green. Does this mean you've chucked Baz over without even telling him? 'Cos if so I reckon it's a mean trick.'

Merle got slowly to her feet and began to undress, replying as she did so. 'No, of course I haven't chucked Baz over. He's me steady boyfriend; I told you so. But Jerry's awful good-looking and he's nice, isn't he? I've heard you say so yourself. The truth is, queen, that I'm lonely. Oh, I know I've got you and Angela, but – but havin' a boyfriend is different. They make such a fuss of you, make you feel you're worth something, take you nice places, buy you meals . . . can you understand?'

'No I can't,' Lottie said bluntly. 'I've heard Louella talking about one of the chorus girls, the pretty one who's usually on the end of the line because she's the shortest. She's going out with the feller they call the stage door johnny, the one Max says is forty if he's a day. Louella said all that girl is looking for is a meal ticket and it sounds to me as if you're after a meal ticket yourself.'

By this time Merle was in her nightdress and beginning to give her hair the obligatory two hundred strokes with the brush, but at Lottie's words she spoke sharply. 'It ain't like that at all and it's cruel of you to say so,' she hissed, for both girls were keeping their voices down, having no desire to rouse the rest of the household. 'I'd like Jerry even if he never took me anywhere, or made me pay for meself when we went to the flicks. If you were a bit older, you'd understand. It's terribly difficult to explain, but d'you remember that big box of chocolates some feller handed in for your mam at the Gaiety, when the audience heard we were going away for the summer season? Well, when they were finished, Louella told Max that she'd sort of got used to having a chocolate, a sort of reward like, after the final curtain, and she wanted to buy some more only Max told her she'd get fat, so she just sort of sighed and said she'd try to do without, and they both laughed.'

'I don't see what that's got to do with you canoodling with Jerry Green, yet still saying you and Baz are going steady,' Lottie said, genuinely puzzled. 'I think you're just making excuses, Merle.'

Merle heaved an enormous sigh and began to plait her hair. This was a lengthy business since she had masses of hair and braided it into at least a dozen plaits every night. Lottie had long ago realised that Merle's beautiful waves were the result of these plaits and admired the other girl's persistence, for no matter how tired Merle was she always plaited her hair before falling into bed. Lottie knew that she herself did not care suffi-ciently about her appearance to take such pains. 'I am not making excuses; I'm explaining, you little idiot,' Merle said crossly. 'What I'm trying to say is, having a bit of a kiss and cuddle before you go your separate ways is a bit like having a chocolate after the finale. It's a little treat and something you look forward to when you get to my age. Only Baz isn't here to give me a kiss and a cuddle and Jerry is. See?' She must have seen Lottie's baffled expression for she gave a smothered giggle and then reached across and squeezed the younger girl's hand. 'I'm sorry; it wasn't a very good explanation, but it was the best I could do. And in a way you're right, or you might be except for one thing. Jerry knows about Baz and he knows this is just what they call a holiday romance. So you see, no one's going to get hurt, not if you keep your mouth shut.'

Lottie sat quiet for a moment, taking in what Merle had said, then she nodded reluctantly. 'All right, I won't say anything to anyone. But if you've told Jerry about Baz, why don't you tell Baz about Jerry?'

'Because it would be downright unkind,' Merle said at once. 'Think how he'd feel! He's stuck in Liverpool on that grimy old station, livin' all by himself in Victoria Court, eatin' his meals with the Brocklehursts and not havin' much fun I bet. And here's us, having the time of our lives at the seaside, with folk pointin' us out in the street, and Mrs Shilling givin' us some of the best meals we've had in years . . . and then you want to drop a bombshell on the poor feller and tell him I'm carrying on with someone else! Which I ain't doin', not really.'

'Right, only don't go too far,' Lottie said. She had heard the expression, though she had little idea of what it meant. 'I've not asked you before, Merle, because it seemed kind of cheeky, but are you coming back to the Gaiety when the season ends? I suppose you must be, if you really mean to go steady with Baz.'

'I'm not sure,' Merle said rather guardedly. 'To tell you the truth it depends on your mam. She's been much better with me in Yarmouth but she were always findin' fault in Liverpool; I couldn't do a thing right, if you remember. So I thought I'd ask her if she means to continue with the three sisters act and if not I'll try the Rotunda, or the Empire, or anywhere else where I might get work. By the time we leave here at the end of September management will be auditioning for people to take part in pantos, so even if your mam doesn't want me I reckon in a big place like Liverpool with plenty of theatres I should be able to find work.'

She slid down the bed as she spoke and Lottie did the same, remarking drowsily as she did so: 'I don't think you need worry about Louella not wanting you. As we were walking home this evening she said we were doing so well that management would likely raise our money because the theatre's packed every night and Max had arranged something . . . I think the word was percentage . . . which will mean more cash coming our way. I don't think she'd have fancied handing over a third of the money if she thought you weren't pulling your weight.'

'Good, that's what I wanted to hear,' Merle droned, her voice already thickening with sleep. 'You're norra bad kid, Lottie. I'll teach you to twinkle when I've got a moment. Night-night now.'

'Night-night,' Lottie said, glad it was a Saturday so that she might lie in on the morrow. She was almost asleep when she heard a mumble from the other bed. She strained her ears and just about managed to make it out.

'I like you better'n anyone else I know,' Merle muttered. 'I wish you really was my sister.'

Lottie had sat up on one elbow, the better to hear what her companion was saying, but now she lay down again, feeling touched and grateful. Keeping her voice very low indeed, she said softly: 'I like you too, Merle, and I wish we were real sisters an' all.' Then she cuddled down once more and was soon asleep.

To everyone's pleasure, the weather was perfect, sunny day following sunny day, but it was often windy, and the girls grew accustomed to arriving at the theatre with wind-blown hair.

September came, and with it some rain at last, to the relief of the fishermen in the cast, who had had poor sport during the very dry spell. 'But I wouldn't be surprised if the rain sets in now for the autumn,' one of the chorus boys said gloomily.

They were all in the green room, having a cup of tea after a matinée performance. He brightened. 'Still, it's grand weather for fishing. My landlady took a bob off of my rent last week when I handed over a couple of sizeable sea bass. It were a surprise, I can tell you, when the show finished and I pulled me lines up and found I'd got a fish on both. She fried 'em for supper – they were really good.'

One of the scene shifters, a local lad, nodded enthusiastically. 'I've had pretty good fishing myself since the dry ended,' he acknowledged. 'But if you want to see real fishing, you should come back here in October when the herrin' are running. The drifters follow the shoals from Scotland right the way down to us here, where our drifters join 'em. The boats come into harbour so heavily laden with fish that it's a wonder they don't turn turtle, and on a Sunday the boats are packed so tight in the harbour that you can walk across it from deck to deck without getting your feet wet.'

'Aye. No one could do a season in Yarmouth without hearing about the October herring,' Jack put in. 'Mrs Shilling told us all about the Scottish fisher girls what follow the fleet from port to port, gutting the fish as they come on to the quays. She says they're so fast that while you blink an eye they've gutted half a dozen.'

The local lad nodded. 'Aye, they're fast all right, and pretty rough, I'm telling you. When they ain't guttin', they walk round the town, knittin' an' talkin' an' laughin', and the rest of us can scarce understand a word they say.' He chuckled. 'But you can always tell when they're comin' towards you by the smell. I reckon they're kippered themselves after following the fleet for so long.'

'You just said the boats pack the harbour on a Sunday; why is that?' Lottie asked curiously. 'The drifters go out on a Sunday – we've watched 'em sail off and come back, haven't we, Merle?'

Merle nodded and the lad gave a crow of laughter. 'Oh aye, you're right there. Nothin' won't keep a Yarmouth fisherman ashore when the shoals are runnin'. But the Scots are different. They think they'd be sent straight to hell if they fished on the Sabbath, so they crowd into St Nicholas's church and the Methodist chapels, even if the sea is like a mill pond and the fish fairly jumpin' to be caught.'

'I wish we could see the fisher girls, though Mrs Shilling says they ain't girls at all, but quite old women,' Merle remarked. 'But though we can't hang around here till October, it might be quite fun to go and take a look at one or two other resorts. Cromer, for instance; I'm told it's a quaint little place.'

Louella, who had been listening to the conversation without much apparent interest, suddenly turned back into the room. 'If you're keen to go and visit Cromer, I'll pay for your bus fares, and a cup of tea and a bun, if you'll take a look at their pier theatre. The Fol-de-rols are playing there, and if you mention that you're from the Wellington I dare say they'd ask you into the green room and you could tell them what good audiences we've been having and find out how theirs have been. It's always interesting to discover how other theatres are faring, but the thought of a bumpy bus ride just to see yet another Norfolk resort is more than I can stomach right now.'

Lottie and Merle invited Angela to go with them but the show at the Britannia was due to finish before that at the Wellington and she was already busy helping her parents to prepare for their move. Accordingly, Merle and Lottie climbed aboard the bus by themselves one wet afternoon and set off.

They were impressed with Cromer, a delightful old-fashioned little town, perched on its cliff high above the beach and the grey and sullen sea. The pier, when they reached it, was much smaller than their own and it was from here that the lifeboat was launched. Naturally enough they examined the theatre with interest, but it was closed until the evening performance started and by then the girls had to be back at the Wellington. So Louella's cunning plan to discover how the opposition were doing had to be abandoned.

As the month advanced, the rain disappeared again and a boating trip on the broads, which had had to be called off, became a possibility once more. Management had cancelled the matinées, since these were poorly attended, which meant that the girls had two more full days off, though they still had to work in the evenings.

By mid-September, everyone was eager to enjoy their last couple of weeks at the seaside. Angela and her parents had already left for their next engagement, so Lottie could either make up a threesome with Jerry and Merle – or with Max and Louella for that matter – or go about by herself. Merle and Jerry always assured her that she was welcome to join them, but she thought this was just politeness and anyway playing gooseberry was not her favourite pastime.

So it happened that, on a particularly pleasant and sunny Saturday morning, Merle announced her intention of spending the day with Jerry, shopping for new shoes, a smart new pleated skirt and a lemon-coloured blouse. Lottie decided that such an expedition would not be her cup of tea at all. She hated shopping and knew that Merle would visit every shoe shop in the town before finally deciding which shoes to buy, so she told her friend that she meant to catch a bus or a train into the country, but would be home in time for the start of the evening show.

Having examined all her options, Lottie decided to walk up to Southtown station and catch a train to Oulton Broad. Oulton was a small village which they had visited earlier in the season. On that occasion, they had taken a picnic to the Nicholas Everett Park. They had walked round a part of the broad, but had not actually hired a boat since neither Merle nor Louella fancied doing so.

Now, Lottie decided that she would enjoy it even more by herself, particularly if she could hire a boat and row a short way. She had never learned to row but thought it would be easy enough, or perhaps there would be a guided tour which she could join. The broads were beautiful and she had been fascinated by the gorgeous butterflies and dragonflies, the neat little water voles and the many breeds of ducks and geese which they had seen from the park.

She was walking down Nelson Road, knowing that presently she would have to cross the river, for the Southtown station was on the further bank, when she glimpsed ahead of her the colourful market stalls and remembered that since it was Saturday the market would be in full swing. She plunged a hand into the pocket of her jacket and fingered her money. She had meant to have a meal at Waller's restaurant, but if she were to buy a picnic from the market stalls it would cost far less and would probably be more fun as well. I won't spend more than a bob, or perhaps one and a tanner, she told herself, as she arrived at the first stall. I'll get some fruit as well, though I'm pretty sure there will be somewhere in Oulton to buy a drink.

She glanced around her, for the market was crowded, and was surprised to hear herself hailed. 'Lottie! Hey, Lottie! What are you doing here? Don't say you knowed I were comin' 'cos I didn't know meself till a couple o' days ago.'

Lottie's heart gave an enormous thump. She swung round and there was Baz, grinning from ear to ear. He was wearing his porter's uniform, but carried a small bag in one hand which he chucked on the ground as she ran towards him in order to lift her up and whirl her round before giving her a kiss on the forehead and standing her back on the ground once more. 'Baz!' she gasped. 'I can't believe my eyes! What are you doing here? Earlier in the season we expected you to come across and see us, but you never did. Oh, Baz, don't say you've lost your job!'

'No, course not; I'm too bleedin' useful for the boss to dispense with me valuable services,' Baz said, grinning. 'But I've not taken so much as a couple of hours off since I started work so when I said I'd appreciate a long weekend to go and see me girl, the boss made it right. Why, I've even got somewhere to lay me head, 'cos one of the porters at Lime Street has gorra brother what works at Vauxhall station and he's lettin' me use his spare room for a couple o' nights. I'm gettin' it real cheap because the holiday season's comin' to an end, so he's only chargin' me a few bob, and that includes breakfast.' He looked around him. 'But where's Merle? I made sure the pair of you would be together.' He glanced down at Lottie and a puzzled look crept over his face. 'You're different,' he said. 'You look . . . oh, I dunno. Older, I think. Prettier, too.'

'It's my hair,' Lottie said quickly, feeling her

cheeks grow hot at the unexpected compliment. 'It's my real colour because Louella doesn't make me have it lightened now. I think it's the only thing that's really different about me.' Her mind was racing furiously, for after her first pleasure in seeing Baz she had remembered where Merle was. What on earth should she say to him? If she told a downright lie, then she had no doubt they would walk slap bang into the couple as soon as they left the market. She wondered whether she could persuade Baz to accompany her to Oulton, but this seemed unlikely. He had undertaken the long and arduous cross-country journey in order to see 'his girl', and was not likely to allow himself to be palmed off with a boat trip.

But he was still staring down at her, a frown beginning to crease his forehead, so Lottie burst into speech. 'Merle? Well, honestly, Baz, if only you'd let us know! You could have sent a telegram! As it is, Merle will be heartbroken to have missed you, but she and a friend have gone off for the day, I'm not sure where. They've gone shopping – she needs some new shoes and an outfit to match – so they could have gone to Norwich, but even if they have they'll be back in time for "Beginners please!" You know what Louella's like about always arriving at the theatre long before your call.'

Baz's face had fallen but now he began to smile again. 'Norwich? I had to change there. There's a river, and some lovely old buildings. What say you and meself catch a train back to Norwich and see if we can run her and her pal to earth? What's her pal's name?'

'J-Jerry,' Lottie mumbled. 'But I don't think . . .'

'Cherry? Nice name. Is she with the theatre? I suppose she must be because I can't see my Merle taking up with a girl who's not connected with the stage,' Baz said. 'Well, what d'you say? Shall we go to Norwich?'

Vastly relieved that Baz had not heard her correctly, Lottie was about to agree when it struck her that Merle might really have decided to visit the city, so she shook her head firmly. 'No, you'll have to count me out, Baz,' she said. 'I'd planned to take myself off to the broads and I don't mean to miss what might be my last chance of a boat trip. Shopping bores me to tears, to tell you the truth, so we'd best go our separate ways.' She smiled at him and was pleased to see his face fall. Absence, it seemed, made the heart grow fonder, or perhaps it would be truer to say that young men are seldom really keen on shopping trips. And though Baz had only had a glimpse of Norwich, he must realise that his chances of running Merle and her friend to earth were pretty slim. If Lottie played her cards right, however, she might yet save the situation. 'You'll have to go back to Vauxhall station. My train leaves from Southtown in ten minutes, so I shall have to get a move on.' She started to move away but Baz grabbed her arm.

'No sense in my going all the way back to

Norwich on a wild goose chase,' he said. 'I'll come with you. I dare say you won't mind my company instead of Merle's for a change?'

'Oh, Baz, I didn't like to suggest it, but it'll be much more fun to have you along,' Lottie said fervently. 'What a good thing I didn't buy any food; now you can perishin' well treat me to a lunch because I know Mrs Shilling will give you a hot dinner with the rest of us before we have to go to the theatre. She's the best cook in the world – her food is prime. And remember, you've got all day tomorrow to be with Merle, right up to bedtime, because there's no show on a Sunday.'

'That's true,' Baz said. 'But I've got to leave first thing Monday morning. It's a helluva journey, with so many changes you wouldn't believe, but I knew it would be worth it to see my Merle.'

'And your dad, and Louella . . . and meself of course,' Lottie said, rather reproachfully. 'And Merle and me have done the journey too, remember.' Before Baz could reply, they were crossing the bridge which led to Southtown station and Lottie broke into a trot. 'C'mon, or we'll miss it,' she panted. 'We have to take the Ipswich train as far as Haddiscoe, where we'll catch the Lowestoft train; that'll take us to Oulton Broad.'

'It sounds a pretty complicated journey,' Baz said breathlessly, as they hurried towards the station.

Lottie laughed as they skidded to a stop in front of the small ticket office. 'It won't take more than twenty minutes to reach Haddiscoe, and then another ten or fifteen to get to Oulton,' she informed him. 'Thank goodness it's such a lovely day. Oh, Baz, we are going to have fun!'

'Well, I reckon we're in for a real treat, queen, and I'm glad I came,' Baz said later as they climbed cautiously aboard the small boat he had hired. Lottie had asked him whether he could row and he had pretended to be insulted. 'I've been rowin' small boats ever since I were old enough to get meself over to the lake in Prince's Park,' he had said. 'We'll buy ourselves some bread rolls, a bag of tomatoes and a chunk of cheese and have a picnic, seeing as how the weather's more like July than September. How will that suit you?'

Lottie had thought it sounded fun, and now she stowed their food under the thwarts and took her seat a trifle apprehensively. Baz had said he could row a boat, but then boys, she knew, thought they could do everything, and suppose he could not row at all but overturned them, forcing her to swim fully clothed to the nearest shore and making it imperative to explain to the boat-owner that the accident had not been their fault? Only five or ten minutes convinced her, however, that he knew what he was doing, and once she was sure of his ability she simply leaned back in the stern and relaxed. The sun was shining, a gentle breeze blew, and the water was so clear that she could see weed moving gently and fish darting to and fro in the crystal depths. Feeling beautifully secure and dreamily enjoying the sunshine on her bare arms she trailed one hand in the water, thinking that people would believe her to be a young lady out with her boyfriend, but she hastily pulled it back inboard when Baz reminded her that there were enormous freshwater pike in the broads, which might mistake her fingers for a delicious snack. 'And what would Louella say if I took you home minus your finger ends?' he asked, grinning and looking so like the old Baz, the laughing boy of the before-Merle period, that Lottie felt all her former affection for him flooding back. 'And talking of snacks, are you ready for a bite, 'cos I've spotted a good place for a bit of a picnic; see those willows? There's like a little cove underneath 'em, and we can tie the boat up to them big roots . . . what d'you say?'

Lottie agreed that she was a trifle hungry and that Baz had chosen a good spot, and presently they disembarked from their small craft and Baz moored her to a willow branch. Then they spread out the picnic and settled down to enjoy their meal in the dappled shade beneath the trees. As well as bread, cheese and tomatoes, Baz had bought sausage rolls, apple turnovers, a bag of jam dough-nuts and a large bottle of ginger beer.

'I say, Baz . . . they must pay porters awfully well, much better than they pay Merle and me,' Lottie said with considerable respect. 'What a feast! Poor Merle, missing all this!'

'Poor Merle, missing all me,' Baz said with mock boastfulness. 'As for me pay, don't forget I've been savin' up for this trip ever since you Laceys left. I can afford to splash out, especially as you assure me your landlady will give me a hot dinner for nowt but a few words of thanks.'

'She will, and if she wouldn't, your father would pay,' Lottie reminded him, sinking her teeth into a sausage roll. She spoke thickly through her mouthful. 'He's ever so generous, is Max. Pass me a tomato, would you? Oh, Baz, just look at that butterfly!'

'Swallowtail,' Baz said casually through a mouthful of his own. 'Did you see that? Wharrever was it?'

'Kingfisher,' Lottie said, trying to sound equally casual. 'Aren't they the most beautiful creatures? I've never seen one before but there's a picture in Jack Russell's book on birds and animals of the broads.'

'Oh aye? Do you realise, Lottie, that we're the only craft on this particular bit of the waterway? Nice, after bein' stuck on Lime Street station all day and havin' to fight me way back home on a tram when I come off shift. Then goin' round to the Brocklehurst's for a meal ... my, how them kids argue and fight if their da isn't home! I tell you what, queen, all this peace and quiet makes me wish things were different.'

'I guess that's how most of us feel,' Lottie admitted. 'We've all had a grand time in Yarmouth and no one much wants to go back to the Gaiety . . . well, we do in a way because all our friends are there, but we'll miss the seaside, and the country. But the pier management have said they'd be glad to have us again for the next summer season, so we'll have something to look forward to.'

'All right for some,' Baz said gloomily. He broke off a bit of his bread roll and threw it into the shallow water, no more than a couple of feet away. Immediately twenty or thirty tiny fish – fry, Lottie knew they were called – attacked it vigorously, reducing it to nothing in seconds. 'But for me it's back to the grind, and saving up for months just to afford one measly week at the seaside.'

'You should do what your dad wants and start learning magic and stagecraft and that,' Lottie said, highly daring, but Baz leaned over and cuffed her lightly, shaking his head reprovingly as he did so.

'You're a fine one to talk! You hated the stage when you were nine or ten, you know you did! You said you hated people staring at you, complained about the hours you had to work and all the rehearsing and missing school . . .'

'Stop, stop,' Lottie said, laughing. 'But it's not so bad now, and at least it means I'll be coming back to the seaside next year . . . probably to Yarmouth. And I don't suffer from stage fright any more, though I know you do, so I shouldn't tease you. Merle was telling me that you'd applied for

a country station – any luck?' Baz looked astonished, as well he might, Lottie thought guiltily,
remembering that Merle had most probably made
this up as well as everything else. To cover her
mistake, she added quickly: 'Or was that someone
else she was talking about?'

'I dunno,' Baz said slowly. 'I might have said I
was going to. I certainly would like a country
station, but there's no chance for a while yet.
Everyone wants jobs like that, you see, and a lot
of them were taken by fellers who fought in the
war and came home with injuries which make
living in a city unsuitable.' He brooded for a
moment, lying on his back and staring up at the
canopy of leaves which moved gently against the
brilliant blue of the noonday sky. 'Lottie, do you
still have them dreams?'

'Which dreams?' Lottie said idly, though she
knew very well what he meant. It would be so
easy to confide in him, to tell him about the most
interesting dream of all, the one she had had after
arriving in Yarmouth. But later on he would meet
'his Merle' once more and they would want rid of
her so that they could kiss and canoodle and she
would wish she had not told. Oh dear, if only life
were more straightforward, less complicated, she
mourned, turning to stare out across the broad.

'You know which dreams,' Baz said reproachfully. 'The weird ones. The ones you thought might
mean something . . . might be part of the years you
lost.'

'Oh, them. I did have one more, but I don't think I'd better talk about it,' Lottie said. 'You'd only laugh and tell me I was bein' silly.'

'When did I ever do that?' Baz said. He sounded hurt. 'I thought the dreams were trying to tell you something, though you weren't sure what. So you had another one, eh? Go on then, start at the beginning and tell me just what happened.'

'It was a long time ago,' Lottie mumbled. 'Those dreams, the important ones, are only really clear for a couple of days after I've dreamed 'em. Then they go fuzzy round the edges. Oh, I can't explain exactly but I lose the thread, if you understand me.'

Baz had been lying on his back, but now he sat up, caught Lottie gently by the shoulders and pulled her nearer to him, so that they could look one another in the eye. 'Lottie Lacey, you think I'll spill the beans to Merle, just because she's my girl,' he said accusingly. 'If I swear not to tell a livin' soul, will that do?'

'Well, all right, I'll tell you as much as I can remember,' Lottie said. 'It was different from the other dreams because in them I never managed to talk to the people I met. I think it was because I was just a baby, but in this dream I was older, perhaps three or four, and the boy I told you about, the one Kenny and I met in Rhyl, was in the dream too. It started off with paddling in the sea . . .'

To begin with, Lottie had not meant to give Baz more than a vague outline of the dream, but once

233

she had started she found the dream coming back as clear and sharp as though she had dreamed it the previous night, instead of weeks and weeks ago. Perhaps it was Baz's interest, but suddenly the dream became important, and Lottie found herself longing to hear his reaction. '. . . so you see, if the dreams are really sort of memories, then I have been in Yarmouth before,' she said triumphantly. 'Though why Louella should deny it, I really can't imagine. I know we did summer seasons before the accident, she's told me so many times, but no one could do a season in Yarmouth – or even a couple of weeks – and then completely forget it.'

As she spoke, Lottie had been looking out across the sparkling water of the broad, but now she turned to look at Baz, waiting for his agreement to her remark. Baz, however, was staring out across the water as well, with a crease between his brows. Lottie frowned too. Of course, Baz did not yet know Yarmouth as she did, but since Merle had admitted he was still in Liverpool she had written him long, descriptive letters about the pier, the town and its many attractions. Surely he must realise that Louella could not simply forget such a memorable place? 'Baz? What are you thinking? I know you've not been into the town, but I promise you . . .'

'It ain't that,' Baz said slowly. 'I s'pose it's possible that you came to Yarmouth with a school trip, or with pals.'

It was Lottie's turn to frown. 'But Baz, I were only a little kid, and little kids don't go off without their mammies.'

'They do, though; and without their dads an' all,' Baz said promptly. 'Look at me. My dad couldn't trek me all round the country with him when he was touring. When your mam or your dad has a job which means a lot of travelling, grannies and aunts and that come in ever so useful. What I reckon is, the old lady who dried your feet for you and put your sandals on is probably your grandmother, or perhaps a great-aunt or something, and when your mam was doing a summer season and you were too small to take along, then your gran, or your aunt, took over. See?'

Lottie nodded. 'I suppose that's possible,' she admitted. 'But why didn't Louella say so?'

Baz shrugged. 'I dunno,' he said. 'But she never talks much about what happened before the accident, does she? Mebbe she feels guilty about sending you off with someone else, even if it were only for a week. Anyway, no harm in asking.' Baz got to his feet and began to collect their belongings. 'Best be gettin' back,' he said. 'We don't want to miss that train.'

They caught the train in good time, and – in Lottie's case at least – snoozed on the way back. She had had a wonderful day and knew Baz had enjoyed it too, and when they reached Southtown station they saw that they were still in good time for Mrs Shilling's five o'clock dinner. It was not a long walk from the station to Nelson Road, and they were actually on the point of turning into No. 55 when Baz gave an exclamation and stopped short. 'Well, if it isn't Merle!' he said joyfully. And then, his tone changing: 'What the devil . . . ?'

Lottie gave a gasp of dismay. Merle and Jerry were coming towards them, hand in hand, and as they drew level with No. 55 Merle turned and flung her arms round Jerry's neck. Lottie heard Baz grind his teeth and his growl would have done credit to an angry Alsatian. He started forward, then stopped short, the hands which he had clenched into fists dropping to his sides. 'Well, Merle, what a surprise,' he said, and his voice had an edge to it which Lottie had never heard before. 'You must introduce me to your friend.'

Merle's face was scarlet and her voice trembled, but Lottie could see she was doing her best to remain calm. 'Baz! Oh . . . this is Jerry Green. When did you arrive? Jerry was kind enough to treat me to a day out . . . he's been awfully good to me and Lottie . . .'

'Oh, awfully good! So good that he let Lottie go off by herself whilst he took you shopping. And you gave him a great big kiss to say thank you, though of course you're barely acquainted,' Baz said sarcastically. 'Well, I'd best be off to my lodgings, but it's nice to have met you.'

He turned rather blindly on his heel, and Lottie turned too, grabbing his arm. 'I'm awful sorry, Baz, but honest to God, Merle and Jerry are only friends,' she said urgently. 'You mustn't go off in a huff. Remember, you're having dinner with us, and then you're coming to the show on the pier. Just give Merle a chance to explain . . .'

By this time, Lottie was trotting along beside Baz, for though he had not shaken her off he had continued to walk rapidly back the way they had come. Lottie peered up into his face, which was very red, and to her horror saw a tear slide down his cheek. 'Oh, Baz, please don't be upset! I'm sure Merle can explain. Jerry don't mean anything to her, except as a friend. She told him the two of you were going steady . . .'

Baz continued to stride on but presently there was the patter of feet behind them, and Merle came running up. Lottie was still holding on to Baz's right arm, but now Merle grabbed his left and between the two of them they managed to pull him to a halt. 'Baz, you've got hold of the wrong end of the stick,' Merle said breathlessly. 'I were only giving Jerry a hug 'cos he'd took me out for the day and bought me dinner 'n' tea, and made me laugh a lot. Usually, we go around in a foursome: Jerry, Angela, Lottie and me.' She turned appealing eyes to Lottie. 'Tell him it's true, Lottie. Tell him Jerry's just a friend and nothin' more.'

'I'll take some persuadin',' Baz said, but Lottie thought he already sounded half convinced. He turned to her. 'Why did you let me think Merle

237

had gone off wi' a girl? If I'd knowed it were a feller, it wouldn't have been half the shock.'

'I told you his name was Jerry, but you misheard, so I thought it were best to mind me own business. After all, you and Merle both told me to do so back in Liverpool often enough,' she ended with a flash of spirit. 'And I did tell you Jerry were just a friend.'

'So you did,' Baz said. 'Well, I'm just a friend 'n' all, so let's go back to your lodgings and have a meal before the show. After all, I've not so much as said hello to me dad yet, and if he knew I'd been and gone without a word, he'd be rare upset.'

Much relieved, Lottie would have released his arm so that he and Merle might walk ahead, but when she tried to pull free Baz would not allow it. 'We're all pals now and nothing else,' he said firmly. 'I must meet this Jerry of yours, Merle.'

'Of course you can, and he'll tell you what I said's true,' Merle said eagerly. 'Oh, Baz, I do love you, and you've not give me a kiss yet.'

She turned her face up to his but Baz, though he smiled, shook his head. 'No, Merle. You've changed; you're a stranger to me now and I don't kiss strange girls in the street,' he said calmly. 'You and I have got a lot of talking to do before we decide what the future holds.'

Chapter Nine

As Lottie had promised, Mrs Shilling did not turn a hair when the girls introduced Baz and asked if he might share their dinner. 'Course he can; this here's Liberty Hall,' Mrs Shilling said at once. 'I've made a casserole of beef and onions, with apple pie for afters.' She smiled up at Baz. 'I hopes you're fond of beef do you'll go hungry, 'cos that's all I've got.'

'It sounds marvellous, Mrs Shilling,' Baz said, licking his lips. 'I've managed to get myself lodgings with a chap I know, but I'll come round as soon as I've finished breakfast tomorrow so I can spend some time with my dad. What time does he get up on a Sunday?'

'He'll be up betimes when he finds his son have come a-visiting,' Mrs Shilling said, twinkling up at him. 'And what about these two lovely young ladies? You'll be wanting to take them out on the spree, no doubt. The pleasure beach will be open and most of the amusements, though not all o' them 'cos at this time o' year it's mainly day trippers and weekenders what come down to Yarmouth.'

Baz was starting to answer when the kitchen door opened and Louella, Max and Jack Russell came into the room. Max shouted, 'Baz!' and pumped his hand vigorously up and down whilst clapping him on the shoulder. He was clearly delighted to see his son and said so, asking eagerly how long Baz could stay and whether he would attend that evening's performance.

Louella kissed Baz warmly and began to scold him for not giving them advance notice of his arrival. 'We would have met you at the station and brought you straight back here,' she said. 'But I dare say the girls have entertained you.'

'Well, Lottie has; we went to Oulton Broad and hired a boat,' Baz said. 'Merle was out shopping with a – a friend, but we had a good day, didn't we, Lottie?'

Lottie was beginning to answer when Jack Russell cut in. 'Have you spoken to Mrs Bob yet?' he asked anxiously. 'She'll mebbe want to stick a few more spuds in the pan.' He turned to Mrs Shilling. 'Ain't that right, Mrs Bob?'

'That's right, Mr Dog,' Mrs Shilling said placidly. 'I've told you before, if you call me Mrs Bob then I'll call you Mr Dog, and you'll have to lump it.'

Jack Russell laughed loudly, then turned to Baz, who was looking distinctly puzzled. 'A bob is just another name for a shilling, ain't it?' he explained. 'I'm a grand one for coinin' phrases, ha, ha; it were me that decided to shorten Liverpudlians to Puddles, which is what everyone in the theatre calls us now.'

'Oh, don't listen to him,' Merle said impatiently. 'You are coming to the show, ain't you, Baz?'

'Of course,' Baz said shortly. Lottie saw Max shoot his son a quizzical glance and guessed he had sensed there was something wrong, though no one else appeared to have noticed. 'But I'll come backstage first, so I can meet everyone. Lottie here is a grand little letter writer; she's been telling me all about the rest of the company and I can't wait to meet 'em.'

'I do try to write regular myself but I dare say my letters aren't that interesting,' Max said humbly. 'Somehow, I'm always so busy . . .'

'Your letters are interesting, but I think Lottie's got the gift of making you see what she sees,' Baz said quickly. 'And you do write regular, Dad. I don't think you've missed a week once in all the time you've been away. In fact it's me that should feel guilty because I'm a rotten correspondent.'

Merle began to speak but was cut off short by Mrs Shilling's clapping her hands briskly and addressing them. 'Off with you to the dining room, Puddles,' she said. 'And you can all take something through with you. Mr Max, you carry the casserole, and you Laceys can bring the veg. Mr Russell, bring the teapot, will you? I'll fetch the rest.'

In bed that night, Lottie thought long and hard over what had happened between Merle and Baz. There was no doubt in her mind that Baz's feelings towards Merle had changed, though it was pretty clear that Merle's feelings for Baz had remained the same. She had done everything in her power to assure him that she felt only friendship for Jerry whereas she felt a far deeper emotion for himself. Baz, however, remained cool and detached. As he had promised, he had accompanied them to the Wellington and met the company; then he had become a part of the audience until the final curtain, when he went backstage once more. Merle had tried to throw her arms round him when they trooped off the stage, but he had eluded the embrace with some skill. One of the chorus girls had giggled and this had made Merle very angry, but it had also made her realise that she was going to have to work at their relationship if she wanted it to return to its old footing.

When the two girls were preparing for bed, Lottie had tried to talk it over but Merle had said pettishly that there was nothing wrong between herself and Baz and that she would thank Lottie to mind her own business. 'I don't know how you dare say that, Merle O'Mara,' Lottie had said, feeling her cheeks grow hot with indignation. 'It weren't you that spent the whole day with Baz, it were me, and all I wanted to say was that he will be in Yarmouth all day tomorrow; he's leaving first thing on Monday. I wondered whether you'd like to ask Jerry to make up a foursome since we're all going to be friends, it seems.'

Merle had glared. 'I've not had a chance to speak

to Baz by myself yet, so I don't know what we'll be doing,' she had said coldly. 'But if there's one thing I am sure of, it's that Baz and me won't want no kid hangin' around. If you want to go out with Jerry, that's up to you, but I can't see him taking to the idea myself.'

'Whatever have I done to make you so mad, Merle?' Lottie had asked, for Merle's tone had been not only cold but also sharp. 'I let Baz think you'd gone into Norwich with a girlfriend and I took him out to Oulton Broad 'cos I was afraid if we stayed in Yarmouth we might walk slap bang into you and Jerry. And I backed you up when you said you and Jerry were just friends, you know I did.'

Merle had sighed. She had just finished having a quick wash and turned to give Lottie an impulsive hug. 'I'm sorry. I know you did everything you could to help,' she had muttered. 'But tomorrow I reckon I've got to have some time alone with Baz, to sort things out. You don't mind, do you, queen?'

'No, of course I don't mind,' Lottie had said, completely won over. 'As soon as breakfast is over I'll slip away; there's lots to do in Yarmouth. Ever since we arrived I've been meaning to start a shell collection, but somehow I've never got round to it. I'll do it tomorrow.'

The next morning, however, Lottie found that slipping away was not going to be so easy. Baz arrived just as they finished breakfast, and she opened the door to him, greeted him pleasantly and would have gone past him and out into the sunny morning had he not grabbed her wrist, saying in a jovial tone: 'Not so fast, young lady! I've got plans for today and they include you. I expect you'll pretend you were just on your way to close the front gate, or to buy a Sunday newspaper, but you aren't going anywhere . . . not until we've made our arrangements, that is.'

They were standing in the doorway and Lottie knew that Merle, whose turn it was to dry the dishes, would have heard Baz's voice and would be listening eagerly, so she drew him into the small front garden, pulling the door almost shut behind her. 'Baz, I've got plans of my own for today,' she said. 'Merle and you need to talk things over and catch up with each other's news. You – you mustn't let what happened yesterday afternoon spoil things.'

'Has Merle put you up to this?' Baz said suspiciously. Lottie shook her head, beginning to disclaim, but he gave her a little shake and overrode her. 'It don't matter whether she did or she didn't. She's not the girl I thought her and that's the truth. If Jerry was just a friend, then why didn't either of you ever mention him?'

'Because Merle was afraid you wouldn't understand,' Lottie said frankly. 'Please, Baz, don't hold it against her. If you won't go out with her alone, then all three of us could do something together.'

Baz shook his head. 'No; it 'ud be downright

embarrassing. She'd keep trying to grab me and I'd want to give her an almighty great shove, and tell her to grab someone else,' he said with a frankness which rivalled Lottie's own. 'When something's over, it's over.'

'But it isn't over,' Lottie said desperately. 'At least, it isn't for Merle. She still loves you, Baz, honest to God she does. It's just that she got so dreadfully lonely . . . and you didn't really answer her letters, and you never visited us either.'

'That's true,' Baz admitted grudgingly. 'I hate writing letters. I didn't reply to you, either.'

'No, and I got pretty upset with you, but you weren't my boyfriend and you were supposed to be Merle's,' Lottie pointed out. 'Look, suppose I tell her she mustn't grab you, would you come out with us then – both of us, I mean?'

Baz laughed, and to Lottie's relief his face showed genuine amusement. 'All right, if that's what you want,' he said. 'But you enjoyed yesterday, didn't you? I thought we might go out there again, only this time I'd hire some fishing tackle and we could take our bathers.'

'Well, we could still do that,' Lottie said, but she spoke doubtfully. 'Only Merle can't swim, you know. I think she'd rather we went round the town. There's lots to do and see. I've told you about most of it, but telling isn't the same as seeing with your own eyes.'

'Right. And now you'd better nip indoors and tell Merle what we've arranged. Will it take you long to get ready? Shall I amuse myself for half an hour?'

'No need; Merle must have finished the crocks by now, so we can come at once,' Lottie assured him. 'You come and wait in the parlour while I tell Merle no grabbing. We'll have a really good day, just you see if we don't.' So saying, she disappeared into the kitchen to tell her friend what she and Baz had agreed. Merle sighed, but said it was fair enough.

There was a little constraint at first as the three of them walked down towards the prom, but since their first call was Barron's Amusement Arcade they soon became very much easier with one another. They played the penny falls without once winning so much as a ha'penny, and they took it in turns to see 'what the butler saw' and also the gruesome hanging of a condemned man, which had Merle shuddering with pretended fear, though Lottie knew perfectly well that she had viewed the exhibit half a dozen times before without turning a hair. There was a rifle range where Baz won a celluloid doll which he said he intended to give to the small daughter of his Yarmouth landlady. This made Lottie giggle and the giggle, in turn, made Baz give her a wink, but fortunately Merle was lining up to throw darts at playing cards and noticed nothing.

Baz treated them to lunch at Langtry's restaurant, which was a thrill for both girls since it was known to be expensive and they had not previously entered its portals. They were very impressed by the starched white tablecloths and shining silver cutlery and by the food, which was delicious and elaborately presented on fine china plates, with the restaurant's name in gold leaf around the edge.

The weather remained bright and sunny and when Baz suggested that they should go down to the beach and hire deckchairs to digest their meal, the girls were not at all unwilling. They followed him on to the golden sand, already crowded with a great many trippers, and collapsed into the deckchairs, though in Lottie's case not for long. Baz had his eyes shut and so did Merle, but Lottie knew her friend well enough to be sure that Merle was not actually asleep, so before she left them, she addressed her. 'No grabbing,' she hissed into the older girl's ear, and saw Merle open one eye and give a wicked little grin.

Lottie threaded her way through the recumbent forms, kicked off her sandals, bunched the skirt of her cotton dress in one hand and walked into the waves. It was lovely! She wished she had brought her bathing costume, but it would not have been fair on Merle. Recently, her friend had felt herself too much of an adult for the beach, complained that sand got into everything, and refused to accompany Lottie even on the hottest day when everyone, surely, must long to cool themselves in the beautiful North Sea. Once she was up to her knees, Lottie glanced back up the beach and was dismayed to realise that Baz was no longer in his deckchair, but striding towards her. He called, but when she took no notice rolled up his trouser legs, removed his shoes and socks, and paddled in after her. 'You thought I were asleep, you little monkey,' he said, but his voice was amiable. 'I wish I'd brought my swimmin' things, then we could have had a proper dip.'

Lottie opened her mouth to remind him that Merle could not swim, then closed it again. After all, this was Baz's one and only trip to the seaside, so why should he not enjoy himself? It was not his fault that Merle would not go in the sea if she could possibly help it.

The rest of the day was spent introducing Baz to the many and varied amusements which the town offered. Several times Merle signalled to Lottie to make herself scarce, and Lottie did her best to comply, but both girls soon realised that it was useless. Baz stuck closer to Lottie than a limpet to a rock and very soon the three of them began to behave more naturally, laughing and joking and even linking arms, with Baz in the middle and a girl on either side.

When they reached the pleasure beach it was growing dusk and many of the attractions were beginning to close. Lottie was well aware that Merle disliked heights – she was not too keen on them herself – and guessed that Merle had noticed Baz was pulling them towards the queue of people waiting their turn to go on the scenic railway. Baz said that if he was to enjoy a ride on the popular attraction, it was now or never, and they joined the queue. 'We'll get a marvellous view when the carriages are at the very top of the highest loop,' he told them. 'All the better because it's growing dusk. But if you really don't want to come, Merle, I'll understand. After all, there's not a lot of spare space in them little carriages. Tell you what, I'll give you some money and you can buy us all a penn'orth of chips while Lottie and meself sample this here scenic railway.'

Lottie could see that this idea did not appeal to Merle at all but at that moment the train they were watching reached its highest point, hesitated, trembled, and then plunged down to ground level. The screams were deafening and Merle gave a ladylike shudder and held out her hand for the money Baz was offering. 'All right, I'll buy a penn'orth of chips each and probably I'll be the only one who can eat 'em because that there ride is enough to turn the strongest stomach,' she observed. She turned to Lottie. 'You won't like it, queen. Why not let Mr Cleverboots here go on alone, then you an' me can enjoy our chips with insides what ain't churned up.'

Lottie looked uncertainly from one to the other, but at that moment the queue began to move forward. A brightly painted little car stopped alongside them, two giggling girls got out and Baz lifted Lottie up and dumped her unceremoniously on the wooden seat, squeezed in beside her and snapped the guard rail into place. A skinny youth came and took the money, Lottie shouted goodbye to her friend, reminding Merle that she wanted salt and vinegar on her chips, and then the little cars jerked and began to move forward.

The climb up the first length of track was slow for the train was fully loaded, and when they reached the top of the incline they felt the full force of the wind for the first time. Lottie looked around her and was amazed by the beauty of the scene. The sea shone like watered silk; lights twinkled in streets and glowed from windows, turning Yarmouth into a fairytale town. Below them, the crowds of people in their holiday best thronged Marine Parade, and the piers jutting into the sea looked like fairy palaces, with their sparkling lights, domes and minarets. Lottie was clutching Baz's arm and starting to ask him if his lodgings were visible from here when their little car tipped over the edge and began its downward plunge. She had not meant to scream or clutch, had certainly not intended to stand up, but the speed and force of their descent was so tremendous that a shriek was torn from her lips and she was jerked upright, so that Baz had to put his arm round her and heave her back on to the seat.

'That was horrid,' Lottie panted, as the train reached the lower level and began to climb once more. 'Oh, Baz, I thought that was the highest hill when we were on top of it, but it wasn't, was it; this one's high – high – higher!' The last word came out as a shriek, but this time Lottie was shrieking for a different reason. The train was gradually gaining height, and as she looked down, trying to pick Merle out in the crowd surrounding the fish and chip van, she saw a face which was as familiar as that of her friend. She half stood up, and as Baz jerked her back into her seat once more she pointed frantically. 'Look, Baz! Look! It's the boy with the golden eyes! He's just in front of Merle, waiting for chips! Oh, Baz, make them stop. I've got to get off, got to reach him before he disappears again.'

'Don't be daft. No one can stop this thing once it gets going,' Baz said. 'Just sit down like a good gal or we'll be in trouble. Who's the boy with the golden eyes, anyway? No one has golden eyes.'

'I just call him that because his eyes are a sort of golden brown, like lions' . . .' Lottie was beginning when the car reached the summit, hesitated for a moment, and then plunged even more horrifyingly than before.

As soon as they were within a few feet of the ground Lottie tried to get out, but Baz grabbed her firmly and shook her. 'Don't be a little fool,' he said urgently. 'The ride only takes a few moments. There's one more hill and then the cars will come to a halt and you can get off like a Christian. You don't want to end up with every bone in your body broken, do you? Now tell me about this boy. Is it someone you knew from Liverpool?'

The railway was climbing the last hill and Lottie

searched desperately for a sight of the boy, then saw him. He was standing quite near the scenic railway now, looking upwards. His face was illumined by the coloured lights which winked and shone all over the pleasure beach and any doubts she might have had as to his identity disappeared. It was the boy with the golden eyes all right . . . oh, if only she could get off this wretched ride and reach him before he disappeared into the crowd once more!

'Lottie. Who is this boy?'

'He's in my dreams; he calls me Sassy,' Lottie said rapidly. 'I met him properly once, but I didn't ask him his name. If I can just get to him . . .'

Their car reached the top of the ride and even as Baz opened his mouth to answer her, speech, breath and practically everything else was whipped away as the steepest and worst descent began. Lottie shrieked because she could not help it and tried to fix the boy with her eyes so that she could find him again as soon as the ride finished, but even as the little car drew to a halt and Baz unclipped the guard rail, she knew it was no use. He would have disappeared into the crowds without even knowing she was there.

She jumped out of the car as soon as it stopped, but Baz detained her, a hand on her arm. 'The boy you dreamed about? I'm getting confused, but I'll do my best to help you, obviously. What was the fellow wearing? What colour is his hair?'

'I only saw him from the top so I've no idea

what he was wearing, but his hair is sort of toffee-coloured, like his eyes,' Lottie said. She was pushing her way towards the fish and chip van as she spoke, hoping against hope that he might have returned to it, but, as she had feared, the only person she recognised was Merle. Her friend came towards them, holding out the bags of chips and pulling a face as she handed them over. 'You were ages,' she said accusingly. 'A good thing we don't work on a Sunday or we'd be in real trouble. Don't blame me if your perishin' chips is cold.'

'We weren't ages,' Baz said, looking slightly surprised. 'We came straight to the fish and chip van to find you.'

'Well it seemed ages, to be left all on me own,' Merle grumbled. 'Where shall we eat our chips? Tell you what, if we walk back along the prom, we could grab a seat in the Marine Parade Gardens. Then I reckon we'd best be getting back to Mrs Shilling, else we'll be good for nothing tomorrow.'

All the while they ate their chips, Lottie's eyes were scanning the thinning crowd, but the boy did not appear again and she had not really expected that he would do so. Indeed, she was beginning to wonder whether she had actually seen him at all, or whether it had been a chance resemblance, or even wishful thinking. She told herself that it could simply have been due to her telling Baz about the dream, so that the boy was on her mind. Yet on the other hand, she had seen him first in

Rhyl, a seaside resort, had dreamed of him in Yarmouth, and now she had seen him again, beside the sea. It was weird. If only she had asked him his name, where he lived, anything that would enable her to find him again! But she had not done so and it was no use regretting the fact. She had been very young on the school trip and anyway, she had not known then that she was going to dream about him. In fact the whole thing was a mess and a muddle and would probably be best forgotten.

'Lottie? You're awful quiet. I told you you wouldn't like that scenic railway; you'd ha' done far better to stick wi' me.'

'Yes I would,' Lottie said thoughtfully. 'If I'd stayed with you, I might have had a chance to speak to that boy . . . did you notice him, Merle? I dunno what he was wearing, but he had very pale, goldy-brown hair and eyes the same colour.'

'Oh aye; there were a young man in front of me in the queue with funny, very light brown eyes,' Merle said carelessly. 'Quite a looker, wasn't he? He had a gal with him and he kept turning his head to talk to her. Then, when he'd bought his chips and were walking back along the queue, one of the little bags slipped . . . he'd bought four or five . . . and I grabbed it just before it hit the ground. He thanked me and grinned – lovely white teeth he had – and the girl he were with went off in the opposite direction, so I guessed they'd just got chatting in the queue, the way one does.'

'I wonder who he was buying for?' Lottie said. She was not particularly surprised that Merle had noticed a young man – she was a girl who did notice men – but was not at all sure that Merle had really encountered the boy with the golden eyes. To Lottie he was a boy, not a young man, but then she chided herself. Years had passed since the meeting in Rhyl. She herself was no longer a child but a young woman, and he had been several years older than she. Dreams, of course, did not take age into account, but if she and Merle really had seen the same person, then he would probably be at least as old as Baz, and probably older. In fact, he would be the young man Merle had described, and not the boy which she herself had thought him.

'Who were he buyin' for? Why, pals of course. But what does it perishin' well matter?' Merle asked impatiently. 'How come you know him, anyhow? Does he come to the theatre? But no, he can't, 'cos if he did I'd know him an' all. Come on, spill the beans! How come you know the feller?'

'Oh, I met him on the beach once,' Lottie said, vaguely but not untruthfully, for she had indeed met him on the beach, though only in her dream. 'He was nice to me, really friendly. He was with his old gran – I think that's who she was – and he helped me make a sandcastle. Only I never asked him his name and when Baz and I were on the scenic railway, right at the top, I was looking for you over by the chip van, and saw him only a few feet from you.'

'Oh, I see,' Merle said, losing interest. 'Well, we'd best be heading for home now, or old Ma Shilling will lock us out.'

'She wouldn't,' Lottie said at once. She was truly fond of their landlady and knew how generous Mrs Shilling was towards her lodgers. 'Merle, would you know that young man again? The one – the one in the queue in front of you, I mean?'

'Why?' Merle asked. She scrumpled the little paper bag which had contained her chips into a ball and lobbed it into a nearby litter bin. 'You ain't interested in boys, you're always saying so.'

'I told you: I forgot to ask his name and I want to know it. If we're coming back to Yarmouth next year, then I'd like to meet him again. Why shouldn't I have a friend, even if he does happen to be a feller?' Lottie said rather belligerently. 'Look at you and Jerry . . . you're just friends, but I reckon if we really do come back next summer, you'll want to get in touch with him again.'

Merle jumped to her feet and gave Lottie the benefit of her most scorching glance. 'You spiteful little cat,' she hissed. 'If Baz hadn't gone off to buy a bottle of lemonade, and heard what you just said, he'd never have understood.'

Lottie, who had spoken quite without thinking, felt the blood rush to her cheeks. Merle was right: what a catty, thoughtless thing to have said! 'I'm really sorry, Merle, it was a stupid thing to say,'

256

she said humbly. She turned as Baz collapsed on to the seat beside her, saying as he did so that he had been unable to find anyone selling lemonade. 'Never mind. If you come back to Nelson Road with us, there'll be plenty to eat and drink there. Mrs Shilling puts supper on the kitchen table each Sunday. It's always cold food – bread and butter, salad and cold ham – and then there's usually a big sponge cake or a bowl of jelly to finish up with.'

Baz agreed to share supper and they returned to Nelson Road to find Max, Louella, Jack and the Melias already in the kitchen, piling their plates with salad, new potatoes and ham. Max grinned at his son. 'It's a shame you've got to go back early tomorrow, but we'll be in Liverpool ourselves in a fortnight so it's not so much goodbye as au revoir,' he said. 'Come on, youngsters, dig in.'

As soon as the meal was over, and Lottie began to stack the plates in the sink – for it was her turn to wash up – Baz said his goodbyes, asked them to thank Mrs Shilling for her hospitality, and set off for his digs. He had barely been gone two minutes, however, when Merle threw down her tea towel and hurried out of the room, calling over her shoulder that she had forgotten something she needed to say to Baz and would not be a moment. She was gone nearly half an hour, and Lottie had washed up, dried and put away all the supper things before her friend re-entered the kitchen, looking flushed and pleased with herself. 'Thanks,

Lottie, for doing my share of the work; I'll do your turn next week. And now let's get up to bed 'cos I'm almost asleep on my feet.'

'Is everything OK between you and Baz?' Lottie asked as they undressed and got ready for bed. 'I guessed you'd followed him, and you looked pretty happy when you came back into the kitchen just now.'

'Yes, we've sorted things out,' Merle said. 'I knew I could make him understand if I could see him alone for ten minutes.' She got into bed and shrugged the covers over her ears. 'Goodnight, Lottie. I'm going to dream about Baz and I bet he'll be dreaming about me. I suggested we might have a weekend in Blackpool together, and he liked the idea.'

Lottie, snuggling down also, hoped Merle was joking, for nice girls, she knew, did not go off with young men for weekends. But then she gave a small and secret smile: I know all about dreams, she thought drowsily, and they won't simply come for the asking. Chances are Merle will dream she's being dragged out to sea by a giant octopus, or having her best dress gobbled up by a whale, 'cos you can't order dreams the way you can order boiled beef and carrots in a restaurant.

For her own part, however, she thought she had a pretty good chance of getting into the dream this very night, if it followed the course of her previous experiences. She had been on the beach and had paddled in the sea. She had dug a big sandcastle and carted water to fill the moat. But the best sign of all was seeing the boy with the golden eyes. Yes, she really should get back into her dream tonight, and if only she could remember, she would ask the boy his name.

In the other bed, Merle began to snore.

Though Lottie had had such an exhausting and exciting day, it had taken her ages and ages to get to sleep. Despite her most earnest efforts – or perhaps because of them – she had lain awake in her small bed listening to the chimes of the church clock until well past three in the morning, when she had fallen at last into an exhausted slumber. It had not, however, been a dreamless sleep. In the middle of her tap-dance routine, one of her shoes had come untied and had flown across the orchestra pit and into the front row of the stalls, where it had inflicted a black eye upon a fat and furious man. With surprising agility, he had leapt the orchestra pit and chased Lottie out of the theatre and along the whole length of the pier. Within six feet of the end, her legs had unaccountably turned to lead, so that the dreadful man had caught her up and tossed her over the rail. She had been wearing an enormous crinoline dress and a poke bonnet, so had sailed down towards the sea, crinoline billowing. But before she could touch the water, a giant octopus had wrapped his arms round her, clearly intending to do her awful harm. But the crinoline had foiled his evil intentions for he had chosen to devour her clothing first, and so difficult had he found it to negotiate such an unwieldy and prickly garment that he had let her go. She had swum desperately to the shore, seeing a tall tower on the promenade, and guessed this must be Blackpool. As she gained the beach, she realised she was naked when holidaymakers surrounded her, oohing and ahhing and telling her she ought to be ashamed, for no decent girl would ever arrive in Blackpool without a stitch on her back.

Lottie did not think she had ever visited Blackpool, yet here she was, apparently having swum all the way from Yarmouth. She looked round desperately for a towel or a shawl, anything to drape her nakedness, and finally seized a striped deckchair, tearing its canvas free from the wood and wrapping it thankfully around her. Before she could feel even slightly safe, however, the man who hired out the deckchairs gave a roar of displeasure, and once more the chase was on. Poor Lottie ran and ran, but the sand was soft and the crowds impeded her progress, and no one can run one's fastest whilst clutching a piece of stiff canvas around oneself. She was near despair, her breath running out and tears pouring from her eyes, when she ran full tilt into someone who clasped her comfortingly, saying as he did so: ''Ello, 'ello, 'ello, what's all this then? Ho, a naked young lady! I can see I'll have to take you to the police station and throw you into a cell.'

Terrified, she looked up, past the familiar black

uniform with its winking silver buttons, and into Baz's face, for it was he. She began to explain that it was not her fault, that an octopus had eaten her clothing, but he was shaking his head at her, his dark eyes sorrowful. 'Nice girls don't go to Blackpool with octopuses for a dirty weekend,' he said reprovingly. 'I'm surprised at you, Lottie Lacey. I thought you'd ha' known better.'

For some reason, this was more than Lottie could take. She wrenched herself out of his arms and shouted at him at the top of her voice. 'You can talk! Why's you here, Basil O'Mara, if it ain't for a dirty weekend? Just you let me alone and get back to Merle before I set that octopus on you.'

Baz grabbed her again and began to shake her and, to her immense relief, Lottie awoke to find herself safe in her own small bed, with Merle bending over her.

'Wake up, queen! Wharrever is the matter? You were havin' a fearful dream . . . more like a nightmare, I reckon . . . and the church clock just struck nine, so if we don't get down smartish we won't have time to grab ourselves some breakfast.'

Lottie sat up. She was trembling and soaked with sweat. She began to tell Merle about the awfulness of her nightmare, then stopped short, having reached the point where she had struggled out of the sea to find herself apparently transported on to Blackpool beach. She realised she could not possibly tell Merle any more, and also knew that she was going to find it hard to look

Baz in the eye when they next met.

'Go on, what happened then?' Merle enquired, clearly intrigued. 'I wonder why the octopus ate your dress, though? Ain't dreams the oddest things?'

Lottie shuddered. 'That wasn't a dream, it was a nightmare,' she said, stripping off her damp nightgown and going over to the washstand. She began to wash vigorously, glad for once of the cold water on her hot skin. She glanced at Merle over her shoulder. 'Look, Merle, you're fully dressed. Go down and tell Mrs Shilling I won't be five minutes.'

'OK,' Merle said airily, banging her way out of the room. She had left the door ajar and Lottie heard her footsteps clattering down the two flights with some satisfaction. If Merle really had dreamed of Baz, she either had forgotten it on waking, or intended to keep it to herself. That meant that Lottie had time to mull over both the nightmare and the absence of her own special dream, which she had been so confident would come to her because she had seen the boy in real life.

Cleaning her teeth vigorously, she decided the nightmare had been at least partly her own fault. She remembered thinking as she got into bed that, far from dreaming about Baz, Merle would prob-ably find herself in the arms of an octopus, so that was one puzzle solved. The other, equally strange until you thought about it, was the octopus attacking her crinoline; but she had imagined that a whale might devour Merle's best dress, and since she had thought it just as she got into bed, sea creatures eating dresses must have been very much on her mind. Then, earlier in the evening, Merle had talked about taking Baz off for a weekend in Blackpool . . . and there you were! Dream interpretation, Lottie decided, was simply a matter of common sense. But she would be very careful, in future, to think calming and pleasant thoughts right up to the moment of falling asleep.

By the time she had reached this conclusion, she was fully dressed except for her shoes. Usually, she made her bed and tidied the room before leaving it, but decided that it would have to wait until she returned later today. Why not? Neither Mrs Shilling nor Louella ever climbed up the last flight of stairs to the attic bedrooms. And besides, if she lingered, she could miss her breakfast. Taking her shoes in one hand Lottie stole out of the room, closed the door quietly behind her and tiptoed down the stairs. How different I am from Merle, she thought rather smugly. The older girl had clattered down the stairs, never sparing a thought for others who might still be trying to sleep. But that was Merle all over. The older girl didn't mean to be selfish or thoughtless and if, later, Louella or Max reproached her for her noisy descent, she would be truly sorry. But it would not occur to her to go quietly unless someone specifically suggested it.

The girls had decided to spend the morning on

the beach. Lottie wondered whether Merle would make some excuse, but by half past ten the chilly wind had dropped and though Merle shivered and grumbled, she consented to share a changing tent with Lottie and the two of them put on their costumes.

Merle refused to go in further than her knees, then retreated up the beach when Lottie went in deeper. The water was not as cold as she had feared it might be, and when Merle came down to the edge of the waves to implore her to come out because she was growing bored and cold sitting alone on the sand, she refused to do so. Why should her pleasure be spoiled because Merle was a water funk?

Lottie swam, and then, to her delight, she saw a familiar figure coming jauntily across the sand. It was Jack, wearing the blue swimming costume which reached to his knees, with a gaily coloured towel draped round his neck. She splashed happily out of the sea and grabbed his arm. Jack gave a start of surprise, but Lottie was pretty sure that this was put on. 'Hello, enjoyin' a dip?' Jack said breezily. 'Thought I'd pop along and have a swim since the weather's turned out fine.' He unslung the towel from his neck and wrapped it swiftly round Lottie's shoulders. 'You're shivering, young lady.' He sat down on the sand and pulled her down beside him. Gazing out to sea, he said reflectively: 'I got the impression yesterday that there were a certain coolness between our Baz and young Merle. In fact, I thought he'd give up on her an' taken up wi' your delightful self, but it seems I was wrong.' He cocked an eyebrow at her, then began vigorously rubbing the towel across her back and shoulders. 'Was I right? About yesterday I mean.'

Lottie heaved a tremulous sigh, suddenly realising how nice it would be to confide in Jack. She had always liked him and trusted him, and now it occurred to her that he had probably come down to the beach actually wanting a word with her. 'Yes, you were right. Baz caught Merle kissing that feller, Jerry Green, that she's been going around with. He was really cross, and wouldn't listen to her explaining that Jerry was just a friend. But he didn't really take up with me, as you put it; in fact I suppose you could say he just used me to annoy Merle and keep her at arm's length.'

Jack pulled a face. 'It's mebbe not a nice way to behave but young fellers in love don't always act the way they should,' he said rather obscurely. He gave the towel a final rub. 'Are you warmer now? Feel like comin' in the sea again?'

'Yes, I'd love to swim a bit more, only I promised Louella I'd never go out of my depth when I was alone,' Lottie said at once. 'You are kind, Jack. I was feeling pretty miserable until you came along. You see, Baz and me were pretty good pals until Merle arrived, and then he went with her, and my friend Kenny has gone off girls altogether . . .'

'It happens, queen,' Jack said comfortably as

they began to wade into the sea. 'But don't you worry about it. If Kenny's the one I think he is he's too young for you, and Baz ain't your type, no matter what you may have thought. You're pretty as a picture, sweet as sugar candy, and bright as a button. If Baz prefers Merle it's because they're two of a kind, and you're in a different league.'

'I'm not, but I'm beginning to feel left out and lonely,' Lottie said dolefully. 'Even my pal Angela has left Yarmouth now, and Jerry – well, he really is Merle's friend, you know.'

'Oh aye. But there's a feller for you out there somewhere,' Jack assured her. 'And he's a corker, I bet. So let's make the most of today's swim – beat you to the end of the pier and back!'

Presently, feeling very much better for both the exercise and Jack's words, Lottie panted up the beach and joined Merle in the changing tent.

In the warm little space Lottie dried and changed, then plaited Merle's hair, knowing that she was making a poor job of it, but feeling there was little she could do to improve her work. Merle had no brush or comb with her so Lottie simply did the best she could. When she had finished she flicked the thick and heavy plait over Merle's shoulder, tidied her own hair with her hands, and followed Merle out of the tent, towels and swimsuits wrapped into a ball and pushed into the string bag in which she always carried her bathing things. They found Jack, who had set up an old ginger beer bottle as a target and was chucking

266

stones at it, awarding himself points for a direct hit. He got to his feet as the girls approached and Merle, good humour apparently restored, beamed at him. 'Well, I declare, the sea isn't so bad after all! Why don't you go down to the pleasure beach and have a go on the rides? Lottie and I want to take a look at the shops after some grub, and you'd find it boring, I dare say.'

Lottie felt her cheeks begin to burn; how could Merle be so rude to Jack? She said, stiffly, that she hated shopping, but Jack, it seemed, was equal to anything. 'You don't want to be saddled with an old feller like me, so if you want me to make meself scarce I'll leave the two of you to your lunch,' he said, and for the first time it struck Lottie that Jack was really not old. He might be about the same age as Louella, and her mother certainly did not consider herself as anything but young and beautiful. She opened her mouth to say something cutting to Merle, but Jack spoke once more. 'Tell you what, we'll have fish and chips at that place in Regent Road, then go our separate ways,' he said.

After the meal, Merle disappeared towards the shops, leaving Lottie – who had refused to accompany her – and Jack to amuse themselves until the show started. They decided to walk all the way along the prom until they reached the mouth of the Yare. There, they sat on a bench and Jack expanded on his earlier theme. 'I suspect you've been unhappy because you think Baz has treated you badly, which, o' course, hurts like hell. But, as I said earlier, one of these days you'll meet someone special, and you'll understand why young Baz – and Merle for that matter – have behaved so shabby towards you.'

Lottie sniffed dolefully and knuckled her eyes, for Jack's kind words had made her see what she had always known really: that she had lost Baz. 'How do you know, Jack?' she asked, as soon as her voice could be relied upon. 'Have you ever liked someone who pretended to like you back, only they didn't?'

'Yup!' Jack said briefly. 'You can't reach my age without fallin' in love at least a dozen times. But it's true what they say: time's a great healer. And now let's walk up to the harbour, see what vessels are in dock, and then I'll buy you tea at a posh hotel. Make you feel like you're a real lady!'

Chapter Ten

It was a rainy day, but the strong wind which had been blowing off the Mersey had dropped, so Lottie, setting out for the theatre – for there was an afternoon casting meeting today – had been able to erect her umbrella without fear of its blowing inside out. She trotted along the pavement, dodging the puddles and apologising every time she hit someone with her umbrella, for it actually belonged to Max and was a good deal larger than her own brolly. When she had gone to the stand in the hall, however, hers had been missing and she guessed that Merle had taken it, for her friend had left the house earlier that morning in order to go and see Baz at Lime Street station during his lunch break.

Despite Lottie's fears, the Laceys, Merle, Max and Jack had settled back happily into life at the Gaiety. Their summer replacements had left as soon as the Yarmouth group returned, and apart from anything else, rehearsals for the pantomime, which would start in early December, had meant that everyone was far too busy for any but fleeting regrets over their lost seaside paradise.

The weather, furthermore, had worsened as

October advanced. Strong winds tore the leaves from the trees, rain gusted sideways along the Scotland Road, and when Louella had said, with some satisfaction, that the thought of the east coast in such weather chilled her to the marrow of her bones, Lottie could only agree. Even in summer the draughts in the Wellington Pier theatre had been notorious and though, in Lottie's experience, the Gaiety would become pretty chilly as winter advanced, she was glad not to have to suffer the buffeting wind and the occasional soakings of sea spray which the Wellington Pier theatre staff had assured her were a regular feature of the place in winter.

Mrs Brocklehurst had cleaned No. 2 Victoria Court until it shone from attic to cellar, and to Lottie's astonishment and delight Kenny had told her, the very first time he set eyes on her, that he was downright glad to see her back. 'I missed you, honest to God I did,' he had said, and Lottie forgave him for sounding so surprised. 'I still muck around with me mates, of course, but most of us have got jobs of sorts, and fellers . . . oh, I dunno, but I've missed you anyhow.'

'I missed you as well,' Lottie had said, some-what untruthfully. They had been sitting on Mrs Brocklehurst's beautifully whitened steps, catching up on each other's news, and she beamed at her old friend, thinking back with pleasure to her lovely summer by the sea. 'But Yarmouth was marvellous, honestly it was. We're going back next year, at least I hope we are. But tell me about your new job, Kenny. Fancy you gettin' one, with the Depression an' all.'

'I'm what they calls a "gofer" at one of the warehouses down on Canning Place,' Kenny had said, his expression lightening a little. 'It's heavy work but I like it. The man I work for, Mr Ridley, is fair and don't give me more work than I can cope with. And the hours ain't too bad; I start at eight and finish at six, wi' half an hour off for me dinner. Sometimes, if the work's slow, Mr Ridley tells me to take an hour so's I can have a look at the shops an' that.'

'It sounds all right,' Lottie had said, trying to infuse her voice with enthusiasm. 'But what exactly does a gofer do?'

'Goes for anything his boss might need, I reckon,' Kenny had said. He warmed to his theme. 'See, the most important thing in the warehouse is gettin' the goods stacked so's you can find them again, and not leaving gaps, because, as Mr Ridley says, every gap is money lost.'

He had gone on to describe in great detail what he did, and Lottie had let her mind wander, though she kept her eyes fixed on Kenny's face, conjuring up such a convincing expression of admiring interest that her friend was completely fooled and continued to expound on the packing of a warehouse until Lottie had grown afraid that sleep would overcome her, and had made a hasty excuse that she had to help her mother prepare a meal.

271

'Hey! Watch what you're doing with that umbrella, young lady. You nearly took me eye out!'

Lottie turned quickly to apologise, almost removing someone else's eye as she did so, and sighed with relief when she recognised Jack. He grinned at her and ducked his head to join her under the umbrella. 'I thought it were you, my little mushroom,' he said cheerfully. He was wearing a flat cap, pulled well down over his eyes, and the yellow waterproof which he had bought in Yarmouth, as well as enormous wellington boots, and now he wagged an admonitory finger under Lottie's nose. 'And this, Miss Lacey, is my umbrella. I didn't fancy walking the streets under that frilly pink one your mam favours, so I resigned myself to a good soaking. And then what should I see, bobbing along the pavement ahead of me, but my brand new umbrella, with the little thief trotting along underneath it, collecting eyeballs as she went.'

'Oh, Jack, I'm so sorry; I thought it were Max's,' Lottie exclaimed, conscience-stricken. 'But I never saw a pink umbrella! Merle took mine – it's brown – so I'm afraid I just grabbed this one. But what was yours doing in our umbrella stand?'

'I lent it to Louella the day before yesterday, only she kept forgetting to bring it back, so since I was in the neighbourhood I dropped round to pick it up. But all I saw was that pink thing of your mam's, and I didn't fancy walking the streets of Liverpool looking like a perishin' rosebud. Mind

272

that puddle . . . too late. Now you're going to have to spend the afternoon with wet feet, and serve you right for thievin' my umbrella.'

Lottie was beginning to apologise all over again when a thought struck her. 'Oh, Jack, you're crazy you are! That pink umbrella is Louella's parasol; it's for keeping the sun off, not the rain. And that's why she doesn't keep it in the umbrella stand but hangs it on the coat hooks.'

Jack grinned. 'Well, I never did,' he commented, steering her down the side street and across the small cobbled yard at the back of the theatre. He opened the stage door and ushered Lottie inside, calling out to the doorman, who was brewing up on his small paraffin stove, that it was 'Only Jack and Lottie Lacey, come to the casting'.

He had closed the umbrella and shaken off most of the excess moisture in the yard and now he took off his waterproof and shook that too, sending droplets of water along the narrow corridor which led to the dressing rooms. He then removed his cap and kicked off his enormous wellingtons and, turning to Lottie, advised her to follow suit. 'You don't want them wet things in your dressing room,' he said. 'Give 'em to me and I'll hang them on the pegs in the boiler room. They'll dry off there in no time. Then best make your way straight to the stage because I reckon everyone else is there already.'

Lottie followed his advice, though she was nowhere near as wet as he, having had the benefit of the umbrella all the way from home. Then she headed for the stage, guessing from the sound of voices that Jack was right and most of the cast were already assembled. The Christmas panto-mime last year had been *Jack and the Beanstalk*. Louella was always principal boy, Jack took the role of the dame, and other members of the cast were fitted in around them, so to speak. Max, who insisted that he could not act, had been the back end of the cow in the previous year's production, and Lottie herself always waded in manfully to any part she was given. For the pantomime was fun, with every seat taken and the audience as eager to be pleased as the cast were to please them. It was fun to have a great many children there too, and Jack played up to them like anything, until the little ones were shouting all the right things at the right moments, and threatening to invade the stage if Louella was in danger.

So Lottie hastened towards the stage with some eagerness. She had heard rumours that the cast were to do *Cinderella* this year, and thought perhaps management would break with tradition and make her and Merle the Ugly Sisters . . . what a laugh that would be! She could imagine Merle's fury and chuckled to herself as she stepped on to the stage. For a moment no one noticed her for Louella was in full voice and obviously very angry about something. ' . . . not tall enough . . . an awful lot of lines to learn . . .' she shouted, 'break with tradition . . .'

Lottie glanced curiously from face to face. Her mother and Merle were both pink-cheeked and bright-eyed whilst management, in the shape of Mr Quentain, was looking extremely embarrassed. 'I only thought – I only thought it would ease the burden, be f-fairer all round,' he stammered. 'It – it just seemed . . .'

'It don't matter, Louella, honest it don't,' Merle said. She was smiling. 'I don't care what part I take, so long as there ain't too many lines to learn. But I fancy my legs is as good as yours any day of the week, even if they are a bit shorter.'

Louella laughed hysterically. 'A bit shorter? A bit shorter?' she said derisively. 'They're not only shorter, they're fa—'

Max cut across the impending insult, though he must have realised, as Lottie did, that Merle had guessed what was coming and was about to refute it angrily. 'Louella, my love, we aren't arguing about the length of your legs, or your ability to play the part; your legs are beautiful and you could play Prince Charming standing on your head. It's just that Mr Quentain thought you might like a change.'

Louella whirled on him; Lottie could almost see sparks coming from her mother's fine eyes. 'A change? Why in God's name should I want a change? We've only ever done *Cinderella* once before.' She turned on Mr Quentain. 'And as for my being Cinderella, can you see me brushing up the stage with a twig broom, hair in rats' tails,

275

ragged dress touching the floor? If, that is, you were envisaging me as Cinderella . . . or perhaps you had one of the Ugly Sisters in mind?'

'No, no,' Mr Quentain said hastily. 'But I'm sure you're right; I'm sure you'll make a perfect Prince Charming.' He glanced hopefully at Merle, whose face was still flushed. 'So that's settled then, to everyone's satisfaction. Louella will be Prince Charming, and Merle will take the part of Cinderella.' He looked around him, his expression so hunted that Lottie had hard work not to laugh. 'The rest of the casting . . . it's all suggestions, mind . . . is written out on this piece of paper. Perhaps you'd best pass it around amongst yourselves whilst I fetch the other copies of the book from the office. I've only brought the one with me.'

He put the sheet of paper down and turned to leave the stage, clearly so eager to be out of range of artistic temperaments that he was almost running. Merle was beginning to say that she did not wish to be Cinderella if it meant learning a great many lines and Louella, sensing victory, was adding to the general hubbub by exclaiming that she would need new doublet and hose this time round, because she had worn the same garments in every pantomime they had performed since the year dot. She hurried after Mr Quentain, jerking his arm and reminding him that had he really cast Merle as the prince, he would have been forced to hire – or even to buy – entirely new clothing for both Merle and herself. Mr Quentain made soothing noises but continued his retreat and Louella returned to the stage to try to get possession of the casting list, but Max, being the tallest and strongest, held it up out of everyone's reach and slowly read it aloud. 'Prince Charming and Cinderella have been sorted out,' he said tactfully. 'Don't worry, Merle: I'm sure you'll see when the book arrives that you don't have many lines, and they're all easy ones to remember.' He turned to Lottie. You're doing Buttons this year, my love; all right?'

Lottie nodded. 'So long as I don't have masses to learn,' she agreed. 'What are you, Max?'

Max grinned. 'I'm the tall, silent Ugly Sister, Lady Arabella Huffle-Duffle, and Jack is Lady Amelioration,' he said. 'That suits me and I know it'll suit Jack.' He frowned at the paper in his hand. 'The chorus are the people at the ball, and Mr Carstairs is the wicked baron, as usual, whilst his wife is the fairy godmother.' Max turned to Merle. 'You wouldn't know, love, but Mr Carstairs is an old actor who lives in a tiny flat above a fish shop. He's a real ham but you couldn't find a better wicked baron if you searched for a year. His wife's a pro too, and does an excellent fairy godmother.'

'He is good, especially if you can keep him off the booze,' Jack muttered. 'Not that he's ever appeared on stage more than slightly jolly; it's Sundays, after he's been paid, that he's liable to bend his elbow a little too freely.'

277

Max, who had obviously overheard the comment, frowned reprovingly before beginning to read the rest of the casting list. 'Well I never did! Jim Henty is the footman who brings round the glass slipper, the chimney sweep in the kitchen scene, and the driver of Cinderella's coach.' He grinned at Jim, who did a juggling act with his wife, Jess, as support. 'You're going to be very busy, and so is Jess: she's down here as the mayor's wife, the chatelaine of the castle and the servant who leads the ponies across the stage when the coach calls for Cinderella.'

'Ponies?' Merle said, pricking up her ears. 'Not real ones, surely?'

Lottie remembered vaguely having been in a pantomime which had included live animals on the stage, but could not remember which one. Before she could speak, Jack chimed in. 'Course they're live ponies; dead ones wouldn't be much use at pulling a carriage,' he said, grinning. 'They're them little Shetlands, usually dapple greys. We hires 'em from a circus complete with trappings.'

Merle turned astonished eyes to Lottie. 'Really? Or is it just Jack having me on?'

'No, he's serious,' Lottie said. Now that Jack had put it into words, she remembered that when she had been no more than seven or eight – too young for any major part in the pantomime – it had been she who was responsible for leading the ponies and their glittering coach across the stage, with Cinderella perched precariously upon the small seat, and Jack following behind, as Buttons on that occasion, with a large shovel and bucket to pick up anything the ponies might deposit. 'Why are you so interested, Merle? So far as I remember, the feller who brings the ponies takes them off as soon as they leave the stage and doesn't bring them back until the next performance. It may be because they're circus ponies, but they're not very friendly. Max always used to cut an apple into pieces and put the bits in my pocket so the ponies would follow me across the stage and out the other side, and I had to give them the apple pieces pretty sharpish or they'd try to take a chunk out of me. Isn't that so, Jack?'

Jack nodded. 'They're a rare nuisance, and not cheap either,' he agreed. 'Some companies do without 'em. They get someone in the wings with a couple of coconuts making trotting sounds, and then Cinderella comes across the stage, making admiring remarks about her glass coach, and Bob's your uncle! But of course the ponies is a great draw for the kids and word soon gets around. Believe it or not, there's more presents for the ponies left with the stage doorkeeper than there is for the cast. Sugar lumps, apples, carrots, even the odd handful of grass gets handed in, and after matinée performances half the audience goes roaring round the back, hoping to see the ponies, 'cos they don't go away when there's a second performance on the same day.' He looked keenly at Merle. 'Like riding, do you?'

Merle nodded vigorously. 'Yes, I do, though not on Shetland ponies.' She giggled. 'I reckon my legs would touch the ground for all dear Louella thinks they're so short.' She glared across at Louella, but Lottie was relieved to see that her mother, Max and the Hentys were in deep discussion, their heads bent over a copy of the script. 'When I were a kid I used to ride the liberty ponies . . . oh, not in the ring, though I did do a bit of that later, but just hackin' round the country lanes on days when there was no performance because the circus was setting up or taking down.'

'Gosh, I never knew you could ride. Aren't you clever, Merle?' Lottie said respectfully. 'I wish I could, but to tell you the truth, the Cinderella ponies rather put me off the whole idea.' She turned to smile teasingly at Jack. 'And you weren't too fond of them either, were you, Jack? Not when one of them bit you on the bum when you bent down to pick up a piece of apple I'd dropped.'

Jack laughed ruefully. 'Ponies is like babies in one way,' he said. 'With babies you've gorra keep shovellin' in food one end – and half the time they brings it up, along with their wind, when they're draped across your shoulder – and the other end messes its nappies. Ponies bite you with the front end, do rude things all over the stage with the back, and kick hell out of you if you're fool enough to get near their horrible little hooves. Oh aye, I'm no horse lover.'

'Well, this time it won't be me leading the ponies

on and off the stage, so maybe I'll manage to make friends with them,' Lottie said hopefully. 'I wanted to like them last time, honest to God I did, but I reckon they knew I was scared of them so they bullied me. This time will be different.'

Merle began to say that she would show Lottie how to deal with the ponies just as Mr Quentain came back on the stage and began handing out copies of the script to each member of the cast. Even the chorus had copies, for though none of them had what might be called a speaking part, they had to know when to exclaim and where in the programme their song and dance routines came.

It was still raining heavily when the cast left the theatre. As Lottie had guessed, Merle had taken her umbrella and was reluctant to share it. 'Someone nicked mine from our dressing room the last time it rained after a performance,' she said aggrievedly, 'and your umbrella's a stingy little thing with two of the spines broken, so there's barely room for me underneath it. You share with Louella.'

'But she's sharing with Max,' Lottie wailed. 'C'mon, Merle; it is my umbrella after all.'

They were still arguing over who should actually hold the umbrella when they reached the stage door. Jack, hovering there, grinned at them and flourished his big black brolly. 'Want me to walk you home, gals? I'll do the decent thing and take you to your very door, then go on me way, though of course if you'd like to invite me in for a cuppa . . .'

This suggestion was greeted eagerly by both girls, for it transpired that Merle wanted to 'nip along to Lime Street station for a word with Baz', and Lottie simply wanted to get home. So they parted company and Jack walked Lottie back to Victoria Court and was invited in for a cup of tea and a piece of Mrs Brocklehurst's fruitcake. Louella, setting tea and cake in front of Max, poured a mug for Jack and soon the four of them were discussing the script, though Max wagged a reproving finger at Jack. 'I know you'll keep ad-libbing, no matter what management says, but don't you dare drag me into it,' he warned. 'I'm a lousy actor, and though I do try to learn my lines your ad-libbing makes cues pretty pointless. If you tell me you want me to do some particular bit of business, like lifting my skirt so's the kids can see I'm wearing thick striped socks and football boots, then I can just about cope, but putting on a squeaky voice and saying a lot of foolishness isn't my long suit and you know it.' Jack laughed, but agreed that he would go steady with the ad-libbing.

Very soon, the cast began to assemble quite early in the mornings for panto rehearsals. Sometimes these went on all day, for management cancelled matinées in November and December. Despite Merle's fears, she soon became word perfect in her part, as was Lottie, and they were able to enjoy rehearsals.

The ponies did not arrive until the dress rehearsal, when Merle, Lottie and Jess Henty decided to ingratiate themselves with the fat little fellows by feeding them sugar lumps whenever their trainer was not looking, for he had made it plain, the first time they met, that they should not titbit his charges who were quite fat enough already. He was a taciturn individual, never speaking an unnecessary word to anyone, and Merle said wisely that he would be the reason that the ponies did not seem to like people much. 'They take after the fellow what trains 'em,' she said. 'But a sugar lump every time we see 'em will soon sweeten their natures, you'll see. They're bright little fellers and the kids'll love 'em.' Since both the little dapple greys had played their parts to perfection, tossing their heads and pulling the light little carriage from one side of the stage to the other without, as Jack said, leaving their calling cards, Lottie thought that Merle was probably right.

The dress rehearsal went extremely well. Lottie's costume as Buttons was a scarlet pageboy suit, with a matching pillbox hat perched on her head. Her neat and shining bob looked just right and she helped Merle to brush out her mass of light brown curls for the ballroom scene, telling her friend admiringly that she looked just grand and would get more cheers than any other member of the cast.

'Except for the ponies,' Merle said with a chuckle. 'One of the little buggers trod on me foot as they were being unbuckled from the glass coach and I swear it grinned at me. Still, Jack's right; word'll get around that we've got real ponies on stage and the kids'll pour in, hoping to see us cope with a pile of steaming dung if nothing else.'

'Thank God it's not elephants,' Lottie said devoutly. 'Now, tomorrow afternoon we do the special matinée with what they laughingly call a selected audience, which means everyone's relatives, landladies, pals and third cousins once removed, to say nothing of hangers-on, come along for free. It's fun and afterwards we all go to a café and management treat us to high tea.'

'Sounds good,' Merle acknowledged. 'I wonder if Baz will be able to make it?'

'Of course he'll be there,' Lottie said at once. 'Everyone wants to see a free show so he'll invite anyone at Lime Street who isn't working. I reckon there'll be engine drivers, signalmen, and all sorts in the audience tomorrow.'

As Christmas approached, enthusiasm for the pantomime increased. 'Jack is the ideal pantomime performer and grand to work with,' Max told the two girls as they left the theatre one frosty night to walk home to Victoria Court. Louella had caught a tram, but Max and the girls liked a breath of fresh air after the show, and so had chosen to walk. 'I was a bit doubtful about how I'd cope with actually having a part in the panto, even though I didn't have many lines, but I'm really enjoying it. And Jack's a big help with my quick change. Louella tries to give a hand but she's pretty busy turning from Prince Charming into my assistant and back again, so Jack's support has been invaluable.'

'He is a nice bloke,' Merle said dreamily. 'At first he used to annoy me, always making fun, but then I realised he wasn't just laughing at me but at everyone, and I stopped minding.'

'There's no malice in Jack. I grant you he's got a wicked sense of humour but he'd never say anything wounding or unpleasant,' Max agreed. 'I hope you realise, young Merle, how lucky we are to be working with a company who all like one another.'

'Yes I do,' Merle said at once. 'When I were working in Scarborough, there was a feud going on between the stage manager and one of the acts. Then two of the chorus simply loathed each other – they were both after the same feller – so if one were in the green room when the other came in, you could feel the atmosphere gettin' colder and colder. Yes, you're right, we are lucky. Ain't we, Lottie?'

Lottie had been gazing up at the dark arch of the sky above, admiring the twinkling stars and the thin sliver of moon, deep in her own thoughts. This evening Jess Henty had had a streaming cold and had been sent home by the stage manager before, as he said, she gave it to every other member of the cast.

'But who'll lead the podies into the wigs?' she had asked thickly, mopping her streaming eyes. 'I

285

suppose the traider could do it, but would he be willig?'

Lottie, standing nearby, had come forward. 'I'll do it,' she said. 'The ponies like me, and anyway they'll follow anyone to hell and back for a lump of sugar. Obviously I can't do the mayor's wife or the chatelaine of the castle because I'm on stage at the same time as them, but Sally is about the same size as Jess so she could wear her costumes and no one's going to notice if the chorus line has seven girls instead of eight.'

This had been agreed, so it was Buttons who had come forward, taken the pony's bridle, and led the small procession slowly across the stage. As they had reached the wings, she had turned the equipage around and gone halfway back across the stage so that Merle might climb into the glass coach in full view of the audience. Then she and her charges had left the stage once more and the tabs had come down for a scene change.

Backstage, she had helped the trainer to unhitch the coach and take off the ponies' fancy trappings, the plumed headdresses and the jingling bells, and as she worked something quite strange had happened. The warm stableyard smell had brought a picture flashing into her mind: the rounded rump of a horse, the big hooves shifting as she squeezed past to attach a hay net above the manger. Then the picture had flickered and died and she had been backstage once more, realising with a start of surprise that she had unbuckled the

286

bridles without even thinking about it; had done it, in fact, as though she had been doing it for years.

'Lottie? We are lucky, ain't we, to work with such a happy company?'

Lottie returned to earth with a jerk, and agreed with Merle as they turned into Victoria Court.

'What's up with you this evening, Lottie?' Merle asked curiously as the two of them were getting ready for bed. 'You've scarcely spoken a word since we got home.'

'Nothing's the matter,' Lottie said at once. She looked thoughtfully across at Merle. 'Only – only halfway through taking the fancy bridles off the ponies, I had a sort of feeling that I'd done it before.'

Merle shrugged and slid into bed, and Lottie quickly followed suit, for their attic room was icy cold and Louella had given each of them a hot water bottle, which they had pushed into their respective beds as soon as they had entered the room. Lottie let the bottle remain near her feet and felt the warmth begin to thaw out her frozen toes. Presently, she would bring the bottle up and cuddle it, and would very soon fall asleep. But Merle was talking. '. . . we've both watched Jess and miserable Mr Monkton harnessing and unharnessing the ponies dozens of times since the panto started,' she was saying. 'So it's not surprising you knew how to do it. It's a good thing, though, because I reckon Jess will be off until the end of the week. I jolly well hope she is, 'cos the last thing

I want is a horrible cold in the head. It's all right for Jess, she don't have to sing, but when I get a bad cold me voice turns into a croak.'

Lottie, already halfway to sleep, murmured drowsily that she supposed Merle was right. Then she began to feel beautifully warm. Memories of the ponies' soft muzzles twitching against her palm as she fed them sugar lumps mingled with the words she had spoken as Merle had climbed into the coach. 'So you're off to the ball, Cinders, leaving poor old Buttons behind. Well, I hope you have a wonderful evening. You'll be the belle of the ball . . . belle of the ball . . . belle of the ball . . .'

She slept.

In the dream she was walking along a woodland path, dappled by sunshine and shadow. She looked around her and knew that it was spring because the leaves on the trees were pale but bright and the grass which edged the path was beginning to show new growth. She continued to walk along and saw ahead of her that the trees thinned so that presently she would be in full sunshine. As always in the dream, she felt wonderfully peaceful and happy, though her senses were sharpened and she used all of them to try to discover where she was and what was happening. As she came out of the shelter of the trees, she felt the sunshine blissfully warm on her neck and shoulders, and saw that she was wearing a skimpy brown blouse and skirt. She listened. Birdsong fell on her ears like music and the chuckling of water told her that there was a stream nearby. She walked on and presently she was beside the river, looking down into its limpid brown depths. There was a good smell here, a smell of water and river weed, with a faint scent of flowers. She looked to her right, away from the river, and saw a bank studded with primroses and violets and felt triumphant; she had known it was spring and here was proof positive.

She went on walking and presently saw ahead of her that someone else was also on the path. It was a boy, and as soon as she set eyes on him she knew who it was: the boy with the golden eyes. He was leading an absolutely enormous horse, ebony in colour, and when he heard her coming up behind him he turned and smiled. 'Hi, Sassy,' he said, sounding pleased but not at all surprised. 'Did you get 'em?'

'Hi, Troy. Course I did,' Lottie said and realised, with some surprise, that she was carrying a string bag which contained a quantity of potatoes and also a good deal of earth. 'The farmer didn't charge me because I gave him a hand catching the pony. His wife wanted to go into town, so they'd got the trap ready but they couldn't catch the little devil.'

'Gran'll think you nicked 'em,' the boy called Troy said calmly. 'But if you tell her straight away what happened it'll be all right because, as she's always saying, she's brung you up to speak the truth. Are you going straight back to her, or will you come with me to set Champ out to graze while we have our dinners?'

'I'll come wi' you, Troy,' Lottie said joyfully. 'Now we're clear of the trees, grazing will be easy to find. And I'm going to pick Gran a bunch of flowers – she do so love to have flowers about her.'

As she spoke she saw, in her head, a neat little room, its windows curtained in scarlet and white gingham; saw also a small blue vase on a table which gleamed with polishing and a tall green water carrier embellished with paintings of roses and lilies. There was writing round the rim but before she had a chance to read what it said her attention returned to the pretty little vase which was empty now but would soon be full of primroses and violets, so that the faint sweet scent of them would fill the little room.

Right now, however, she, the boy and the horse abandoned the path and began to climb a grass-covered slope. Where it dipped into a tiny dell a stream bubbled and it was here that Troy unwound a long length of rope attached to a spike, the other end of which was fastened to Champ's rope halter. He stamped the spike into the ground with his heel and gave the horse an affectionate smack on the rump as it lowered its huge head and began to graze. 'No need for the tether really; there's enough grass in this hollow to last the old feller for days. But Gran's a stickler for playing fair,' he said. 'If the farmer happens by he'll likely not see him, tucked away in the hollow down here. But if he does spot the old boy, he'll see the tether and know that Champ won't go wandering off into some other field, where mebbe young corn is sprouting.' He turned away and began to climb out of the hollow once more, with Lottie close behind him. 'Race you back,' he shouted suddenly. 'I'll give you a start as far as the gate 'cos you can't expect a six-year-old to beat a feller of twelve.'

Lottie gave a shriek of excitement and set off at a fast run and then the scene blurred and grew small, and she awoke in her own bed to discover that at some stage of the night her lovely hot water bottle had slipped out of her arms and on to the floor. It was still pretty dark and she thought, crossly, that it must have been the noise of the stone bottle hitting the linoleum which had woken her. She reached out a hand and felt the bottle, but it was only lukewarm, so morning could not be far away. She still felt comfortable and knew that it was because she had been in the dream and had managed, without any conscious effort on her part, to learn the boy's name. Troy. It was a very unusual name, but then he was a very unusual boy.

She still had no idea why she dreamed the dreams and was puzzled by the clarity and reality of them. She had been certain at first that they must be the missing years which she could no longer remember, but that had been when she was just a child, and now she was not so sure. After all, Louella had denied all knowledge of a girl named Sassy, so Lottie had not even asked if she remembered a boy with golden eyes. But now that I've got a name for the boy, maybe it will ring a bell with Louella, Lottie told herself hopefully. Oh, I wish I could get back into the dream again! The sunshine was so warm, and the primroses and violets smelt so delicious.

She had half sat up in order to feel her hot water bottle, but now she cuddled down the bed again. I'll think about spring, and flowers, and a big horse called Champ, she thought drowsily, and I'll think about Troy and his gran, and the little, little room with the bright curtains and the gleaming wooden table. The room had smelt of beeswax polish and apples . . . she was drifting into sleep when she remembered that she had never actually been in that room, but had merely seen a picture of it in her head when she had told Troy she would pick a bunch of flowers for Gran. Aren't dreams the strangest things, she thought. Oh, Lord, I'll never get back to sleep if I can't get my feet to warm up; they're just like two blocks of ice. She curled up, wrapping her toes in the folds of her long winceyette nightdress, and presently slumber claimed her once more.

Lottie did not see Louella at breakfast, so she had to wait until they met at the theatre to ask the all-important question which had been on her mind all day. The three women were in their dressing room; Louella was making up her face whilst the other two scrambled into their costumes. Buttons was easy – all Lottie had to do was powder her nose and apply a very little makeup – but Merle had to have her long hair carefully combed into rats' tails, her hands and cheeks smeared with ash, and her bare feet dirtied. Not unnaturally, Merle moaned a great deal about her appearance in the first scene and was heartily glad when, as the pantomime progressed, she was able to dispense with the dirt, even though her clothing remained ragged. It was not until after the interval that her fairy godmother appeared, and she was able to don the magnificent silver and white ball dress, and to have Lottie brush out her mass of light brown curls.

But now, everyone was ready and waiting for their cue. Louella turned away from the mirror at last and Lottie took a deep breath. 'Louella, do you remember me asking you if you knew a girl called Sassy?'

Louella frowned, then removed a speck of powder from her enormous false eyelashes. 'No, I can't recall . . . was it someone you met in Yarmouth, darling?'

'Oh, Louella, I told you! It was in Rhyl, on that school trip. A boy with golden eyes called me Sassy, only I didn't learn his name. Well, to tell you the truth, he ran off before I could ask. But I saw him again in Yarmouth, and this time—'

'—you did ask,' Louella completed for her. 'So go on, what's his name, this boy with golden eyes?'

Lottie hesitated. Suddenly, Troy seemed an

extremely silly name, but having said so much she didn't mean to back down. 'He's called Troy,' she said defiantly. 'Do you know him, Louella?'

Louella shook her head. She was standing in front of the full-length mirror, as she did every night, whilst waiting to go on stage. Actually, her first appearance was as Mr Magic's assistant when they did their act in the kitchen of the wicked baron's castle, but fortunately both costumes were rather similar, so changing was not nearly as difficult for her as it was for Merle. 'Roy? Did you say Roy? I do seem to remember someone called Roy when we were working in Rhyl,' she said slowly.

'Not Roy,' Lottie said impatiently, hearing her own voice rise with annoyance. It was so typical of Louella to mishear what her daughter had said. 'I said Troy, T-R-O-Y. Do you know someone called Troy?'

'No, sorry,' Louella said. She bestowed her sweetest smile on her daughter, chucked her under the chin and headed for the door. 'I'm just going to help Max into his dress because "Beginners please" will be called in ten minutes and if I don't he'll arrive on stage with his wig askew and half his buttons undone.'

When she had gone, the two girls simply stood where they were and stared at one another. Then Merle gave a little crow of laughter. 'Your mam is incredible,' she said. 'Did she really think you said Roy? I heard you say Troy, and I wasn't really listening. Not that she was lying, because I'm sure she wasn't. Have you ever noticed that when your mam wants to tell a whopper her voice sounds quite different? It's – it's softer, and sweeter somehow.'

'No, I don't think I have,' Lottie said slowly. 'Or perhaps I have noticed – her voice changing, I mean – but didn't realise it was for what you might call a purpose.' She sighed. 'Sometimes I'm really stupid.'

Merle shook her head, then picked up the bass broom which leaned against the wall by the door, just as the prompt boy's voice came hollowly down the corridor, calling: 'Beginners please, five minutes.'

'No, you aren't stupid, it's just that your mam doesn't use that voice to you very often, if at all, but she uses it to me all the time. Whenever she says I've done well, or asks whether I've had a nice day out, her voice goes quite different.'

Lottie laughed; she couldn't help it. 'Next time she says something to you, I'll make a note,' she said, as Merle pushed the door open and hurried along the corridor towards the stage. Lottie turned back to check herself in the long mirror, thinking wistfully how nice it would have been had her mother recognised the name Troy and been able to fill her in on details, such as whether it was the boy's first or last name, and where she had known him. However, it was comforting to know that Louella had not lied to her, for Lottie trusted Merle, who was extremely shrewd over such matters.

And anyway, all was not lost; if she and Louella had worked both in Rhyl and in Yarmouth, then the chances were that others had done the same. Come to think of it, Jack Russell had mentioned the number of times he had worked on the Wellington Pier. Now that she had a name she could ask everyone whether they knew, or had come across, anyone called Troy. Satisfied, she picked up her own particular prop in Scene I – a tin of Brasso and a yellow duster – and made for the wings.

As December advanced, everyone settled happily into their pantomime routine. Merle and Lottie, as the youngest members of the cast, undertook to do the messages for anyone who needed help and this was often Mr and Mrs Carstairs, who hated the icy weather and grudged having to go shopping for food. They always tipped the girls for carrying heavy bags up the steep little staircase to their tiny two-roomed flat, which was useful with Christmas presents to buy.

Max had gathered the cast together ten days before Christmas, to remind them of the scheme which had been inaugurated some years previously to make Christmas buying less of a chore. 'Each of us buys one really nice present, to the value of a shilling; it's surprising what you can get for a bob if you put your mind to it. The men wrap theirs in blue paper and the girls, of course, wrap theirs in pink. Then all the presents are placed in the big beer barrel which is one of the props in the castle kitchen, and someone, me usually, hands them round on Christmas Eve. Now I say this every year, but I don't mind repeating myself in a good cause. Some folk fish out an unwanted gift from a couple of years back, rewrap it and put it in the barrel. This is a mean trick and frowned upon; understand?'

Several members of the chorus had giggled, but Merle had told Lottie she thought it was a really good idea and they had decided to shop together for all their presents the following day.

Lottie awoke next day telling herself that if it was raining, she would jolly well cuddle down under the covers and have a lie-in until the weather cleared, so she did not know whether to be glad or sorry when she saw that the day was cold but clear. Sunshine fell in a pale beam through a crack in the curtains and when she informed Merle, in ringing tones, that she had best get up for they had a deal of shopping to do, the older girl moaned but sat up, knuckling her eyes, and very soon the pair of them were clattering down the stairs and heading for the kitchen.

When they reached it, they found Louella making porridge whilst Max sat in front of the fire toasting slices of bread. Both adults looked up and greeted the girls cheerfully as they entered, and Lottie remembered that her mother and Max – and Baz as well – would also be doing their Christmas shopping today. Indeed, when Baz entered the kitchen five minutes later she half expected Merle to say that she would rather shop with him, but this did not prove to be the case. To be sure, Baz did suggest that he might accompany the girls, but Merle immediately vetoed the idea. 'Two's company, three's a crowd,' she said chirpily. 'Besides, it don't matter if Lottie sees what I'm buying because I don't plan to get hers today, but I do mean to get yours, Baz, so we'd best go our separate ways.'

'We could meet for a bite to eat at Lyons Corner House on Church Street,' Baz said hopefully.

Merle looked wistful but shook her head resolutely. 'No. We'll mebbe shop straight through and get ourselves a high tea later.'

'Well all right then, we'll meet for high tea,' Baz said. He was not used to being brushed aside by his Merle.

'No we shan't; I told you, we want to concentrate on shopping. I don't want to have to watch the clock, and nor does Lottie. Remember, Baz, we've only got this one day, whereas you can shop evenings, when we're on stage.'

The two girls were sitting at the table, eating buttered toast and drinking tea, and now Baz joined them. He sat down next to Merle and squeezed her hand. 'Awright, queen, if that's how you want it,' he said. 'My shopping won't take more'n an hour at most; us fellers is so much more organised than you females. I'd bet a pound to a penny that you'll traipse from shop to shop, picking things up and putting 'em down again, haggling with shopkeepers, changing your mind a dozen times and in the end going back to buy the very first thing you saw. Now us fellers know what we want, find who's selling it cheapest, buy it and go home again.'

Everyone laughed, but Merle said severely: 'How like a man! If you buy the cheapest thing on the shelves for me you'll get a Fry's chocolate bar and nothin' else in your perishin' stockin'.'

Lottie, who knew that Merle intended to buy Baz a pair of beautiful lined leather gloves, smiled to herself and presently, breakfast finished, she and Merle set off. They had decided to go round the big shops first, where they could earmark the things they would like to buy. Then they would go round the smaller shops and market stalls searching for the same goods at, hopefully, greatly reduced prices. Knowing Merle's intentions, Lottie found a grand pair of leather gloves for what she considered a very reasonable price in George Henry Lee's, and pointed them out to her friend, but Merle looked at the price label, whistled softly beneath her breath, and then said she would bear the gloves in mind but would buy nothing until they had examined the goods on display in Paddy's market. 'But this is for Baz. He's your feller,' Lottie pointed out, rather shocked, for she had not imagined that Merle would stint on a gift for her boyfriend. 'Still, maybe you're right. What are you getting your Uncle Max?'

'Coloured handkerchiefs, or mebbe just one coloured handkerchief,' Merle said. She slid a sideways glance at Lottie. 'To tell the truth, I've gorra be careful with me money because I've been thinking. I really must see my family for a couple of days before Christmas, and so what with the train fare and a few presents for my parents and little cousins, I'll need all the pennies I can save.'

The two girls had just entered Lewises, where Lottie intended to buy a tiny phial of her mother's favourite lily of the valley perfume, since Lewises was the only shop which stocked the make Louella liked. She had been wistfully examining the wonderful array of perfumes, soaps and scented talcum powder on display, but at Merle's words she turned startled eyes upon her friend. 'You're going home! It would mean you'd miss two or three performances just before Christmas. Oh, I know Betty would understudy for you, but it isn't the same.'

'I reckon you can do without me for a couple of days,' Merle said vaguely. 'Are you going to buy that perfume or aren't you?'

'All right, all right, I'll buy it,' Lottie said. 'But you'd better tell everyone you'll be away for a couple of days. You will be back in time for the party on Christmas Eve, won't you? Louella's already put her name down for a fine big bird, and a ham, and you wouldn't want to miss that.'

'That's right,' Merle said, as a shop assistant came bustling up. 'I'll be back before you've had time to miss me. I might even do it in a day if the trains run right.'

Lottie paid for the tiny parcel which the shop lady obligingly wrapped in silver and white paper, then the two of them turned away. 'Where shall we go next?'

Merle examined her list. 'I think we'll try Bon Marché next,' she said. 'Goodness, I've only bought two presents! We shall really have to get a move on.'

The girls managed to do all their shopping, separating for a short while in Bunney's in order to buy a present for each other, and then they made their way home.

That evening, Lottie gave Merle several openings in which she could have admitted that she intended to go back to her family for a couple of days before Christmas. Merle, however, failed to take her up on any of them. She was very quiet, replying in monosyllables when anyone spoke to her and telling Baz, quite snappishly, that if he asked any more prying questions about their shopping, he would be lucky even to receive that chocolate.

'Oh, Merle, you are in a bad mood,' Lottie said reproachfully. 'And you've not told anyone – except me – that you're going back to Blackpool to see your family.'

Baz, looking thunderstruck, exclaimed at this. 'You can't abandon me so near Christmas,' he said. 'It's all very well you making threats about chocolate bars, but two can play at that game. Tell you what, though: if you're set on going, why don't I come with you? I doubt it would cost me more than a few bob since I work for the railways, so if your mam and dad could let me lie on the floor in a blanket . . . ?'

'No they couldn't. There's scarcely room to swing a cat in the caravan. Even my going back will be awkward,' Merle said crossly, then she rounded angrily on Lottie. 'See what you've done? I haven't said anything 'cos I've not let me parents know what's happening yet, but you had to go and spill the beans, didn't you?'

Lottie was bewildered. 'You never said you wanted it kept secret. And anyway, what difference does it make?' she demanded. 'I dare say Baz would have suggested going with you whenever he found out that you were going away . . .'

'And that means missing a performance and alerting your understudy,' Louella said, her voice cold. 'Really, Merle, how can you be so thoughtless? And when, pray, do you intend to return to the fold? I'm sure Mr Quentain will be at least as interested as I am in your intentions.'

'Now, now, Louella, there's no need to be so sharp,' Max said. 'Merle has a perfect right to want to see her family at Christmas time. As for letting her understudy know, isn't that the whole point of having an understudy? If Merle was took ill on a Saturday lunchtime, her understudy wouldn't get much advance notice, would she?'

Louella sniffed. Lottie knew her mother hated it when Max took Merle's side, but for her part she realised he was right. Understudies were always anxious to step into their principal's shoes and Betty, a mere member of the chorus, would treat the news of Merle's absence with delight, not apprehension. But it was different for Baz. Ever since Merle's return from Yarmouth, he and she had just about been inseparable, and being calmly told that Merle would not be around must be hard indeed. What was worse, his suggestion that he might accompany her had been scorned. Yes, it was hard on Baz.

The whole family were sitting round the kitchen table with their food in front of them and Lottie looked covertly from face to face, realising as she did so that the usual comfortable friendly atmosphere which accompanied mealtimes had been completely dissipated by her revelation and Merle's response. Louella was upset because she felt Max had snubbed her, Max was cross because Louella had found fault with his niece, Baz was upset because his offer to accompany Merle had been rejected and Merle herself, frowning darkly, was cross with just about everyone. Lottie began to wish that she had not opened her big mouth, but told herself that if Merle had wanted the secret kept, she should have said so. And anyway, now that she considered the matter, Lottie realised that whenever the revelation had come it would have brought dissatisfaction in its wake.

Quietly, she began to eat her meal again and after a moment or two the others followed suit. Max, ever the peacemaker, began to talk of other things and suddenly Merle put down her knife and fork and reached across the table to take Baz's hand. 'I'm real sorry I was so horrid to you, chuck,' she said softly. 'You're the best pal I've ever had and it were mean to say there wouldn't be room for you. Tell you what: next time I go back I'll take you with me, I promise. I don't really want to leave the panto but me mother keeps askin' when I'll be comin' home. So you see . . .'

'Whyever didn't you tell us that at once, darling?' Louella said. 'I'm so sorry I reproached you; I simply didn't understand. But you are quite right, of course. Families are very important over Christmas and I'm sure your Uncle Max and myself are proud to think of you going to such trouble.'

Max, vastly relieved, leaned across and kissed her cheek. 'That's very generous of you, Lou,' he said, beaming. He got to his feet. 'Who wants apple pudding and custard?'

Chapter Eleven

In the end, Merle left them one day and returned on the next. Not knowing which train she would be catching, Lottie had been unable to meet her at the station but she went down to Lime Street on the off chance. Baz was delighted to see her, though he was not able to advise her from which train Merle would descend. 'It were nice of you to come along, queen,' he said. 'Tell you what, me dinner hour's due in twenty minutes. What say we slips out and goes along to the café further up the street? I'll mug you to a cup o' tea and one o' them giant sausage rolls, then we can have a bit of a chat. It seems ages since you and I had a chance to talk.'

Lottie said, rather tartly, that there had been plenty of chances only Baz had been too busy with other things – or people – to take advantage of them, but Baz only told her not to cry over spilt milk, which did not seem a particularly apt reply. Then he led her out of the station and they hurried along Lime Street, which was as busy as usual, and into the café of his choice.

As soon as they were comfortably settled, Baz began to question Lottie about her dreams, but on this occasion she decided not to satisfy his curiosity.

'I haven't had a dream for ages,' she said firmly, crossing her fingers beneath the table. 'I dare say they were all nonsense anyway. I mean, Louella had never heard of a boy called Troy, and . . .'

'What d'you mean, Troy?' Baz asked, his face alight with interest. 'D'you mean that boy you saw at the pleasure beach in Yarmouth? I knew he was the boy you'd met in your dreams, of course, but you never got near enough to ask him his name.' He leaned across the table and gave her a shake. 'You met him again, didn't you? C'mon, tell your Uncle Baz.'

Lottie was beginning to say, coldly, that she did not know what he was talking about and that he should jolly well mind his own business, when she suddenly gave a squeak and jumped to her feet. 'It's Merle! Her train must have come in a few minutes ago!' Baz, who had half risen to his feet, was looking round wildly, so Lottie pushed him down into his chair once more. 'I'll fetch her in here; no doubt she'll be glad of a cuppa and a bite to eat,' she flung over her shoulder as she made for the door. 'You sit tight or the waitress will think we're leaving without paying our bill.'

She hurried out of the café and along the pavement and soon caught up with her friend, who was hampered by her suitcase. Merle jumped when Lottie grabbed her arm but did not object when the younger girl seized her case and told her that she and Baz had a window table in the Black Cat café and had been looking out for her. 'How were your mam and dad and the cousins?' she asked, as they turned in to the café. 'I bet everyone were really thrilled to see you. Did you get some nice presents? I'm sure your suitcase is heavier than when you left.'

'Oh, presents . . . Christmas,' Merle said vaguely. 'I said I'd not open 'em until the twenty-fifth . . . yes, I had a grand time, ta.' She greeted Baz with a smile, but pushed him back into his seat when he tried to stand up. 'Have you ordered me a pot of tea, chuck? I'm gaspin' for a drink; I've been travellin' since the crack of dawn so's I'd be in time for the show. I take it everything went off OK?'

'Yes. And I ordered another pot of tea and a sausage roll, because I know you like 'em,' Baz said. As Merle sat down beside him, he leaned across and kissed her cheek. 'It's good to have you back, queen; we've missed you, haven't we, Lottie?'

The waitress arrived with the tea and sausage roll, and Merle began to pour herself a cup. 'It were nice of you to come an' meet me,' she said, addressing herself to Lottie. 'When I got off the train I looked everywhere for Baz, 'cos I knew if he were on duty he'd keep an eye open for me, but of course no luck. Then I saw young George and asked him where you were,' she continued, now addressing Baz. 'In fact I thought he were you for a moment; two young porters looking very much alike.' She gave Baz a cheeky grin, and Lottie realised it was the first time her friend had smiled since her arrival in the café. 'He said as how it were your dinner hour an' you'd gone off with a young lady. I were just about to call you a rotten flirt, to take up wi' someone else while me back were turned, when he said as how it were Lottie Lacey, so that were all right.'

Lottie and Baz both laughed. 'If you're going to make a habit of headin' for home every time we get a bit of holiday, then you'll find I will take up with someone else,' Baz said, mock-threateningly. 'I can't have me best girl leavin' me in the lurch all summer and then again at Christmas.'

'Oh, I doubt I'll do it again,' Merle said. 'As for next summer, who knows? When the panto finishes everyone has a fortnight's holiday and then things are pretty slow until Easter. At least, that's been my experience, and I reckon the Gaiety is no different from other theatres once the bad weather sets in.'

'You're right there,' Lottie said. 'But I'm sure management will want you once the winter holiday's over. Oh, Merle, don't go running out on us! I've missed you something rotten. Isn't it funny how things change? When you first came I didn't think I was going to like you much – you did snub me whenever you got the chance – but now you're me best friend and I'd hate it if you went away. Besides, "The Three Lacey Sisters" is ever so popular and everyone loves your modern dance routine.'

'Oh, Lottie love, you aren't the only one who likes things the way they are,' Merle said. 'By the way, how did my understudy do? She's nice is Betty but I don't believe she would even try to take my place as a Lacey sister if I quit the show.'

Lottie smiled reassuringly. 'No, of course she wouldn't; taking the part of Cinderella was just about all she could manage. Her actions were fine but her voice wasn't really strong enough to reach the folk in the gallery, so we'll all be glad to have you back.'

'That's nice,' Merle said. She finished off her sausage roll, dusted her hands, and reached for the teapot. 'Just one more cuppa and then we'd best be off. I want to get rid of my suitcase before we go to the theatre.'

'I wish I could walk you home and carry your case,' Baz said rather wistfully as the three of them stood on the pavement outside the entrance to the station. 'But I dare not be late. Can you make a note of the dates when you'll be takin' your winter holiday, queen? I'll try to get some time off during that fortnight; it should be easy enough because no one else on the station is going to want a holiday in the middle of winter.'

He had carried her suitcase and, when she reached for it, retained his grip. 'It's all right, love. I'll put it in the ticket office and bring it back with me when I come home after work.'

Merle, however, told him that this would not do at all. 'There's stuff in there I need now, before

309

the next performance,' she said firmly. 'I'll see you after the show, Baz, but thanks for the offer.'

Lottie thought that Baz meant to argue the toss, but at that moment a loud voice shouted: 'Porter! Come along, young O'Mara, let's be havin' you! There's work to be done,' and Baz sighed, squeezed Merle's hand, and disappeared into the busy station.

As Lottie had said it was good to have Merle back, for though Betty had done her best she was not a natural actress, which Merle had proved herself to be. So it was a relief to all concerned when Merle slipped back into the role. Lottie was pleased to notice that Louella, who had seemed unimpressed by Merle's performance, now said openly that Max's niece was a real trouper and one with whom she was happy to share centre stage.

Despite the fact that all the theatres in Liverpool were showing a pantomime, the Gaiety had full houses for every performance. Many members of the audience came back several times to see the show again. Lottie could not help wondering why and thought it might be due to the presence of the Shetland ponies, but Louella disabused her. 'It's Jack, not the ponies,' she assured her daughter. 'Haven't you noticed how he keeps changing his routines? It used to drive Max mad, but he's grown accustomed and now he even adds his own two penn'orth when he can think of something appropriate. Liverpool folk have always loved Jack, him being as much a Liverpudlian as they are themselves, so they'll come to see him again and again, and lucky for us that he's with the Gaiety and not at the Rotunda or the Royal Court.'

After that conversation, Lottie had kept an eye on the audience and often stood in the wings to listen to Jack and Max as they joked and fooled around. Jack was the nicer of the Ugly Sisters, who would have helped Cinderella if that had been possible; Max was merely very foolish indeed. Mr Carstairs, as the wicked baron, would come sneaking across the stage, intent on capturing Jack's hand puppet, a toy dog named Fluff, which Jack used as a foil in several of his routines. Jack would say innocently: 'Well, the wicked baron's gone off to Blackpool today, so Fluff and I needn't look out for him.' Then he'd sit down on a very low stool and begin to chat to the audience. Naturally, at this point, the wicked baron would come creeping across the stage in order to give the children the opportunity to shriek: 'He's behind you!' Whereupon Jack would activate Fluff who would leap up and down and bark, whilst Jack looked over the wrong shoulder, fell off the stool with wails of pain, or simply told the children they were all mad as hatters, since everyone knew the wicked baron was many miles away.

The last performance of the pantomime was on a Saturday, and was followed by a party on stage before the company went their separate ways for their fortnight's holiday. It was a grand occasion, with the band playing modern dance tunes and everyone talking at the tops of their voices. The ponies and their trainer had left after the last curtain call – and there had been many – but everyone else was present. There was a lot of kissing and cries of goodbye and plans to meet up, for though a good few of the artistes now lived locally most had family or friends in other parts of the country whom they would visit in the course of the next two weeks. Merle meant to visit her parents again, for the circus, too, was enjoying a rest from the constant touring which it undertook for most of the year. They were still in Blackpool, for that town was a popular resort even in midwinter, and the circus did not close.

'Why don't you take Baz with you?' Lottie asked idly. The management had just declared the buffet open – it was set out in the green room – and she and Merle, plates in hand, were circling the long table which positively groaned with food, helping themselves. 'He's got the time off, you know . . . oh, not the whole fortnight, but at least a week of it.'

Merle looked thoughtful. 'I suppose he might like to come with me, only it's such ages since I saw my family that I'd feel a bit mean bringing someone else along,' she said. 'Of course I want them to meet Baz sometime, but it's a bit soon, don't you think?'

'No I don't,' Lottie said bluntly. 'And what's more, it isn't ages since you saw your family. You visited them not long before Christmas, and that was only just over three weeks ago.'

Merle giggled and clapped a hand to her mouth. 'Yes, of course, but that was just a flying visit,' she said. 'Well, I'll think about it. I can't say fairer than that, can I?'

Baz, who had been working a late shift at the station, joined them at this point. He put a brotherly arm round Lottie, kissed Merle's cheek, and then began to pile a plate with goodies. 'What'll you think about?' he enquired. 'If you're doing any thinking, young lady, I want to hear about it. I say, wharra spread! Good thing you're off for the next fortnight 'cos if you two tried to get into your costumes tomorrer I reckon Buttons's buttons would be poppin' off right left and centre, and Cinderella would need more'n a wave from her fairy godmother's wand to get that there ball gown fastened at the back.'

The rest of the evening fairly sparkled with jollity and mirth. Jack Russell and Max, in their ordinary clothes, danced a languorous waltz together, making even the stagehands double up with laughter. And Louella, Merle and Lottie performed a version of their own act in which each girl only used one leg, causing almost as much hilarity as that which had greeted Jack and Max.

When they finally made their way to Victoria Court, they were worn out but extremely happy. Max had his arm round Louella, and Baz was cuddling Merle. This might have been awkward for Lottie save that Jack Russell, who lived further up the Scotland Road, walked back with them, telling Lottie how he meant to spend the next two weeks, and making her laugh so much that she got the hiccups and had to stop and hold her breath until they went away. This meant that she and Jack fell a good way behind the others, and presently Jack stopped teasing and asked Lottie seriously what she and her pal intended to do for the next two weeks. 'I expect your mam will go around with Max; they'll want to rehearse, of course, 'cos Louella's a perfectionist. So if you want a bit of advice, young lady, I'd say you could do worse than go off and visit friends or relatives for a week or so. At least that way you'll get some rest from the theatre.'

'I don't know what I'm going to do,' Lottie admitted. 'Merle's off to Blackpool to visit her parents. I think she'll probably ask Baz to go along with her, and since I don't mean to play gooseberry, I shan't be accompanying them.'

'What about relatives?' Jack said. He peered into her face, looking so anxious and so comical that Lottie had to smile. 'Everyone has relatives, chuck. Your dad was one of a large family, and then Louella must have relatives of her own – she didn't just appear on this earth fully fashioned, so to speak; she was born, like the rest of us. So she must have a mam or a dad lurkin' somewhere in her background. Don't she talk about them from time to time?'

Loyalty forced Lottie to say that indeed her mother did sometimes talk about her parents, though in fact she had only done so once. 'They were a Mr and Mrs Henning, only they're both dead,' she explained. 'They farmed on the Wirral somewhere, and when they died they left what little they possessed to Louella. I think she must have been an only child – well, I'm sure she was – so I've no uncles or aunts, not on Louella's side at any rate.'

'Well, wharrabout your dad's relatives?' Jack persisted. 'I know old Alf had brothers. Why don't you tell your mam you'd like to visit 'em? I shouldn't think she'd object; she might even go with you.'

Lottie stopped short and stared incredulously into Jack's face. She had thought for a moment that he must be joking, but now she saw he was serious for once. 'Jack, my dad died when I was a few days old, which means he's been dead for fifteen years and never, in all that time, has Louella tried to get in touch with his family. I suppose they may live in Cornwall or Scotland, or somewhere far away, or maybe they blame Louella for Alf's death, because it's not just one way, you know. We get a heap of Christmas cards every year, but they're always from theatre folk. To the best of my knowledge, we've never had so much as a line from the Denhams. When I was little – if you can call seven little – I asked Louella several times why my grandparents never sent me a card or a gift on my birthday or at Christmas. She said they had cast Alf off when he went on the stage and had no interest either in herself or in me. I thought that were pretty odd – everyone likes grandchildren – but Louella said they had plenty of grandchildren already and didn't need another.'

'I see,' Jack said thoughtfully. By now they had reached Victoria Court and Lottie expected him to leave her and continue on his way, but instead he caught hold of her arm, drawing her to a halt. 'Didn't you make pals when you were in Yarmouth?' he asked. 'Well, I know you did; you were always going around with that girl from the Britannia. And there were other folk, I'm sure. Wharrabout visitin' them, eh?'

Lottie thought of the tedious cross-country journey, and of Yarmouth out of season. The pleasure beach would be closed, the swing boats shrouded in canvas; the bright booths along Marine Parade would be barred and shuttered. From what local people had said, it would be freezing cold, with the wind coming straight from Siberia. And anyway, where would she stay? She did not have enough money for decent lodgings and now that she came to consider the matter, almost all the friends she had made had been theatre folk. Some of them, she knew, had hailed from Yarmouth, but most were from away.

She said as much to Jack, who pulled a rueful face but let go of her arm and pushed his cap to the back of his head. 'Aye, you're right,' he said.

'Well, if you're lonely and need a bit of company, you know where I live.'

He was turning away when Lottie called him back. 'Jack! I've just realised . . . you *knew* my father, didn't you? You called him Alf and know he had brothers . . . but *when* did you know him? Was it before I was born? I'd love to know a bit more about him, only asking Louella is a bit awkward. She's liable to burst into tears and rush out of the room, and of course if Max is there . . . well, I don't like to say too much. It seems tactless, somehow.'

Jack looked wary. 'Aye, I knew your dad. Alf was a real friend and one of the best, and I'd have talked to you about him before only I wasn't sure how much Louella wanted you to know. But you're fifteen now, a young lady, and if you don't care to ask your mam I reckon I could fill you in on a few details without upsetting either of you,' he said quietly. 'Tell you what, queen, if you come to Mrs Parrot's place around noon tomorrer, I'll take you out for a spot of lunch and we'll have a good old crack. Alf and me were about the same age, which means I'm old enough to be your father, so no one won't think it odd if we meet from time to time. Does tomorrer suit you, or have you other plans?'

'Tomorrow suits me just fine, Jack,' Lottie said recklessly. She knew her mother had planned to rehearse some changes in the Lacey Sisters' act, knowing that Merle would be off to Blackpool in two or three days. But Louella will just have to lump it, Lottie thought rebelliously as she waved Jack off and turned in to the court. It's about time I asserted myself. Louella's always telling me I'm a young woman; well, now she'll have to realise that I'm a young woman with a mind of my own.

She crossed the court rapidly and went into the kitchen. Everyone was sitting round the table drinking cocoa, though no one had helped themselves to the plate of shortbread biscuits, not even Baz, whom his father often accused of having hollow legs. Lottie, herself sated with party food, apologised to everyone for her lateness, explaining that she had been chatting to Jack. Then she made herself a mug of cocoa and sat down at the table, eyeing her mother challengingly as she did so. 'I shan't be rehearsing tomorrow, Louella,' she said briskly, taking a sip of her cocoa and then standing the mug down with a thump. 'I've some business to attend to, so I'll be out most of the day.'

She looked round the table. Louella was staring at her, her mouth at half cock. Max looked equally surprised, and Merle's expression was almost shocked. She would be thinking of her own imminent departure and wondering whether she would have to rehearse with Louella alone: a prospect which would not please her. Baz was the only one who was grinning, and when he caught her eye he gave a surreptitious thumbs-up sign. Louella, however, burst into speech. 'And what business might you have, pray, that is more important than my rehearsal? I had to book the stage, you know, because others will need to rehearse new routines as well. After six weeks of pantomime we're all a bit rusty and need to polish our acts.'

'Yes, queen, and don't forget I shall be leaving for Blackpool next Thursday or Friday,' Merle put in. 'I don't mean to rehearse more than a couple of times before I leave because I shall have an awful lot to do. Couldn't you put off your business, whatever it may be, until I'm gone?'

'Of course she can' and 'No I can't' came simultaneously from Louella and Lottie, Louella adding: 'Don't be difficult, darling; there was a good deal of competition for stage time. A lot of the cast will be leaving Liverpool on Monday, so you see ... '

'If the rest of the cast are going off, then you'll be able to book the stage for Monday or Tuesday with no bother,' Lottie said sweetly. She stood up and gave a large and rather artificial yawn. 'Golly, I'm tired. If you don't mind I'll be off to bed, because I'm having an early start in the morning.'

She left the room, ignoring the hubbub which broke out behind her, and took the stairs at a run, smiling to herself. She really had put the cat among the pigeons, but much she cared! And she had no intention of telling anyone, not even Merle, that the important business was merely having lunch with Jack, whilst he told her as much as he could remember about her father.

Jack reached Mrs Parrot's house and let himself into the kitchen through the back door. His landlady was a widow in her late sixties, but as spry as many a much younger woman. She had three lodgers, all men, and treated them like sons. She cooked their favourite meals, washed and darned their socks, listened to their stories and encouraged them to confide in her when they had troubles. Two of her lodgers were from the theatre, Jack of course hailing from the Gaiety, Derek Danby from the Royal Court, whilst Mr Gluhowski was a retired seaman who had chosen Liverpool as his home rather than returning to his native shore.

When Jack entered the room the other lodgers and Mrs Parrot were sitting round the table, enjoying the late night supper which their land-lady prepared and set out every day except Sunday, but Jack waved aside the offer of refresh-ment. 'I'm full to burstin', thank 'ee,' he informed the company. 'It were the last night party, you know, and the grub were grand. Management surpassed itself.' He pointed an accusing finger at Derek. 'You had a last night party too, I'll be bound, yet here you are feeding your face. Well, be warned: you'll look a lot more like Fatty Arbuckle than Errol Flynn by tomorrow morning.'

'Shan't,' Derek responded rather thickly through a mouthful of sandwich. 'Anyway, I'd rather be fat than a cradle snatcher.'

Jack grinned, and sat down on the only vacant chair. 'I guess you saw me with young Lottie,' he said genially. 'Poor kid, it don't seem to occur to the others that she's a bit left out like. Louella walks with Max, puttin' their heads together over the latest theatre gossip, Merle walks with Baz, billin' an' cooin' like a couple o' turtle doves, and Lottie trails after 'em, not likin' to join either pair. I saw them as I left the theatre so I hurried a bit to catch Lottie up and we had a grand old chat.'

'A likely story,' Derek jeered. 'You want to watch it, Jack. Older fellers what fall for pretty young girls are doomed to disappointment.'

Mr Gluhowski, tucking into a slice of rich fruitcake, swallowed, wiped his mouth, and then addressed the two younger men. 'Vot nonsense you do talk, Mr Derek,' he said. 'Ve all know that Mr Jack is true to the voman he has alvays loved and that is Miss Louella, and not her little daughter.'

Jack flushed darkly, considered denying it, then changed his mind. 'I admire Miss Louella greatly; she is a dedicated performer who puts her work before anything else,' he said stiffly. 'But as I'm sure you know, she's in love with Mr Max and never so much as glances in my direction.'

'But that doesn't stop you from being in love with her . . .' Derek began, then caught a glare from Mrs Parrot which made him break off. 'Sorry, Jack. I guess you aren't in love with either of them,' he muttered. 'Besides, it were old Gluepot who started talking about love, not meself.'

There was a moment's uncomfortable silence and then Mrs Parrot spoke. 'If you've all finished here, you can be off to your beds while I clear away and wash up,' she said briskly. 'Mr Jack, you were last in, so you can give me a hand.' She turned to her other two lodgers. 'Be off with you,' she said, though not unkindly. 'Tomorrow's Sunday so I'll be serving breakfast at half past nine instead of half seven; don't be late for it.'

As soon as the other two had left, Jack began to clear the table whilst his landlady poured hot water from the kettle into the tin washing-up bowl. 'Thanks, Mrs Parrot,' Jack said sincerely, taking the gingham tablecloth over to the back door and shaking the crumbs into the cobbled yard. He turned back into the room. 'I – I do admire Miss Lacey but she's as good as married to Mr Magic, so I don't have any sort of chance there. As for Miss Lottie, I'm not in me dotage yet. She's a nice little kid, but even at fifteen she's young for her age, and I believe she badly needs a friend. She didn't take to young Merle when the older girl first joined the company, but over the summer they grew real close. Only now of course Merle's got a regular boyfriend, and poor little Lottie is on the outside looking in. I used to know her father years ago, and she's desperate to learn a bit more about him herself. So she's comin' round here tomorrow mornin' and I promised her I'd tell her what I can over a spot o' lunch.' He looked anxiously into his landlady's small face. 'Did I do wrong to suggest it? Will folk talk?'

Mrs Parrot clattered the last of the plates on to the draining board, dried her hands on the roller towel which hung from the back door, and shook her head. 'No one won't say a word. They'll think you're an uncle taking his niece out on the spree,' she said at once. 'Mr Derek was trying to get a rise out of you and old Mr Gluhowski didn't think before he spoke. Why, I don't believe he's ever been in the theatre – except as a member of the audience – in his life, so where did he get the idea that you were in love with Miss Louella? I think he was just trying to put a spoke in Mr Derek's wheel, make him look a fool like.'

Jack grinned ruefully. 'Fact is, the old feller hit the nail on the head,' he admitted. 'Oh, I'm not in love with Louella in the way it sounds, but I do admire her. I've tried very hard never to let it show and I'm sure no one in the theatre has the foggiest idea, but it seems I've not been that successful. I wonder if anyone else suspects?'

Once more Mrs Parrot shook her head. 'Mr Jack, you're far too sensitive and it don't do,' she said. 'I've known you longer – a good deal longer – than either of me other lodgers, and I didn't have the faintest idea that you liked Miss Louella any more than you liked, say, Doris Lavery, what plays the piano, or that little chorus girl – Annie, wasn't it – the one you took to the fillums a couple of times.'

'Well, if you didn't guess, I reckon I'm safe enough,' Jack said, greatly relieved. 'I'd hate anyone at the Gaiety to know I had a soft spot for Louella, because I've always felt sorry for chaps sufferin' from . . . dammit, whatever is it called . . . oh aye, unrequited love. And anyway, I'm not, because I reckon I've got a crush on Louella, nothing more.'

'Well, there you are then,' Mrs Parrot said placidly, refilling the kettle. 'Glad we sorted that out 'cos I like me lodgers to feel comfortable with one another. Now, Mr Jack, do you fancy a hot water bottle? It's mortal cold out and I reckon the sheets will feel like ice when you first gerrin bed. I'm takin' one up myself.'

'If I were a real tough guy I'd refuse your kind offer and shiver half the night, but I ain't a tough guy, so thanks very much, Mrs P,' Jack said gratefully, and presently climbed the stairs to his room. Five minutes later he was in bed where he cuddled his hot water bottle and refused to let himself imagine that he was cuddling Louella Lacey.

Lottie turned up bright and early on Jack's doorstep next morning. The day was both cold and overcast, but within ten minutes of setting out Jack's jokes and good humour made it seem sunny and special. Since they could scarcely have lunch at ten in the morning, Jack suggested a ride on the overhead railway, followed by a brisk walk along Seaforth Sands to give them an appetite for their meal.

They carried out this plan and Lottie discovered all over again, as she had in Yarmouth, what a truly nice person Jack was. He went out of his way to put her at her ease, kept up a constant flow of small talk so that there were no awkward pauses, and made her talk about herself, her hopes and ambitions. She was shy of telling him much at first, but presently found herself chatting quite freely, and when they got on to the subject of her life before the accident she began to tell him about the dreams. Then, horrified, she pulled herself up short, saying lamely that she did not know what had come over her. 'They were only dreams after all,' she said feebly. 'They didn't mean anything. Besides, I've only had one since Yarmouth.'

'Odd though,' Jack said thoughtfully. 'But then so far you've only told me about the first dream you had. I take it there were more?'

'Ye-es, a couple more, but they were all nonsense,' Lottie said uneasily. What an idiot she had been! She and Baz had agreed that no one, save themselves, should be told about the dreams and here she was blabbing to Jack as though he could possibly be interested.

It seemed, however, that he was. 'Nine out of ten dreams are nonsense,' he agreed now. They were walking along the sands and had to keep their heads close for otherwise the strong wind blew their voices away. 'But I read a book once . . .'

Lottie jumped in immediately, seeing her chance to change the subject without hurting anyone's feelings. 'No, did you?' she said admiringly. 'You actually read a book . . . quite a scholar, aren't you?'

Jack laughed. 'You stole that joke from me,' he said accusingly. 'What I meant to say before you interrupted was that I read a book about ancient

Egypt, and in them days people used to have what they called "true dreams". They were usually dreams about what would happen in the future, mainly concerning pharaohs, battles and such, but the folk who had 'em were revered by others as soothsayers and one of 'em, a woman it were, insisted that in her "true dreams" she could smell and feel and taste, which you can't do ordinarily, when you are asleep. And when you were describing your dream you said you felt the wind on your cheek and felt the rubber teat of the bottle against your lips, and tasted the sweetness of the milk. I reckon what you had were a "true dream".'

Lottie struggled with herself for a moment. She both liked and trusted Jack, was sure he would never break a confidence, yet could not bring herself to talk any more about the dreams. She had asked him, weeks back, if he had ever met anyone named Troy, but he had thought long and hard and had finally shaken his head. He had not even asked why she wanted to know and she thought it would be best if she changed the subject now.

'I can't talk against this wind. Besides, isn't it time we turned back?' she shouted. 'Anyway, if you remember, it's you who's supposed to be telling me things, not vice versa.'

She half expected him to argue, but he simply nodded and turned round, pulling her with him. Back on the overhead railway they discussed the pantomime and next year's summer show in Yarmouth, but when they were ensconced in the canny house of his choice and had been served with a helping each of steak and kidney pie, mashed potatoes and cabbage, he took a deep breath and began.

'Your dad and meself met when we were both no more than seventeen or eighteen, and trying to make our way on the stage,' he said. 'He grew up on the Wirral but we were both determined to be in the theatre and we chose the Gaiety because it's smaller than the Royal Court or the Rotunda, and in them days management made their own stars, you could say. Well, what I mean is, the big names – Marie Lloyd, Harry Tate and Little Tich – went to the big places which could pay them big money, so Alf and meself thought we had a better chance at the Gaiety. To start with, Alf were props and I were lighting.' He smiled reminiscently, his gaze fixed dreamily on the middle distance. 'Only then a touring repertory company came to the Gaiety to do a couple of weeks whilst the permanent people had some time off. They needed what you might call dogsbodies, lads who would shift scenery, sit in the prompt box, sell tickets and do walk-on parts. The money weren't much to write home about, but me and Alf jumped at it. The rep company were pleased with us and took us with them when they left – for experience, you know. We had a grand time, too. Alf was always good fun and of course we saw a great deal of the country. By then Alf and I had considerable stage experience and could do all sorts. Then the Gaiety theatre needed a comedian and a magician, or a conjurer; the stage manager wasn't fussy so long as he had a full show.' He chuckled. 'Believe it or not, Alf and I tossed a coin to see which of us would start in trying his hand at magic; we both reckoned we knew enough jokes to get us through, but magic needed something more. As you know, Alf won the toss, but even if he hadn't I reckon he'd have ended up doing the magic bit because he had the steadiest hands of any man I knew, and he took to the magic business like a duck to water, same as I took to comedy in me own small way. Only at first he used one of the chorus as his assistant and she were useless. She were on the short side and clumsy! Many a time I've heard your dad threaten that if she made one more mistake he really would saw her in half, no kiddin'. And then one evening, after the show, this gorgeous young girl turned up. She were that lovely, I reckon every feller – or all them that weren't keen on other fellers – fell in love with her. Alf and meself were as bad as anyone, but Alf had one big advantage over the rest of us. He were dead good-looking, tall and slim but wi' broad shoulders, and he needed an assistant, for the last time he had bawled his girl out she'd left in floods of tears, vowin' never to return. So of course, he offered the job to your mam and she were ideal. Perfect, in fact. She had marvellous looks, oodles of charm, and – oh, I dunno, a sort of freshness which were very appealing. So appealing that within six weeks

Alf had asked her to marry him, and the rest is history.'

Lottie drew in a deep breath. 'And that beautiful young girl was my mother,' she said reverently. 'Gosh! She always says she was only seventeen when she had me, so that means you knew her when she was only a year older than I am now. Did she call me Lottie right from the start? I know I were christened Charlotte Sarah but I expect Lottie went better with Lacey; I mean, Charlotte Lacey is a bit of a mouthful, isn't it?'

'I reckon you're right,' Jack said, rather doubtfully, after a short pause. 'Only I disremember Louella usin' your name much. She called you baby, sweetheart, little darlin', stuff like that. It must have been when she decided to take you into the act that she thought Lottie went better with Lacey. Yes, that'll be it.'

'I see,' Lottie said, nodding her head. 'But Jack, you've said you were fond of her, so why didn't you ask her to marry you after Alf was killed?'

Jack had been staring into the distance, but now he rubbed his nose thoughtfully, then ran a hand through his crisp grizzled hair. 'After your dad died, you and your mam simply disappeared,' he said slowly. 'She had left the theatre of course whilst she gave birth, and I always reckoned she couldn't abide the thought of returning to the place where she and Alf had met and fallen in love. I wasn't the only one who tried to trace her, but none of us had any luck. I'm telling you, when she turned up at the Gaiety one sunny morning in June, six years after she had left, to say that she had her own act and wanted Mr Quentain to give her work, you could have knocked me down with a feather. She was still pretty as a picture and she recognised me at once and was pleased as Punch to hear that I was now the company comedian and comfortably settled in Liverpool.

'She was working in Rhyl for a magician, but she said he wasn't a bit like Alf; he was a bully and she hated him, and she was afraid for her little girl – that was you, Lottie – so she planned to escape from him by getting another theatre to take on her act. She knew the magician would be mad if he found out, and might attack you as well as herself. She had worked out a song and dance routine with you, and hoped someone at the Gaiety would remember her and give her work, which is what happened, of course.

'And there was Max, tall and handsome and remarkably like Alf, needing an assistant. He said he would give her a trial and Mr Quentain said kids were always a big draw, so even if Max didn't take her on, he definitely would. Of course she had to work out her time with the feller in Rhyl, so she planned to come to us in October, when the holiday season were over.'

'Thanks Jack; I feel a lot happier now I know a bit more,' Lottie said gratefully as Jack finished his tale. 'But why did Louella stay in Rhyl for another four months if she hated the magician so much?'

'Because she had signed a contract with the Pavilion,' Jack explained. 'She needed the money since in those days you were only a kid and she had to pay someone to look after you when she was on stage late.' He grinned at her, then beckoned to the waitress. 'What say we round off our meal with a helping of apple pie and custard? Or you could have a slice of Bakewell tart.'

Lottie walked thoughtfully back to Victoria Court very much later in the afternoon, thinking over what she had been told. Jack had taken her to the Walker Art Gallery, saying that it was always comfortably warm inside since great paintings had to be kept at an even temperature, but they had not discussed the past again, and when they parted at the entrance to the court Lottie had thanked him for a lovely day and had gone indoors determined to say nothing. She could not imagine why her mother had been so secretive about her own early life in the theatre, then concluded that Louella was not one to dwell on the past, particularly if it was sad. However, she deemed it wisest not to admit that Jack had been telling her how he and her father had met. If anyone asked, she would simply say someone had asked her out for a meal and then they had spent the afternoon at the gallery. She did not think her mother would be sufficiently interested to cross-question her, and Merle would only be curious if she suspected Lottie of having a young man.

Letting herself in through the front door and

heading for the kitchen, Lottie smiled to herself. Merle was always nagging at her to get herself a boyfriend, so that they could go around in a four-some. If she knew Lottie's mysterious friend was Jack Russell, she'd likely die laughing; but at least it might stop her nagging.

The family were in the kitchen, Merle laying the table, Max slicing bread and Baz buttering it, whilst Louella was rather inexpertly carving a cold leg of mutton. Lottie guessed that they had had it roast at dinnertime, but thought her own meal to have been infinitely superior: she was not a lover of mutton. Everyone looked up as she came in and Lottie braced herself for questions or reproaches, but Louella had clearly forgotten her grievance of last night. 'Hello, darling,' she said cheerfully. 'Did you have a nice day? I've booked the stage for tomorrow afternoon and Tuesday morning, so we can all have a lie-in, and Merle's bought her return ticket to Blackpool, so she can leave on Wednesday or Thursday, whichever suits her best.'

'Wharrabout me?' Baz said, but he was smiling. 'I'd rather she went Wednesday, 'cos I'm off for the whole of that week, Wednesday to Wednesday. I've not had time to buy myself a return ticket but I'll do it as soon as Merle makes up her mind when she's leaving. And then I'm hoping I'll pay a good deal less than a normal passenger. Gee, I'm looking forward to visitin' a circus as one o' the family, you might say. Merle reckons they'll show me all sorts, even let me ride one of the liberty horses, only she'll have to have me on a lead rein, 'cos they're valuable, them animals.'

'You can't ride,' Lottie pointed out practically, fetching the plates from the Welsh dresser so that Louella could carve a helping straight on to each one. 'Still, I'm glad you're going, Baz, even if it does leave me in the lurch.'

Max looked up, having cut the entire loaf into beautifully even slices. 'There won't be much point in you and Lou rehearsing once Merle goes,' he said. 'So you'll have some time to yourself for once, queen. Do you good.'

Lottie agreed that this was so, but when the meal was over and she and Merle were getting ready for bed in their own room, she told Merle she would miss her horribly and had no idea how she would spend the next couple of weeks.

'You could go out with your new feller,' Merle said slyly, and then burst out laughing at Lottie's hunted look. 'It's all right, queen, I know it were only Jack Russell. Baz and meself went out for a bit of jolly – that's to say we took two seats on the overhead railway – and as we were climbin' aboard we saw you and Jack gettin' off. I waved like fun but the pair of you had your heads together and were chattering away, so you never saw me. Were you with him all day, or did you meet someone else later?'

Merle was already in her nightdress, sitting up in bed and staring interestedly across at her young friend. Beside her their bedtime candle burned in its holder, and Lottie realised that Merle was in the mood for a chat. Hastily she donned her own nightie and climbed into bed. 'I were with Jack all day,' she said. 'He told me quite a lot about my dad – Louella never mentions him, you know – and quite a lot about Louella, too. Did you know the three of them met for the first time right here, in the Gaiety? She was awfully young and pretty, Jack said; well, she was only seventeen when I was born. I reckon, from what he told me, Jack had hopes in that direction himself, but Alf was a magician, and he needed an assistant who would look good in tights and sequined bust bodices. He employed Louella and then asked her to marry him, so I suppose Jack had to look elsewhere. I felt really sorry for him, but you know how he is: he made a joke of it.'

Merle's head bobbed in assent and her shadow, huge and flickering in the candlelight, nodded too. 'Yes, Jack don't wear his heart on his sleeve,' she observed. 'What else did he tell you?'

Lottie related the story so far as she knew it herself and added Jack's theory that after Alf's death Louella had been unable to face returning to a place where she had once been so idyllically happy.

Merle nodded wisely. 'Yes, of course. It weren't just that everyone in the theatre had known her and Alf as a couple, it would be the theatre itself. Oh, your poor mam! She must have been dreadfully unhappy, but at least she had you.' She gave

334

Lottie a quick, almost furtive glance which, in the flickering candlelight, was difficult to interpret. 'Though for meself, I'd say a baby weren't so much company as an extra responsibility.'

'You're right there. I'd rather have a puppy any day,' Lottie agreed. She leaned over and snuffed the candle wick between a wetted thumb and fore-finger. 'Night-night, Merle, sleep tight.'

Chapter Twelve

Lottie had expected to miss Baz and Merle horribly, but instead she found herself almost enjoying her independence. There were a number of things she had always meant to do, but had somehow never got round to, and she found that though she missed Merle there was a good deal of satisfaction to be gained from doing what she wanted, when she wanted, without having to consult anyone else. Furthermore, fond though she was of Merle, it had to be admitted that her friend was almost always late for whatever outing they planned. Merle's appearance was important to her and she could – and did – spend ages in front of the mirror, combing her hair into different styles, trying on different combinations of clothing, or even running through her entire stock of shoes before choosing which pair to wear. So, though Lottie told herself, rather guiltily, that it would have been fun to go around with Merle, she knew she would not have had time to do all the things she wanted to do.

On the first day of Merle's absence, Lottie caught the ferry to New Brighton, and though the funfair was closed and the amusements shuttered she enjoyed exploring the town, having a fish and chip dinner at a café on the promenade, and then wandering for miles along the hard, wet sand. Mindful of what Jack had told her about the Denham family, she then spent three or four days exploring the Wirral by bus, intrigued by the pretty villages and the gently rolling countryside. She went to the city of Chester twice and, greatly daring, introduced herself to a young lady on the haberdashery counter in Brown's whom she had heard another shop assistant call Miss Denham.

Lottie hung around by the haberdashery counter until the young woman was free, when she went shyly forward, asked to see some lengths of scarlet ribbon and finally plucked up her courage to put the only question which seemed appropriate. 'My name is Lottie Denham. My father was Alf Denham, but he was killed when I was only a baby, so I never knew him. I know he came from the Wirral . . . I wonder whether you and I might be related?'

The young woman looked pleased. 'I don't remember anyone ever mentioning an Alf Denham,' she said. 'But of course if he died when you were born I'd only have been a kid myself at the time and probably wouldn't remember. I've heaps of relatives, mostly cousins, and of course not all of them are Denhams since my grandparents had seven daughters and only two sons. What did your father do? Most of our family farmed.'

'Alf joined the theatre as a magician . . .' Lottie was beginning when a tall stout woman, with upswept grey hair and a large, curved nose, interrupted.

'Miss Denham, if your customer does not care for any of those ribbons, perhaps you might attend to somebody else; we do have other customers, you know.'

The girl murmured an apology, her cheeks scarlet, but managed to mutter to Lottie as she began to replace the ribbons in their drawer beneath the counter that she would be taking her lunch break in thirty minutes and would go to the Kardomah café and await Lottie there.

Lottie went, full of delighted anticipation, but when the two girls parted she was no wiser. Miss Denham admitted she had never heard of Alf, and frankly doubted whether any member of her family could possibly have become a magician. 'It sounds great fun and the sort of thing that would have been talked about, but to own the truth, Miss Denham, my relatives are a very ordinary lot. Still, if you'll give me your address, I'll drop you a line if I find out anything.'

Lottie was disappointed but told her that she herself was on the stage and had taken the name Lottie Lacey. 'It would be nice to keep in touch, for I'm sure we must be related, even if we're only second or third cousins,' she said. 'Do you ever visit Liverpool? If so, come along to the Gaiety theatre – to the stage door, I mean – and ask to see me and I'll get you complimentary tickets for the show.'

The two girls parted and Lottie thought rather sadly that nice though Miss Denham had been, she doubted whether she would keep in touch. From the other girl's conversation, it was clear that the Denhams were an enormous family, scattered all over the world, and fond of one another's company. There was always something happening – a wedding, a christening or a funeral – and visits between different branches of the family were commonplace. With so many cousins, aunts and uncles, she thought it doubtful that her new friend would be particularly interested in acquiring another relative, but comforted herself with the thought that at least she had done her best. Unfortunately, she had not asked Miss Denham for her Christian name, nor for her address, so the first move would have to come from her.

Lottie had visited Chester on the day that Merle and Baz returned from Blackpool, which was a bit of luck because normally Louella asked her about her day and Lottie did not wish her mother to know that she had been trying to trace her father's family. However, Baz and Merle swept in just as the evening meal was being served, Baz in particular full of the events of the past week. 'I've never thought much of the stage, as you know,' he said, reaching for the bread and butter, eyes sparkling. 'But a circus! There's a hundred different jobs you can do, mostly looking after the animals, which means you'd be working out of doors. I only decided on the railways because it meant I wouldn't be shut up in an office or a shop or a factory, but so far I've been stuck in Lime Street station, which is just like a huge factory really. Every time a job comes up in a country station, I think about putting in for it, only mostly they're miles away, which would mean livin' in lodgings, and that would cut down on me savings as well as meaning I couldn't see my Merle every day.'

'Thank you, kind sir,' Merle said, dimpling at him. 'But if you worked with the circus, you wouldn't be able to see me every day either, because I've no intention of going back to that sort of life. I know circus folk mostly go into digs during the winter and stay in one spot if they possibly can, but for the rest of the year they're on the road, living in caravans, performing in a different village every two or three days; then at night they pull down and travel on to the next field, or village green, or whatever.' She shuddered expressively. 'And you hardly ever see a decent shop and most of the food is fried, which is murder for me waistline . . .'

Max laughed. 'We all eat too much in the winter; it's something to do with stoking up so that we can withstand the cold,' he said, then turned to his son. 'What exactly were you thinking of doing in the circus? As you know, both myself and Louella worked in circuses at one time, and very happy we were. But there's no denying that you get better paid and have an easier life in the theatre, as well as being able to live in your own home. Oh, I know we go into digs during the summer season, but at the back of your mind there's the comfortable knowledge that you do have a place of your own waiting for you.'

Louella smiled at Max across the table. 'Pass me the salt, chuck,' she said. 'I don't want to spoil your fun, dears, but now Merle's back I think we ought to have one proper rehearsal before the theatre opens to the public on Monday. Does Friday suit everyone? We can start the rehearsal at nine in the morning and be through by lunchtime.'

Merle looked sulky. 'But management have called a full dress rehearsal on Saturday, for every member of the cast and all the backroom people,' she pointed out. 'Surely that will be rehearsal enough? Baz and I have had a pretty hectic week; I wouldn't mind a couple of quiet days before Saturday.' She turned appealing eyes on Lottie. 'Don't you agree, queen? I'm sure you must know all the new numbers by heart, same as I do.'

Lottie did agree but knew it would be pointless to say so. When Louella tightened her lips like that, it meant she had already made up her mind. Still, there was no harm in trying. 'It does seem a bit much, Louella,' she said mildly. 'After all, management give us these two weeks so we can have a winter break.'

Louella snorted. 'What's wrong with honing our

act to perfection?' she asked, then leaned over and slapped Max's hand chidingly when he laughed. 'It's all very well for you, Max, most of your act is silent, but we have six new songs to do as well as a variety of dance steps.' She turned her most ingratiating smile upon Merle. 'Tell you what, poppet, suppose we start at nine, and work until half past ten; would that suit you?'

Mollified, Merle said that that would be fine and Lottie could not help chuckling to herself. How cunning Louella was! She must have booked the stage already, had probably fully intended to rehearse for only an hour and a half, but because she must have guessed that the girls would object she had suggested a full morning's work and had pretended to allow herself to be persuaded into the shorter session.

And on Friday, when the rehearsal was over and she and Merle had cleaned off their makeup and changed into street clothes, Lottie admitted to her friend that Louella had been right. They had not forgotten any of the songs, or the dances, but their timing was not what it had been. At the beginning of the rehearsal the act had been ragged, but after an hour and a half of concentrated effort it was running as smoothly as a well-wound watch, and all three of them felt better knowing they would have nothing to be ashamed of at the dress rehearsal next day. Even more satisfying was the fact that others had booked the stage to rehearse after the Lacey

Sisters, and had applauded spontaneously as the girls left the stage.

Back in their dressing room, Louella positively glowed. 'You've both done jolly well,' she told them. 'Max and I have a new angle, a really clever one, which you'll see on Monday, but other than that our act scarcely changes at all. Oh, Max produces pigeons from his top hat one day and rabbits the next, but it's all sleight of hand and doesn't need anything but practice. Now off with you. Enjoy your last day of freedom!'

As January slid into February the weather worsened and full houses became a thing of the past. Lottie noticed that Merle was quieter than usual, and not such good company. She had taken to going off by herself for hours at a time and once Lottie, going up to her room to fetch a jumper for it was cold in the kitchen, had found Merle lying on her bed, clutching her pillow and weeping. She had immediately dropped to her knees and enveloped her friend in a warm embrace. 'Whatever is the matter, chuck?' she had asked gently. 'Don't say Louella's been getting at you again! I thought that was all over weeks and weeks ago. You've not split up with Baz, have you?'

Merle had sat up and reached for her handkerchief. She had mopped her reddened eyes and blown her nose before giving a rather watery smile. 'Can't a girl have a good cry without you thinkin' the worst?' she had enquired, jerking a

343

thumb at the book lying open on the floor by the bed. 'I've been reading *Uncle Tom's Cabin* . . . oh, it's so sad, Lottie.'

Lottie, who knew the value of a good cry over a book, had accepted the explanation and thought no more of it, and when, a few days later, management cut the matinées saying it was not worth heating the theatre for such small audiences, she and Merle had been quite glad of the extra time off, though Merle pulled a face when she realised she had to take a cut in salary as well. Now that Lottie was heading for sixteen years of age, her salary was paid direct to her, although both she and Merle handed over a good deal of their money to Louella for their keep, which was only fair.

'The weather will get better – and houses too – once Easter arrives,' Louella assured anyone who would listen. 'Yes, we'll all be raking in our full salaries then.'

Although the winter had been cold and very wet, they had only had a few days of snow, and now that it was a little warmer great banks of fog came rolling in from the Mersey, so half the cast were coughing and no one much liked going home alone after the performance. Consequently, they usually gathered in the green room to drink a sustaining cup of cocoa after the show and to arrange their walk home in groups, rather than ones or twos. Merle had thought this precaution unnecessary but Lottie reminded her that Liverpool was a busy port.

'Folk have been known to walk into the Mersey and drown,' she told her friend. 'And then there's sailors who come ashore and have too much to drink. They're on the lookout for bad girls – you know, prossies – and when they're fuddled with the drink they can't always tell good girls from bad 'uns. When the weather's fine and clear you can see them coming and take a different route, but when the fog's really thick you could walk slap into a group of them and before you know it you're in trouble.'

The reason Merle objected, of course, was because she liked to walk down to the station and then come home with Baz, but once the dangers had been explained she saw the sense of leaving the theatre together with other players, though she and Lottie, and occasionally Max and Louella too, often hung around outside the theatre until Baz came up, whistling and self-confident, when his shift ended.

A poor week was followed by a wretched Saturday. The audience was so sparse that Jack descended to the footlights and invited everyone to come into the first couple of rows, and this improved matters a little. But then George, who dressed as a cowboy and sang of the Wild West, tripped and fell as he strode on to the stage, landing heavily on his ukulele and crushing it beyond repair.

As if that was not enough, Merle turned right in their first number when she should have turned

345

left, bumped into Lottie, and the pair of them got the giggles so badly that they infected the chorus, who could hardly dance for laughing.

Louella was angry and berated Merle, calling her unprofessional and childish, and Merle, sobering up and promising to be good, then made a mess of her rendition of the Charleston, though Lottie didn't think the audience noticed. Louella, however, commented bitterly that she was surrounded by silly little girls who cared nothing for the Laceys' reputation, and was still smouldering when the tabs were lowered for the last time and the rest of the cast headed for the green room.

Lottie and Merle, about to follow suit, were prevented from doing so by Louella, who said ominously that they were to remain on stage since she wanted a word with them. She then swept off, her brow furrowed, leaving the two girls still in the costumes they had worn for the curtain call, glancing apprehensively at one another.

'Your mam's in a real foul mood tonight,' Merle observed. 'She can't believe I turned in the wrong direction on purpose, surely?' She hugged herself, for the stage was extremely draughty and the fog, which was a real pea-souper, had managed to penetrate right inside the building so that everyone, though putting a brave face on it, must have longed for the show to end. 'What say we go back to the dressin' room and change into our street clothes? I wouldn't mind puttin' me coat on an' all. If she's givin' the chorus a wiggin' she'll be gone for at least another ten minutes.'

Lottie considered. 'Tell you what, I'll go and fetch our stuff and bring it back here,' she said. 'We can slip our coats on and then take them off again if she wants us to show her how we came to collide earlier. You stay here, because you know what Louella's like: she'll want to give you lots of advice and if she has to hang about on the empty stage she'll be so mad she'll make our lives a misery for weeks.'

Merle agreed to this and presently Lottie returned, clutching their street clothes, which she dumped on the edge of the stage. Merle came towards her and Lottie noticed that not only was the older girl shivering, but she looked extremely pale – not well at all, in fact. 'Are you feeling all right, Merle?' she asked anxiously. 'I think perhaps we ought to get changed and start for home. It's a horrible night and if you go down with this flu that someone said was going about, then we really shall be in a fix.'

'OK. You'd better find Louella and tell her how sorry I am, though . . .' Merle whispered, her voice muffled by her costume, which she was pulling over her head. Lottie helped her out of it and Merle dropped it on the floor and stood there in her silky petticoat, looking so white and ill that Lottie was suddenly frightened.

'Here, put your coat on whilst I sort out . . .' she was beginning, even as Merle gave a little moan and fell to the floor. 'Merle!' Lottie gasped. She went down on her knees beside her friend and shook her shoulder. 'Dear Merle, do wake up!' Merle made no sign of having heard, so Lottie scrambled to her feet. 'I'm going for help,' she said breathlessly. Thoroughly frightened, she ran towards the wings just as Louella swept on to the stage. She did not appear to have noticed Merle, lying in a crumpled heap with a pile of clothes on the floor nearby, for Lottie had dropped everything to go to her friend.

'Where's that girl gone?' Louella demanded sharply. 'I told you both to wait on the stage, but isn't it just typical of Merle to go her own way! I suppose she's gone to meet Baz, choosing to ignore my instructions . . .'

'Oh, Louella, she's there,' Lottie said, pointing. 'It's so bitterly cold . . . she was white as a sheet . . . I was just going to help her into her coat when she fainted; at least, I think she fainted. At any rate, she fell down and didn't move when I called her name.'

Louella's eyes widened. 'Fainted? Oh, I suppose she'll say she's ill, which is why she made so many mistakes . . .' she started, just as Merle's eyelids fluttered open and she tried to struggle into a sitting position.

'What – what happened?' Merle said. She glanced down at herself and then began to cry. 'Where's me clothes?' she wailed. 'Am I dreamin'? Oh, I feel so funny . . . God, I'm going to be sick!'

'Not on the stage, you're not,' Louella said

grimly. She hauled Merle to her feet, put an arm round her for support, and gestured Lottie to do the same. 'Never mind her coat, just get her off the stage and into the wings. C'mon, Merle, you can make it!'

Lottie thought her mother was being really cruel, for Merle was beginning to retch and to moan, but in fact they managed to get her to the nearest fire bucket, fortunately only half full of sand, before Merle actually vomited and Merle was not ungrateful.

'Thanks, Louella, Lottie,' she said as soon as the paroxysm of vomiting was over. 'I never should have ate them potted shrimps at teatime, but somehow I really fancied them, even after Jack had said he thought they tasted a bit queer.' She looked around her as Louella and Lottie lowered her into an ancient wooden chair. 'But why's I in me petticoat?' She shivered violently. 'I'm bloody near dead of the cold.'

'I imagine you were getting changed when you came over queer and fainted,' Louella said. 'You were still on stage because the pair of you had been playing around during the act, instead of concentrating.'

Lottie had returned to the edge of the stage to fetch the pile of clothing and now Louella snatched Merle's skirt and jumper from her daughter and began to heave the jersey over Merle's head. 'Stand up a minute, and hang on to me while you step into your skirt,' she said briskly. 'And don't think that a little thing like a fainting fit is going to get you out of a good ticking off, because . . .'

Louella was helping Merle into the skirt as she spoke. It was a garment fastened at the side by three buttons, but when she endeavoured to do them up Merle said quickly: 'They don't work any more, Louella; the skirt has shrunk something dreadful. Use the safety pins.'

Lottie, staring, saw that the skirt had indeed shrunk, saw also that Merle had enlarged the waist by employing six of the enormous safety pins more normally used for fastening babies' nappies, and even as the thought occurred, Louella spoke. 'You wicked girl!' she said venomously. 'You're pregnant . . . you're havin' a bleedin' baby! If you'd spoke up early enough you could have gone somewhere and got rid of it, but by the look of you it's too late for that, and you've never said a word to anyone. Well, my girl, that's your career down the drain! As soon as we get back to Victoria Court you can pack your things and go.'

Lottie was so astonished that she simply stood there, staring at Merle, and saw her friend's face begin to turn first scarlet and then, as the colour drained from her cheeks, white as a sheet. Louella tapped an impatient foot. 'Well, Merle? Do I have to ask who the father is?'

Large tears welled up in Merle's eyes and trickled down her pale cheeks. 'I'm not having a baby, I'm not, I'm not,' she said desperately. 'How can you say such things, Louella?'

'Because it's true, and you must know it,' Louella said angrily. 'I should have guessed a long time ago except that I thought you were a decent girl. But now you've proved me wrong. You're a slut, Merle O'Mara.'

Merle gave another wail and Lottie stepped forward and put her arm round her friend's shaking shoulders, eyeing her mother defiantly. 'She's not what you called her because of course Baz must be the father,' she said. 'I know they're not very old but I'm sure they love one another, and anyway, you're always telling people that you were only seventeen when I was born. Merle's eighteen, so why shouldn't she have a baby? If she is having one, that is.'

'Because she's not married, that's why,' Louella shouted. 'And I'm not having her lumbering about the stage like a great clumsy elephant, and ruining our act. She's got to go and the sooner the better.'

Lottie had been half aware of a movement in the wings behind her, and Max chose this inauspicious moment to come forward. He stood behind his niece's chair, one hand on her shoulder, the other smoothing the rumpled curls away from her hot, wet face. Across the top of Merle's head, he eyed Louella coldly. 'What did you call my niece, Louella? If my son has got her into trouble, should you not save your abuse for him? And then there's myself, of course. My brother is a strict Methodist, and he put Merle in my charge, made me promise that I'd see she kept to the straight and narrow. If

351

you want to apportion blame, then you had best put a good deal of it to my account.'

Lottie saw colour begin to blotch Louella's neck and spread across her face as her mother smiled ingratiatingly at Max. 'Oh, dear, you weren't meant to hear any of that because I – I didn't really mean it. I'm afraid I lost my temper . . . in fact, I can't remember what I did say.' She turned hopefully to Lottie. 'It was the shock, and the realisation that I would have to train someone else to take Merle's place.' She turned back to Max. 'I really am sorry, Max. I never should have said what I did.'

'It's Merle to whom you should apologise, if you think an apology can help,' Max said stiffly. He looked down at his niece, still huddled on the hard wooden chair, her arms folded defensively across her breast. 'Merle, my dear, Louella has said terrible things, but one charge she made I think you must answer. Are you expecting a baby?'

'I'm very sorry for what I said, Merle,' Louella said glibly.

Once again, there was an interruption. Footsteps hurried along the corridor into the wings and Baz, whistling cheerfully, came on to the stage, closely followed by Jack. Baz looked around him in some surprise. 'Hello, 'ello, 'ello, what's all this then? I know I'm late but the fog's that thick you can't see your hand in front of your face, and my torch battery is giving out, which didn't help matters. When I arrived, I went straight to the green room, but the fire's out and there were no sign of you. Jack was still there, trying to find one of them gold cufflinks what his father left him. When I asked him where you were, he said he thought he'd heard voices coming from the stage, so here we are.' Baz glanced around him, apparently becoming aware of the strange stillness caused by their arrival. 'What's up?' he said again. 'You're all very quiet, which ain't usual; cat got your tongues?'

Merle was the first to speak. 'Louella thinks I'm – I'm in the family way,' she said. 'I wondered if I was at Christmas time, only I went and saw someone who said I wasn't. Only none o' me clothes fit any more – Mrs Jones has put extra panels in all me stage costumes – an' this evening, I fainted. So – so, maybe I am, after all.'

Baz looked thunderstruck. 'But we haven't – we didn't – we always said we wouldn't do nothing that could get us into trouble, and we've stuck to it,' he said. His face went very red but Lottie, watching closely, guessed that this was embarrassment and not guilt. 'It must be a mistake, queen. There's things you have to do to get a baby and we've not done 'em.'

'Then if you aren't the father, who is?' Louella said bluntly. She turned to Merle, who shrank back as though she feared the older woman would strike her. 'Who's the father, Merle? How far gone are you? I'd say five or six months.' She glanced apologetically at Max, giving him a sweet, lopsided smile. 'We've got to get at the truth, Max,'

353

she said. 'We can't all go on livin' a lie, as Merle has been.'

Max's brows drew together, but before he could speak Merle heaved a deep sigh, straightened her shoulders, and looked slowly round the circle of people, all of whom were staring at her intently. 'I'd better start at the beginning,' she said drearily. 'It were in Yarmouth, during our summer season . . .'

'Jerry!' and 'That bleedin' red-headed feller what I caught you kissin' . . .' came simultaneously from Lottie and Baz.

Merle, however, shook her head. 'No, it weren't Jerry. It were Alex.'

'Alex?' The name came from more than one throat.

But Merle nodded a trifle impatiently. 'That's right, Alex, the ventriloquist on the Britannia. I was a fool to be taken in by him, but after the first time I realised he were a bad lot. Well, Jerry said he always went after young girls and then dropped them, because he's a married man, you see. Actually, he's been married three times and has seven children.'

Lottie stared at her, open-mouthed. 'And you – and – and he . . . you let him . . . oh, Merle!'

At the sorrow in her friend's voice, Merle burst into tears once more. 'It were only the once,' she sobbed, mopping her eyes furiously, 'and when I started feelin' sick in the mornings and funny most of the day, I told you I was going to Blackpool and instead went all the way to Morecambe to tell him

I thought I might be havin' a baby.' She sniffed dolorously, peeping at Lottie through swollen eyelids. 'Only when I told him, he said to cheer up 'cos it were impossible for a girl to get pregnant her first time and besides, he said he took precautions. Then he said if I were having a baby it would have to be Jerry's, only I told him Jerry and me were just friends. I thought he couldn't meet me eye, but like a fool I believed him and came home much happier, only there weren't no sign of me monthlies and then a couple of weeks ago me clothes stopped fittin' me. I told myself the material were cheap and had shrunk . . .' She turned desperate, tear-drenched eyes up to her uncle. 'But I were beginnin' to believe Alex had lied to me when Louella went for me this evening.'

There was a short silence whilst everyone digested this. Then Jack cleared his throat and stepped forward. 'If you asks me, and I know you haven't and I'm goin' to put in my two penn'orth anyway, you'd best stay with the act while you train a replacement, then you must go home to have the baby and come back afterwards. It's a pity you can't make it all legal, like, by marryin' the father, but mebbe you'd sooner have the child adopted. Folk do, I know, unless of course you want to keep it.'

'Of course I don't want to keep it; I don't want to have it, come to that,' Merle wailed. 'Havin' a baby hurts, an' lookin' after it will ruin my career . . .'

Louella snorted. 'Your career is ruined already, young lady, so far as the Lacey Sisters are concerned,' she said bitterly. 'I simply can't agree to your remaining with the act now that we know you're in the family way. And if you hope to come back afterwards, you're out there. I'll train someone else and you can just find yourself another job. I know you keep saying it were just a one night stand . . .'

Merle promptly burst into tears once more and Max came out from behind her chair and glared at Louella. 'How dare you speak to my niece like that!' he thundered. 'Merle was seduced by an older man, a thing which has happened to many a decent young girl. I heard you earlier, remember; I came into the wings to tell you to hurry because the fog was getting thicker and I heard you call Merle dreadful names. You were berating her as though she was a dockside whore, instead of a child who fell into the clutches of a wicked, greedy man. Well, you've dished yourself this time, my girl, because I'm not at all sure I want an assistant who treats a member of my family like dirt.'

'Max, how can you?' Louella wailed. Tears formed in her brilliant eyes but were dashed impatiently away. 'I've already apologised, both to you and to Merle . . . what more can I do?'

'An apology isn't much use when it's closely followed by more abuse and the threat of being kicked out,' Max commented. Merle stood up and Max took both her hands in his and gave them a

356

comforting squeeze. 'Jack's right though, my love, you'll have to go home and tell your parents, explain what happened. If you decide to have the baby adopted, that is your decision, but perhaps your mother will take it on; parents frequently do, I know. In either event, you can then come straight back to the Gaiety. If Louella won't have you, you can be my assistant.'

'Oh, Uncle Max, I can't tell me parents. Dad would kill me, you know what he's like,' Merle said. 'Let me stay here! I'll have the baby, get it adopted, and come straight back to work. I swear it.'

'No you will not!' Louella shouted, clearly throwing caution to the winds. She turned to Max. 'As for her assisting you, Max, I won't be cast aside through no fault of my own.' She looked challengingly at him. 'I'm sure audiences will be thrilled to see a pregnant woman being sawn in half, and of course management will greet the idea with cries of delight, so if you're threatening me, Max O'Mara, two can play at that game.'

Max was helping Merle tenderly into her overcoat, adjusting her felt hat, and wrapping her long blue scarf round her neck and the lower half of her face, but as Louella finished speaking he turned towards her, his eyes glittering dangerously. 'Now the truth is beginning to come out, so perhaps it's time I said a thing or two myself,' he said evenly. 'Have you ever wondered why I've never asked you to marry me, Lou, even though

357

we've shared a house for more than eight years, though never a bed? It's because I've always known that you disliked babies, had no time for children and were jealous – yes, jealous – of young people. Despite what you probably believe, I do mean to marry one day. I've always wanted a settled home, somewhere in the country, with a bit of land so I can keep hens, goats and pigs. And I want an easy-going, comfortable wife, who'll give me two or three children. I don't want a woman who shows off her figure night after night on the stage, and thinks more of her own career than of mine. And now you've proved my point: not only do you dislike the young, but you're cold-hearted through and through. I wouldn't marry you now if you were the last woman on earth!'

'Max O'Mara, how dare you speak to me like that! And it's not true that I don't like babies. I loved Lottie when she was small, didn't I? But as for marrying, why, after tonight I wouldn't have you even if you asked me.'

Max did not deign to reply but Baz, looking extremely uncomfortable, said quietly: 'I think this discussion – if you can call it that – has got out of hand. It's time we went home anyway. Tomorrer morning things won't seem so black.'

Jack, looking almost equally uncomfortable, nodded vigorously. 'You're right: I reckon things have been said by all parties which they'll regret when tempers have cooled.' He crooked his elbow invitingly, and smiled at Lottie. 'You come along

358

o' me, chuck; I'll see you to your door.' He turned to Louella. 'You take my other arm, queen, and we'll venture out into this bleedin' fog, or it'll be mornin' before we're home.'

'I'll come wi' you, Dad,' Baz said. He went towards his father, but Merle, who had been clutching Max, broke away and ran over to Lottie. Her face was still swollen and tear-stained, but she was no longer crying.

'I'm coming wi' you, Lottie,' she announced with surprising firmness. 'I think Max and Louella need to get things sorted out and they can't do that if I'm around.'

Lottie expected Max – and her mother for that matter – to refuse the suggestion, but to her very real surprise Louella suddenly broke free from Jack and ran to Max, clutching his arm. 'You were right. I said wicked things to Merle, things I didn't really mean. You say I think of nothing but my career, but what else have I got to think about? I'd love to be married, with a baby and a nice little cottage in the country.' She looked pleadingly up into his face. 'Can we talk?'

Lottie had never heard such desolation coming from her mother, nor such pleading, and Max was obviously touched by it. 'Yes, we'll talk,' he said gruffly. He glanced around him: Merle was clutching Lottie, and Baz and Jack were hovering protectively near the two girls. 'Are we all agreed?' he asked. 'Then let's get going.'

The six of them left the theatre and plunged into

359

the fog. It was thick and yellow, and even through the scarf wrapped round her nose and mouth Lottie felt the breath catch in her throat. The four of them were spread across the width of the jigger, but when they turned into Scotland Road there were still enough people around to mean that they had to split into three couples, to avoid bumping into others.

Lottie would have kept close to Jack and Baz, for though their torches scarcely illumined the pavement at their feet at least they gave some light, but Merle dragged on her arm, causing her to fall behind. 'Lottie, you've been a good pal to me, and if I'd knowed for certain I were havin' a baby I'd have told you days ago, honest I would,' Merle whispered. 'It were ever so good of Uncle Max to take my part and try to force Louella to have me back after the kid's born, but in a way I see your mam's problem. Once I get really big I shan't be able to do half the routines, so she'll have to employ someone else, and if the other person goes down well and is cheaper than me, I wouldn't really blame her for not wanting me back. But I can't go home to my parents, honest to God I can't. My dad's always said that circus people are far more moral than theatricals, and he'll think this proves it. He never did like the act I did before I came to the Gaiety.' She gave a small breathless giggle. 'He said I were flauntin' me body and no good would come of it. So you see, if I do go home, there wouldn't be no question of me comin' back.

He'd put his foot down. And he wouldn't let me have the kid adopted, either. He'd say you've made your bed and now you must lie on it.' She pulled Lottie to a halt beneath a lamp post and stared helplessly into the younger girl's face. 'What'll I do, Lottie? Oh, how I wish I'd never set eyes on bloody Alex!'

Lottie opened her mouth to say that for her part she wished Alex had never set eyes – or anything else – on Merle, then closed it again. 'Don't you think you might go home and have the baby, and then bring it back here?' she asked. 'I mean, if Louella really does like babies, we ought to be able to look after it between the three of us.' She hesitated, then spoke more resolutely. 'Come on, we've already lost sight of the others and it's dreadfully cold. We'll talk it over once we're warm and snug in our beds.'

Merle pouted, but took Lottie's arm once more and set off into the fog. 'But I want to tackle Uncle Max as soon as we get indoors,' she said. 'If he can pay for my keep until I start work again, then I could have the baby in Victoria Court and my dad need never know. It's – it's just Louella who could be difficult, though if she really wants to catch Uncle Max, then she must have realised by now that the way to do it is to accept me and the baby with open arms. So I wondered, Lottie, if you'd prove what a real pal you are and tell your mam how things stand. I reckon she does love Max, so she might even put up with me in order to get him legal, like.'

'There is Baz to consider, though,' Lottie said, after some thought. 'No matter what you say, Merle, most folk are goin' to think the baby is Baz's because so far as they know he's been your boyfriend ever since you joined the act, which is gettin' on for a year. They'll think he's managed to wriggle out of marrying you, given you the go-by, and they'll think Max has gone along with it as well. So don't you think it would be fairer if you went home?'

'I hadn't thought of it like that,' Merle said, after a longish pause. 'Oh, Lottie, I'm just as selfish as Louella in my own way! I've not given a thought to poor Baz, and it must have been a terrible shock to him, yet he never reproached me or said nasty things about me; he left that to Louella,' she added with a flash of humour.

'Baz is a really nice feller. But to be honest, Merle, I think he was too shocked to say much,' Lottie said. 'And anyway, what with Louella and Max bawling each other out, and you crying and trying to tell everyone what had happened, Baz wouldn't have been heard even if he had spoken up.'

Merle gave a small giggle. 'He is nice; and much too good for me,' she said with unwonted humility. 'I wish I'd had a chance to speak to him alone because he's the one person – apart from you, love – who deserved to know the truth.'

'But you didn't really know for sure that you were pregnant until this evening,' Lottie pointed out. The two girls had been walking with arms

362

linked, but now Lottie stopped, and Merle followed suit. 'We've been walking for ages, Merle. I'm sure we should have reached Burlington Street by now. The trouble is, the fog's so thick you can't even read the names of the shops, but I'm sure we've crossed over half a dozen side streets whilst we were talking. D'you think we ought to go back?'

'Heavens, I don't know,' Merle said. 'I wonder what time it is? I don't know if you've noticed, but when we first turned into Scotland Road there were quite a few people about, but we've not passed anyone for ages.'

Lottie had dragged her companion to the side of the road and now she swung her round so that they were both staring at the nearest building. 'We've gone wrong somehow, because this ain't a shop, it's a terraced house,' she said. 'Oh, Merle, the fog's far too thick to read the street names; even the numbers of the houses are difficult to see, and there isn't a light on anywhere. We've gone wrong somewhere and I haven't got a clue where we are!'

Chapter Thirteen

The walk home had been meant to give Max and Louella a chance to talk things through but in the event they were silent, simply making their way through the thick fog and longing to reach Victoria Court. Louella was thinking miserably how badly she had handled the whole affair, and Max was apparently wrapped in his own reflections. They were recalled to the present, however, when Baz came up behind them and jerked at his father's arm. 'You are in a brown study, Dad,' he said reprovingly, 'or don't you intend to go home tonight? It's a good thing Jack noticed that you'd gone straight instead of turning into Burly.'

'Was it Burly? I didn't realise,' Max said vaguely. 'I've had my mind on other matters, believe it or not, and I dare say Louella wasn't watching the street signs too closely either.'

'You can't see 'em up there,' Baz said, indicating the upper floors of the shops and dwellings they had passed. 'I wonder if I ought to stay here and wait for the girls? Only the truth is, I've a deal of thinking to do before I see Merle again. I'm not blaming her, mind,' he added hastily. 'But I still feel a bit awkward, like.'

'You must,' agreed his father. 'And you'd have to be a perishin' saint not to feel angry as well. But Merle's only young, when all's said and done. I reckon she was seduced, tricked into doing what she did, so don't blame her too much, old feller.'

Louella, who had not spoken, suddenly let go of Max's arm, to which she had been clinging, put out a hand and patted Baz's shoulder. 'You've behaved really well, Baz, ever so much better than I did,' she said humbly. 'I'm sure your father's truly proud of you.' She hesitated, then plunged on rather wildly. 'But has this put you off Merle for good? I mean, if you wanted to make everything respectable . . .'

'My son is not going to marry at the age of eighteen to cover up another man's misdeed,' Max said stiffly. 'I wonder you should even suggest it, Louella.'

Louella immediately began to retract, but as they fumbled their way through the thick fog and into No. 2 Victoria Court, she changed her mind. 'I was only trying to help when I suggested that Baz might want to marry Merle despite what's happened,' she said, keeping her voice small and diffident. 'I know it isn't the ideal solution and of course it wouldn't be necessary if Merle went home to have the baby . . .'

'She doesn't want to go home, and knowing her father as I do, I'm not surprised,' Max cut in. 'He's a really good man, but very strict in his ways, and I'm sure Merle is right: he would never consent to her putting her child out for adoption. So I think it best that she should stay with us until after the baby's born. Then she can . . .'

'That's just my point,' Louella said quickly. 'No matter what we tell people, everyone is going to think that Baz is the father. They'll wonder why you, Max, haven't insisted that he marry Merle. And the more Baz denies it, the more people will talk behind our backs.'

'I don't care about gossip,' Baz said at once. 'And folk know Dad doesn't tell lies, so that's all right.'

Max had been filling the kettle at the sink but now he carried it across the room and set it on the fire, before turning to give his son a rueful smile. 'Louella's got a point,' he said quietly. 'We're in a bit of a cleft stick here because I don't want Merle to have to go back to her father, but on the other hand I won't have you made a scapegoat for something you didn't do. I'll sleep on it, see if something occurs to me.'

'Well, I do have a suggestion,' Louella said. She tried to keep her voice steady, but it trembled in spite of herself. 'There are . . . places which take in young girls who get into trouble; they arrange adoptions, if that's what the mother wants. I'm not suggesting Merle should go to a home in Liverpool, but there are others. I know there's one in Rhyl because it's where that chorus girl went – the one we found crying her heart out quite early in the season, when she realised she was expecting.

Merle could go there, have the baby adopted, and then come back to us and no one any the wiser.' She looked appealingly at Max. 'I'd give her her old job back, truly I would, Max. I'm really ashamed of the way I spoke to the poor kid and I'll never reproach her again, honest to God I won't. And I'm sure Lottie and myself could keep the act going until Merle could rejoin us.' She looked hopefully at Max, then let her gaze move over to Baz, and was relieved to see that though they both looked thoughtful, neither seemed displeased; in fact Baz was nodding his head slowly.

'I think you've hit on it, Louella,' he said. 'I dare say it ain't the ideal solution, but it's the best one we're likely to find. Don't you agree, Dad?'

Max nodded. 'I think you're right,' he said. 'She needn't go yet, although she must leave before she begins to show. But one thing: I've heard tales about those homes so I'd rather pay for the child to stay in lodgings until the birth is near. Then she can go into a private nursing home. I'm sure they'll arrange the adoption, just as a home for bad girls would do.'

'I'll help with the cost,' Louella said eagerly.

Max cast her a grateful glance. 'Thanks, Louella. You know, it's really lucky that no other member of the company has any idea of what went on tonight. For once we should bless the fog for sending the cast home sharpish.'

'Don't forget Jack knows,' Louella reminded him. 'But he won't tell. He's a real good sort is Jack.'

'Aye; Jack's true blue and will never stain,' Max agreed. At that moment the kettle began to hiss and Louella spooned cocoa into five mugs, whilst Max picked up the kettle and carried it across to the table.

Baz watched for a moment then glanced at the clock above the mantel and whistled beneath his breath. 'Wherever have those perishin' girls got to?' he asked anxiously. 'Me and Jack hurried to catch you up when we saw you had walked straight past Burly without giving it a second glance, but I disremember how far behind us the girls had fallen by then. Still, if they made the same mistake as you and continued on up the Scottie, Jack would put them right.'

Max frowned. 'They should have been here by now, though,' he observed. 'Unless, of course, they went into Jack's lodgings with him . . . they might have done that when they realised they had a fair walk back to reach Victoria Court.'

'Yes, that's possible,' Baz conceded and Louella saw that the worry had left his face. 'I expect Jack would want to nip in and tell Mrs Parrot not to lock up. Then they'd mebbe have a hot drink and Jack would walk them back home, 'cos he's a real gent, is Jack. And that means they'll arrive here any minute now.'

Through the thickening fog the two girls stared at one another in dismay. If they turned back and tried to retrace their steps, they could be in a worse muddle and might end up on the docks. Neither girl owned a watch but both knew it must be very late indeed. Although they had done their best to hurry the second half of the performance because of the worsening weather, it had almost certainly been ten o'clock, or not far off that hour, when they had taken their last curtain call. Then there had been the bustle of departure as the rest of the cast left the theatre, whilst Lottie and Merle hung about on the stage, waiting for Louella to return so that she could scold them. After that, of course, there had been the row, and then the slow fumble through the fog, in the course of which they had lost first their companions, and then themselves.

'What'll we do, Lottie?' Merle asked, sounding as though she, and not her companion, was the younger. 'What'll happen if we just keep on? We've gone a good way down this road, so we should soon come to a junction, and then one of us will have to climb on to the shoulders of the other one, and maybe from there we'd be able to read the street name.' At this ridiculous suggestion they both laughed and somehow laughing made their predicament seem less frightening.

'Yes, we have come a good way,' Lottie said thoughtfully. 'And if we're right and it's past eleven o'clock, maybe nearer midnight, most folk will be tucked up in their beds, which is why there's no lights showing in the windows we've passed. But folk round here are used to the fogs coming off the Mersey, so if we find ourselves still lost in ten minutes or so, I think we'll have to take a chance and bang on the nearest door. Still, if we keep walking we might find ourselves in an area we know, or at least an area I know. It's different for you, you didn't grow up in Liverpool, but I got to know it pretty well from visiting school friends and getting the messages and so on.'

Accordingly the girls walked on, but this time they talked very little, both concentrating on trying to recognise their surroundings. Presently, however, Lottie gave a squawk of dismay. 'Oh, Merle, we've gone wrong again! This is a court and not one of the ones I know, either. We've followed the pavement right under the arch – which we couldn't see because of the fog – and if we keep on walking we'll meet the wall which makes every court into a dead end. I think the time has come to ask for help, because Max and Louella will be worried sick.'

'So will . . .' Merle began, then stopped short, and Lottie guessed she had been about to say 'So will Baz' and had suddenly remembered the rift in their relationship.

They had linked arms, for both warmth and comfort, and now she slid her hand down and squeezed Merle's fingers. 'It's all right, goose, of course Baz will worry when we don't turn up. In fact I'm sure the two of you will sort something out once you've had a chance to talk. And here's a bit of luck, I spy a lighted window, so somebody's still up. Come along. As soon as we know where we are we can start planning our route home.'

Feeling rather self-conscious, the two girls climbed the steps up to the door and banged the knocker. Its echoes resounded and Lottie was about to bang again when she heard shuffling foot-steps approaching, and presently the door was opened, though no more than six inches, and a voice said: 'Oozat knockin' at me door in the miggle o' the night?'

Lottie hesitated. Her name was unlikely to mean anything to the person on the other side of the door, but she decided to give it anyway. 'I'm Lottie Lacey and this is my friend Merle O'Mara. We took a wrong turn somewhere in the fog, and now we're completely lost. We can't even see the street names 'cos the fog's got so thick, and our folk will be worried sick.'

The door opened a good deal wider to reveal a tiny old woman, wrapped in a long, drooping black shawl and wearing beneath it a rusty black skirt. Her skin was seamed and brown and she grinned at the two girls, revealing gums but no teeth, then gestured them into the hallway. 'Well I never did; if it ain't the Lacey Sisters,' she said in a high, cracked voice. 'I've been comin' to your shows since you were just a kid, young Lottie. And what's you doin' astray on a night like this?'

Lottie began to speak but the old woman cut across her words. 'No, no, don't tell me now; you must be fair frozen. There's a good fire in me

371

kitchen and the kettle a-hoppin' on the hob, so you'd best come through and then you can tell me what's what while I mash the tea.' She led them into a pleasant and very clean kitchen, with rag rugs on the floor, a couple of ancient basketwork chairs drawn up before the stove, and firelight and lamplight flickering on the whitewashed walls. 'Take off your coats or you won't feel the benefit when you goes out again,' she instructed, and when this had been done she gestured them to the two easy chairs. 'Sit yourselves down, young ladies, while I make us a nice cuppa. I were about to have one meself, 'cos you ain't the only ones what've been out in that fog, though I didn't go far enough to lose meself. This here is Isobel Court and me granddaughter – she's a good girl, she is – lives in Frederick Court, no more'n twenty yards further along Burnet Street. She had a babby a couple of weeks ago and I'm givin' a hand, like. I went round to cook . . .'

Lottie however broke in, too surprised to remember her manners. 'Burnet Street? Ye gods, we're miles out of our way! Oh, Lor', we must have wandered down Hopwood and then just kept following the pavement along . . .' She turned to Merle. 'It'll take us ages to find our way back to Burlington Street and Victoria Court, if we ever do!'

'I can guide you back to Hopwood meself, fog or no fog, and once you're there you must count the side turnings until you reach the junction –

which is the Scottie of course – then you just turn
right, and count every side street you cross again
until you reach Burly.' As she spoke she had been
pouring three mugs of tea, and now she handed
two of these to her guests, put the third down on
the kitchen table, and hobbled over to the
cupboard beside the sink. She came back with a
large tin which proved to contain a fruitcake, and
got to work with a wicked-looking carving knife,
talking all the while. 'Me name's Ada Donovan,
but everybody calls me Donny, and I've led an
interestin' life,' she said. 'I'm a widow, have been
for twenty years, though I only moved here when
I retired. Before that I worked the canals, first wi'
me husband, then wi' me two sons. But a coal
barge is hard work and the day come when I
couldn't be useful, so the boys rented me this
house. I was near me daughter, which was handy,
and as I've already told you me granddaughter's
just about on me doorstep, and me friends from
the canal visit me when they're loadin', so all in
all I couldn't be better off.'

'That's nice,' Lottie said politely, accepting a slab
of cake. 'And I gather you come to the theatre
sometimes since you recognised my name?'

'Oh aye, I come most weeks,' the old woman
assured them. 'I gets free tickets in winter when
the panto season finishes and you're a bit quiet
like. You see, me sister's eldest boy married the
wardrobe mistress, and she gets what she calls
"comps" from time to time, what means they're

373

free, though I reckon you know that.' She beamed at Lottie. 'I used to come special to see you and your mam, 'cos you were such a sweet kid, all blonde curls and big blue eyes. Mind you, I were surprised when your hair turned dark so sudden, and your mam became your sister, along with this 'ere other gal, but I reckon that's thee-ay-ter for you.'

Lottie smiled at her. 'My hair always was dark,' she said gently. 'But Louella thought that because we were mother and daughter we ought to look more alike, so I had my hair bleached. She really is fair-haired, though she does lighten it a little.'

The old woman nodded slowly. 'Aye, now you mention it, when I first saw you your hair were dark. But that really were a long time ago. Now eat up that cake and drink your tea, then I'll walk you to the end of the road. I'd like to keep you longer because to have two stars of the Gaiety sittin' in me very own kitchen, suppin' tea and eatin' cake, is like a dream come true. The Lacey Sisters is me favourite act, though I like Mr and Mrs Magic as well, but when I tell my daughter I've met you, talked to you like you was just anybody, she'll probably think I'm goin' off me head.'

Both girls laughed, but Merle said gently: 'I'm sure your daughter will believe you, if you explain what happened . . . the fog and us gettin' lost, I mean. I don't know whether we mentioned it, but we wandered for ages without seein' a single light

374

in any window. It were dead lucky for us that we ended up in Isobel Court and saw that someone was still up.'

The old woman had perched herself on one of the upright kitchen chairs. 'Lucky for you I don't sleep so good any more,' she observed. 'I don't usually tek to me bed till well after midnight, and even then I can't always sleep.' She gave the girls a quick, twinkling glance. 'To tell you the truth, I don't see no point in trudging up all them stairs to a cold room and a colder bed. So quite often I dosses down on that there couch; if you look underneath it you'll see there's blankets and a piller stowed away there. That way, I keep nice and warm all night and I nips out o' bed when it begins to get light, pokes up the fire, and pulls the kettle over the flame. I can have a nice cuppa while I wash in the sink, and since I'm already dressed in me underthings, I lays me skirt and that over one of the chairs before the fire, and dresses meself in the twinkling of a bedpost. Only don't you go tellin' no one,' she added, 'because me daughter don't see it my way. She's not lived aboard a canal barge since she were a child, where there's only one room, you see.'

She beamed at them and Lottie suddenly realised why the old woman's face was so brown and furrowed with wrinkles. If you lived an outdoor life for many years, your skin turned leathery; Louella had often been heard to remark on the injurious effects of too much sunshine. If

375

Mrs Donovan had spent all her working life aboard a canal barge, it would account for the state of her complexion.

'We won't tell a soul,' Merle assured their new friend. She drank the last of her tea and stood up, gesturing Lottie to follow suit. 'It's been ever so nice meetin' you, Mrs Donovan, and I don't like to ask you to venture out on such a night, but we really must be gettin' home. So if you wouldn't mind . . .'

'Course you does, course you does,' the old woman gabbled. She kicked off her old felt slippers and thrust her feet into a pair of stout boots, then reached down a number of shawls which hung on hooks on the back of the kitchen door and began to muffle herself in them. She was surprisingly quick and was ready before Lottie and Merle had scrambled into their own coats, buttoned up and wound their thick scarves about them. Mrs Donovan then picked up a lamp, lit it, and set off briskly towards the door. She accompanied them as far as Hopwood Street and they thanked her profusely, both for the refreshment they had enjoyed in her house and for seeing them safely on to a main road.

To Lottie's relief, the fog was already beginning to thin and she had no doubt that they would find their way home safely. Indeed, they had barely turned in to Scotland Road when they saw two well-muffled figures coming towards them. 'It's Baz and Uncle Max, come to search for us,' Merle said joyfully. 'Oh, they must have been most dreadfully worried; I just hope they aren't going to be awful cross.'

When Max and Baz greeted them, however, it was clear that relief was their main emotion. 'I was beginning to wonder whether you'd wandered into the dock area,' Max said, giving both girls a hug. 'As for your mam, Lottie, she was nigh on hysterical, saying it was all her fault for keeping you out late. Now come along, best foot forward, otherwise you're not going to get any sleep at all before morning. And while we walk, you can tell us how you come to be such a long way from home. We thought at first you must have gone into Mrs Parrot's place with Jack, but we knocked the old girl up – Jack must sleep like the dead – and she assured us they'd not seen hide nor hair of you. By then, though, the fog was beginning to lift, so we simply kept on searching. Now tell us your side of the story.'

The two girls explained, making the most of their fright when they had realised they were lost, and praising Mrs Donovan for her kindness. 'We'll have to make sure she comes to the Gaiety whenever she wants to and gets a complimentary ticket every time,' Lottie said. 'She was so nice, Max, and a really keen theatregoer. She first started coming to the theatre when I was just a kid; she remembered my hair changing colour and everything!'

'I reckon you two girls ought to club together and buy her a box of chocolates,' Baz said, speaking for the first time. 'Everyone likes to gobble chocolates whilst watching a performance.'

'What a good idea, Baz,' Merle said eagerly. 'We'll do it, won't we, Lottie?' She was walking beside Baz, but Lottie thought her friend had not liked to take Baz's arm and Baz, whilst not appearing to avoid her, had still managed to keep a little distance between them. 'Lottie? Did you hear what I said?'

Lottie blinked, then spoke apologetically. 'I'm sorry, I think I'm sleepwalking, but I did hear, and I agree, of course. Tomorrow's Sunday, but we'll go out first thing on Monday and buy some. We can take the comps to her at the same time.'

Louella was delighted to see them when they came into the kitchen. She hugged both girls exuberantly and told them she had put hot bottles into their beds and would make them a nice cup of cocoa to warm them up. 'And I think I've solved your problem, Merle,' she said. 'There are really nice places, full of kind understanding people, who take girls who've got into trouble and look after them until their babies are born. Then they arrange the adoption and everything, and the girls can take up their old lives where they left off.'

Merle looked doubtful and cast an appealing glance at Max. 'Is that what you want me to do, Uncle Max?' she asked.

Max nodded. 'It's for the best, darling Merle; I'm sure it is,' he said gravely. 'This way, we shall avoid any trace of scandal – we'll tell folk you've had to go home to look after your mother. And when you return, everything will be back to normal.'

Merle looked hunted. She turned to Baz. 'What do you think, Baz?'

'I agree with Louella and my dad,' Baz said quickly. 'It is for the best, honest to God, Merle. No one will know anything; you won't have to say a word to your pa and before you know it you'll be back here, one o' the Lacey Sisters, and doin' all your modern dance routines, as though you'd never been away.'

Lottie thought he had meant to give Merle an encouraging smile, but somehow it didn't quite come off and Merle turned away quickly and went to the table to pick up her mug of cocoa. 'I think I'll take this up to bed,' she said, not meeting anyone's eyes. 'I'm that tired, I could sleep for a week. You comin', Lottie?'

'Hang on a minute, I didn't mean . . .' Max was beginning anxiously, but Merle had already left the room, so Lottie turned and smiled apologetically.

'Sorry, Max, but it is true that we're both absolutely exhausted,' she said. 'And talking, when you're tired out, is never a good idea. You can give us all the details at breakfast.'

Max looked worried. 'Yes, but I wouldn't want Merle worrying all night because we'd not explained properly . . .' he began, but Lottie shook her head.

'Don't start, please, Max, because I'm far too tired to listen properly,' she said firmly. 'Goodnight, one and all – see you at breakfast.'

By the time Lottie got upstairs Merle was already in bed, having clearly not bothered to wash. Lottie did not blame her: the bedroom was freezing cold and there was a thin film of ice across the top of the ewer, so she gladly followed Merle's example, ripping off her own clothes and dropping them on the floor before bounding between the sheets. It was lovely to find the bed well warmed and she remarked to Merle that they should soon be asleep, adding that no one was likely to wake them early on the Sunday morning, since they had had such a nasty adventure in the fog. 'Though it didn't end nastily,' she added. 'Mrs Donovan was ever so nice. And – and it does look as though Louella and Max mean to do what's best for you. Louella must have agreed to have you back after the baby's born, and it would be awkward, you know, if you stayed here with us, to hide your – your condition.'

Merle mumbled something, but her voice was muffled by the pillow and Lottie had to ask her to repeat what she had said. Merle gave an exasperated yelp, and shot upright in bed. Her eyes were very bright and she looked extremely angry. 'I am not goin' into one of them awful homes, like Effie Evans did,' she said positively. 'Uncle Max don't know nothin' if he thinks they's nice to you in them places. Effie went when she were seven months gone and they hired her out as a scrubbin' woman, and the people she was made to work for treated her like dirt. When her time come, the staff bullied her, smacked her across the face, and told her she was a dirty little slut and if she died in childbirth it would be no more than she deserved. I bleedin' well won't get sent to somewhere like that. I'll kill meself first.'

Lottie was genuinely alarmed. She, too, had heard horrible and frightening stories about 'homes for bad girls' and she sympathised with her friend, but never before had Merle threatened to harm herself, and Lottie thought she had sounded as though she meant it.

'Don't be so foolish, Merle,' she said, in a scolding tone. 'If you explain to your Uncle Max how you feel, I'm sure he'll understand. And now we'd better get to sleep or we'll be a couple of wrecks in the morning.'

'I'll never sleep,' Merle wailed. 'I'm far too upset. I never thought me uncle could be so heartless, and as for Baz ... well, I'm just glad he ain't me boyfriend any more now that he's shown himself in his true colours. As for that Alex, I just wish there was some way I could get me own back on him. It ain't fair, is it, Lottie? A feller persuades you to do what you know is wrong and then he just walks away. Well, if we do go back to Yarmouth next summer, I'll make him suffer, see if I don't.'

Lottie, who had sat up in bed when her friend

did, snuggled down again, feeling greatly relieved. If Merle was talking of revenge and next summer, then it seemed unlikely that she meant to do away with herself immediately, and in Lottie's experience things always looked better in daylight. And presently she heard something almost more reassuring: Merle was snoring gently.

Despite the fact that she was exhausted, or perhaps because of it, Lottie found it extremely difficult to drop off to sleep. Her mind was too active, going over and over the events of the day and wondering what to do for the best should Max prove adamant and insist that Merle enter a home for bad girls. She was after all in his care and only her father could overrule him, since Merle would not be twenty-one for another three years.

Having wrestled with that problem in vain, her thoughts then turned to Louella. She had known for a long time that Louella desperately wanted to marry Max, and had wondered why Max had never proposed. He had said it was because he wanted children and Louella did not, but Lottie thought there must be more to it than that. She had watched Louella back-pedalling with some embarrassment, for she was sure it must be as clear to everyone else as it was to her that Louella's sudden change of heart was a last-ditch attempt to wring a proposal of marriage from the handsome and easy-going Mr Magic. Lottie, however, did not think that her mother would succeed in her aim. Max might say he wanted a comfortable wife and a cottage with roses round the door but if this was so, why had he never got himself a lady friend amongst the many girls who hung around the stage door in the hope of seeing him? Why did he go everywhere with Louella, who was anything but a comfortable woman? No matter what she might tell him in order to win his favour, Max must know, as Lottie did, that Louella was a player through and through, and would never give up her place in the spotlight for anyone, not even for Max.

When the first faint lightening of the sky began to show through their thin bedroom curtains – and Merle's snores were at their loudest – Lottie gave up all attempt to sleep. Naturally, as soon as she did so, slumber overcame her and she found herself in the dream.

She was very happy, but that went without saying, for she had known nothing but happiness whenever she entered this particular dream. She was in a wood, with a basket hooked over one arm and a headscarf tied under her chin. She looked into the basket and saw she had been collecting sweet chestnuts, and even as she realised this saw the prickly husks at her feet, and the gleaming nuts, half hidden by the gold of fallen leaves. It's autumn, Lottie told herself, and these nuts will be for Gran. She looked around her, at the close-crowding trees and the leaf mould beneath her feet, then she listened. Water, chuckling and gurgling somewhere ahead. Lottie smiled to herself.

Next, she sniffed; what could she smell? Woodsmoke definitely, the loveliest smell in the world on an autumn afternoon, even when there was no sunshine and the wind was getting up. There was another lovely smell too, which made Lottie's mouth water. It would be one of Gran's marvellous stews. And now she remembered that Troy had gone to get potatoes since Gran was running out. Lottie looked down at her basket just as the freshening wind brought more nuts tumbling down, and the smell of Gran's stew, brought to her by that same wind, made her scrabble hastily for the nuts. She was hungry, and once Troy had handed over the potatoes they would take old Champ out of the wood and into a meadow where he might graze until they were ready to move on. Lottie snatched up another couple of handfuls of chestnuts, swearing softly as she pricked herself on an obstinate husk. Then she hurried through the trees towards the delicious smell, enjoying the scent of the woodsmoke as it blew against her face.

Gran had chosen a clearing in which to light her fire and cook their meal, but to Lottie's astonishment she was not alone. There was a woman with her, thin, elegant and, Lottie supposed, beautiful. But there was something in that fine-featured face, perhaps it was the set of her lips, which made her feel wary, so Lottie remained in the shelter of the trees, watching the scene before her.

The strange woman seemed to be doing all the

talking, emphasising each point she made with a wagging forefinger, laying down the law, but at last Gran managed to interrupt. 'How did you find us, missus?' she broke in. 'I've not been in touch for years, knowin' you didn't have much interest . . .' Suddenly Lottie saw light dawn on the old woman's face. 'It were that newspaper chap, weren't it?' she asked. 'He come when the farmer telled folk that an old woman an' a couple o' kids had saved his place from bein' burned down. That's right, ain't it?'

There had been a dreadful thunderstorm, Lottie remembered, with lightning arrowing to earth and no rain as yet, and the three of them had seen the barn burst into flames as they came down a nearby hill. They had rushed to the farm, made the family aware of what was happening, and had helped to douse the flames. She remembered Troy saying that there had been an article in the paper . . . but what had that to do with this stranger?

Lottie went forward hesitantly, not liking to interrupt, but Gran surged to her feet as soon as she saw her. When Lottie was near enough, Gran drew her close and put an arm about her shoulders. 'Good girl, Sassy. I see you've picked a mess o' nuts. We'll roast 'em over the fire this evenin' 'cos I know you're mortal fond o' chestnuts.'

'I do love 'em, Gran,' Lottie, who was now Sassy, agreed at once. 'But I thought you were goin' to make that beautiful cake . . . I know it's a lot of trouble but it keeps well, and . . .'

The woman interrupted, giving Gran a reproachful glance as she did so. 'Sassy! My own dear little girl! I don't suppose you remember me because it's a long time since I came to see you . . .'

'The best part of six years,' Gran said belligerently. 'And since Sassy had her sixth birthday back in the summer, it ain't likely that she'd reckernise you, is it?'

The woman shot her a darkling look. 'It's not my fault that I haven't managed to visit more often,' she said defensively. 'You were always following the fairs and circuses when I knew you first, so naturally I searched for you in Rhyl, Yarmouth, Scarborough . . . oh, all over. It wasn't until I read the article in the paper that I realised I'd been on the wrong track all along. As for not coming to see the child, I don't have the sort of job I can simply abandon whilst I go visiting, which is why I – I lost touch.'

Gran snorted. 'I'm no hand at writin', but for the first few years me grandson Troy dropped you a line whenever we moved on so's you'd know where we was. Only you never replied.'

The woman coloured. 'Well, yes, but I'm always busy; as I said, when you're holding down a decent job you can't just up sticks and leave 'em in the lurch. If I'd done that, I'd have been out of work in two shakes of a lamb's tail, and the money would have stopped coming, which wouldn't have pleased you, I'll be bound.'

It was Gran's turn to colour, but her face turned

bright red, Lottie knew, from rage and not embarrassment. 'What money?' she asked derisively. 'Oh, I grant you, money did come at first, only pretty soon the gaps between your bits o' money got longer and longer, and it's a good two or three years since we've seen a penny.' The arm round Lottie's shoulders tightened momentarily. 'But I never thought you'd come a-looking for our Sassy. If she'd been fourteen or fifteen now, I'd understand, but a kid of six . . .'

It was at this point that Troy came whistling into the clearing, stopping short when he saw the woman and glancing quickly from Gran to the stranger, and then back again. 'What's up?' he asked. 'We ain't trespassin'; the woods is free to anyone, and old Champ is tethered where he can reach sweet grass but won't do no harm to nobody.'

He had addressed Gran and it was she who answered him. 'Nothin's up; this – this lady has come a-callin' and is about to leave,' she said grimly.

But the woman shook her head. 'I'm not leaving without my daughter,' she said firmly. 'And she's still my daughter, no matter what you may say.' She held out a beguiling hand. 'I'm your mammy, Sassy, and I want you to come and live with me in the city,' she said coaxingly. 'I shall buy you beautiful clothes and a bicycle, and you shall have lots of toys and games, as well as a great many friends. I'll teach you to dance and sing, and though I suppose you'll have to go to school because you need to learn to read and write—'

'I can read and write; Troy taught me,' Lottie interrupted rudely. 'And I'm not going anywhere with you. I live with me Gran – and Troy – and we like things as they are.' She looked down at herself in her old blue jumper, which was more darn than anything else, at her ragged scarlet skirt and her bare feet which were so tough that she could walk across the forest floor without pain. 'And these are my workin' clothes,' she added defiantly. 'I've got decent stuff for special occasions and I don't need nothin' else.'

'You'll need a great many smart clothes when you live with me,' the woman said. 'You must understand, Sassy, that I am your mother and you are a six-year-old child. You think you have a choice, but you are quite wrong. To be sure, I was forced to hand you over to Mrs Olly here when I was offered a good job in the theatre, but that doesn't make you any the less my own child. So you'll come with me when I leave here, and though it may seem strange at first I promise you'll be truly happy.'

Poor Lottie shrank closer to Gran but Troy stepped forward and spoke directly to the woman. 'You've done without our Sassy for six years; why d'you want her now?' he said bluntly. 'We guessed you'd come for her when she was fourteen or fifteen, old enough to earn, but she's only a kid. You can't possibly have any use for her.'

The woman sighed. 'I don't have to explain to you,' she said coldly. 'You can't be more than twelve or thirteen yourself.' She turned to Gran. 'The truth is, I've been doing a mother-daughter act with a little girl called Lottie; we got along just fine but unfortunately her mother, who was French, realised what an attraction the child was. Michelle was a singer with the same company and she and Lottie moved back to France. It was too bad; it took me the best part of six months to teach Lottie all the songs and dances, and now her wretched mother is reaping the reward. I looked around me for someone to take her place, and—'

'And remembered you had a daughter of your own, even if you'd not set eyes on her since she was a few days old,' Troy said bitterly. 'And now you want her back and you don't give a damn about Gran, nor about Sassy either. She's happy with us, but she won't be happy with you. She's a country girl now; she knows nothing about cities. Just let us alone, will you?'

The woman looked undecided and Gran said: 'Grub's ready. You'd best join us, missus. But I think the choice must lie wi' Sassy here.' The woman began to speak, but Gran hushed her. 'Eat first, talk later,' she said, suddenly brisk.

Lottie was so absorbed with what was happening that she scarcely noticed when the scene before her began to blur and a fine white mist crept up between the trees. She realised she was on the

389

verge of waking and fought to get back; she simply must know what happened! 'Please, please,' she whispered to whoever sent the dream, 'please let me go back, if only for a minute.'

And she did go back. The scene before her had changed and she was with the boy, Troy. The weather was wild, the wind roaring through the trees like an express train, the rain driving into their faces, and Troy was talking to her with great earnestness. 'I'm taking you into the village because Gran was forced to say I would. That woman really is your mother, you see, for all she handed you over to Gran all those years ago, so we can't just refuse to let her take you. The plan is that you'll meet her at the Swan With Two Necks, where she's putting up. You know your mam's an actress? Well, she's appearing in Blackpool at the Palace theatre, so that's where she's going to take you. She told us that much, though she claimed to have forgotten the address of her lodgings, but that won't matter. Gran has sewn some money into the hem of your coat, but I'm sure you won't need it; it's just for emergencies, like. Can you remember the plan we made?'

'Of course I can,' Lottie said fervently through chattering teeth. 'I am to pretend I like it and do everything my mother says for five whole days. Then on the sixth day I must make an excuse to wander round to the Tower. It is the biggest thing in Blackpool and everyone knows it and will direct me. You'll be there, or maybe even Gran, and you'll take me somewhere safe where that woman won't ever think of searching.'

Troy nodded approvingly. 'You've got it. You're a bright kid,' he said. 'I wish we could get to you sooner but it'll take us all of five days to reach Blackpool from here. By the way, if something happens and we don't arrive on Saturday, we'll be along on the Monday, 'cos Sunday is everyone's day off. Gran says your mam may think about searching for you but the panto season is coming up and she'll need to train someone else for her double act, so she won't search for long.'

'And Gran will send her a letter saying she's got me safe, and I'm best with her, and happier,' Lottie said contentedly. 'Don't worry, Troy, I shan't forget. I'll be outside that Tower next Saturday – that's right, isn't it?'

Troy nodded and squeezed her hand. 'You're the best and bravest kid in the world,' he said. 'I'm proud of you, and so's Gran.'

By now they had reached the outskirts of the village, and presently they entered the main street and Troy stooped and gave her a quick kiss on the cheek, then a gentle shove between the shoulder blades. 'There's the Swan, and your mam's already out there, waitin' for you. See her?' he said. 'Keep your pecker up, littl'un, and remember, it won't be for long.'

The journey which Lottie and her mother then undertook was a complicated one with several changes, and during the course of it Lottie acknowledged that the woman had really tried to be nice to her. She had bought her sandwiches, fruit and a bottle of ginger beer, and had tried to explain about the life which she loved and for which she needed Lottie's help. 'I've always done a double act and that's why I wanted you, my own little daughter,' she had said earnestly. 'I can't go on alone and honestly, pet, you'll love the life once you get used to it.'

Presently, the train slowed and stopped, and the woman helped Lottie down on to a busy platform. 'Where do we go now?' Lottie asked, for she had seen the sign 'Liverpool Lime Street' and thought that they must be changing trains yet again. 'I'm tired; is it much further?'

Her mother, who had told Lottie to call her Louella, laughed. 'No more train journeys, you'll be glad to hear,' she said gaily. 'We'll catch a cab and be home in five minutes.'

They emerged from the station on to a crowded street and Lottie looked round her wildly. 'Where's the Tower?' she asked baldly. 'And the sign on the station said Liverpool, not Blackpool.'

'That's right; this isn't Blackpool,' Lottie's mother said abstractedly. 'I was boasting a bit when I said Blackpool. I'm working at the Gaiety theatre in this town and so will you be in a week or two.'

For a moment Lottie could only stare whilst fear mingled with cold fury in her breast. Then she swung the small bag she carried, which contained her few possessions, and hit the older woman squarely in the stomach, causing her to teeter and crash into a passer-by. Then she darted into the roadway, her only thought escape. She heard the scream of brakes, saw the streetlights reflected in the puddles as she slipped, and then there was a tremendous bang, an instant of excruciating pain, and darkness descended.

Chapter Fourteen

Lottie awoke, trembling and soaked with perspiration. For a moment she was completely disorientated, imagining herself still lying in the roadway with the rain beating down on her and the roar of traffic stilled whilst voices shouted and, somewhere, a woman screamed.

Then she became aware of the warmth of her bed and the lighter square of the window to her right. Slowly, gradually, she was able to acknowledge that she was in her own room, and that she was safe. It had only been a dream after all. She snuggled her cheek into the pillow and then sat groggily upright, her heart beginning to beat very fast. It had not been a dream; it had been a recollection. She had remembered at last!

She had often wondered whether the dreams, which seemed so real, could possibly have any connection with her six lost years, but because her mother had lied to her – yes, she knew now that Louella had deliberately lied – she had convinced herself that the dreams were just that and nothing more. Yet always, at the very back of her mind, she had believed them, had known that Gran was a real person. Even now, she could feel Gran's fat, cushiony bosom and strong arms round her when she needed the comfort of a hug. As for Troy, she had known he was real in her present life, but had not managed to work out why someone she had met only once should appear in her dreams. Well, she knew now.

Lying there, as the light slowly strengthened, she began to relive the dreams and thus the first six years of her life. She had been handed to Gran as a very tiny baby, only a few days old, by Louella. She could understand in a way why her mother had been forced to part with her. It would not have been easy to continue a stage career with a very young baby to look after, and no husband to support her. But why lie about it? She realised now that all her dreams had been pictures of her past, tiny incidents sometimes, which had actually happened. Champ was as real as Gran and Troy; the scene on the beach had really taken place ... and the fact that Jack Russell had said she was a natural swimmer was, surely, the best confirmation of all, because Troy had taught her to swim the very first time they had visited the seaside together.

And then, of course, the whole thing became clear. Louella had been returning to Liverpool, and the Gaiety theatre, with a daughter she scarcely knew. She could not have realised that Lottie meant to run away as soon as she was able, could not have understood, either, that the lure of the stage was not something felt by everyone. She would soon have begun to see, however, that though you can take a horse to water you can't make it drink, for this would most definitely have applied to young Lottie, because all she had wanted had been to return to her old life with Gran and Troy.

So when the accident had happened and Lottie's memory had been completely erased, Louella must have heaved a huge sigh of relief. What was more, now that Lottie thought about it, her mother had done just what the doctors had forbidden: she had taken every opportunity to tell Lottie about those missing years. Only what she had told her had been a tissue of lies, which Lottie had accepted because it had never occurred to her for one moment that her mother was not speaking the truth. Naturally enough, this meant that when her memory began to function, presenting her with pictures of her true past, she had dismissed such memories as mere dreams.

As she lay there, staring at the ceiling above her head, resentment began to grow. Louella had been ruthless in her pursuit of what she wanted, never giving a thought to Gran, pretending she had never known anyone named Troy, steadfastly denying that either she or Lottie had ever visited Yarmouth. Lottie had believed her mother when she said she had to bleach her daughter's hair so that they looked more alike, but now Lottie was sure this had been a ruse. The blonde hair had made Troy back off, thinking she really was someone else . . . in other words, it had been a disguise.

There were other things, too. She did not know what her real name was, but Gran and Troy had called her Sassy and she remembered, now, that Louella's first child assistant had been called Lottie. So even my name is not my own, she thought miserably. Louella took my past, the people who loved me, the name I was known by, and simply bundled them out of sight for her own convenience. Oh, God, and Gran must have thought I'd taken to the life! What else could she think, when she waited and waited in Blackpool, and I never came? That was what Troy meant when he came up to me in Rhyl and accused me of letting Gran down . . . and it's ten years ago. Oh, God, what must I do, what must I do?

She scrambled out of bed, ripped back the curtains, and went over to the washstand. She splashed water noisily into the basin and began to wash. Behind her, Merle groaned and sat up. 'Whazzamarrer?' she said thickly. 'Wazza hurry?'

Lottie had soaped herself all over; now she was rinsing off, trembling with a mixture of cold and fury. She removed the last of the soap and began to rub herself dry, then turned to Merle. 'I've remembered,' she said. 'You know, the six years before I had the accident. And – and everything's changed. Louella's been lying to me for the past ten years. I'm going to have it out with her.'

She was dressing and Merle promptly heaved

herself out of bed and began to drag her own clothes on, not bothering with a wash. 'If you're going to challenge Louella, then I don't mean to miss it,' she said, beginning to brush out her tangled curls. 'But what happened, Lottie? Did them six years just come floodin' back? Are you sure you haven't been dreamin'?'

'Positive,' Lottie said briefly. She did not mean to explain about the dreams to anyone right now. 'It's – it's a bit as though there was a door in my head which has been closed and locked because I believed there was nothing behind it except for what Louella had told me. Only every now and again I'd see something – or someone – which seemed familiar, and I'd ask Louella about it. She put me off each time, but I was getting increasingly doubtful about what she told me and then, when I woke this morning, the door in my head flew open and the things which had really happened came tumbling out.'

'Gosh!' Merle said in an awed voice. 'How do you feel? It must be like going around for years with a heavy pack on your back, and then suddenly finding it's slipped off.'

Lottie laughed. 'Yes, it's a bit like that,' she admitted. 'But at the moment I'm so furious with Louella for all the lies she told that I've not really taken in anything else.'

She set off across the bedroom and clattered down the stairs, Merle close behind her. But with her hand on the doorknob she turned to face her friend, feeling the colour draining from her cheeks. It was all very well to talk about having it out with Louella, but she had no proof. If Louella continued to deny everything . . . but it would make no difference, not now. Very soon she would be Sassy again and even Louella would not dare to deny the change of name which she had forced upon her daughter, doubtless for fear that if she used the name Sassy her child's memory would come flooding back.

Lottie took a deep breath, turned, and walked into the kitchen. As she did so, she felt Merle's hand slip into hers, and her friend said in a low voice: 'Be brave, love, and don't let her get away with any more lies.'

Louella was at the stove, stirring porridge, and Baz was toasting bread and passing the slices to Max, who was stacking them up on a plate. To Lottie's surprise, Jack Russell was also present. He grinned at her cheerfully. 'I brung a dozen eggs what I bought off of me landlady's cousin, and invited meself to breakfast,' he said, before either girl could speak. 'So it's scrambled egg on toast for brekker this morning. Hope you're hungry as hunters!'

Lottie was opening her mouth to reply when Merle dug her in the ribs. Louella turned away from the stove and began ladling porridge into the dishes arranged around the table. 'I'm glad you two are up, despite your late night,' she said briskly. 'I want the pair of you to come down to

the theatre with me.' She turned a smile of ingratiating sweetness on Merle and her voice dropped
a couple of tones. 'Darling, I want you to instruct
Lottie in your modern dance routines. I promise
you she'll only be doing the dances whilst you're –
you're temporarily away . . .'

Because of what Merle had told her, Lottie
recognised the sudden infusion of sweetness in her
mother's tone and it helped her to come to the
point at once. 'Louella, I want some explanations,
please. For a start, where's my birth certificate?'

Her mother stared, then shrugged and once
more her voice changed its tone. 'Your birth certificate? Darling, I haven't the foggiest notion, but
why on earth do you want it? It seems a strange
thing to ask for on a Sunday morning, when we're
all about to enjoy scrambled eggs.' She turned to
Jack. 'It was so good of you, Jack, to buy them. It's
true, isn't it, that Mrs Parrot's cousin owns a farm
on the Wirral? That means that they'll be really
fresh; a rare treat for us townies.' She had
continued to ladle porridge as she spoke and now
she gestured to everyone to take their places at the
table. 'Eat up! There's milk in the blue jug and
sugar in the bowl, not that you should need either
because this is the creamiest porridge I've ever
made.'

Max, Baz and Jack took their places, but Lottie
and Merle remained standing. 'I want my birth
certificate, Mother,' Lottie said firmly. 'You are my
mother, I take it?'

Pink colour gradually crept up Louella's neck and dyed her face. She said stiffly: 'You know I prefer you to call me Louella. And now do get on with your porridge, darling, because I can't start scrambling the eggs until those plates are scraped clean.'

She was trying to sound jokey but Lottie, knowing her well, could hear the underlying strain, so she ignored her mother's words and actually held out a hand and snapped her fingers, right under Louella's nose. 'I want my birth certificate,' she said steadily. 'And I want the truth so I'm going to tell you a story. My name isn't Charlotte, or Lottie, it's Sassy, and you gave me away when I was only a few days old.' Standing there in the kitchen, she proceeded to tell the story of the first six years of her life as she now knew it, and had the satisfaction of seeing Louella go alternately as red as a turkeycock and as white as a sheet. No one else was eating their porridge; they were all staring at her, open-mouthed. Even Baz, who knew about the dreams, looked astonished.

When Lottie got to the meeting in the clearing, Louella actually burst into speech. 'It's all nonsense, stupid nonsense!' she shouted. 'Who's been talking to you, filling you up with lies? As if—'

'You have; been filling me up with lies, I mean,' Lottie said resolutely. 'You sat by my hospital bed and told me I'd been your partner, singing and dancing and helping you with the act. Whilst anyone might still recognise me as Gran's Sassy, you would never do a summer season, though Max frequently begged you to do so. You made all sorts of excuses, Louella, but they were just excuses. You knew that Gran and Troy were often at the seaside in summertime, and you didn't want to meet them, or rather you didn't want me to meet them. You only agreed to go to Yarmouth because I was older and you thought I looked quite different. You thought that if Gran had walked up to me and called me Sassy, I'd not have known who the devil she was, so you assumed you were safe . . .'

At this point Max broke in, though his voice was tentative. 'But Lottie, darling, I've met performers who worked with Louella and Lottie when you were no more than three or four. How do you explain that?'

'Easily,' Lottie said. 'My mother hired a little girl called Lottie for several years. But the little girl's own mother realised how popular the child was and took her away with her, back to France. It was then that Louella decided to reclaim me, having been quite content to leave me with Gran for the previous six years.'

'But – but how did you find out?' Jack Russell broke in. 'I know you said your memory has come back, but a baby of a few days old don't remember nothin', not so far as I know.'

'When my memory returned, I remembered Gran telling me, when Louella came and snatched me back, that she'd thought of me as her own child since Louella had handed me over when I was only a few days old,' Lottie said steadily. Abruptly, she turned to her mother. 'Do you want me to leave here now and come back with someone who can confirm every word I've said? Or would you try to say they were telling lies, too?'

At the thought of such a confrontation, Louella's courage deserted her. She began to babble, saying that she had had no choice. She had had a little baby she could not look after, and almost no money. She had been offered a job with a circus, as the magician's assistant, with the possibility of other work. She would share a caravan with a couple of the girls who rode the liberty horses, but there was no room for a baby. Mrs Olly – the woman Lottie called Gran – told fortunes and travelled all over the country in her funny little caravan, with her young grandson. She was about to leave for her winter quarters, since the circus only wanted side shows in the spring and summer, but she promised to let Louella know where she was so that Louella could send her money for the baby's keep and visit whenever she had the time.

'It seemed the ideal solution,' Louella said tearfully. 'Everyone assured me that Gran – they all called her Gran – was marvellous with children and would take care of my baby as though she was her own.' She looked defiantly round at her speechless audience. 'Can't you see I had no choice? Max, you must understand.'

'In a way, I can see your predicament,' Max admitted. 'But remember, Louella, I've been in a very similar position myself. Baz was three months old when my wife left me – left us, I should say – but it never crossed my mind to hand my little son over to anyone else. Of course I employed people to keep an eye on him when I was actually performing, but otherwise I simply did my best. When he was teething, or had the colic, I scarcely slept . . . but you don't want to know that. All I'm saying is, I wouldn't have handed Baz over to anyone else for a thousand pounds.'

'But I've told you, I had no choice,' Louella insisted. 'There was no room in the caravan for a baby, and – and I've never been good with kids. I thought it was best that little Lottie was brought up by someone who understood babies. And of course I meant to visit her as often as I possibly could.'

'But you never did visit, not once in six years,' Lottie reminded her. 'You did send money at first, but even that had stopped by the time I was three or four. Then, just when you'd lost the first Lottie – the one who wasn't really your daughter – you had an enormous piece of luck. You read an article about us in the paper, Gran, Troy – he's her real grandson, incidentally – and me, how we'd seen a nearby barn struck by lightning. We went and warned the farmer, and helped him fight the fire. The feller from the newspaper said Mrs Olly was a fortune-teller, and Sassy and Troy her grandchildren, and that was enough to put you on our

404

trail. You followed us because you needed a child for your act, and I was just about the right age. You can't pretend you loved me, or you would have visited, if nothing else.'

She turned to Max, who was listening, his face impassive. 'Then I had that awful accident and Louella thought she was in the clear. I was in hospital for weeks and weeks and Louella filled in the six years I'd lost with lies, which of course I believed. But that's all over now. I've remembered everything and I'm going back to Gran.'

Baz got up. 'So that was it,' he said softly. He turned to his father. 'She's been telling me bits and pieces for years, but we neither of us realised it was her memory coming back because we both believed the things Louella had told her.' He turned back to Lottie. 'You'll go off in search of them? Gran and Troy? I wish to God I could come with you, but jobs is like gold dust, and I dursen't leave mine, not even for a few days. If I knew . . .'

'No need. I'm going with her,' Merle said quietly. 'I ain't goin' into one o' them homes, and I bet that were one of Louella's fancy ideas 'n' all.'

'It wasn't; that's to say I did suggest it, but everyone agreed . . .'

'Forget it,' Merle said. 'It's my life and I'll live it the way I bleedin' well choose. I'm goin' to pack my gear.' She turned and was across the hall and halfway up the stairs, with Lottie close on her heels, when behind them, in the kitchen, bedlam broke out, with Max shouting, Louella beginning

405

to have hysterics, and Jack and Baz, from the sound of it, doing their best to calm everyone down.

In their own room, both girls snatched their belongings from drawers and cupboards and began to cram them into the holdalls they had used for their Yarmouth venture. But it was very soon obvious that this would not do. 'Our arms will break from the weight,' Lottie said practically, trying to heave her holdall off the floor. 'Best just take the essentials: warm stuff, no frills.'

It was astonishing, once they had made up their minds to pack only practical garments, how quickly they were ready. Lottie packed soap, flannel, toothbrush and toothpaste, and finished off with her folded towel, then turned to her companion. 'Ready?' she enquired.

Merle nodded dumbly, and without more ado both girls clattered down the two flights of stairs into the hall below. They would have avoided the kitchen but the door shot open as they reached it and Lottie realised that their coats still hung on the hooks and their thick boots stood by the dresser. A quick glance round showed them that Louella was no longer in the room. Only Max, Baz and Jack stood there, all looking deeply troubled. Lottie, well aware that the three men had had nothing to do with either Merle's predicament or her own, dumped her case on the floor and went over to Max to give him a hug. 'I'm awful sorry you had to hear all that,' she said in a low voice. 'I didn't mean to turn you against my mother but when I realised ... when my memory came back ... and I suppose you'd have learned the truth in the end anyway.'

'Not from Louella he wouldn't,' Merle said.

Max released Lottie with a pat on the cheek. 'It's all right, flower; you've probably done me the best turn one person can do another,' he said. 'I'd almost made up my mind to ask Lou to marry me, which would have been the biggest mistake I'd ever made.' He turned to Merle. 'I wouldn't have put you into an ordinary home, you know. I were goin' to find a private one, 'cos when you pay down your money, I believe they really do treat you very well,' he said.

'I'm sorry, Uncle Max, because I'm sure you think that sending me to one of them homes is the best thing you can do, but perhaps I really am a circus girl at heart. I think I'd die in one of them places.'

'Well, you go with your pal now, but if you change your mind and want to have the baby in some sort of nursing home, just drop me a line and I'll see you right.' He dug a hand into his pocket and produced a couple of notes and some silver. 'Look, leave your cases here, take this money and go for a bit of a day out. Then come back here for tonight and tomorrow morning, first thing, we'll all go down to the post office and I'll draw out some of my savings. You can't go off with scarce a penny piece to your names.'

Merle took the money gratefully, but both girls

shook their heads at the notion of returning to Victoria Court. 'We're going now, Uncle Max. We've both saved a bit in our own post office accounts, but when that runs out we might get in touch,' Merle said. 'You agree, don't you, Lottie?'

'That's right, because at the moment I feel I never want to set eyes on Louella again,' Lottie said frankly. 'She's – she's so clever, Max. She'll try to talk me into staying; she'll appeal to my better nature because both of us walking out means the end of the Lacey Sisters, and if she tries to remind me that she's been a good mother to me for the past ten years ... no, I can't come back.'

Jack, who had been following the conversation closely, cleared his throat. 'But it's true, isn't it, Lottie?' he said gently. 'Your mam has been good to you for the past ten years. You wanted for nothing and she's taught you a trade, as a performer. When you wanted money for little extras, she always shelled out, even if she grumbled a bit. I know Mrs Brock helped with the cooking a couple of times, but your mam always made your favourite dishes ... Then there was a grand cake for your birthday every year, smart new shoes, or a nice thick coat for Christmas ...'

'I know, Jack, but she would have done the same for anyone to keep them in the act,' Lottie said obstinately. 'I've never loved the stage, not the way Louella does, but I really did love Gran. What she must think of me ... oh, I can't bear to remember how I let her down!'

'Well, don't think too badly of your mam, queen,' Jack said quietly. 'She's a gifted performer, a real trouper, and perhaps theatricals ain't quite like other people. It's a tough profession and maybe it's made Louella hard, but underneath I'm sure she loves you. Can't you forgive her and try to get in touch with this old woman without leavin' Louella in the lurch?'

'Don't appeal to her better nature, Jack, because it ain't fair,' Baz broke in. 'Lottie will come back one day, won't you, chuck, same as Merle will, once she's – she's able. They've got the old woman's name and the boy's too, so they might find them easier to trace than you'd think. And they'll keep in touch, won't you, girls? You can ring the theatre from time to time and ask to speak to Max or Jack, and you can send us postcards, or even letters, so we know how you're gettin' along.' Surprisingly, he put both arms round Merle, gave her a gentle squeeze, and then kissed the top of her head. 'I'm sorry I've not been more help, love,' he said gently. 'But everything's happened so fast. Mebbe it's best for you and me to be parted for a while, so we can sort ourselves out.'

Merle gave a watery little giggle. 'I do love you, Baz, but maybe you're right and we need to go our separate ways until after the kid's born. I'm real sorry I let you down. We'll keep in touch.'

She bent and picked up her holdall and Lottie, following suit, saw Jack cock his head on one side and then go over and snatch their coats and hats

409

from the hooks, gesturing to them to pick up their winter boots. 'I just heard a thump from upstairs; I reckon Louella will be down in a couple of minutes,' he said. 'Better not meet whilst tempers are still a trifle frayed.'

The girls hurried down the passageway and out of the front door. Lottie was surprised into a gasp as the cold air struck her. She turned to take her coat from Jack only to find him closing the door gently and descending the three well-whitened steps. He helped Merle into her coat, handed Lottie hers and then put on his own. 'I'm comin' with you,' he said, in answer to Lottie's surprised look. 'I'll explain as we go.' He looked down at the thin shoes which both girls wore. 'Shove them silly little slipper things into your bags and put on them nice warm boots,' he advised. 'By Jupiter, you don't half choose the right sort o' weather to run away in.'

'We aren't running away,' Lottie objected, as Jack began to shepherd them out of the court. 'Neither of us are. We're leaving because we have . . . things to do.' By now they had reached Burlington Street and Jack took Merle's bag from her.

'Whilst I'm with you, I'll carry this,' he said. 'And you two can each take a handle of t'other 'un. I've heard it said that a gal in the family way shouldn't go heftin' heavy stuff.'

'It ain't heavy at all, really, but thanks anyway, Jack,' Merle said, as they reached Scotland Road.

'Hey, why's we turnin' left? I reckoned we'd be headin' towards the city centre.'

'We're going to my lodgings,' Jack said briefly. 'Where had you planned to go, eh? That bit of money Max gave you might buy you a room for the night, but it wouldn't buy you food, and not one bit of them lovely scrambled eggs so much as got to the table, lerralone down your throats. I'm a bachelor, so a good deal o' me money gets purraway for me old age, but I don't have no truck wi' banks. I keeps me cash hid away in an old sock, under me mattress, so I'm a-goin' to shell out to you young ladies, secure in the knowledge that if I ever needs it I'll gerrit back from one o' you.'

'It's awfully good of you, Jack, but we can't possibly . . .' Lottie was beginning, but Merle elbowed her sharply in the ribs.

'You're a prince, Jack,' Merle said gratefully. 'When Baz said that about jobs bein' like gold dust, I remembered someone sayin' that this here is what they calls a depression and it'll get worse, not better. The rich people at the top of the heap uses the Slump as an excuse to get rid o' employees an' pay the rest as little as they can get away with. Who'd have thought the Wall Street crash would have affected us? Of course we mean to work as we go, and maybe when we find Mrs Olly she'll need us to earn our keep an' all, so we're real grateful for your offer and we'll accept it gladly.' She nudged Lottie again. 'Ain't that so, queen?'

Lottie, having had time to think it over, agreed fervently that it was indeed so, but refused to go inside Jack's lodgings when he invited them. 'The fewer people to know we're leavin' home, the better,' she observed. And when Jack handed over what seemed like a substantial sum, she threw her arms round his neck, and gave him an impulsive kiss. 'Everyone always says that theatre folk are generous, and you've proved it. Oh, Jack, you're the best friend anyone could ever have, and we'll pay you back one day, honest to God we will,' she said breathlessly. 'We promised to keep in touch and so we shall, but I'd better tell you that none of our letters or postcards will have our address on, or any clue to our whereabouts, because I'm afraid if Louella knew where we were, she'd come after us. I am her daughter, after all.'

'And you're not so very old,' Jack pointed out. 'But I wouldn't give you away to your mam, you know that.'

'I do know it, but what you don't know you can't reveal, even by accident,' Lottie said, crossing her fingers behind her back. She would have liked to be able to trust Jack but thought his affection for Louella might cause him to waver, for her mother could be very persuasive. No, it was best to stick to their guns and never give an address.

For a moment, the three of them stood in silence on the pavement, surrounded by the white mist of their breath. Then Jack gave each of them a brisk hug. 'Good luck,' he said, before stepping back into his landlady's hallway, and the girls set out for the nearest tram stop.

Jack's money, still in an ancient grey sock, was shoved deep inside Lottie's coat pocket, and its weight gave her a comfortable feeling of security. They climbed aboard the first tram to arrive, but when the conductor called, 'Fares please!' they looked at one another in some consternation.

'Sunday trains aren't like weekday ones, and I bet you ain't certain where you mean to start this search,' Merle muttered as the conductor approached. 'Quick, what stop shall I say?'

'Oh, say Lime Street,' Lottie said quickly. 'There's cheap lodging houses round most stations so we'll book into one of them for the night, but we'll go straight to the station now and check on timetables. If you've no objection, I'd like to start my search at Rhyl, because that's where I first saw Troy in real life, not in my – my memory. All right by you?'

The girls reached Rhyl at around three o'clock on Monday afternoon. It was another chilly day and they spent a considerable time touring the town and enquiring about prices, and finally went for the cheapest room available. The landlord, dark-skinned and sour-faced, told them that bed and breakfast would be half a crown. 'But we don't want breakfast,' Lottie said quickly, seeing a chance to save some money. 'How much for just the room?'

'I telled you: half a crown,' the man said, glaring at them. After a moment's thought he added: 'Each.'

Lottie would have said nothing, but Merle gave a bitter laugh and half turned away. 'You'll say leg in a minute,' she remarked. 'Half a crown a leg.'

Lottie giggled, getting ready to run, but greatly to her surprise the man gave a reluctant grin. 'You ain't as green as you're cabbage-lookin',' he remarked. 'All right, half a crown for the room. It ain't much and there's only the one bed, but it'll be big enough for a couple of skinny kids, I dare say. And now you'd best come in and take a look at it. How long d'you mean to stay? Is it just the one night?'

'We don't know,' Lottie said truthfully. 'I'm searching for my gran and my cousin Troy. If we find them quickly, we may only be here the one night; it depends.'

They had been following the man up two flights of rickety stairs as they talked, and now he flung open a small door and revealed their room. Needless to say, since they were in the attic, the ceiling sloped so sharply that even Lottie could not stand upright, but had to bend her head. The room contained little apart from an ancient brass bedstead, a rickety chest of drawers and a wash-stand, but to Lottie's surprise the bedding, though worn and patched, was clean, and the floorboards showed no trace of dust.

'Well?' the landlord said; his momentary amusement had clearly evaporated and from his impatient tone he was keen to get back to his own quarters, wherever they might be. 'Are you taking it? I want me money in advance, mind.'

'Yes, we'll take it,' Merle said, fishing a half-crown out of her pocket and handing it over reluctantly. 'But we'll want a key to that there door because we've got to leave our holdalls here whilst we search for our gran.'

The landlord pocketed the money and turned away. 'There ain't no key as you'd see if you'd eyes in your head,' he said nastily. 'There ain't no keyhole, so is it likely there'd be a key? But at present you're the only lodgers so your stuff'll be safe enough.'

'In other words, if we lose anything we can tell the scuffers that it was you what took it,' Merle said amiably, following him out of the room.

They descended the first flight of stairs and the man turned on the landing to grin at them. 'That's right; but I doubt you'd be believed. I've been runnin' this 'ere lodgin' house for twenty years and no one's accused me of dishonesty yet. Well, if you're only here for one night, no point in tellin' you the house rules, but I'd best mention you're not allowed to cook food in your room and the lavvy is in the yard at the back. I'll show you.'

Once outside on the pavement again, the two girls smiled at one another. 'I say, Merle, you are brave,' Lottie said admiringly. 'I'd never have dared to speak out like you did.'

'Ah, but you've not spent your life touring the country and having to tackle landlords and land-ladies, fighting your corner with folk being prejudiced 'cos they reckon circus people are gypsies,' Merle said. 'Of course when I were a kid, me mam and dad did all the bargaining, but I suppose I took in more'n I realised because when I went off with me two pals to do our Sisters act I knew just how to treat anyone tryin' to do us down.' She glanced around the street, then linked her arm in Lottie's. 'Which way to the prom?' she remarked. 'I reckon our search should start there.'

Rhyl was not a big town and the couple for whom the girls were searching would have stood out in people's memories, Lottie was sure, so by the end of the day they were pretty certain that Gran and Troy were not in Rhyl. As they made their way back to their lodgings with a newspaper-wrapped bundle of fish and chips, Merle was inclined to be depressed, but Lottie said she thought they had made a good start. 'We've learned that young people can't help us much, but older ones actually remember a circus which used to come every August, and had a fortune-teller who sounded just like Gran,' she reminded her friend. 'I know everyone says that the fortune-teller who's come to Rhyl recently has been young and sharp-featured, but that only means Gran's not with that particular show any more. We could try Llandudno, Abergele,

Prestatyn . . . only so far as I know, none of those towns are visited regularly by a circus.'

'Well, the seaside does seem the best bet,' Merle acknowledged as they unlocked the front door of their lodgings with the key their landlord had given them. They scuttled quietly down the hall and up the stairs, and shut the door of their room behind them before shedding their coats and checking that their holdalls were still beneath the bed where they had left them, and did not appear to have been touched.

'Let's wrap ourselves in the bedding and eat our suppers,' Lottie said. 'I wish we could lock the door. If there was a chair we could jam it under the handle . . .'

She and Merle had both slumped on to the bed, but at her words Merle got up, put her finger to her lips and left the room. A minute later she was back, carrying an old kitchen chair. 'It were in the room opposite,' she said, jamming the door closed with the back of the chair. 'There you are, safe as houses. And now let's get at them fish and chips!'

Despite the tiring day they had had, however, Lottie did not find it easy to fall asleep. Long after Merle was snoring gently, she lay staring at the cracks which ran across the ceiling, for the curtains were thin and the moon shone through them, illumining the room with a ghostly grey pallor. Eventually, however, she did sleep, and pretty soundly too.

417

In fact she only awakened to daylight and the sound of someone sobbing. She opened her eyes and for a moment could not imagine where she was. Then she glanced blearily around her and remembered: she and Merle were in lodgings in Rhyl, and her friend, who had been quite cheerful and optimistic for most of the previous day, must have remembered her situation. She sat up, meaning to give Merle a hug and tell her that all would be well, but even as she did so Merle put her arms round Lottie and said bracingly: 'Whatever's the matter, chuck? Oh, don't tek on so; I'm certain we'll find 'em before too long!'

Lottie stared at her friend, then put tentative fingers up to her own cheek. It was wet with tears. 'It was me crying, then,' she said wonderingly. 'But I thought it was you ... I must have been dreaming.'

'You were,' Merle said. 'You ... well, you were talking about Louella ...'

All in a moment, Lottie remembered. She had been dreaming about the Gaiety theatre. In her dream, Louella had had to explain to Mr Quentain that The Three Lacey Sisters were no longer an act, and Mr Quentain had turned Louella out. She had seen her mother, shoulders drooping, walking dejectedly away from the theatre, despair in every slow dragging footstep. 'What am I to do?' her mother had said, in a small, hopeless voice. 'I know it was wrong to abandon my baby, but what choice did I have?'

Then, in the manner of dreams, Max had been there, walking along beside her mother, talking earnestly. 'You won't be able to manage when you have only the money I pay to my assistant coming in,' he was saying, in a matter-of-fact voice. 'Is there nothing else you can do? I suppose you could launder sheets and tablecloths for the big hotels . . .'

'I couldn't possibly do work of that nature,' Louella had cried. 'Oh, Max, I know I was wrong to leave my baby with that old woman, but since getting her back again I've really, really tried to be a good mother. I don't know whether I succeeded – I suppose not, since Lottie's run away from me – but I truly did try. And now that she's gone, there's a dreadful ache in my heart and I miss her more than I can say.'

Then the dream had faded and Lottie realised that the tears she had shed had been for Louella, and not for herself. She looked at Merle. 'I thought I hated Louella but I don't believe I do,' she said slowly. 'And I don't believe she hates me, either. So I've made up my mind that when I go back to her, I'll always call her Mam, never Louella, and I'll make her listen to me and tell me the absolute truth, always. Then we can be a proper mother and daughter, even though we may never live under the same roof again, because I mean to live with Gran, you know.'

'Good for you, love,' Merle said. She hesitated, then went on. 'But darling Lottie, has it never occurred to you that – that ten years is a long time, and Mrs Olly may be . . . may be . . .'

'May be dead, you mean,' Lottie said. 'Yes of course it's a possibility, but if she was, I – I think I'd know. And now we'd best get dressed because we'll want to be moving on today and it's broad daylight. Why, it could be noon!'

'Well it ain't; I heard a clock strike eight just before I woke you,' Merle said. 'So you were dreaming about Louella. Why were you crying then?'

'Oh, it was a silly dream,' Lottie said, beginning to wash. 'I dreamed Mr Quentain and Max told her she'd have to take in washing.'

Merle laughed. 'I can just see Louella doing that,' she said, taking her friend's place at the washstand. 'I wonder if the old bugger would sell us half a loaf and let us make ourselves some toast at his kitchen fire? Because I don't mean to go without me brekker, not now that I'm eating for two.'

It was a cold day towards the end of February. Max came into the kitchen, talking as he did so, then stopped short. Louella was before him, making porridge, whilst Baz cleaned his shoes, whistling. Max looked at Louella intently. 'You've been crying,' he said gently. 'I thought you would have come to terms with it by now . . . Lottie's leaving, I mean. I told you, young Merle's got a sensible head on her shoulders and she's been raised in a hard school. Circus folk are grand but they're always on the move and ordinary towns-people think they're gypsies and treat them accordingly, so Merle has had to be tough. And remember, Lottie never said she was going for good; I'm sure she means to come back just as soon as she's explained things to this Mrs Olly you mentioned.'

'Oliphant, that's her real name,' Louella said. 'But everyone calls her Mrs Olly.' She began to ladle porridge into the dishes she had stood ready, then banged the pan back on the stove and turned away from the two men. 'I can't get used to there being only three of us,' she wailed. 'I miss them both, but losing Lottie is like losing an arm. I can't stop thinking about her, wishing I'd told her the truth, only of course if I had I'd have lost her earlier.'

'It doesn't follow,' Baz said, his spoon poised halfway to his mouth. 'Oh, I don't deny she would have wanted to go back to Gran, but I'm sure between you you could have worked something out. Why, Gran could have come and stayed nearby every summer season so that Lottie could do her act yet be with both of you.'

'Well, it's no good wishing, because I didn't do it at the time and it's a bit late now,' Louella said. She came over to the table and sat down, pulling a dish of porridge towards her, then pushing it away. 'And the worst thing is the worry. I've never been a worrier but now, not knowing where she is or what's happening to her . . .'

'Eat that porridge,' Max said firmly. 'The girls have written, so you know they're all right even though you can't reply because they won't give you an address. It's early days, Louella, and Mr Quentain isn't going to want a singer-dancer with legs like matchsticks and a face as long as a wet weekend. You're always fond of telling us you're a pro, a real trouper; now's the time to prove it!'

Chapter Fifteen

It was a cold spring, and as the girls continued their search it became imperative that they should work. They had tried all the larger East Anglian seaside resorts without success, though a good many people – the older ones – remembered Gran and Troy from years back. Some reckoned she had retired, others that she had perhaps joined a travelling fair. 'There's tiny fairs what don't do the big resorts at all, but go from village to village from March to October, and then lays up somewhere snug to overwinter,' one elderly man told them. 'Come to think, she and the boy appeared on the scene around ten years gone. She must ha' done something before then, though I misremember her ever referring to it. Maybe, as she got older, she went back to her roots, so to speak.'

This was bad news for the girls and that evening, as they lay huddled together in the single bed in a cold and rather dirty lodging house, they discussed what best to do. 'We need to earn some money badly; I know we've had bits and pieces of work in every town we've stopped in, but it really isn't enough. We want a job that will last weeks, not days, and will pay well enough to cover food, lodgings, and a little bit over,' Lottie said. 'There don't seem to be many jobs about anywhere but I think if we ask folk to employ us – say we'll do anything – then someone may take us on. Only I don't fancy sleeping out again now that it's got so bitter.'

Merle, pulling the thin blankets up to her chin, shivered and agreed that sleeping out was no longer an option. Some time previously they had received a tip-off from an elderly woman who remembered Gran and Troy and also the winter quarters of the fair which had last employed the old lady. 'Mrs Olly told fortunes and the lad did just about everything: he took the money on the bumper cars, lifted the kids on and off the horses on the galloper, barked for the side shows and helped wi' the takin' down and puttin' up,' she had said, smiling. 'He were a grand lad. He looked after the old gal real good; well, I suppose you could say they looked after each other. Yes, I reckon if you make your way to King's Lynn you'll mebbe find 'em, or at least get news of 'em.'

The girls had taken her advice but no amount of questioning had helped in their search. Even then, the caravans had been drawn into the shelter of a nearby wood and the amusements tucked away under canvas. The field in which the fair overwintered was several miles from King's Lynn and by the time the girls had finished questioning the fair folk night had been drawing in. The thought of tramping back into town and then

424

having to search for lodgings was daunting, and it was then that Lottie had her bright idea. 'It doesn't look as if it's going to rain,' she said. 'I reckon if we crawl under the canvas and curl up in one of the cars, we'll lie snug enough until morning and it'll save us a night's rent.'

They had done this for a couple of nights but then had felt impelled to move on and had not been sorry to do so, for they were not the only ones who sheltered beneath the canvas covers. Scuttlings and squealings indicated that rats and mice also appreciated having a roof over their heads, and there were spiders and earwigs in residence as well.

So now Merle agreed fervently that work was infinitely preferable to sleeping rough. 'If it snowed, we'd be found dead by morning,' she said. 'But there's a big café in the town centre and they get real busy around lunchtime, when folk come out of the offices and factories to get themselves a bite to eat. They might need girls to wash up or wait on; you never know.'

They were in luck and worked for a couple of days at the café in question, but when they left on what turned out to be their last evening to go back to their lodgings, they ran into an ugly situation. A group of girls accosted them, forming a circle round them and demanding to know what they were doing, taking jobs from local girls and working for a pittance. 'My mum's cook assistant in Heyworth's Dining Rooms and she says you're so desperate you let the old feller pay you half cash an' half grub,' she said accusingly. 'He sacked me an' Rita here, as well as Dottie and Mabel, because he said we weren't satisfactory, took food when he weren't watchin' and flirted wi' the customers. But we were all right until you come along, and now we wants our jobs back.'

She was a tall heavy girl and not the sort, Lottie and Merle realised, to sympathise with their plight. Lottie, however, tried to explain. 'We're searching for our gran and we need to make some money before we can move on . . .' she began, but she got no further. The tall heavy girl swung her arm and her fist connected with Lottie's head, knocking her to the ground. Lottie got groggily to her feet just as another girl began to batter Merle, and all might have gone very badly for them had not Merle's face gone suddenly white as a sheet before she slumped to the ground.

'You wicked, horrible creatures!' Lottie shouted, bending over her friend's inanimate form. 'She's expecting a baby and if you've killed either one of them, I swear I'll see you hang!'

Several of the girls looked shamefaced, but the ones who had lost their jobs were made of sterner stuff. 'We won't touch either of you if you'll go,' the big heavy girl said. 'We don't want the likes of you stealing our jobs an' takin' the bread from our mouths.'

Merle was beginning to come round; she sat up, stared, then seemed to remember where she was and what had happened. 'We're moving on all the time,' she said wearily. 'We'll go, won't we, Lottie?'

'And gladly,' Lottie said through clenched teeth. She wished she could hand out a few clacks herself but knew she was not nearly strong enough, for weeks of poor food and worry had already taken their toll.

They moved on the next morning but went first to the café to explain why they were having to relinquish their jobs and to ask if they might have the money they had earned for their two days' work. 'I didn't oughta pay you a penny 'cos you're lettin' me down,' the proprietor grumbled. 'But the rest of the staff say you worked well while you were with us so I've put a bit extry into the envelope.'

Both girls thanked him profusely and set off for the railway station. 'I still reckon it's time to put our search aside for a while, get ourselves work of some sort, and begin to put money aside for when your baby's born,' Lottie said, when they reached the station and began to scan the timetables in a glass-fronted case. 'It ought to arrive in four or five weeks, shouldn't it? We don't want to find ourselves in some tiny hamlet with no doctor for miles, 'cos I've never delivered a baby and I don't mean to start now.'

'I'm losin' track of time,' Merle admitted. 'But I think I'm due in May. What's the date now?'

'It's the end of March, I think,' Lottie said. 'Won't

it be grand when the warmer weather comes, Merle?' She turned her friend so that they could both look out through the station entrance at the rain which was driving along the pavement. 'What we need right now is a big city where there's still some work around, even if it's not very well paid.'

Merle agreed, and after some further discussion they bought two single tickets to Leeds. As they settled into their seats, having already deposited their holdalls on the rack above their heads, Lottie thought that for the first time in their wanderings they were heading towards home. Oh, Leeds might be a long way from Liverpool, with a good deal of wild and hilly country in between, but it was the first time they had turned their faces westward since they had left Rhyl, and Lottie thought wistfully of the warm kitchen in Victoria Court, the enthusiastic applause of the audiences at the Gaiety and her weekly wage packet, taken for granted once but never again.

Merle's mind must have been running on the same lines for presently she spoke thoughtfully. 'When all this is over, Lottie, when I've had my baby and you've found your gran, I'd go back and work for Louella for nothing, so I would. I never realised how lucky we were to have proper jobs and a proper home. I know Louella didn't like me much at first, and she was awful cross when she found out I was in the family way, but me own mother would probably have reacted similar. The trouble was, I knew I'd been a fool but I should have known I'd done wrong and deserved all the things Louella said of me.'

'But you didn't . . . deserve what Louella said, I mean, because she said you were a bad girl, and bad girls go with more than one feller and aren't a bit sorry except when they're caught out,' Lottie said. There was a short pause and when she spoke again it was almost grudgingly. 'I suppose you'll say it was the same for me, that my mother lied for my own good. I dare say living in a little old caravan and going round fairs and circuses and such was Louella's idea of hell. She's always loved the stage and wanted me to love it too, wanted me to have a proper home, nice clothes, good food. So she told lies, and when I found out I never gave her a chance to put things right herself. Maybe if I'd stayed, she would have helped me to find Gran.'

Merle nodded slowly. 'We acted hasty,' she agreed. 'But if we hadn't we'd never have known what a hard old world it is. I reckon leaving Liverpool was the best thing in the long run. And going back . . . oh, it will be wonderful! They'll be pleased to see us so they'll give us a grand welcome and I reckon everyone will appreciate us more too, because we were good, Lottie: slick an' professional. I bet the girls who've took our places get the rough side of your mam's tongue five nights out of six, and that don't make for a good act.'

'And what about Baz? Will he welcome you with

open arms?' Lottie asked. 'Do you want him to, for that matter?'

Merle frowned down at her hands lying in her lap. 'I don't know,' she said slowly. 'There's lots of pretty girls in Liverpool. By the time we get back he could be – involved – with one of them. And d'you know what, Lottie, we ain't the same two girls what left Victoria Court. So Baz and I will have to play it by ear, I reckon.'

'Fair enough,' Lottie said. 'Then we must simply do our best to stay independent, because it would never do to have to crawl home with our tails between our legs, or write asking for money.'

Merle agreed fervently. 'So we must find work, no matter how hard, and it would be nice to get decent lodgings for a change.'

'I say, I've just thought! There are bound to be theatres in Leeds. You might get a job backstage and I might fill in if one of the chorus is ill . . . something like that, anyway.'

'Wish you were right, but I doubt it,' Merle said. 'Oh, Lottie, if only!'

They reached Leeds and saw that it was indeed an enormous place, but even so there was a queue for every job going and the wages paid were very little better than they had been in smaller towns. There were theatres, but none were looking for employees and Lottie realised, ruefully, that their appearance was against them. Down-at-heel shoes, worn clothing and untidy, overlong hair was unlikely to make any management keen to employ them.

However, they managed to get work in a large bakery, though their lodgings were some distance from their place of employment and bakery employees started work at three o'clock in the morning and worked right through to three or even four o'clock in the afternoon. The money was good, however, and both girls speedily realised why. Working in the Earlham Bakery was sheer hell. At first they had revelled in the warmth after the icy cold of the night, but very soon they were not warm but horribly hot, with sweat pouring down their faces and their clothing damp with it. The bakers were all men. Merle and Lottie were little better than slaves, for they had to pick up the heavy trays of loaves and take them through to where they stood in the warm to prove, and then over to immense ovens which stood against the rear wall. The trays were slid on to the oven shelves, the timer was set and the cooked loaves were carried to the tiny rear scullery, where they were placed on cooling trays before being taken through into dispatch, who were responsible for delivering the bread to the chain of Earlham shops throughout the city.

However, there were some perks to the job. Misshapen loaves and pastries and cakes which were slightly burned, or in some other way less than perfect, were occasionally given to the girls, who took them back to their lodgings and handed

431

them to their landlady, who would then serve them with their evening meal.

The big disadvantage of the job was the distance the girls had to walk through the icy night to reach their place of employment, for there were no trams or buses running at two o'clock in the morning. They always tried to get to bed no later than six o'clock, which gave them a good eight hours' sleep before they had to stumble out and begin the long walk to work. But Lottie noted how pale and weary Merle was growing and determined to try to search for easier work as soon as she could do so. Neither girl wanted to change their lodgings for Mrs Piggott's house in Duncombe Street was clean and comfortable, and she was a good cook, providing them with a hot meal at night and a pan of porridge, kept hot in a hay box, to line their stomachs before they set off for the bakery.

They had lodged with Mrs Piggott for nearly three weeks and spring was making itself felt when they emerged from the house in Duncombe Street one morning to find a thick and blanketing fog enveloping everything. Leeds was an industrial town and the fog made both girls gasp and cough as they stepped on to the pavement. 'This is hateful,' Lottie said, dismayed. 'It was bad enough in Liverpool when the fog came down, but at least it rolled in from the Mersey and smelt of the sea rather than of factory chimneys, brickworks and the tannery. What's more, we don't know this place well enough to risk getting lost.

D'you think we ought to go back home until it clears?'

Merle, however, shook her head decidedly. 'Can't risk it; we need the money,' she pointed out. She smoothed a hand across the curve of her stomach. 'I know I don't show very much but I feel the size of an elephant, and the kid is forever kicking hell out of me so I reckon it might arrive any day. I shan't be able to work for a week or two then, so we must earn while we can. C'mon, best foot forward!'

'Well, if you're sure,' Lottie said doubtfully. 'Is this the main road? Gosh, the fog's made the paving stones awful slippery. Be careful, Merle!'

'I'm always careful, because I don't want to flatten the kid,' Merle said cheerfully. 'Where's this, d'you reckon? Oh well, we're bound to see a building we recognise sooner or later. Or perhaps the fog will lift.'

They walked on for a while in silence. Lottie listened to the drip, drip, drip of water descending from the eaves of houses they passed, and the muffled sound of their own footsteps. They were used to meeting almost no one at this hour of the night and saw few lighted windows, but somehow tonight was even worse than usual. Not a cat or a dog was abroad; no vehicle passed them, and presently Lottie sat down on a low brick wall and Merle followed suit. 'We're lost, Merle,' Lottie said. She tried to make her voice calm and despised herself for the tremble which she could not control. 'We were daft to keep going – we should have turned back. D'you remember our last night in Victoria Court, when we got lost in the fog? Well, at least there was one person still up, whereas here . . .'

Merle sighed. 'It were my fault, Lottie. I should have listened to you. But there's no point in us sittin' here freezin', an' we can't turn back because we don't know which way is back, if you foller me.' She shivered suddenly and got slowly to her feet, holding out a hand to her companion. 'I've got to keep movin', else they'll find me dead body lyin' on the pavement when the fog lifts,' she said. 'You never know, we might see a lighted window . . . oh my Gawd!'

'What is it? Have you seen . . .' Lottie was beginning when she realised what had caught her friend's attention. It was the gleam of water. She turned to Merle with a feeling that was almost relief. 'It's the perishin' canal! Well, at least we know where we are,' she said. 'How far is the canal from Duncombe Street? If we were to turn right and follow it, keeping to the towpath, wouldn't we end up quite near Mrs Piggott's place?'

'I don't know,' Merle admitted. 'When we first came here and were job hunting, I remember seeing the canal but not taking much notice, though I'm sure there were factories and warehouses all along its banks. Tell you what, whichever way we walk we'll find barges moored, and we may even find someone still awake who might be able to tell us the way back to Duncombe Street. In fact, it 'ud be worth wakin' someone up, even if they were angry, to find out where we are.'

Accordingly, the girls set off along the towpath, and as they walked they talked about that other fog and the woman who had come to their rescue. 'It's odd, isn't it, that she had spent all her working life on the canals and here we are, close by one and just as lost as we were that other time,' Lottie said presently. 'It's almost as though we were guided to the canal.'

Merle snorted. 'And I suppose, if we do find someone still awake, she'll turn out to be an enthusiastic theatregoer,' she said scoffingly. 'Still, if all bargees are as kind and helpful as her . . .'

'She might have been especially nice because she remembered us at the Gaiety,' Lottie said dreamily. 'She remembered me when I was quite a little thing.'

'How d'you make that out?' Merle asked curiously. 'I don't remember her saying she knew you when you were very young.'

Lottie frowned. Where had she got the idea that Mrs Donovan – yes, that was her name – had known her as a very young child? She struggled with the thought for a moment, then the old woman's exact words popped into her head: *When I first saw you your hair were dark. But that really were a long time ago.*

Merle was talking but Lottie clapped both hands

over her ears, closed her eyes and concentrated fiercely. When Mrs Donovan had first seen her, she had had dark hair, but Louella had insisted that her hair be bleached as soon as she arrived at the Gaiety. Therefore it must mean that Mrs Donovan had known her when she had been living with Gran, and this in turn meant that she had been searching in all the wrong places because she had assumed that Gran had always been with circuses and fairs. Feverishly, she cast her mind back over the dreams and saw again Champ's big rump, heard the sound of water and saw the woods and meadows through which they had travelled, often in high summer, autumn or spring. At such times of year, fairs and circuses would have been travelling the country and had Gran been with them there would have been a great many people about. She remembered the campfires and the lovely stews which Gran had cooked over them. Everyone knew that caravan dwellers cooked their meals outside over open fires when the weather permitted, but so of course did the bargees who travelled the length and breadth of the country aboard their painted craft. She remembered the tiny living room in her dream, which she had assumed to be a caravan, but now she believed to have been the cabin of a canal barge. She should have guessed when she had seen the bucket with flowers painted on its side!

'Lottie? Wharrever is the matter? There's a barge chuggin' up behind us. Can you hear it? If we

436

wave and shout, mebbe the feller aboard will draw over and we can find out where we are.' Merle looked curiously at her friend. 'What's up? Ten minutes ago you'd clapped your hands over your lugs and looked so fierce that I dursen't say a word, an' now you're grinnin' from ear to ear. Somethin's pleased you. You might tell me what it is – I could do wi' cheerin' up.'

Lottie turned eagerly to her companion. 'We've been lookin' in all the wrong places,' she said breathlessly. 'It won't mean much to you – it didn't to me at the time – but Mrs Donovan told us she'd worked the canals and she said she knew me when I was just a kid. I reckon when Louella stopped sending money Gran took to the canals to keep her off our trail and I bet she's gone back there now. Oh, Merle, I believe we're on the right track at last!'

Both girls assumed that when they reached the bakery they would be in trouble, but this did not prove to be the case. Everyone was late, grumbling about the fog and saying that they should not be expected to come to work in such conditions. Two of the men lived on the outskirts of Leeds and cycled in each morning and they were even later than Lottie and Merle, so the girls found them- selves actually doing some of the baking, which gave them a chance to exchange a few words from time to time.

'What do you want to do now you think you

437

know where that gran of yours is to be found?' Merle asked as she and Lottie weighed out ingredients.

Lottie was enjoying herself, finding the work far more interesting than their usual boring and repetitive tasks, but she was still unsure of what their next move must be and said so, keeping her voice low. 'We did geography at school and we once had to draw a map of the British Isles, with all the rivers and canals marked in blue crayon,' she said. 'Merle, I'm telling you there's hundreds of miles of waterways all over the country. It may be simpler to search canals and question canal folk than it was to do the same with circus and fair people, but it still won't be easy. I've been thinking and thinking and I reckon our best bet will be to go back to Liverpool and ask Mrs Donovan if she can remember the name of Gran's boat and where we would be likely to find her. Only – only I don't want to walk into anyone who knows us, not until I've found Gran.'

Merle stopped for a moment. 'I know what you mean. We want to go back successful, an' if we go now they'll think we're a couple of failures,' she said.

Lottie seized a ball of dough and pressed it into one of the waiting tins, then did the same with another. She carried them into the hot kitchen to prove and then returned to her friend's side and began weighing out once more. 'Look, Merle, we've stuck together through thick and thin but

438

now you've got to think about that baby. Oh, I know you want nothing to do with it but it's got to come out, whether you like it or not, and you don't want to go giving birth in Liverpool where you're known to half the population, if not more,' she said. 'I think you should stay here. Mrs Piggott knows you're pregnant and has accepted that you're a widow, and you liked the doctor and that young nurse you saw at the hospital, didn't you? I reckon you should stay in Leeds, even though I'll miss you horribly.'

Merle looked frightened. 'But I can't have the baby at Mrs Piggott's house; I'll have to go into hospital,' she said. She gazed at the little Woolworth ring on the third finger of her left hand. 'Only – only I didn't tell the people at the hospital that I wanted the baby adopted and when I tell them they'll guess, won't they?'

'No, of course they won't,' Lottie said bracingly. 'You can tell them you need to earn your living and can't cope with the baby as well.'

'But Lottie, hospitals ain't like them homes what Uncle Max wanted me to go in . . .' Merle was beginning when one of the cooks came over to their table.

'Jake's in,' he said, grinning at them. 'You might as well continue with the bread, then he can start on the fancies. When you've done the big loaves, you'd best make bread rolls with the remainder of the dough.'

The girls had no more opportunity to discuss

439

their problem until they were going home that afternoon, when the subject which had been on their minds all day could be talked over in private. 'I'm going to make a clean breast of it to the young nurse what lives a few doors off from Mrs Piggott – tell her I need to have the baby adopted,' Merle said. 'I'll say I were on the stage and explain that I can't afford to keep it because babies and theatres don't mix, and I need to work. She's bound to know how one goes about findin' a kid a good home.'

Lottie laughed. 'You make the baby sound like a stray puppy,' she said. 'Don't go telling her you aren't a widow, though.'

'Course I shan't,' Merle assured her. 'When will you be leavin' to go back to Liverpool?'

'Tomorrow,' Lottie said at once. 'You'll have to explain at work and pick up my wages as well as yours. Lucky it's Saturday so we'll get the whole week.'

'You wouldn't like to stay on just for a few more days?' Merle said wistfully. She was still looking worried and Lottie guessed that the idea of giving birth amongst virtual strangers must be a frightening one. 'The trouble is, I really don't know when I'm goin' to pop, never havin' done it before. So a few days mightn't be enough.'

'Tell you what, I'll come back to Leeds just as soon as I've spoken to Mrs Donovan,' Lottie said, inspired. 'Why, I shan't be gone more than two or three days.'

They returned to Mrs Piggott's, and when they had explained to her that Lottie was returning to Liverpool for a short time they received another surprise. 'You'll be going by train no doubt, 'specially if you're in a hurry,' their landlady said placidly. 'I've a brother-in-law what visits Liverpool reg'lar and knows it well, but of course he don't need no train bein' as how he's master of a canal barge. They plies to and from the mills, tekkin' great bales of cotton from Liverpool in one direction and finished material in t'other.'

Lottie could hardly believe her ears. 'Your brother-in-law works the canals? I wonder if he'd know my gran,' she said. 'Her name's Mrs Olly.'

Mrs Piggott shrugged and continued to pour tea into their mugs. 'As to that I couldn't say, but I should think it likely, though there's a great many canals, as you doubtless know. But I thought you said your gran told fortunes at fairs and circuses around the coast.'

'Yes, that was what Merle and I believed,' Lottie admitted. 'But now we think it quite likely that she's gone back to her former trade, which was working a barge on the canals. In fact, that's why I'm returning to Liverpool, to trace someone who knew her in the old days.'

'I see,' Mrs Piggott said. She pushed two mugs of tea towards the girls, then turned to the oven and produced a large pie. 'Meat and tater,' she said briefly. 'Sit yourselves down and I'll serve.'

*

Despite Lottie's hopes of leaving the following morning, she had agreed with Merle to spend a day or two preparing herself for her journey. It would enable her to collect her week's wages, for neither girl could afford to say goodbye to the money they had earned, and Merle had pointed out that their boss would not willingly hand over one person's cash to another. 'And if he realises you ain't comin' back, he'll hang on to it like grim death,' Merle said. 'Besides, as soon as we finish work we can both go down to the canal and see if we can get news of your gran.'

There had been pleading in her voice as well as practicality, so Lottie had agreed to put off her departure until Monday, and so far all had gone smoothly. When they had received their wages, Lottie had explained – untruthfully but earnestly – that she had had a letter from a relative telling her that her mother had been taken ill. This meant that she must return to Liverpool to see for herself how things stood, but she hoped to be back in a couple of days. 'So if you could see your way clear to keeping my job open . . .' she had said hopefully, and had not been unduly perturbed when the boss had replied grumpily that he'd see how things went.

'If there's a strong young feller or a sturdy girl recommended, then I aren't tekkin' 'em on just for a couple of days, so you can kiss your job goodbye,' he had said nastily, adding in a less aggressive tone: 'But folk don't like the three a.m.

start so mebbe you'll be back afore someone else teks over.'

Lottie had thanked him humbly, and she and Merle had caught the tram back to their lodgings, both a good deal happier to think that Lottie had a bit of money for her journey. 'Only I'll have to pay Mrs Piggott for the coming week,' she said as they jumped down from the tram and headed towards their lodgings. 'I'm going to ask her the name of her brother's boat. It 'ud be grand if he would let me work my passage all the way to Liverpool. Train fares are expensive and though I know tramps sometimes ride a train by hanging on between the carriages, I don't fancy doing it myself.'

Merle shuddered at the mere suggestion and, as they reached the house, pointed out that her friend might offer to work her passage on any canal boat going in the right direction.

Lottie thought this a good idea and suggested that they hurry to their room, eat the sandwiches they had bought, and then go along to the canal. 'Why, I'd even work on a coal barge if it meant a free trip to Liverpool!' she said exultantly.

When they reached the canal they walked beside it until they came to a part of it where a good many craft were moored whilst they discharged cargo or took more on board. The bargees were busy and there was quite a lot of bad language as the long craft were manoeuvred in and out of places alongside the quay, but Lottie managed to shout her query about Gran to a number of the men.

Almost invariably their reply to her question was one of their own. 'What's the name of her craft? What goods does she carry? Does she work the Leeds to Liverpool regular? If it's a fly boat – they're the craft what ply twenty-four hours a day – then it would be engine driven.'

'When are you going to ask one of 'em if you can have a lift, working your passage like?' Merle whispered. 'Ask someone who's unloading an' if he says yes, then we'll have time to rush home an' pick up some of your stuff. Go on, Lottie, don't be an idiot.'

'Oh, but I don't know how long it takes to get from Leeds to Liverpool by water, and they all seem pretty capable and not in need of help,' Lottie replied, in an agony of indecision. 'I wish there were more women about.'

'They're in the cabins gettin' a meal, or off into town to buy grub,' Merle said. 'Or they might be stablin' the horses. I seen some women leadin' horses up that side street and since there ain't no grass for 'em to graze on, I reckon they buy 'em a net of hay an' stick 'em in the stablin' until they're loaded up an' ready to leave. But if you ain't goin' to ask we might as well go home, 'cos I'm gettin' perishin' cold standin' here while you dither.'

Horrified at the idea of being abandoned, Lottie went boldly up to the nearest canal boat and addressed the woman at the tiller. 'Please, missus,

I've got to get back to Liverpool – me mam's ill – and I've no money for the train fare. Could you do with a helping hand? I can't pay much but I'd do my best to earn my keep.'

The woman grinned at her: a flash of surprisingly white teeth in a face which was brown and leathered by constant exposure to sun, wind and rain. 'No, me lass, we'm fully manned. Me daughter sleeps in the rear cabin and between us we manage just fine. Howsoever, old Nat's missus were took bad down at the Liverpool docks, and I dare say he'd be glad of a hand. Want me to ask him for you?'

'Oh, yes please,' Lottie said eagerly. What a piece of luck to have picked on someone so kind! 'Have I time to rush back to my lodgings and fetch some gear? Which is Mr Nat's boat, by the way?'

'His barge is the *Lucky Lady* and he's horse-drawn,' the barge woman said. 'His craft is the third one in line, waitin' to take up a berth, so you'd be all right for an hour at least. But I'd best nip down there and have a word.'

She was only gone a few minutes and Lottie watched anxiously as she spoke to a short, stout man at the tiller of the craft she had pointed out. He stared across at the two girls, grinned and raised a hand, and then the barge woman was hurrying towards them. 'You're on,' she said cheerfully. 'He says to bring some grub along 'cos he's no time for shoppin', and to be back in an hour 'cos once he's loaded he wants to leave immediately, seein' as how his wife weren't too good when he left her.'

Immensely heartened, the two girls tore back to their lodgings. Lottie threw a few things into her holdall, then kissed Merle goodbye and, when her friend showed a tendency to weep, reminded her that their parting would not be a long one. 'I'll be back before you've had a chance to miss me,' she said cheerfully. 'Take care of yourself, Merle, and don't go having that baby whilst I'm away.'

Leaving the house, Lottie went straight to the nearest corner shop. She bought several tins of corned beef and luncheon meat, a bag of potatoes, three loaves of bread and a pound of cheese. She crammed these goods into her holdall, then added four large onions, a few apples and a quarter of tea and was about to pay for her purchases when the shopkeeper suggested that she might like a couple of tins of condensed milk, since she was obviously off on a bit of a holiday. Lottie examined her money carefully and decided that the shopkeeper was right. She knew little about the canal but thought it unlikely that fresh milk would be available, though she supposed that their journey would take them through farming country for at least a part of the time. Her knowledge of canals, however, was confined to that section in Leeds which she and Merle had walked along, and to the Scaldy in Liverpool, where the boats loaded and unloaded by Tate's enormous factory, and these were both very built-up areas.

She reached the *Lucky Lady* well inside the time limit she had been set and jumped aboard, throwing her holdall ahead of her. The barge had now moved up into second place and Nat greeted her with obvious relief. He was a short, stocky man, probably in his late thirties or early forties, Lottie guessed, with coarse straw-coloured hair which stood up like a coxcomb on his round head, very bright blue eyes and a gap-toothed grin. But his face was friendly and cheerful and already he seemed well disposed towards her. 'Good gal. We'll be loadin' in ten or fifteen minutes an' I'll be downright glad of a bit of help,' he said in a strong Liverpudlian accent. 'Me wife's a good deal younger'n me an' I reckon every bit as strong. Did old Betsy tell you what were up wi' Mrs Trett?' He held out his hand. 'I'm Nathaniel Trett, by the way, but you can call me Nat; everybody does. How d'you do?'

'I'm Lottie Lacey and no one's told me anything about Mrs Trett, save that she was taken ill in Liverpool,' Lottie said, shaking his proffered hand. 'I hope it's nothing serious?'

Nat chuckled. 'She's havin' a baby,' he said proudly. 'She wanted to have it aboard the barge, but I were happier when she agreed to go into hospital. She's a fine healthy gal, but it's her first, you know, so I reckoned she were better with a doctor to hand.'

'That's a coincidence,' Lottie said, smiling at him. 'My friend – the girl you saw me with

447

earlier – is expecting a baby any day now. In fact I'm hoping that it may have arrived by the time I get back to Leeds.'

'Well, even if the missus brings the baby back on board when we dock in the 'Pool, I dare say we'd be glad of your help on our return journey,' Nat said hopefully. 'I reckon the kid will take up most of her time, so if you're wantin' to return to Leeds, we'd be glad to bring you.'

'Thanks very much; I may be grateful for another lift,' Lottie said. 'What do want me to do, Mr . . . I mean, Nat? I've been working in a bakery so I'm pretty strong, even if I don't look it.'

The boat in front of them, now fully laden, began to move away and Nat, who had come up to the prow when Lottie jumped aboard, hastily returned to the tiller at the rear of the boat, and gestured to a bystander to give him a hand getting it into position for loading. 'You'll find a tiny rear cabin; put your gear in there,' he shouted to Lottie. 'There's blankets and a bit of a piller in there already 'cos we take on extra help from time to time. You'll be snug enough when we stop for the night. Ever tacked up a barge horse?'

Lottie hesitated. Had she ever tacked up any sort of horse? She was almost sure she had at least helped to do so, but no use to say she could and then discover she couldn't; better to be frank. 'I've not done it for ages,' she called back. 'Maybe you'd better come along and make sure I'm doing it right.'

448

Nat frowned. 'I dunno why I asked you that,' he said, as he jumped ashore and began to tie the mooring rope round a handy bollard. 'Betsy never said you were a canal girl . . . well, you ain't, or I'd know you, so why should I think you might be able to tack up a horse?'

'My gran has a barge and I think I probably helped her from time to time when I was small,' Lottie said guardedly. 'I wonder if you know her? Her name's . . .'

But Nat was beginning to load the boat with the help of two or three men who had been standing by. Instructions were being shouted, boxes moved so that the boat rode the water evenly, and in the general hubbub Lottie's remark went unregarded. Indeed, she was soon pressed into service so she had no further chance to ask Nat whether he knew Mrs Olly until the pair of them were heading for the stables, when it was actually Nat who brought the subject up. 'You said your gran were a bargee, didn't you?' he enquired. 'What were the name again?'

'Mrs Olly,' Lottie said briefly. She had thought the work in the bakery hard but realised now that loading a barge was harder. She ached in every limb and was longing to be able to sit down and relax, preferably over a nice hot cup of tea. 'I don't know the name of her boat, or what goods she carries, but the horse she had when I was small was a great old black called Champ.'

Nat's brow cleared. 'Oh, yes, Mrs Olly. Course

449

I know her; nice old body. Gorra grandson what helps with the boat, and the boat's called the *Girl Sassy*. They take mixed goods, groceries and such, from village to village, all the way from Liverpool to Leeds and back. You've heard about her accident, of course.'

Lottie's heart, which had leapt with excitement and joy, abruptly descended into her boots. 'An – an accident?' she faltered. 'No, I've not heard about any accident. We – we lost touch years ago – it's a long story – so I've had no news of her, save gossip. Was she much hurt?'

Nat looked embarrassed. He rubbed his nose with the back of his hand, then replied hesitantly. 'Last I heard, she were real bad. They took her into hospital. I'm not sure what happened after that 'cos once a body leaves the canal there's no one to pass on the news. But the *Girl Sassy* will be laid up somewhere. I've not seen her these past six, eight weeks. The lad couldn't manage her alone, I reckon, and anyways, he'll want to be with his gran while she's so poorly.'

Lottie stared at him, her eyes round with dread. 'She's – she's not dead, is she?' she asked in a trembling voice. 'Oh, Nat, don't say she's died before I've had a chance to explain.'

Nat gripped her shoulder reassuringly. 'I ain't heard no word to that effect, but o'course she's an old lady and the accident, from what I've heard, were real nasty. She were goin' ashore at one of the villages, half on and half off, if you understand me, when she slipped on some ice and fell into the water. The boat swung and crushed her against the quay; it's a bad thing to happen to a man in his full strength, lerralone an old lady. But now you know a bit more detail, you can ask for news from every boat we pass.'

'I'll do that, and thanks so much, Nat,' Lottie said as they entered the stables. 'I hope to God she's still alive because I must explain what happened to me years ago.'

'You'll have to tell me an' all,' Nat observed, beginning to get the horse's tackle down from the hooks. 'There's nothin' like a good story when you're snugged down for the night, with a hot meal inside you and the wind howlin' round the barge.' He began to ease the head collar over the animal's muzzle. 'Now watch what I do, then you'll have some idea, so if you're called on to tack him up yourself, you'll mebbe only make half a dozen mistakes.' He chuckled at his own words, but even as he spoke he was working on the horse, and Lottie, looking on, knew that she had seen someone doing this before; had helped, small though she had been. It's coming back, she thought to herself, as she and Nat, one on either side of the enormous bay horse, returned to the *Lucky Lady*. I'm remembering, just as I thought I would.

'I'll take the tiller and you can lead old George here,' Nat said as they reached the boat. 'There's nothing to leading the horse while we're in built-up surroundings, but once we get into the country

451

he'll mebbe want to crop the grass on the towpath so then we'll put his nosebag on. But right now you should be able to manage him, and as soon as we're clear of the city I'll moor up so we can have a mug o' tea and a jam butty.'

Later that evening, when Nat decided they had gone far enough, they stabled the horse and Lottie cleaned vegetables and cooked them over the bright little stove in the cabin. She mashed a quantity of fine big potatoes with a knob of butter, then opened a tin of corned beef and mixed that into the potato. She served the food into two dishes, adding some of the carrots and swede which she had cooked after finding them in one of the cabin cupboards. Nat's eyes glistened when he saw the food. 'Honest to God, I've not seen a decent hot meal since I left Mrs Trett in hospital, and that looks real grand,' he said appreciatively. 'Corned beef hash is one o' me favourites. Now I've a bottle of Flag sauce and a jar of pickled onions stowed away under the seat to your right. Fetch 'em out an' we'll have ourselves a real feast.'

'I don't know how you managed on the way to Leeds without your wife to give a hand,' Lottie said as they finished their meal. 'Who got the food ready, sorted the fire, boiled the kettle and so on?'

Nat pulled a wry face. 'No one did, mostly. I had a lad along to help but the fire were out a deal of the time and we made do with cheese sandwiches and water,' he told her. 'The boy were only nine. He'd got left with his gran in Burscough, to give her a hand like, 'cos she'd not been too well, but as soon as she improved he wanted a lift back to his mam and dad's boat.' He grinned at Lottie. 'It were a bit of luck for me, 'cos wi'out him I'd ha' been hard pressed.'

'And what about the journey back from Leeds to Liverpool?' Lottie enquired. 'I don't see how you could have managed alone.'

Nat's grin broadened. 'I'd have had to hire someone, an' even a lad costs,' he admitted. 'I put the word about that I'd need someone to give a hand, so you were a real bonus. You see, us bargees ain't exactly overpaid for the work we do. In fact, we couldn't carry on if it weren't for our famblies. They's unpaid labour like, so when someone falls ill it's short commons an' hard times all round.'

'I see,' Lottie said slowly. 'Then why do you do it? I mean, there must be easier ways of earning a living.'

Nat snorted. 'Haven't you heard of the Slump?' he asked. 'The newspapers say it's the start of a depression, whatever that may mean. But we mostly own our boats, and when you come down to it, it's all we know. Besides, it's a free sort of life. We comes and goes at our own speed and as you'll see, we travels through some rare fine country. I admit there's times when it's a bit hand to mouth – in winter 'specially – but there's other times, summer and autumn mostly, when there's free food on every side. Blackberries, wild apples, nuts, besides rabbits and hedgehogs for the pot.

And farmers aren't a bad lot; they'll sell us fresh milk, spuds, all sorts, a deal cheaper than in the shops, and turn a blind eye to us diggin' up a couple o' turnips, or the odd swede.' Nat settled himself comfortably into his seat and beamed at his companion. 'And now, young lady, it's your turn. Tell me what brought you to the canal after so long, and how you come to lose touch with old Mrs Olly.'

Chapter Sixteen

May 1930

Although the weather in Leeds had been cold, it grew warmer as the barge moved onward. Lottie chafed at the slow speed of the *Lucky Lady*, but felt a little better when a fat and friendly barge woman, met in a village shop, told her that Gran had been taken to the Northern Hospital in Liverpool. 'It's a grand place, so it is,' she assured Lottie. 'There's many a bargee been taken in there after a nasty fall, what's come out right as rain a week or so later. Did you say she were your gran, pet? I disremember her havin' more than the one child, and I never heered Troy had a sister.'

'She's my adopted gran,' Lottie admitted rather breathlessly. She and Nat were delivering a box of margarine and two sacks of flour to the shop, and the goods were very heavy. 'My mam works in the theatre and couldn't look after me, so she handed me over to Gran – Mrs Olly, I mean – and she brought me up until I was six or seven. Can you tell me how to reach this hospital?'

The old barge woman laughed, but shook her head. 'Not I, pet. But the moment you reach Liverpool there's a dozen folk what'll put you on

455

the right road. Oh aye, they all know the hospital, don't you fret.'

That night Nat bought a rabbit from a man with a lurcher, and Lottie made rabbit stew, the smell of which made her think nostalgically of Gran's wonderful cooking. Nat had opened up a potato clamp and taken half a dozen splendid spuds, so the meal would be a satisfying one, though Nat had been guilt-stricken and vowed to pay the farmer back on their return journey. 'But the weather's too foul tonight to go searchin' out a farm just to hand over a few pennies,' he said. 'Thank God we've done the Bingley Five Rise; it were no joke at the time but it'ud be a deal worse in heavy rain.'

'Is it raining?' Lottie asked, for she had been in the cabin ever since they had moored up.

Nat chuckled, and when the kettle boiled began to make the tea. 'It's pourin' down, but up here in the high Pennines you can get all sorts,' he observed. He grinned at her. 'Before you know it, we'll be seein' the dear old Mersey glintin' in the sun and I'll be admirin' me new son or daughter. They say some women have trouble birthin' their first child but I'm hopin' Mrs Trett'll be like her mam; she had eleven children, easy as poddin' peas, the missus told me. '

The remark made Lottie think of Merle and she said as much to her companion. 'But I don't know when Merle's due, so no point worrying,' she finished.

She was sleeping in the tiny rear cabin, and when she settled down for the night she thought again of Merle and of the imminent birth. Unlike most of her friends, Lottie had no younger brothers and sisters, and had not realised until Nat had put his feelings into words that a first baby was any different from a tenth. But she pulled the blankets up round her ears, knowing that she could do nothing to help Merle now.

Sighing, she told herself that the instant she had found Gran and explained about her accident, she would borrow money from someone and catch a fast train back to Leeds. Having gone over and over what she should do, this seemed the most sensible course, though she was aware that Nat would not agree, and presently she fell asleep, to dream of babies, theatres and canal boats all night long.

Merle, meanwhile, was not enjoying her enforced loneliness. She had known of course that she was growing increasingly fond of Lottie, and despite the fact that the other girl was a good deal younger than herself, she had begun to rely on Lottie's common sense. She had kept her job at the bakery but dreaded the lonely walk to work through the dark streets, and after only two days was beginning to think that it was just too risky. She kept imagining herself being bludgeoned to death for whatever was in her pockets, and thought that though the money was good, no job was worth dying for.

On the third day of Lottie's absence, she voiced her fears to Mrs Piggott, who was sympathetic. 'A gal in your condition didn't ought to work at all, certainly not at a job which involves heavy liftin',' she said. 'Suppose you start giving birth to that baby on your walk to work . . . have you thought of that, eh? There must be other jobs you could do, just for the few weeks before the birth.'

'Well, I'll have a go at getting something a bit easier, something which would mean a tram ride in both directions,' Merle said. 'But I suppose I'll have to work my week out, else I won't have enough money for me rent.'

She had half hoped that this ingenuous remark might lead to Mrs Piggott's offering to forgo the money Merle paid her, but though the older woman might sympathise Merle knew, really, that she was not a charitable institution.

Accordingly, next afternoon, when she finished work at the bakery, she did the rounds of small local shops, without success. Feeling horribly lonely and unwanted, she did not go back to Mrs Piggott's house, but wandered down to the canal. Oh, if only she had gone with Lottie, how much happier she would have been! Of course there was the risk of being recognised in Liverpool, but that no longer seemed such a terrible thing. She could have kept out of sight, and if Lottie did find her gran, then surely the old woman would not grudge a place under her roof to Lottie's friend? Then Merle remembered that Gran had a canal boat, which might mean she could bring the pair of them back to Leeds. Why on earth hadn't she thought of that earlier? Lottie had promised to return to the city in time for the birth, so if she had thought of it before, they could both have gone to Liverpool on the *Lucky Lady*, helping out not only on the journey from Leeds, but also on the return trip.

There was one snag, however. They had managed to scrape up enough money to pay Mrs Piggott a retainer to keep Lottie's bed free until the younger girl returned. But if she had lost both her lodgers, she might easily have been tempted to let their room to someone else . . . and of course their well-paid though hateful jobs in the bakery would have gone. She was pretty sure the firm could not do without two workers and would have to replace them, no matter how reluctantly.

Merle was still hanging around the canal quayside when she recognised a figure cleaning down the decking of a nearby barge. It was the woman who had introduced Lottie to Nat and the *Lucky Lady*. Impulsively, Merle approached her. 'I dunno if you remember me, missus,' she began, 'but you told my pal about a feller who needed help on the Leeds to Liverpool journey, 'cos his wife were in hospital . . .'

The woman beamed. 'Course I remembers you, pet,' she said. 'But if you're lookin' to see your pal, she won't be back for the best part of two weeks ... no, I tell a lie, 'cos they've been gone four days so mebbe she'll reach Leeds a bit sooner'n that. The old *Lucky Lady* ain't a fly boat, you see ... them's the ones that travel by night as well as by day. Now if she'd ha' took a job aboard a fly boat, she could ha' been back much earlier.'

'Oh, I see,' Merle said rather dully. 'I don't suppose you know of another boat what's short-handed?' Even as she spoke the words, Merle wondered why on earth she had uttered them. She had good lodgings in Leeds, a friend in Mrs Piggott, and a hospital bed booked for when her labour started. What was more, she did not imagine anyone would want to take on a helper who might give birth at any moment. She grinned apologetically at Betsy. 'Sorry, sorry, I know the answer to that one. The thing is, I'm missin' me pal and I'm in a job which starts at three in the morning so I can't catch a bus or a tram, but have to walk. It weren't too bad when there were the two of us, but to tell the truth I don't know as I can stick it much longer only – only I need the money and – and ...'

To her horror, Merle heard her voice begin to wobble and felt tears brim into her eyes and trickle down her cheeks. She half turned away, reluctant to let the woman see how upset she had become, but Betsy stepped ponderously down from the deck of her boat and flung an enormous arm round Merle's trembling shoulders.

460

'Look, we've lost four days already – engine trouble – but we're headin' for the Liverpool docks with a cargo of general merchandise. Maud – that's me daughter – has gone ashore to get some grub what we're short of, but she'll be back in mebbe ten, fifteen minutes, and then we'll set out. Maud and me share the main cabin but if you don't mind squeezin' into the little rear one, you're welcome to a ride up to Liverpool. And if that baby comes betimes, well, I've helped many a woman what's misjudged her time to give birth, so I dare say you could be in worse hands than old Betsy's.'

Merle could not believe her luck and was stammering her thanks when she suddenly remembered that she had given notice neither to her landlady nor to her employer, and that there was money owing. She hesitated, but only for a moment. Oh, the sheer joy of meeting up with Lottie again . . . perhaps she might even see Baz, tell him she still loved him, ask him if he had missed her. Quickly, before she could change her mind, she went aboard the barge, which she now saw was called the *Wanderer*. 'Thank you ever so much, Betsy. I'll come as I am,' she said. 'Only I'll have to write a quick note for me landlady because she's been awful good to us. I – I suppose you've not got a piece of paper and a pencil you could loan me?'

Pencil and paper forthcoming, Merle scribbled a short explanatory note, fished a penny out of her pocket, and wrote Mrs Piggott's name and address on the other side of the paper. Then she beckoned to a small and very dirty boy who was hanging around on the quay. 'Will you take this note round to the address on the back?' she enquired. 'I'll give you a penny . . . no, tuppence . . . if you'll take it straight away.'

The boy hung back, his expression rueful. 'I can't read, missus,' he said huskily. 'But if you tell me the address, I'll go straight round.'

Merle was happy to do so and saw the urchin off with a lightening of the heart, for she liked Mrs Piggott and had no wish to cause her anxiety.

She had barely returned to the barge when a young woman crossed the quayside and stepped aboard, staring very hard at Merle as she did so. 'Who are you?' she asked gruffly. 'And where's me mam?'

'Me name's Merle and your mam's gone below to brew a pot of tea,' Merle said shyly. 'I guess you're Maud. Your mam's offered me a ride back to Liverpool so if there's anything I can do to help, please tell me and if I can do it, I will.'

By the time the *Lucky Lady* reached the Appley Locks, Nat and Lottie were working as a team; indeed, Nat told his young friend that anyone would think she had been born to working a canal barge.

'Well I was in a way,' Lottie said as the big wooden doors of the last lock swung shut behind them. 'I know I was only a kid at the time, but

462

even quite small kids can deal with the locks once they're strong enough to turn the key. And haven't we been lucky with the weather these past couple of days? Constant sunshine and not a drop of rain, and wild flowers bursting into bloom everywhere. It makes the work much easier when the weather's good, doesn't it?'

Nat agreed that this was so, adding that spring was a good time to bring a baby into the world. 'I shall buy Mrs Trett a big bunch of lilac before we reach Liverpool; she's mortal fond o' the scent,' he added. 'She puts it on the middle of the table when we're havin' a meal, and in the window when we ain't, so folk can see it as they pass along the towpath. Of course I'll have to pay for it, but I don't grudge it. By 'eck, there's nothin' like a wife goin' off for a few days to mek her husband 'preciate her.'

This made Lottie laugh as she pointed out that Mrs Trett could scarcely have been accused of 'going off', but Nat, though he joined in her laughter, said that for whatever cause, he and his missus had never been parted before and he sincerely hoped that it would be a good while before they were parted again.

'Don't you fancy a large family then?' Lottie asked. 'I should have thought it was a case of the more the merrier.'

Nat shook his head. 'That's not for me and the missus; too many mouths to feed and not enough space,' he said decidedly. 'Two kids would be just fine with say a couple o' years between them.' He jerked his chin at the shore along which they were passing. 'This here's Parbold; nice little village. If you're carryin' grain and want it ground into flour, there's a windmill in Parbold what does a grand job, and a bit further on there's the Ring o' Bells pub. The landlady there's got a fine bit o' garden and I reckon she'll sell me a big bunch o' lilac; there's a tree grows close to her back door, so we'll stop off for half an hour or so.'

This seemed like a good idea to Lottie, though she warned her companion that he might well meet someone who would tell him of the arrival of his new son or daughter. Nat had confided, as they passed through Wigan, that he did not mean to let anyone tell him the news but would hear it for the first time from his wife's lips. 'I ain't a superstitious man but I reckon it'ud be bad luck to get the word from anyone but the missus,' he said, looking shyly at Lottie. 'So if you'd not mind visitin' the Ring o' Bells an' buyin' the lilac for me, I'd be rare obliged. I'll moor up just afore the junction and stay in the cabin while you run back to the pub.'

Lottie agreed to do this, though she could not help wondering how they would manage to get all the way from the junction to the canal basin down by the Stanley Dock without meeting someone who knew Nat and would holler out any news he had acquired. This was a particularly busy stretch of the canal, with villages almost running into one another, so the risk was obviously great.

464

When she put this theory to Nat, however, he grinned but shook his head. 'The missus is in a maternity hospital a fair way from the canal, and unless another bargee's wife is in the family way no one's likely to go a-visiting. Her pains came on her sudden an' I had a deal o' goods to deliver, so there ain't more than half a dozen folk at most who know where she is right now.'

He had been at the tiller whilst Lottie alternately led George – who did not need any help since he knew every inch of the towpath – or nipped down to the cabin where she was preparing their evening meal. As she emerged, her face flushed from bending over the cooking pot, Nat pointed ahead. 'Here's Burscough coming up,' he said cheerfully. 'Burscough is a real bargee village. It's a grand little place and the cottages an' houses crowd all along the canal, so when a feller and his wife want to retire it's usually to Burscough that they come. Many o' these houses have been in the same family for years and years, passed down from father to son like, when the pa's too old to handle the barge no more, and the son's eager to tek over. My old dad lives a bit further along and normally we'd stop off for a cuppa and a chat, but I dursen't do that in case he's had news from my missus. So if he's about, I'll just give him a wave as we go by.'

'Won't he be hurt and think you're avoiding him?' Lottie suggested. 'After all, we're a fair way from Liverpool still, so why should he know any more than anyone else?'

Nat shrugged. 'Likely you're right, but I don't mean to chance it. That there's his house, the one wi' the red-painted shutters. See?'

Lottie saw the house and at the same moment, as Nat steered the barge into midstream and turned his face somewhat ostentatiously away from the houses beside the towpath, she saw something else: a woman, hurrying away from the canal, head down, walking fast for someone clearly not in the first flush of youth.

Lottie knew her at once, without the shadow of a doubt, knew the shape of her, the way she walked . . . Even her clothes, a heavy black skirt and a maroon blouse, with a patched grey shawl flung across her shoulders, were as familiar to Lottie as the back of her own hand. She shrieked: 'Gran! Oh, Gran, it's me, Sassy! Wait . . . I'm coming!'

And before she had thought, she had jumped, jumped clear across the widening stretch of water which separated her from the towpath. She might have made it, landed safely, but behind her Nat shouted in alarm and before her the old lady took absolutely no notice, but continued on her way. Lottie turned her head to tell Nat that it was her gran, her own gran, that she would know the old lady anywhere, and as she did so her feet grazed the bank, failed to land squarely, and she plunged into the water, striking her head sharply on a mooring post, scarcely feeling the pain of the blow or the coldness of the water. Her last thought was that she must not give way to the swirling darkness which encompassed her; she had seen Gran! She must ... she must ... and Lottie lost consciousness.

She came round muzzily to find herself back in the dream. She was being rocked in a reed cradle and a woman was bending over her, brown-faced, brown-eyed, with a fine beak of a nose and a wide generous mouth. A roughened hand stroked down the side of Lottie's cheek, then smoothed back the hair which draggled across her forehead. 'Gran?' Lottie said thickly, and was surprised to find that she could talk, that she was not a baby in a reed basket as she had supposed. 'Oh, Gran, I do love you so, and I never meant ... I never would have ... I'd have come back like I promised only I was knocked down by a bus an' lost me memory. I didn't know who I was, or where, or why.'

'That's all right, me love, you can explain when you've got over that bump on the head,' the old woman said, her voice thinner than Lottie remembered it, but still the same much-loved voice. 'Whatever did ee mean, a-jumpin' across half the canal the way you did? I didn't see it meself but Troy did. He said you'd have made it, save that you turned your head when the cap'n of the *Lucky Lady* yelled out to you to stop. Old Nat can't swim, few bargees can, but Troy's as at home in the water as on land, and he realised what was happenin'. That was how he come to fish you out afore you was drowned-dead, foolish one!'

467

'Troy? But I never saw him,' Lottie muttered, reaching out to grasp the old woman's hand and holding it as though she would never let it go. 'Where was he?'

The old woman chuckled. 'He were right behind me, carryin' the shoppin', like the good lad that he is,' she said. 'But I reckon you only had eyes for me, same as I've only had eyes for you, ever since Troy carried you into my cottage and laid you on the sofy.'

'Cottage?' Lottie said dreamily. 'But you've got a canal barge. Nat told me it was called the *Girl Sassy* . . . that was my name, wasn't it? Only when Louella came and took me away she told me my name was Lottie, like that other girl, and I believed her.'

'Yes, well, you would,' a voice said, and Lottie looked past Gran and saw the boy who she now knew was Troy, smiling at her. 'Mothers don't usually lie to their kids, but I reckon your mother had a good reason. When you're well enough you can tell me and Gran all about it, but for now just you rest. I guess you're warm enough with all the blankets off Gran's bed piled on top of you, and the fire a-blazin' in the grate as though we'd robbed a coal barge. You're in Gran's best nightgown; I reckon there's room in there for three girls, but Gran don't carry spare clothin' for kids who fall into the water just outside her cottage.'

Lottie laughed rather feebly and tried to sit up, then put a wavering hand up to her brow. 'My

468

head feels as though it were splitting,' she said. 'What happened? And where's the *Lucky Lady* and Nat Trett? I remember jumping for the shore all right, but after that . . .'

'After that there weren't nothin' to remember,' Gran said firmly. She heaved herself to her feet, for she had been squatting on a small stool to be closer to Lottie. 'Your head hit a mooring post and into the water you went . . . and out you come when Troy dived in and hauled you ashore. And now I reckon you'd be all the better for a nice cup of my hot cordial. As for Nat, as soon as he knew you were alive and a-goin' to be fit as a flea, he got back on the *Lady* and headed for Liverpool once more.'

'Oh, yes, of course he would. His wife's having a baby,' Lottie said. 'I do hope she's all right – and the baby too.'

'Aye; she had a fine little boy a week or more back,' Gran said at once. 'I opened me mouth to tell Nat only he shook his head like a dog wi' fleas in its lugs so I kept me gob shut. A superstitious lot, bargees, but he'll have heard the news for himself by now I reckon.'

Merle felt the first pains early one morning when the barge was moored just outside Skipton. They had visited the town for supplies the previous day and had moored up under some willows which overhung the canal. They had gone to bed betimes after a hard day's work and at first she hoped the

469

pains were indigestion, or the result of carrying heavy parcels. She lay quite still in the tiny rear cabin of the *Wanderer*, but after half an hour of increasing discomfort she realised, with a pang of pure horror, that this was the real thing, though heaven knew she had yearned for it long enough. Telling herself that she would soon be her own familiar shape and that birth was a perfectly normal event, she emerged from the cabin and walked with considerable care along the planking, for it had been drizzling during the night and the deck was slippery. She tapped timidly on the double doors which led into the main cabin where Betsy and Maud slept, then entered. Betsy did not stir when the sudden onrush of cold air swept in, but Maud sat up on one elbow and knuckled her eyes. 'Whazzup?' she said thickly. 'It's the middle of the night, ain't it? Oh, Gawd, you haven't started wi' that perishin' baby, have you?'

'I think I have,' Merle said. She had meant to sound nonchalant, but the words came out in a squeak. 'It's me back; it's fair breakin'. Does that mean what I think it does? If so, would it be all right to wake your mam?'

As it happened, waking Betsy wasn't necessary. She had shrugged herself deeper into the covers, her head disappearing beneath the blankets like a tortoise into its shell, but she must have been listening for she suddenly sat up, rubbed her eyes and addressed both girls, her voice heavy with sleep. 'Whazzup?' she said, just as her daughter had done. 'Don't say the perishin' baby's started at last?' But even as she said the words, she was scrambling out of her bunk and reaching for the garments she had taken off the night before.

'I think it is; starting, I mean,' Merle said timidly. 'We're miles from the hospital, ain't we? What'll we do, Betsy?'

'Sit yourself down and I'll fettle the fire an' make us all a cup o' tea,' Betsy said briskly. 'And you must watch the clock over the mantel and time your pains, me duck. When they gets to be comin' every three or four minutes, then that's a sign the baby's ready to put in an appearance; we'll go back to Skipton, just in case.' She smiled at Merle. 'Fancy a cuppa now, me luv?'

Gran insisted that Sassy, as she must call herself now, should not tell her story until she was completely well. 'I aren't goin' to blame Louella for tellin' you untruths because that's all in the past and anyway, I'm sure she thought she was doin' it for the best,' she said firmly. 'You talked in your sleep last night, a-mumblin' about never goin' to Blackpool, and all sorts which didn't make sense, so I'll thank you to stay in that bed, quiet like, and give yourself a chance to get over your ducking.'

Troy was in the cottage kitchen, skinning and jointing a rabbit. He turned to grin at Sassy, wagging an admonitory finger. 'Don't you argue with Gran, young lady, 'cos I'm tellin' you, you'll come off worse. Besides, she's right; you'll tell your story a good deal better after a few days' rest and several good nights' sleep.'

'Well, I guess you're right. To tell you the truth, I've still got a crashing headache,' Sassy admitted. 'And I feel a bit as though I've been put through a mangle.' She forced a laugh. 'Otherwise I'm just fine,' she ended.

Troy laughed too, but shook his head chidingly. 'And it ain't as if you slept well last night, young Sassy, 'cos you bloomin' well didn't. You had awful nightmares, you talked and muttered and shrieked; I came through twice to help Gran get you back on to the sofa, and you were real distressed. It were a good thing Gran's nightie was so much too long for you, 'cos your feet kept getting tangled up in the hem when you tried to get out of your blankets.'

Lottie giggled. 'I remember now; I thought I was back in hospital and they were trying to keep me from Gran and you, Troy,' she said, rather shyly. 'And I expect you're right. It'll take me a while to recover completely and then I shall be better able to tell you and Gran what happened to me after Louella took me away from you.'

A few days later, Gran helped Lottie to dress in her own clothes, which had been washed and neatly pressed, and then they all sat down to breakfast in the cottage kitchen. It was a good breakfast: bacon and eggs and fried bread, and Gran's homemade marmalade, the very taste of which took Sassy back ten years. But as soon as the meal was over and the crocks washed up and put away, the three of them sat around the fire and Gran bade Sassy tell her story, right from the time Louella had carried her off until the moment she had spotted Gran on the towpath. 'Since it's clear that you've recovered from that bang on the head, judgin' by the way you ate your breakfast,' Gran said. 'And you slept sound as a baby last night, which is always the sign of a quiet mind.'

Sassy settled herself more comfortably in her chair and began, glad to be able to tell her story at last, though she had to remind Gran and Troy that the facts as she now presented them had been unknown to her until very recently.

When the story was over, Troy smote his forehead with one hand. 'That explains a lot,' he said. 'You've just reminded me of that time in Rhyl, when I saw you trottin' along the promenade with one of your classmates. I *knew* it was you, Sassy, but when you looked at me as though I were a total stranger, and said your name was Lottie . . . and then there was your hair, such a bright blonde . . . well, I let myself believe that the likeness was just an extraordinary coincidence. They say everyone has a double, and for ten or fifteen minutes after I left you, I thought that really must be the explanation.' He looked at her quizzically, one brow rising. 'But I didn't mean to go back to Gran without finding out where you came from and what you were doing in Rhyl. I turned back to where we'd met and asked folk if they'd seen a pretty little girl in a blue gingham dress, with long blonde hair threaded through with scarlet ribbon. Several people had seen you, or thought they had, but no one could give me any more information, and in the end I gave up.

'Gran and me were with a fair what sets up every year on the outskirts of the town – she were telling fortunes and I ran the hoopla stall – and when I told Gran how we'd met, she was convinced you really were her little Sassy. She knew Louella bleached her own hair and thought it very likely that she'd bleached yours as well; a disguise to stop us finding you, she thought. But when I told her you'd not seemed to know me, she was . . . well, she was a bit cast down. We thought your mam must have brought her act to Rhyl, so for a couple of weeks we haunted the theatres and went round all the lodging houses. Believe it or not, it didn't occur to us that you were a day tripper for ages, and by the time it did – occur to us, I mean – it was too late. You had disappeared, and our time in Rhyl was almost up. So back we went to Burscough and the *Girl Sassy*, and set off with a barge full of cotton, heading for Leeds. After all, we didn't know you'd lost your memory, so we thought that if you wanted to come back to Gran, you'd mebbe make for the canal.'

'But I didn't remember the canal at all . . . I mean it was never in my dreams,' Sassy explained. 'I had it firmly fixed in my mind that Gran told fortunes and went round the fairs, so of course when I started looking, I never even thought of the canal. But you know all that; I've told you already.' She turned impulsively towards the old woman. 'If only I'd realised! At one time I was actually in the cabin of the *Girl Sassy* in my dream, but I'm ashamed to say I thought it must be the inside of a caravan. You see, I mainly dreamed of woods and meadows because I suppose that was what I missed most. But now it's your turn, Gran, to tell me what's been happening to you and Troy for the past ten years.'

'Oh, we just got on with our lives, you could say, though I think the both of us were always searchin' for you, my love,' Gran said comfortably. 'We soon found out that Louella never was, and never had been, in the show at the Palace theatre, but at first we just thought she were boastin' a bit and was appearin' somewhere not quite so well known. We wasted time combin' Blackpool before we realised that neither of you were there. So we went back to the canal and gradually, over time, I came to believe that we'd see you again when you were old enough to break away from your mam.

'Then, four or five years ago, I had a good offer for the caravan, so I sold it and we took to the barge full time. Tellin' fortunes is all right when you're young, but as you get older it takes it out of you, and the money ain't regular, not by any means.' She beamed at Sassy. 'So now we're up to date, except for one thing. What's been happening

475

to that there little pal o' yours? When were her baby due, d'you know?'

Sassy felt a stab of guilt. She was truly fond of Merle, but the sheer wonder of finding Gran and discovering her past had put the other girl's plight out of her head. She said as much, adding that the baby was due any time and saying, rather reluctantly, that she supposed she ought to return to Leeds now that she was feeling more like her old self. 'Only I'll have to borrow some money, Gran . . .' she said. 'The fact is, we were pretty well spent up by the time we reached Leeds and I had to pay Mrs Piggott to keep my room while I came in search of you. To tell you the truth, I don't imagine that poor Merle is still working at the bakery. The work was horribly hard but it was the long walk through the dark streets that we both hated, and I can't imagine Merle doing it by herself.'

'I should hope not!' Gran said rather sharply. 'As for lending you money, flower, I've got a nice little nest egg put by which will be yours and Troy's one day, so you're welcome to borrow whatever you need. However, I still don't think you're well enough to undertake a long train journey, even though Troy would be happy to go with you, I dare say. Give it another day or two. And then of course you must go back to Liverpool. You'll need to discuss your future with Louella – don't shake your head, my love, you know very well that you owe her an explanation at the very least, because although she lied, you are her daughter, and I'm sure she loves you deeply in her own way.'

'Yes, I'll go and talk to her, but I want to be with you, Gran,' Sassy said wildly. 'You're in charge of the *Girl Sassy*; couldn't you find me some useful work to do aboard?'

Gran opened her mouth to reply, but Troy cut in, his eyes sparkling. 'Ah, but Gran won't be *Girl Sassy*'s number one from now on, that will be my job,' he said proudly. 'You know she's been in hospital? Well, the doctors there told her she'd got to take it easier, steer clear of the hard physical stuff. She'll arrange for our cargoes and do the paperwork, cook the meals and so on, but she won't tackle the locks, nor move the cargo; she'll stay aboard in the warm. We talked it over and agreed I should hire a lad as soon as she was well enough to leave the Burscough cottage and come back aboard the barge; then we'll go off down to the docks to pick up our next load, which is bales of cotton. But of course employing a feller raised another problem, because Gran has to sleep in the main cabin with the big bed and the fire and that, and there ain't room in the rear cabin for two lads; we don't have a butty boat, you know. But if you're serious, Sassy, and really will come aboard, I reckon we'll manage just fine. You and Gran can share the main cabin, leaving me the little one in the stern, and I'm sure you'll soon do as well as, or better than, any lad we could employ.'

Sassy beamed ecstatically. 'It's what I've always wanted, only I never knew it,' she said.

Gran, however, shook an admonitory finger. 'Only if Louella don't need you,' she said firmly. 'You're a grand girl, Sassy, and there's nowt I'd like better than to have you back where I feel you belong, but if your mam's career depends on you, then we'll have to think again.'

'But she's got Merle, or she will have as soon as Merle's had the baby and got it adopted,' Sassy said. 'Oh, Gran, I know what you mean because I do love Louella, despite the lies she told me. But she's managed without me for all this time . . .'

'You don't know she has, me love,' Gran said gently. 'You've written to her but you never gave her your address, so she couldn't write back. She's mebbe been in real trouble, needing help . . .'

Sassy had been lounging comfortably in her chair, but at these words she shot upright. The thought of Louella in trouble brought her out in a cold sweat and she knew, suddenly, that even though it might break her heart, she would go back to the stage sooner than see her mother suffer hardship. 'You're right, Gran,' she said humbly. 'If she really needs me . . . but I'll contact Merle first, then we can both go back to the Gaiety together and face Louella.'

Gran nodded her approval. 'Good girl; I knew I wasn't mistaken in you,' she said. 'And if you do have to go back to Louella, I'm sure it won't be for ever, because you can always help her to train someone up to take your place. And now let's talk of other things. Have you been aboard the *Girl Sassy* yet? What do you think of her?'

'No, but Troy's going to give me a tour later today,' Sassy said. 'Do you still have Champ? I did love the old feller.'

Troy and Gran both shook their heads. 'No, he's retired now. We got the *Girl Sassy* fitted with an engine three or four years back, and though we miss old Champ, the engine's a real improvement,' Gran said. She chuckled. 'No nosebag, no hay net, and no tramping to and from the stable block, oh aye, it's made life easier.'

'Except when the blamed engine goes wrong, which happened a lot at first,' Troy observed. 'But it's like everything else; you grow accustomed. I reckon I know as much about engines now as any feller on the canal, and I can usually sort out a problem before it has a chance to get serious.'

'Well, I don't know anything about engines, so I shan't be able to help you there,' Sassy said at once. The realisation that the knowledge she had remembered thanks to Nat would be wasted was rather a blow, for she had loved Champ and had looked forward to seeing him again.

But when she said as much, Gran chuckled and leaned across to squeeze her hand. 'You'll learn about engines when you're back with us, same as we've all had to do,' she said calmly. 'And you'll see old Champ again, next time the barge reaches Pinfold. You and Troy can take the old feller a handful of carrots; he's in a meadow not fifty yards from the canal.'

'I'd love to do that,' Sassy said, beaming at her companions. She turned to Gran. 'I hate to leave you, but I'm beginning to feel truly anxious about Merle. Do you think Troy and me should go to the station tomorrow? We can get the train times and leave for Leeds as early as possible the following day. Then with luck we should get back here by evening.'

Gran nodded decidedly. 'I think you should,' she said. 'I wish I could go with you but I'd only hold you back.'

Sassy got to her feet and walked across to pull the kettle over the flame. 'And now let's have a nice cup of tea,' she said cheerfully. 'Oh, I can't wait to explore the *Girl Sassy*, because I'm sure it'll be only a matter of time before I'm able to become a member of the crew.'

After the midday meal that day, Troy and Sassy walked further along the bank to where the *Girl Sassy* was moored and climbed aboard. Troy explained that the boat was not ready to sail so the cupboards, coal bunkers and water tanks were empty, and of course the fire was out, but even so, Sassy was enchanted with the craft. Looking round the tiny cabin brought her dream vividly to mind and she could not imagine why she had assumed it to be a caravan. Now that she saw it in reality, it could not have been anything other than a comfortable cabin. The pretty checked curtains at the windows, the scarlet covers on the seats either side of the central table, which would make up into a double bed, the brilliantly painted kettles, pots and buckets, all positively shouted of the canal. Troy pointed out the cupboards beneath the pull-out bed, which would hold sheets and blankets as well as Gran's thick shawl and the leather boots which she would need for deck work but would not dream of wearing inside the cabin itself. Naturally, the bedding had all been removed along with spare clothing and so on, for the *Girl Sassy* had been laid up, Troy told her, for two months and had not been due to sail for another week.

'When we go, the barge will have everything we need aboard, and the cottage will be thoroughly cleaned out with everything we leave behind packed away,' Troy explained. 'I shan't do anything about employing a lad until we know whether or not your mam needs you.' He put out a hand and gave Sassy a playful cuff. 'Drat Gran's sense of fair play; I'm sure we need you a great deal more than Louella does, but as Gran says, Louella *is* your mam and anyway, if you do have to go back to her, it won't be for ever. Now, if you've seen everything you want to see below, we'll go on deck and you can peep into the stern cabin.'

They scrambled up on deck and Sassy asked rather anxiously where the lad would sleep if she were forced to remain with her mother for a while. 'Because it seems as though I'm letting someone down, whatever I do,' she said worriedly. 'If only Merle has had the baby and got it adopted, then she and I can help Louella to train someone else ... or maybe Merle herself will be enough – I mean they can do a mother and daughter act, or even a two sisters act, without me being involved.'

'If you ask me, a woman who can manage alone for months probably doesn't need either of you,' Troy said bluntly. 'As for the lad, d'you see the dog kennel, up on the roof? We used to keep oats and that for Champ in there, but now it contains a tent and a sleeping bag. If push comes to shove, we can erect the tent on the bank alongside the *Girl Sassy*, and a young feller can sleep in that. Of course it wouldn't do in winter, but with spring advancing and summer just round the corner, it'll be comfortable enough.'

'Yes, I suppose ...' Sassy was beginning when a shout which was more like a shriek echoed across the water.

She glanced up and saw a barge approaching at a leisurely pace, whilst a small figure clutched the tiller and began to pull the boat round towards the *Girl Sassy*. Behind her, Troy's voice said: 'What the devil? Do you know anyone aboard the *Wanderer*?'

'No, of course I don't. Apart from Nat, the only people I know on the canal ...' Sassy was beginning, when she stopped short and uttered a shriek even louder than that emitted by the figure at the *Wanderer*'s tiller. 'Merle! My God, it's Merle!'

Chapter Seventeen

It was indeed Merle, and presently there was a joyful reunion aboard the *Wanderer*. Betsy came up from the cabin and she and her daughter moored the barge against the bank, and then, with great tact, went off to visit Gran so that Merle and Sassy could exchange stories. Troy stayed aboard the *Girl Sassy* but he kept glancing towards the other barge and Sassy had the comfortable feeling that he would come to her aid if she needed his help.

Sassy hugged Merle tight, tears of relief and joy running down her cheeks, for she had worried about the other girl a good deal and the sight of her had reawoken all her old fondness for her friend. But as they drew apart Sassy realised, suddenly, that she had been able to hug Merle without having to avoid her friend's bump. 'Merle, you've had the baby!' she exclaimed. 'Was it a boy or a girl? Has it gone to nice people? Oh, but I'm sure it has because you'd make certain of that.'

Merle stared at her, eyes rounding with astonishment. 'Gone to nice people?' she echoed. 'She hasn't gone anywhere, she's far too little. She's below in the cabin, fast asleep. Betsy thought it would do me good to get some fresh air and she knew I was looking out for the *Lucky Lady*, so I left Veronica – I've called her that because her eyes are as blue as the wild veronica which grows alongside the canal – and came to the tiller.'

'Oh! But – but you said you were going to have the baby adopted,' Sassy said, staring at her old friend. 'Does this mean you're going to keep her? I don't think Louella will be too pleased, though I know she said she'd take you back once the baby was born.'

Merle sniffed. 'I'm not worried about Louella,' she said. 'But you must come and see my little Veronica, then you'll understand why I couldn't possibly let her go to anyone else.' She led the way down into the cabin and tiptoed across to a small makeshift cot, which had clearly once been a drawer. The child was invisible, but Merle folded back the blanket to reveal her daughter's red and crumpled face. 'There you are: Veronica O'Mara, me own little daughter,' she said proudly. 'Ain't she the prettiest thing you ever did see?'

Sassy, who thought the baby looked uncommonly ugly, opened her mouth to make some joking retort, then glanced at her friend's face and saw that Merle was absolutely serious. She really did think the red-faced, swollen-eyed, almost bald infant was beautiful. So Sassy perjured her soul and said faintly: 'What a little darling! No wonder you want to keep her. But Merle, love, you surely don't mean to stay aboard the barge for ever? What'll you do when you reach Liverpool?'

'Oh, can't you guess? I'm going back to Merlotto's Circus in Blackpool,' Merle said.

'But – but . . .' Sassy stammered. 'You said – you said . . . your mam . . . your pa . . .'

Merle giggled. 'I know. I were terrified they'd be furious and I dare say they will be,' she said candidly. 'Pa will shout and Ma may shed a tear or two, but they both love babies and you know they'd never turn me out, not really. I'll gerra good tellin' off, which I guess I deserve, but then they'll do everything they can to see me and Veronica right. Why, in three or four months I'll be doing me act again and Ma will give an eye to Baby, so that's all right.'

'That's grand, and I'm truly glad for you,' Sassy said sincerely. 'But it may put Louella in an awkward position because I believe she thinks you're returning to the Gaiety. And what about Baz? Do you still . . . well, do you still like him?'

'Oh aye, he's real nice, but I don't suppose he'll be interested in me any more,' Merle said. She did not sound unhappy, and leaned over the cot to tuck the blanket round her daughter once more. 'Men – unmarried ones – aren't really interested in babies, you know.'

'But won't you pop into the Gaiety before you go to Blackpool?' Sassy asked rather desperately. 'I really think you should, dear Merle. You ought to tell your Uncle Max, as well as Baz and Louella, you know.'

Merle straightened up and led the way out of

485

the cabin and back on to the deck. 'I've written a letter . . . well, three letters,' she said. 'One was to you, in case we missed you on the canal, so I shan't need to post that, but the others are to Louella and Baz, explaining matters.'

'Yes, a letter's all very well, but it would be far better if you went along yourself. I'll come with you, Merle, because we've both got some explaining to do,' Sassy said. 'If you don't mean to rejoin the act then I suppose I may have to do so, for a while at any rate. I really can't let Louella down.'

'No, because she's your mother, but she's not mine,' Merle said unanswerably. 'Besides, she never really liked me, you know she didn't. I don't think she'll be at all sorry to go back to the mother-daughter routine with just the two of you. Anyway, as I told Betsy, they've managed without us for simply ages, so surely they can go on doing so?'

Sassy shrugged. 'Who can say? Management might have refused to let her do a solo act, and then all she would have would be magician's assistant. Oh, *do* come back with me, Merle. Once the *Wanderer* docks in Liverpool, we can be at the Gaiety theatre in half an hour.'

Merle, however, shook her head decisively. 'No, I can't do that because I'm not going as far as Liverpool. I'm getting aboard a train at Burscough Junction station. I'll have to change at Preston but I should be home before dark. You see, now that May has arrived the circus will soon set out on

486

tour. I must get back to Blackpool before they go, I really must.'

Sassy looked at the mulish set of her friend's mouth and gave in gracefully. 'Yes, I'm sure you're right. If you'll give the letters to me, I'll deliver them for you,' she said.

She gestured to Troy and he came aboard the *Wanderer* with alacrity, holding out his hand to her friend. 'I'm Troy, and you'll be Sassy's pal Merle,' he said as they shook hands. 'I couldn't help hearing what you've been saying since you come up on deck and it's a shame you can't go with Sassy to the Gaiety, but you're right, of course. You must get home before the circus moves on. And anyway, since I'm going with Sassy, I dare say we'll manage to explain why you aren't able to visit them in person.'

Merle beamed at him. 'You're going with Lottie?' she asked. 'Oh, that's grand that is; it makes me feel much better. And you called her Sassy, just like your barge!'

'It's her name,' Troy said. 'Well, her real name's Sally, but when she were just a bit of a kid she called herself Sassy, and it stuck.'

Merle stared, a puzzled frown etched on her brow, then it cleared. 'Of course! Lottie – I mean Sassy – has described you to me so many times since we left Liverpool that I should have recognised you. At first she thought she was dreaming, but then she met you – in Rhyl, wasn't it? – and I reckon she's been searching for you ever since.

I'm so glad that the pair of you have met up at last. And is your gran all right? Everyone on the canal knows her so when we stopped to ask about you, Sassy, folk told us that your gran had been in hospital but was much better, and was staying at her cottage in Burscough. That's why Betsy put me on the tiller, because she hoped you'd be in Burscough, too, and we might spot each other.'

'And so we did,' Sassy said contentedly. 'You must come ashore and meet Gran, and bring little Veronica. Then we'll walk you to the station and put you on the train. Isn't that so, Troy?'

Troy nodded as Merle disappeared into the cabin and reappeared with the baby tucked into the crook of her arm. He turned to Sassy. 'And tomorrow we'll catch the train ourselves, and find your mam and talk things through,' he said. 'I mean to explain to her how important it is to have you back on board the barge as soon as possible, because Gran isn't getting any younger.'

'I never thought I'd feel so terrified,' Sassy said nervously as she and Troy crossed the Scotland Road and headed for the theatre. They had popped in earlier in the day – as soon as they arrived in Liverpool, in fact – only to be told that the cast would be rehearsing for a couple of hours from three in the afternoon. 'Your mam's bound to be here then, Miss Lottie, because she's a stickler for getting things absolutely right,' the stage doorkeeper had told Sassy. 'You could try getting her at home, I suppose, but you might not be too popular if you did so. Now that she doesn't have you and Merle and the lad to feed, she lies in until two in the afternoon, so you'd best return to the theatre just before three o'clock.'

'Oh!' Sassy had said, taken aback. 'But why isn't she feeding Baz? I dare say Max would just as soon have a decent lie-in, but Baz would have to be at work at the normal time. Still, I suppose he can make his own porridge and brew a pot of tea.'

The stage doorkeeper had looked shifty. 'You'll find things have changed a good deal,' he had muttered. 'But it ain't none of my business to go tellin' tales out of school, so I'll leave you to hear what's been a-goin' on from Louella's own lips.'

'Oh, Mr Kemp, do tell,' Sassy had wheedled. 'If things have changed, is it for the better or for the worse? Don't leave me in suspense for another three hours.'

'Depends on your point of view, like,' the stage doorkeeper had said gruffly. 'And more than that I will not say. Go and get yourself a butty and a cuppa, and time will soon pass.' He had eyed Troy curiously. 'Who's your pal? I don't reckon I see'd him before.'

'Oh, sorry, Mr Kemp. This is Troy Davison,' Sassy had said. 'He's an old friend. Well, we'll take your advice and go along to Dorothy's Tearooms for a snack.'

Over a plate of sandwiches and a large pot of

489

tea, Sassy had encouraged Troy to talk. 'Remember, you know about me now,' she had told him. 'But all I know about you really is the things I dreamed, even though I know now that they were really memories of true events. So start at the beginning, Troy, and tell me about yourself.'

For a start, Troy explained how he had come to live with Gran instead of with his own parents. They had been circus folk, trapeze artistes, working many feet above the ground in the big top, and had left Troy, then aged two, with his maternal grandmother whilst they toured on the Continent. There had been a train crash. It had been several weeks before Gran had learned that her daughter and son-in-law had been killed, and naturally she had immediately assumed all responsibility for her little grandson.

'How dreadful for you; you must have been heartbroken,' Sassy said sincerely, but Troy shook his head.

'My dear girl, I were two years old. I adored me gran – who wouldn't – and couldn't so much as remember the colour of me mother's eyes, though I did have a photograph of them both, so there's no need to feel sorry for me! For several years, Gran and I worked the fairs and circuses, touring the country in our little green and yellow van and making friends wherever we went. To tell you the truth, the only thing I missed was another young pal aboard and then, when I were six, you come along.' He grinned at her. 'I thought me prayers had been answered, because I were too young to know where babies come from and every night, for ages, I'd been asking God for a little brother or sister. So when Louella handed you over, I felt she'd given you to me as much as to Gran. You were a lovely kid, full of fun; even as a baby you were always laughing and gurgling. When you went . . . but it doesn't do to go over the bad times. And now you're back, and we're going to forget the ten years we lost, ain't that so?'

'I can't forget them altogether because I had some happy times with the theatre,' Sassy admitted. 'But all the time I knew something – or someone – was missing, though I didn't know what. Now tell me about the barge, because I'm not too sure how Gran came to change from fairs and circuses to being a bargee.'

'She inherited it from an uncle when you were only a few months old,' Troy explained. 'I was too young to help much, though I could lead the horse and open some of the locks, so for years the barge was only used occasionally, sort of as a holiday, whilst the fortune-telling was what you might call work. But when I was sixteen or so, Gran decided that life on the gaff was too irregular so we became full-time bargees.'

'I see. And now we'd best be moving on since it's almost a quarter to the hour,' Sassy said. 'Thank you for explaining, Troy. I understand much better now.'

A few moments later, they were approaching

the Gaiety, Sassy clinging tightly to Troy's hand. What should she do if Louella shouted at her . . . come to that, what should she do if Louella cast herself into her arms and vowed they should never part again?

But Mr Kemp was holding open the stage door and telling them to go straight to the green room. 'Your mam ain't here yet, but when she turns up I'll tell her there's a visitor to see her, and she'll come straight through,' he said. 'Good luck, young 'un, and don't look so scared! I dare say your mam will welcome you wi' open arms.'

This was scarcely comforting since it was what Sassy most dreaded, but she nodded briskly and went past him. In the green room, she filled the kettle whilst Troy lit the Primus stove, and by the time she heard footsteps approaching there was a pot of tea brewed and several cups set out in readiness. Sassy plumped herself down on the small sofa and Troy took a chair opposite. Then, with fast-beating heart, she stared apprehensively at the opening door.

Louella entered, a bright artificial smile on her face which faded as she realised who awaited her. Then she gave a muffled scream just as Sassy jumped to her feet and hurled herself into her mother's arms. The two hugged tightly, and Sassy heard Louella murmuring words of delight and relief. After a moment they drew apart, both probably feeling equally self-conscious. 'Oh, Lottie, my darling, you've kept your promise and come back to me,' Louella said tremulously. 'Oh, but it's so good to see you again. I've worried and wondered . . . but who's your friend?'

'That's Troy. He's Gran's real relative,' Sassy said. 'And you mustn't call me Lottie now, Mam, because I've gone back to being Sassy.' She led her mother over to the sofa and sat down beside her. 'You've had my letters, so you know pretty well all that's happened to me, but of course I never gave you an address, so you couldn't write back. Mr Kemp says there have been changes . . . oh, Mam, I do hope nothing awful's happened! He seemed to think Baz wasn't with you any more . . .'

'That's right. Max and Baz have both left Victoria Court, and the Gaiety theatre,' Louella said. 'Baz went soon after you and Merle left; he said it was no fun living here without you two girls. He managed to get a job with the post office – as a postman in fact – on the Wirral, and I believe he's very happy there. As for Max . . . it'll be a shock to you, my love, but – but Max has found himself another assistant. Well, it would be more truthful to say he's met a young woman and – and they're going to be married.' She pulled a face, but, to Sassy's relief, seemed more amused than upset by the news she was imparting. 'Oddly enough, Anita – that's her name – was employed by me to try to take your place, darling. I admit she has a very sweet singing voice and, curiously, she's extremely like me to look at: same height, same colouring, same neat figure. We were doing very well, only after a few weeks I caught a really heavy cold and it went on to my chest. I lost my voice completely – I could only croak. And Max, very rightly, sent me off to Brougham Terrace to see that nice Dr Watson. He gave me cough mixture and told me to go to bed and stay there for at least a week because if I did not I might permanently damage my voice. I must say Anita was grand. She continued with the song and dance routine – Betty, from the chorus, joined her in that – and she took over as Max's assistant. I couldn't work for two whole weeks and apparently that was long enough for Max and Anita to fall in love, though I didn't realise what was happening until dear old Jack told me to use my eyes, and I began to see what was going on.'

'I think that's awful, absolutely awful,' Sassy breathed. 'I always thought you and Max would marry one day. I think this Anita took advantage of your absence to steal poor Max.'

Louella laughed, but shook her head. 'I fell for Max mainly because he was tall, dark and handsome; really very like your father to look at,' she said. 'And as for Max, he never pretended to love me, you know. He let me share the house in Victoria Court because he was sorry for me and also, I suspect, because a woman in the place made his life very much more comfortable. Of course at first I felt as you do, but I very soon realised it was all for the best. Max wouldn't remain at the

494

Gaiety, he said it wasn't fair on me, so he put my name on the rent book for Number Two, took a job with a theatre company in Llandudno, and then . . .'

At this point the green room door opened again and Jack Russell came into the room, rubbing his hands briskly and talking as he did so. 'Well, well, well, I hope someone's got a brew a-goin' 'cos this feller's dry as a bone, woof, woof, and absolutely dyin' for a . . .' He broke off, staring at Sassy, then rushed across the room to lift her off the sofa and give her a smacking kiss on the cheek. 'Well, if it ain't our little Lottie! We've been that worried, queen, but I can see you've not been half starved, nor homeless, nor none of the other things your mam were afraid of. Oh, I know your letters said over and over that you were fine, but Louella were convinced you weren't tellin' the whole story and were probably havin' a hard time of it!' He stood her down, and turned to point at Troy. 'Who's your young man? I don't recall you mentioning a handsome young feller in your letters what had swept you off your feet. And where's Merle?'

Sassy felt her cheeks grow hot and saw the colour steal into Troy's face. Trust Jack to put his foot in it, she thought wrathfully, forgetting how good he had always been to her. 'His name's Troy and he's been a real pal to me,' she said rather coolly. 'I'm sorry if Louella worried, but I wrote at least once a week, sometimes twice, telling you that Merle and I were doing fine.' She turned to

Louella. 'Oh, I've got a letter for you from Merle, Mam, and don't tell me not to call you Mam because I'm going to do just that from now on; there have been too many lies, and sometimes even little white ones can cause confusion and trouble.'

As she spoke, she fished the letter addressed to Louella out of her pocket and handed it to her mother. Louella ripped open the envelope and pulled out the solitary page it contained, looking rather worried. But as she read, her face cleared. 'Well, what wonderful news,' she said joyfully. 'Merle's had a dear little baby girl and she's going back to live with her own parents. Nothing could be better, because to tell the truth, there's no place for her here.'

'Does that apply to me, too?' Sassy said, hardly daring to hope. 'You see, Mam, I've . . .'

'Darling, there will always be a place for you beside me, because you're my own darling daughter,' Louella said. 'But – but things have changed. You see, when Max left . . .' She turned to Jack. 'Darling, can you explain?'

Jack grinned at Sassy, struck an attitude, then went across and put an arm round Louella's shoulders. 'Meet Mrs Russell, me wife and me new partner,' he said proudly. 'I reckon you know I've loved your mam from the first moment I met her, but I never thought there was a chance for me, not while Max was around. Then he went and I were astonished at how well your mam took it; no tears, no fuss, she just gorron with her act like the real

496

little trouper she is. So I popped the question and she made me the happiest feller on earth.'

'Oh, Jack, Mam, I'm so happy for you,' Sassy said, beaming from ear to ear. 'But what about the act? I take it Jack isn't sawing ladies in half, or using the vanishing cabinet!'

Jack laughed, but shook his head. 'No, but I'd been thinking for a long time that I could do with a partner meself; I'd worked out a brand new act, but it needed a pretty woman what were a clever actress too. It goes like this: I'm the comic toymaker and your mam takes the part of the beautiful doll what I made. The beginning of the sketch is real funny because she has a big key in her back what I winds up, only something goes wrong with the mechanism and she spins round, knocking toys off the shelves and walloping me in the breadbasket with one leg . . . I tell you it's a real scream and the audience loves it. Only then she falls to the floor in a crumpled heap and when I tries to rewind her nothing works, so I picks her up and kisses her and she comes to life as a real woman, not a mechanical toy. Management love it, and so do the punters. So you see, although I'm sure we'd gladly welcome you back . . .'

'Oh, Jack, Lottie – I mean Sassy – is an even better actress than I am,' Louella said eagerly. 'She could be another toy . . . or she could do the modern dance routine that Merle did, as a separate act . . .'

Troy had been silent, following the conversation

with eager attention, but now he interrupted. 'Sassy's got a job waitin' for her,' he said quietly. 'And it's a job she'll really enjoy. Gran and meself own a barge on the Leeds to Liverpool canal, only Gran's not been so well recently, so she's not allowed to do any of the hard work. If Sassy's agreeable, we'd like to take her as the third member of the crew, and naturally she'd have a third share of the profits. But, of course, it's Sassy's choice. Gran and meself wouldn't want to influence her one way or t'other.'

Louella turned to stare incredulously at her daughter. 'Work aboard a canal barge?' she almost squeaked. 'Hefting heavy goods, out in all weathers, leading the horse along muddy towpaths in autumn and fighting your way through snow in the winter? Oh, Sassy my love, that's no life for a pretty, talented girl like you.'

'But it's a grand outdoor life, Mam, and I've already had a taste of it and loved every moment,' Sassy said gently. 'I was on the canal before, you know, and I loved it then as well. As for leading the horse along the towpath, you're way out there! Gran had her barge converted from horsepower to engine power a few years back, which has done away with a lot of the slog.' She grinned at Jack. 'It sounds like hard work, but it's the freest sort of life you could imagine. The barge putters along through the most glorious countryside. We buy provisions from the farms and villages that we pass and everyone knows everyone else, not like the theatre where the audience is always changing. So if you can truly manage without me, then I'll be back on board the *Girl Sassy* before you can say knife.'

'Darling, you can't mean it,' Louella said. She shuddered eloquently. 'All that sun and wind will ruin your complexion in a month. I'm sure you're just saying you prefer the canal because Jack seemed to imply that you weren't wanted . . .'

Jack made an inarticulate sound, but Sassy flew to his defence at once. 'You're quite wrong, Mam. I'm sure Jack would welcome me if I wanted to return to the theatre, because he's always been a true friend to both of us. But I don't want to come back. I've had years of working in stuffy auditoriums, wearing garish costumes and pretending to be happy, happy, happy, when quite often I've felt more like crying. You're a born actress, Mam, but the truth is, I'm not. Maybe I'm a throwback, or maybe those six years spent with Gran changed me, but the thought of working in the theatre again makes me feel quite desperate. Oh, I still love you, and I'm very fond of Jack, but I don't mean to come back. Once it's in full working order, the barge will dock in Liverpool every few weeks, and I'll make time to nip up to the Court and see you both, but now I know you don't need me, I'm going to do what *I* want and work the canals with Troy and Gran.'

Louella stared very hard at her daughter, an anxious frown creasing her brow, but then it faded

499

and she began to smile. 'You might say the wheel has turned full circle,' she observed. 'My mother wanted me to marry the farmer whose property adjoined ours, but I kicked over the traces and became an actress. Now you're doing the same, only in reverse. And if you're half as happy as I've been, you'll be a very lucky girl. Don't think I'll try to stop you, sweetheart, because ever since you've left us, and made me look facts in the face, all I've ever really wanted for you is your happiness.' She turned to Troy, holding out her hand. 'We've never been properly introduced, Troy, but you've clearly grown into a dependable young man. Take care of my daughter; she's the only one I've got.'

Troy nodded solemnly and put an arm round Sassy's waist. 'I will,' he said steadily. And then, just for a moment, the oddest thing happened. Sassy saw a picture of herself and Troy standing side by side in front of the little altar of a church. She was looking up at him as the words 'I will' came from his lips, but then the picture faded and she was kissing Louella, and hugging Jack, promising to see them again soon.

Then she and Troy, hand in hand, left the theatre and were running, running, making for the life that they both loved, aboard the *Girl Sassy*, with Gran.